Heaven Sent

Heaven Sent

Christina Jones

ISIS
LARGE PRINT
Oxford

First published in Great Britain 2007
by
Piatkus Books Ltd.

Published in Large Print 2008 by ISIS Publishing Ltd.,
7 Centremead, Osney Mead, Oxford OX2 0ES
by arrangement with
Piatkus Books Ltd.

British Library Cataloguing in Publication Data
Jones, Christina 1948–
     Heaven sent. – Large print ed.
     1. Chick lit.
     2. Large type books
     I. Title
     823.9'2 [F]

ISBN 978–0–7531–8058–7 (hb)
ISBN 978–0–7531–8059–4 (pb)

Printed and bound in Great Britain by
T. J. International Ltd., Padstow, Cornwall

To my beautiful daughter Laura
with all my love

Acknowledgements

With continued deep gratitude to all at Piatkus — especially my kind, gentle and very patient editor, Gillian Green, who may weep over my working methods in private but bravely never lets it show in public. She also makes me laugh. I doubt if I do that for her.

Many thanks also to the various people who helped with the research for this book:

Fantastic Fireworks (www.5nov.com) and especially Jonnie Alden who helped me with the pyrotechnic details and some wonderful samples and examples. I had so much fun! The funeral planning was particularly enjoyable. The pyro expertise in HEAVEN SENT is all his — the errors are all mine.

Maria Tchorzewska for the mustelid info, and for allowing me to spend so much quality time with her lovely ferrets, especially the gorgeous Hector who morphs into Suggs in this book.

Steve Green for all the technical details — I couldn't have done any of this without him.

Butler and Wilson (www.butlerandwilson.co.uk) who not only provide me with my crystal jewellery fix but also satisfy Clemmie's earring obsession in *Heaven Sent*.

My very own YaYa Bordello who wishes to remain anonymous but who is an absolute star.

And, of course, much love and many thanks to Dr Neel Tank BDS (Bristol) (www.mldp.info) who came up with the title of this book at a rather inebriated firework party.

CHAPTER
ONE

Clemmie Coddle fell in love with Guy Devlin on the same day as she set fire to her feet.

Last May Day morning, in the shed at the back of Coddle's Post Office Stores in Bagley-cum-Russet, Clemmie's incorrect measure of aluminium and carelessly haphazard lighting of a portfire had ignited her safety boots when she'd least expected it.

Last May Day evening, at Fern and Timmy Pluckrose's wedding reception on Fiddlesticks' village green, Clemmie, hobbling around with bunny slippers on her scorched feet, had clapped eyes on Guy Devlin for the very first time, and — whoosh! — had rocketed dizzily through each of the seven heavens and sky-high into all-consuming love.

As Fern and Timmy's magical celebratory evening culminated in a superb musical firework display provided by The Gunpowder Plot — Guy's company — Clemmie's fate was sealed. Her throbbing feet were forgotten.

She and Guy Devlin were *meant* to be together.

He was not only heart-achingly gorgeous, but also a pyrotechnician par excellence; *she*, while not so totally convinced of her physical attributes, had been obsessed with the breathtaking rainbow magic of fireworks for as long as she could remember, and had dabbled with making her own mixtures of exquisitely coloured gentle explosives since receiving a chemistry set for her eighth birthday.

It was, as far as Clemmie was concerned, a lifelong firework match made in the heavenly periodic table.

Now, more than five months on from both incendiary incidents, Clemmie's feet — merely lightly fricasseed and, like her fingers and eyebrows and hair, used to being similarly mistreated over the years — had healed remarkably quickly. Her heart, on the other hand, was still showing no inclination whatsoever to join in.

Behind the reception desk of Hazy Hassocks' Dovecote Surgery on a chilly October morning, carefully arranging a couple of dozen buff folders into a house of cards while lost in her favourite recurring fantasy of exploding rainbow fireworks with Guy Devlin choreographing her very own pyrotechnic inventions to the strains of Rossini, Clemmie lifted another batch of patient notes and smiled wistfully to herself.

Just one more folder . . . There! Fantastic! Best ever! Three storeys and not even a wobble . . .

Clemmie had been well aware of Guy Devlin and The Gunpowder Plot before May Day, of course. Everyone was. That is, everyone in Winterbrook and Hazy Hassocks and Bagley-cum-Russet and Fiddlesticks and — well, all of her native Berkshire and probably most of Hampshire and Oxfordshire too. The

Gunpowder Plot was the best-known fireworks company for miles around, and Clemmie had watched the genius-level pyrotechnics with a mixture of admiration, awe and envy, on many occasions.

Guy Devlin democratically fired jaw-dropping displays for both the rich and famous and the broke and unknown across the south of England. Guy Devlin, Clemmie already knew from the local girlie gossip, was allegedly stunningly good-looking and drop-dead sexy and had hordes of beautiful women falling at his feet and all points north.

She'd heard all this many times, but still nothing could have prepared her for her first glimpse of the six foot plus, lean, black haired, blue-eyed, simply stupendous reality on May Day. Nothing could have prepared her for not just his beauty, but his outrageous flamboyance. He looked, Clemmie thought carefully, like a madly romantic cross between a Johnny Depp pirate and Adam Ant in his dandy highwayman guise

As pyrotechnicians, by necessity, remained mostly invisible during their work, Clemmie reckoned spotting Guy Devlin for the first time was as thrilling as for a dedicated twitcher catching an inaugural and unexpected glimpse of a pair of practically extinct Squeaking Frilly Wood Chuffs.

The fact that Guy Devlin hadn't actually noticed her — either on May Day or any day since — was a bit of a blow, but not a major stumbling block. He would, she knew he would, just give him time and opportunity . . .

Of course there was also the additional drawback of the tall, raven-haired, glamourously sultry woman who had been practically glued to his side on May Day evening. All black leather, killer heels, batwing eyelashes and glossy pout, she'd looked like an updated Mrs Peel. Clemmie sighed again. Still, given Guy's reputation, by now the latter-day Avengers-woman was bound to be a fling of the past.

Oooh, one more folder and she'd have managed four storeys! That would make it a record . . . There, steady . . . Oh, yesss!

"Clemmie!" The eldritch shriek of Bunty Darrington, Dovecote's head receptionist and harridan, screeched round the doctors' waiting room. "Clemmie Coddle! What exactly do you think you're doing?"

Clemmie, rocketed out of her reverie, jumped and groaned as the house collapsed and folders scattered untidily across the desk. "What? Oh, sorry . . ."

"*Sorry?*" Bunty Darrington roared. "And what exactly is *sorry* supposed to mean? Do you mean 'excuse me?' or 'I beg your pardon?' Or was that supposed to be a one word apology?"

At the first sign of a verbal fracas, the patients in the Dovecote Surgery's holding area all looked up in eager anticipation. This was clearly something to take their minds off the biting October wind outside, their ailments, the posters on the wall which listed symptoms they certainly hadn't had when arriving but knew they had every one of now, and the high-pitched wails of three small children dressed like divas all trying to fit into the Wendy House in the corner.

"Well?" Bunty quivered inside her tweed two-piece. "I'm waiting."

4

"Then you're in good company and in exactly the right place," Clemmie said brightly, "seeing as this is a waiting room. No, sorry — er — I mean — that was a sort of joke, Bunty. A joke."

Bunty Darrington's ginger eyebrows rose into her grizzled ginger fringe. Bunty didn't do jokes. "Really? Was it? I can't hear anyone laughing, can you? And let me remind you that this is neither the time nor the place for levity. And I asked you a question."

The waiting room leaned forward.

"Actually you asked me loads. But I only remember two: what I was doing and what I meant by sorry." Clemmie flipped through the tumbled folders. "Sorry was an apology — although I'm not sure what for. And I was filing."

Bunty Darrington's lips stretched themselves with difficulty over her large teeth. "*Filing*? Don't you give me filing, my girl! You were playing — *playing* — with those folders! Confidential folders! Highly confidential patient notes! And you were daydreaming again, weren't you? Admit it."

The waiting room was agog. Sore throats, creaking knees, aching feet and gippy tummies were forgotten. Even the mini-divas had stopped tugging at one another's candyfloss pink tiaras to stare.

Clemmie gazed down at the demolished house of folders and sighed. Bugger Bunty. Caught in the act. Daydreaming was possibly a hanging offence in the Dovecote Surgery. She beamed. "Well spotted. Not much gets past you, does it Bunty? Sorry — again. Oh,

5

and that's sorry as in apology just in case you were in any doubt."

"And that's insolence of the first order!" Bunty stomped up to the desk on her cushion soles. "Not for the first time, either. I'm sorry Clemmie, but I'll have to report this."

A ripple of lights on the desktop intercom momentarily spared Clemmie from any further vitriolic onslaught. Flicking switches, she listened, ticked her lists and cleared her throat. "Cynthia Avebury for Dr Murray. Alec Smart for Dr Khan. Beyonce Winterbottom for Dr Lowry."

No one moved. The youthful Beyonce Winterbottom, one of the mini-divas in the Wendy House, preened and flounced at the mention of her name, but her equally youthful and equally multi-sequinned mother made no attempt to claim her daughter. All eyes were still riveted on the reception desk.

"Come along!" Bunty clapped her hands. "Don't keep the doctors waiting! Mrs Avebury! Mr Smart! Hurry along there! And you, too — er — Beyonce."

Reluctantly, the three patients disappeared through the archway towards the surgeries.

As the remainder of the waiting room regrouped, Bunty Darrington straightened her extremely tight jacket. "I shall go and see Ms Peacock this very minute, Clemmie. She will be sorely disappointed. She's championed you ever since we took you on. No one else thought you were suitable. No one else here wanted you."

Thanks. Clemmie pulled a face as Bunty waddled self-importantly away towards the practice manager's office. Thanks a bunch . . .

It was true, of course, and she knew it, but it still wasn't the sort of thing a girl needed to hear.

The remaining patients, aware that the floor show was temporarily over, went back to snuffling and coughing and staring at the information-plastered walls, clearly wondering if they now had the beginnings of a goitre, something virally rampant, or if that scarily anatomical diagram could possibly relate to their own bodies. Clemmie tidied the scattered folders, pushed her wayward dark red hair back into its barrette, disentangled a few chestnut strands from her large hooped earrings, and awaited her fate.

She didn't have to wait long. Bunty waddled back to the desk, smirking.

"Ms Peacock will see you now — no, don't fiddle with those notes. I'll take over here — and I don't suppose you've answered one phone call have you? And what about Mrs Jenkins? Is she still in the lavatory? Have you checked? She's probably gone to sleep again. It doesn't take thirty-five minutes to produce a sample, especially not at her age."

Aware that the remainder of the waiting room was again watching her humiliation with a sort of gruesome glee — it was clearly far better than reality telly — Clemmie squeezed past Bunty and headed for the practice manager's office.

"Come in!" Pam Peacock shouted.

Clemmie shut the door behind her and smiled. "Sorry about this, Pam. Bunty's on the warpath again and I know she's —"

"Sit down, Clemmie," Pam Peacock peered through her varifocals. "I'm not going to be able to sweep this one under the carpet. Please sit down, dear."

Clemmie sat, the folds of her long velvet skirt pooling round her boots, the trailing lace cuffs of her boho blouse hiding the nervous crossing of her fingers.

Pam Peacock, sadly misnamed Clemmie always thought, being one of those wispy beige women who thought wearing a touch of muted taupe was daring, pulled a doom-laden face. "There have been too many complaints for me to ignore them. True, mostly from Bunty; but she does hold sway here, as you know."

"But the other receptionists —"

"Haven't complained, no," Pam fiddled with her spectacles. "Not individually, that is. And certainly not directly to me. However, they've had several little grumbles to Bunty on the quiet I believe. All grist to her mill, I'm afraid. You know how much Bunty dislikes your, er, individual way of dressing and your cheerfully irreverent attitude — she's been gunning for you for a very long time. And, sadly, not entirely without reason. You've been here for just over six months and in that time . . ."

Pam proceeded to list a catalogue of Clemmie's wrong-doings from the personnel file in front of her. Clemmie, who'd heard it all before, didn't really listen. Individually, she knew they were only minor misdemeanours caused by square-peg syndrome, but

8

no doubt lumped together they sounded far worse. It was better not to hear them. So as Pam's voice faded into the background, Clemmie allowed her attention to stray.

She'd never intended to become a doctors' receptionist. Like most things in her life since the age of fifteen, she sort of drifted into it. When she was fifteen, the firm her dad worked for had relocated from rural Berkshire to Thurso on the northernmost tip of Scotland. It had been mutually decided that Clemmie should remain in Bagley-cum-Russet, living with her aunt and uncle, so as not to disrupt her schooling.

Clemmie, unfashionably enthralled by chemistry, a genius at science and OK-ish at everything else, had happily moved into the Post Office Stores, retaining the continuity of her life in the village. She'd vaguely imagined that after A levels (all sciences; all As), or maybe after uni (Cambridge), she'd move north to be with her parents again. It simply hadn't happened. It had been so much easier, after gaining her degree, to simply come back to the place she'd always known as home, to be with the friends she'd had since babyhood. There was, of course, the issue of making the most of her impressive education; but as Clemmie didn't want to really do anything with her life except invent decorative explosives, the opportunities were limited.

As the majority of the world's fireworks are now made in China and shipped globally for the pyrotechnic companies to buy in ready-built bulk, her thesis and lifelong expertise in concocting chemical cocktails wasn't anyone's urgent must-have.

So, after university and before the Dovecote Surgery, she'd been briefly, and on various occasions, a waitress, a barmaid, a filing clerk, a taxi driver, a data inputter, a lollipop lady, a cleaner, a kitchen hand, a trainee estate agent, a dental nurse, a lab technician — and, of course, a shop assistant in Bagley-cum-Russet Post Office Stores.

With her first-class degree in chemistry she should have gone straight into ploughing some sort of research furrow at best, or teaching science to bored teenagers at worst. If only she hadn't gone back to live with her aunt and uncle in Bagley-cum-Russet after university and lost her momentum . . . If only she'd really wanted to do something other than make fireworks . . . If only she'd never lived in Bagley-cum-Russet to start with . . . If only Sukie and Chelsea and Phoebe and Amber hadn't persuaded her to go to Fern and Timmy's wedding reception . . . If only she'd never fallen in love with Guy Devlin . . .

". . . and so, unfortunately . . ." Pam had the look of someone who is going to tell you've failed your driving test, your blood tests are positive, you owe a fortune in income tax, and your husband's run off with your best friend all on the same day. "Unfortunately, Clemmie, I'm left with no alternative but to issue you with a written warning. Is there anything you'd like to say?"

"Loads." Clemmie smiled sadly. "You've always been lovely to me, Pam. And I'm really grateful to you for getting me this job, but —"

"Your heart's never been in it?"

10

Her heart? Clemmie shook her head. No, her heart had never been in the Dovecote Surgery. Her heart was currently rampaging somewhere in Winterbrook — the nearest largish town to Hazy Hassocks — at The Gunpowder Plot with the beautifully mad, deliciously bad and definitely dangerous to know Guy Devlin, inventing the most wildly sensational firework displays ever staged.

"Something like that," Clemmie said. "And honestly, Pam, Bunty and I are never going to be able to work happily together, are we? And I'm probably going to commit some other perceived clerical sin pretty soon and then, because of the written warning, you'll have to sack me — which will be awful for us both, so shall we just cut out the middle man?"

"There's no need —"

"There's every need." Clemmie stood up. "Thanks for being such a good sport. I'll miss you. I'll just go and clear my desk — metaphorically, of course as I don't actually have one."

"I'm so very sorry." Pam stood up and offered a pale, beige hand. "I personally think you've been a breath of fresh air and the patients love you. I do wish there was some other way. Good luck, Clemmie. Have you any idea what you're going to do next?"

"None at all," Clemmie said, far more breezily than she felt. After all, at almost thirty a girl should surely have some sort of life plan mapped out, shouldn't she? "It's quite exciting in a way."

Out in the waiting room, the remaining patients immediately perked up as Clemmie emerged.

11

Bunty, perched on the stool behind the reception desk with her tweed haunches overflowing, looked up in quivering anticipation. "Right. Now, young lady — you get back here and knuckle down. I hope Ms Peacock has put you straight on your behaviour. First, you file all these notes, then go and check in the lav for Mrs Jenkins, and after that you can man the phones over lunchtime, then —"

"Sorry to interrupt you." Clemmie beamed, shrugging into her ancient oversized mauve mohair cardigan. "But you're going to do all that yourself. I'm off."

"Off?" Bunty's shriek vibrated round the walls. "I think not, young lady. You've forfeited your right to a coffee break, I'm afraid. And Julia won't be on until one so you'll just have to —"

Clemmie gathered her few possessions together and shoved them into her battered bejewelled basket. "No Bunty. I mean I'm OFF. Leaving, packing it all in, departing this surgery. I am now an ex-receptionist."

The waiting room was agog.

"She sacked you?" Bunty howled. "Nooo! She wasn't supposed to sack you! How am I supposed to manage out here without a full complement of staff! You can't go!"

"Can and am." Clemmie swung happily towards the door. "But please don't blame Pam for this. She didn't sack me. I quit. 'Bye, Bunty."

The waiting room, rising to its feet, gave Clemmie a rousing Hazy Hassocks cheer as she left the surgery.

CHAPTER
TWO

Well, Clemmie thought, weaving in and out of the mid-morning shoppers milling on the pavement of a blustery Hazy Hassocks High Street, another failed career move.

This was becoming quite a habit. So, what to do next? Go home to Bagley-cum-Russet, pop on her tabard and start serving the villagers in the Post Office Stores as if she'd never been away? Or stay in Hassocks and make the most of what the High Street had to offer?

If she stayed she could rush into the Faery Glen and get roaring drunk; or spend a couple of hours in the local tea shop, Patsy's Pantry, cramming down her body weight in carbs; or visit Beauty's Blessings and let Jennifer Blessing massage away the shame of losing yet another job. And as most of Clemmie's friends worked in and around Hazy Hassocks, staying and wallowing was very tempting.

She could find Sukie on her aromatherapy rounds, drag Amber away from Hubble Bubble, haul Chelsea out of Big Sava, tempt her best-friend Phoebe from Pauline's Cut'n'Curl, ring Fern at the Weasel and Bucket, and indulge in a long girlie lunch ranting over the injustices of life, the mysteries of love and the meaning of the universe.

Or, of course, she could simply look for her next job.

It was, Clemmie decided, quite empowering. Life stretched out like a blank canvas. She could choose to do simply anything . . .

A particularly vicious and chilly gust of wind sent the urban tumbleweed dancing around her feet, and she pulled her long fluffy cardigan closer round her. Eeeek! A quick glimpse in the reflective glass window of the building society showed her hair blown into a bird's nest, her earrings hooked drunkenly into her collar, her nose glowing scarlet and her mascara smudged under her eyes. It was always so demoralising, she thought, skillfully manoeuvring round a cluster of pensioners chatting by their shopping trolleys, imagining yourself as looking carefree and stylishly bohemian and then being faced with the awful reality that you wouldn't look out of place in a soup kitchen queue.

Maybe before she hurled herself on an unsuspecting job market, she ought to go back to Bagley and tidy up a bit. She was just retracing her steps to retrieve her car from the Big Sava car park when she heard her name.

"Clem! Clemmie! Wait!"

Clemmie turned. And smiled. And waited. Phoebe, her oldest friend, had emerged from the fondant pink door of Pauline's hairdressing salon and was waving energetically. Phoebe always did everything energetically. Clemmie assumed that was why they'd been such good friends since toddling days. They were opposites in practically every way. Phoebe was always smart,

14

always on time, always organised, always on the move. Phoebe got on with stuff — she didn't waste time daydreaming about fireworks, or concocting pretty chemical mixtures, or, for that matter, falling in love with total strangers.

Phoebe had had the same job since school, and the same boyfriend for the same amount of time. Phoebe, who had a penchant for tarots and astrology, was about as unscientific as it was possible to get. Phoebe was everything Clemmie wasn't and she loved her dearly.

"Hi." Phoebe, looking exquisitely neat with her sleek blonde bob and her sleek pink Cut'n'Curl tunic, fell into step beside her. "You're out early. Has Bunty the Bitch Woman sent you to Patsy's Pantry for cream cakes? Is it someone's birthday?"

"No and no. You couldn't be wronger," Clemmie said airily. "What about you? On your way to the Pantry?"

"Yep. Three ham and salad baps and a cheese and onion roll. Pauline's got a tricky perm on the go and needs sustenance. The other girls were busy and I haven't got another appointment for half an hour so I volunteered because it's better than picking hair out of plugholes."

"So you've got time for a coffee?" Clemmie pinged open Patsy's Pantry's frilly-curtained door and inhaled the gorgeous fragrances of fresh coffee and newly baked bread. "And a bit of a chat?"

Phoebe headed for the counter and nodded over her shoulder. "As long as it's quick. Pauline won't be able to eat until she's sluiced off the perming lotion so we've

15

got about fifteen minutes. You grab a table — I'll pay. Any food? Sorry — stupid question."

By the time Phoebe returned to the window table with two cups of Patsy's version of cappuccino and a matching pair of Danish pastries, Clemmie had beamed happily at the rest of the Pantry's clientele. Most of them were patients at Dovecote and of the age where they took morning coffee after removing their coats, but still wearing their scarves, hats and gloves, and although they'd known each other for decades, always addressed one another as Mr Biggs or Mrs Pentelow.

"You've been sacked again, haven't you?" Phoebe sat down and attacked her Danish with perfect teeth. She didn't even spray crumbs or make a mess on her tunic. "Or did you walk this time?"

"Both, really." Clemmie bit into her pastry and immediately managed to shed squishy bits of it over her face, her cardigan and the table. "Not that it matters. It was only ever a stop-gap. Next time I'll find something really, really suitable."

Phoebe laughed. "I've heard that before. Jobs and men — you're always going to find the right one next time."

Clemmie licked her fingers and tried to shake crumbs from her sleeve. "Oh, the man thing's sorted —"

"You can't keep claiming Guy Devlin as a solution to your singledom," Phoebe interrupted. "He's almost definitely attached, you've never even spoken to him and he doesn't know you exist. We've been through this over and over again for the last five months. It's not real, Clem. It's like fancying a pop singer or film star when you're a kid. Not real — and definitely not love. What you've got is a bad case of fantasy lust. Real love has to be reciprocal, and you have to know someone inside out and —"

"Sorry." Clemmie washed down the Danish with a swig of cappuccino and knew she'd now have froth *and* crumbs on her upper lip. "I don't agree. Oh, I know you and Ben have been together for about nine hundred years and you know what he's thinking before he does and you finish each other's sentences and all that — but I don't want your cosy kind of love. It's a habit. And boring. I want burning passion. No, I always knew," she sighed dreamily, "that when I met the right man it would be like an instantaneous explosion. Like a heavenly combination of magnesium and aluminium and sodium salicylate: all bells and whistles and flashes of brilliant colour. And when I saw Guy, it was."

Phoebe chuckled through her coffee. "Bless. Hopefully the poor bloke will never cross your path again and you'll get over it — blimey, though — you haven't been stalking him, have you?"

"No! Course not! How sad do you think I am? There's no need for stalking. We'll meet again. I know it. We're two people in a small area who love the same things. It's logical we should be together. I'd almost say it's fate, if I believed in such things — which I don't. However, I do think it's our destiny to be together."

"Now you sound scary. Fate and destiny are more my areas than yours." Phoebe frowned. "God — you haven't been *dabbling*, Clem, have you? You haven't asked someone to put a spell on Guy Devlin? We both know there's enough odd stuff going on in the local villages, and I can think of a good half a dozen people who'd advocate chanting a bit of an incantation or mixing up a potion to make your dreams come true."

There had always been all sorts of rumours about the goings-on in the cluster of sleepy villages which nestled in the folds of the Berkshire Downs. Here in Hazy Hassocks, Mitzi Blessing had practically moved into rural myth territory with the inexplicable effects of her Hubble Bubble herbal cookery; the nearby hamlet of Fiddlesticks held long-standing beliefs about astral magic — and Amber, who lived there, swore that the star-wishing had completely transformed her life. Then, of course, there was Sukie brewing her aromatherapy massage potions in Pixies Laughter Cottage just down the lane from the Post Office Stores in Bagleycum-Russet. They'd been blamed and claimed for a whole raft of recent romances.

"Including you?" Clemmie laughed, using her spoon to remove the frothy dregs from her coffee cup. "And your Madame Zuleika fortune-telling act?"

"I've never called myself Madame Zuleika — and it is not an act!" Phoebe looked indignant. "I'd never use my cards to manipulate anyone!"

"Shame." Clemmie grinned unrepentantly. "I'd never say no to a bit of manipulation — but you're OK, Phoebes. Calm down. I know your card-sharping isn't in the same league as some of the really witchy stuff that allegedly happens round here."

"Now you've assured me that I'm on the right side of paganism, I'm calm." Phoebe drained her coffee cup. "And I know you'll laugh and you always say no, but I could do you a reading."

"And I wouldn't believe a word of it, any more than I believe in herbal folklore or moon-baying or love potions. I'm a scientist." Clemmie mopped the coffee froth from her chin. "I only believe in logic, principles and things that I can prove absolutely. I'd never dabble in any of this phoney practical magic rubbish."

"Excuse me?" Phoebe flicked non-existent crumbs from her tunic. "Just how many insults are you going to hurl? My hobby is neither phoney nor magic. Astrology is an ancient art —"

"Yeah, right. Give it an 'ology and it assumes an air of respectability. Your card tricks and things are good for a laugh at parties, but it's hokum, Phoebes, and you know it."

"You believe what you like." Phoebe wrinkled her nose. "But I promise you, if you knew Guy Devlin's star sign, I could chart your astral path against his and tell you whether or not you'd ever get together."

"Course you could, dear," Clemmie teased. "So, probably, could Mystic Meg or Justin Toper or Russell Grant, but I choose not to consult them because I already *know* that one day Guy and I will meet again and he'll fall in love with me and we'll live happily ever after: all without any magical intervention."

"And precisely where do your pure scientific logical provable principles come into play in this scenario, then?" Phoebe wiped the flakes from the table top into a neat pile. "Remind me again."

"A heaven-sent opportunity will present itself." Clemmie grinned. "Put scientifically, it's simply a pyrotechnic chemical combination of the elemental contents of the periodic tables and the rainbow colours of the seven heavens."

"Hippie tosh!" Phoebe sniffed, sweeping the pastry flakes into her napkin. "Scientific-babble bunkum!"

They giggled together. Then Clemmie leaned across the table. "If you'd listened more closely in our chemistry lessons, not to mention the religious education ones, instead of exchanging soulful glances with Ben across the classroom and pouting and hitching your skirt up to groin level, you'd know exactly what I was talking about. Love, after all, is universally acknowledged as a chemical reaction. So, my love life is going to be just fine, thank you — mind, if your astrology could tell me where to get my next job, I'd be very grateful."

"That's easy." Phoebe smiled. "And you don't need a reading for that. Stop messing about and use your degree. Any of the schools round here would snap you up. They're crying out for chemistry teachers — you're the only one of us that went to uni, and Cambridge at that — and you've completely wasted your education. Stop playing around with fireworks in Molly and Bill's shed and do something with your life."

"Phoebes!" Clemmie was stung. "That's a bit harsh."

"But necessary." Phoebe stood up. "You're thirty this year. You've probably had thirty jobs and thirty short-term relationships. In the blink of an eye you'll be forty — we'll all be forty — and it'll be too late for you."

"No it won't," Clemmie grumbled, as they left the cosy warmth of Patsy's Pantry to be assaulted by the cutting wind on the High Street. "Sixty is the new forty so that gives me another entire lifetime. And anyway, look at all the olds we know — Mitzi was over fifty when she started Hubble Bubble and fell in love with Joel, and Zillah Flanagan got married at fifty-five, and Joss Benson has just rediscovered her lost youth and fallen in love at nearly pensionable age, and Topsy in Bagley is getting married to Hilton and they're both over eighty and —"

"And they're not you." Phoebe's no-nonsense bob swung neatly in the breeze. "And they all had other really full lives first. You're still messing around. Look, it's because I'm your best friend that I can say all this. I care about you. I want you to be happy and fulfilled. Everyone else in our gang is settling down, getting to grips with careers and marriage and —"

"Oooh noooo! Spare me the happy couples bit." Clemmie linked her arm through Phoebe's. "And I promise I'll consider exploring the teaching thing. OK?"

"OK," Phoebe agreed. As they reached Cut'n'Curl, she went on, "And could you promise not to slag off my astrology too?"

"Nah. That's asking far too much — even from your best mate."

★ ★ ★

Molly was behind the counter in the Post Office Stores when Clemmie arrived back in Bagley-cum-Russet and didn't break stride in dishing out dolly mixtures. "Hello, love. Been sacked?"

"Well, it was mutual really." Clemmie paused in struggling out of her baggy cardigan and disentangling her hair and her earrings. "How did you know? Did Phoebe ring you and snitch?"

"No." Molly bagged up liquorice allsorts at the speed of light. "Simple deduction. You're usually home at five-fifteen — it's only just gone twelve. You're clearly not ill, and your eyes are shining. I've seen it all before. What happened?"

Clemmie fastened her tabard. "Same as usual, really. Sorry — you've got me back under your feet. Anyway, shall I take over here and you can get on with the Post Office stuff. Uncle Bill looks like he's had enough."

They both glanced across the shop. Bill Coddle was nose-to-nose through the slatted security glass with the gaunt elderly figure of Topsy Turvey.

"She's probably just diagnosed his touch of indigestion as an aortic aneurism," Molly chuckled. "You know what Topsy's like on all matters medical. He'll cope for a while longer, you come round here and have a hug."

Clemmie sank gratefully into Molly's cushiony arms. Molly had always been a lovely mother-substitute whenever life had been less than wonderful; never critical, always understanding — probably too much so, Clemmie thought. She and Uncle Bill had been so proud when she'd graduated from Cambridge and had never voiced their disappointment that things had pretty much gone downhill for her after leaving uni. If Molly and Bill had nagged her more, maybe she'd have stopped drifting aimlessly years ago. But no, she shouldn't and couldn't blame them. Her fecklessness and lack of ambition were all down to her.

"Any idea what you're going to do next?" Molly asked soothingly. "Mind, you could do what everyone else round here does: work Up the Atomic or Down Tesco."

"I've already done Down Tesco once. I wasn't very good on the checkouts or anywhere else. I don't think they'd give me a second chance — and it was because Dad worked Up the Atomic that he's now in Thurso and I'm here and you're lumbered with me. Actually, Phoebe said I should take this opportunity to use my degree," Clemmie said when she'd extricated herself from her aunt's arms. "I thought I might make some enquiries about becoming a teacher."

"But is teaching what you really want to do?" Molly said as, side-by-side, they tackled a baying mob of Bagley youngsters who were clearly keen to spend their dinner money on a sugar rush. "I know it would be good if you could use your degree seeing as you were so brilliant at university. What about starting up your own firework company? Is that a possibility? Everyone knows it's the only thing you really care about."

"Oh, I wish!" Clemmie grimaced as she took a handful of sticky coins in exchange for sherbet lemons from a child with a suspiciously moist nose. "But that's out of the question. I'd need a huge amount of capital and a massive bank loan and proper business plans and secure premises and all sorts of things like that. I haven't got a brass farthing — and anyway, The Gunpowder Plot has cornered the market round here. I couldn't compete; I'd be bankrupt within a year. No, if I'm going to make something of my life it looks like it'll have to be teaching."

"Surely you'd have gone in for teaching straight after university if it had been a proper calling, though?" Molly persisted sensibly. "Oh, I know you were talented at chemistry, and you still enjoy experimenting in the shed — but all those children who probably detest science? All those children full stop."

Clemmie grinned. Her aunt, childless by choice, always professed to loathe children — but she'd turned out to be a superb stand-in mum for Clemmie, and the kiddies of Bagley-cum-Russet adored her.

"I'm not even going to pretend that teaching is my vocation," Clemmie said as she wrestled with the top of the jar of pineapple chunks, "but it would certainly solve several problems. And the best teachers at my school were those with an obsessive enthusiasm for their subjects who made learning fun, so it might be OK." She gave up on the pineapple chunks and shrugged at the slackjawed child in front of her. "Sorry, it won't budge. How about pear drops? No — oh well, suit yourself."

"You'll never make a salesperson, that's for sure." Molly removed the jar of pineapple chunks from Clemmie, gave the top a sharp rap and opened it with ease. "There — look, love, why don't you go and ring whoever you have to, to find out about teaching. Strike while the iron's hot and all that. Me and Bill will manage fine here."

So, half an hour later, in the sanctuary of her shed at the back of the Post Office Stores and armed with her mobile, various telephone directories, several newspapers and an out of date *Times Educational Supplement*, Clemmie made tentative enquiries about marrying her degree with her passion and embarking on a whole new career.

It was all very disappointing.

It seemed that she wouldn't be able to just walk into Winterbrook Comp and take up the chemistry cudgels. She'd have to return to college for at least a year and take a teaching certificate, after which no guarantee existed that she'd find a teaching post locally. And because of the National Curriculum there were apparently very strict rules about exactly what she'd be teaching. Chemistry, yes, after a fashion, but possibly not to start with, it was more likely to be general science with a mixture of physics and biology thrown in too.

"How's it going?" Bill Coddle poked his head round the door. "Safe to come in? I've brought refreshments."

"You're a star." Clemmie struggled out of her ancient cushiony armchair and took the tray. "I'll just move the iron filings and this box of aluminium."

Bill settled himself on a rickety stool in the corner where Clemmie kept her test tubes and sparkler wires and an odd box of chemical bits and pieces which everyone in Bagley-cum-Russet prayed wouldn't spontaneously combust.

"I'm sure Health and Safety would have a fit if they ever investigated this shed," Bill chuckled, biting into a fat cheese and tomato sandwich. "They bustle about in the shop fretting over weights and measures and hygiene, not knowing there's enough stuff in here to blow the entire village sky high."

"Hardly." Clemmie swallowed her cheese and tomato with relish. Despite the earlier Danish pastry, she was ravenous. As always. "There's nothing more inflammatory here than in the average basic chemistry set. Just a bit more of it. And none of it commercial. Oh, these sarnies are gorgeous — being unemployed always makes me hungry."

"Being unemployed has nothing to do with it. You've been a gannet ever since you were born," Bill passed a second plate across the workbench. "No idea how you stay so skinny."

"Inherited fast metabolism," Clemmie said happily, reaching for a chocolate éclair. "But clearly not from the Coddle side of the family."

"I'm just comfortably plump." Bill patted his expansive waistline. "Just like your dad. We Coddles are all apples. Your mum now, she makes a whippet look chubby. Must be where you get it from. So, are Winterbrook Comp going to let you loose on terrifying their pupils into submission?"

"Doubtful. It looks as if you and Auntie Molly might have to put up with me for a bit longer. If I'm going to be a teacher I won't even be able to get into a college to do a diploma in education until next year and —"

It took several more éclairs and two mugs of tea for Clemmie and her uncle to thrash out the finer points of further education. The best plan, they agreed, would be for Clemmie to continue to put out feelers about teaching, see what happened, and maybe look for yet another temporary job in the meantime.

Plus ça change, Clemmie thought, but at least she'd be able to tell Phoebe that she'd tried.

"I've got the *Winterbrook Advertiser* here," Bill said. "Why don't you have a skim down the sits vac?"

"Thanks, I will. But somehow I doubt if there'll be the answer to my prayers: *Pyrotechnic company seeks chemistry graduate assistant for devising new fireworks and firing sensational nationwide displays. Six fig salary. Penthouse and limo thrown in.*"

"More likely to be shop work or something at a call centre with awful shifts," Bill agreed. "But you know you can live here for as long as it takes, Clem love, don't you? At least you don't have to worry about having a roof over your head while you sort out what you want to do."

"You and Auntie Molly have always been wonderful to me." Clemmie hugged her uncle. "You've done far more for me than I deserve — and one day I'll pay you back for all this, I promise."

"Don't be daft." Bill picked up the depleted tray. "We've never wanted anything other than to see you happy. Just see if you can find another more suitable job, Clem. That Bunty Darrington at the surgery was always a nasty piece of work, even as a girl. She was a bully at school, and once a bully, always a bully. You're best out of there."

As Bill closed the shed door, Clemmie sighed. The Coddles, with their love and their cosy cocoon, made it so very easy for her to drift. She spread the *Winterbrook Advertiser* across her workbench and picked up her pen.

"So," Phoebe narrowed her eyes across the sticky table, "what's your next step in the career life plan? I hope you appreciate I've given up a night in the hot spots of Winterbrook with Ben for this."

"This" was an impromptu get-together that evening, at Clemmie's suggestion, in the less than auspicious bar of Bagley-cum-Russet's only pub — the Barmy Cow. As pubs went it had been left behind in the early twentieth century, and was avoided by anyone with a modicum of self-preservation. Clemmie only went there when she craved solitude.

Run by Hilton, Savoy, Dorchester and Claridge — the ancient Berkeley brothers — who were standing shoulder-to-shoulder behind the dusty bar and threatening to outnumber the customers, the Barmy Cow was the haunt of the very old, very lonely, very short-sighted Bagleyites. As the majority of the punters were of the generation who took smoking as one of the social graces, the smoking ban in pubs had threatened to pull the Barmy Cow's plug completely. To avoid a clash of bankruptcy and anarchy erupting at the same time, the Berkeley Boys had cleverly improvised by turning the separate adjoining off-licence vestibule into a "smoking club". It explained why a continual stream of elderly people kept shuffling off clutching their drinks, disappeared through a tiny locked door, and returned several minutes later smelling like they'd emerged from a kippering shed.

"I'm sure Ben'll survive without you for an hour or so." Clemmie swirled the cloudy liquid in her glass which passed for house white in the Barmy Cow. "And I owed you something for the Danish and cappuccino this morning — and an apology for being such a mardy moo."

"I've known you long enough for the mardy moo bit not to matter a jot, and as for repaying me for this morning," Phoebe frowned around the almost-deserted bar, "this place is the pits. Couldn't we have gone to the Weasel and Bucket in Fiddlesticks? Or the Faery Glen in Hazy Hassocks?"

"Too many people we know likely to be in those. All nicely paired up: Lulu and Shay, Amber and Lewis, Sukie and Derry, Chelsea and Nicky, Fern and —"

"And you don't want to be reminded that you're the only jobless lonely heart in the village?"

"Exactly. Anyway, moving swiftly on — on the jobless front, I've phoned four of the sits vac in the *Advertiser*, got two application forms on the way, turned down one on the spot as working night shifts in the security industry really didn't sound like me, and —" Clemmie bravely drained her glass without flinching and beamed triumphantly at Phoebe — "I've got an interview at the other one in the morning."

"Oh, great. What is it?"

"Actually, it sounds pretty dull. Mainly computer work. For some small business on the Winterbrook trading estate. The woman on the phone just said they needed someone to handle their data inputting and routine office stuff, that sort of thing. It's only for six months — maternity leave or something. I'm OK with basic computing, and the hours are fine."

"Sounds promising."

"It does, but if I get it, it'll probably be mind-numbing, and I'll be immediately plunged into office politics with a crowd of women who've worked there forever and wear sensible shoes, and there'll be some terrible old lech of a boss whose never heard of equality and thinks sexual harassment is a perk."

"That's right." Phoebe stood up and headed towards the bar for refills. "Look on the bright side, Clem."

Clemmie pulled a face. Then turned it into a rather manic dazzling smile when she realised she was being watched closely by half a dozen ancient Bagleyites, including Topsy Turvey, who were returning from the smoking room to play cards in the corner by the fireplace. It wouldn't do to alienate Molly and Bill's regulars.

Still, whatever the following morning's interview might or might not bring, Clemmie knew she wasn't in a position to turn anything down. And it was a heaven-sent opportunity to make another fresh start, and it might even be a really nice place — and a lovely little job — and she'd still have plenty of time to indulge in her firework fantasies, not to mention daydreams of Guy Devlin, wouldn't she?

"You're smiling," Phoebe said, returning with two more cloudy glasses. "You look weird."

"Cheers. Actually, I was just thinking that tomorrow is another day."

"Welcome to Cliché City," Phoebe said as they clinked glasses. "And let's hope those words do you a lot more good than they did Scarlett O'Hara."

"Scarlett, if you remember, grabbed every opportunity by the throat and made the most of it. She was a girl after my own heart, and I promise you'll be the first to know how things go tomorrow and — oh, yeurgh!" Clemmie spluttered. "This wine's got little dead frogs in it!"

"The Berkeley Boys said we'd had the last of the wine. That's martini — cut-price because Dorchester reckons they might have had it since 1986 — and those are allegedly olives."

"Ah, the high life." Clemmie hooked out the olives and watched as, rock-solid, they rolled like marbles into a greasy groove on the table top. She raised her glass again, leaning back on her rickety chair leaving her feet anchored disconcertingly to the sticky floor. "Cheers, Phoebe. Anyway, one thing's for sure — whatever happens tomorrow, it's got to be better than this, hasn't it?"

CHAPTER
THREE

The next morning was leaden-skied, misty and bitterly cold. At just before ten o'clock Clemmie, shivering in her best interview outfit of long black skirt and green velvet jacket, with her best Butler and Wilson faux-emerald chandelier earrings twinkling amidst her wild hair, paced up and down outside the small grey breeze-block office on one of the inner-maze roads of the Winterbrook trading estate.

It was totally deserted. There were rows of cars outside the neighbouring units, and no doubt all sorts of amazing businesses being serviced by hordes of eager workers behind their closed doors — but at number 19, where her interview was due to take place, there were no signs of life at all. Having already checked if she'd misheard and that she should be at number 90, Clemmie had discovered that the units petered out after 50.

So, she was in the right place at the right time, but number 19 had a dark blue door and a tiny blackout-blinded window, and nothing else. Not even a nameplate. Not that a nameplate would have helped much as the woman on the phone hadn't disclosed the company's name. Clemmie was beginning to have serious doubts about the whole venture.

Obviously it had been some sort of scam. A time wasting practical joke. Shivering even more and feeling distinctly irritable, she checked her watch again. It wasn't looking very hopeful that anyone from the unnamed company was going to turn up. After another five slow minutes went by, she headed back to her car. It always seemed to amuse her friends that Clemmie's car was a basic black Peugeot hatchback. They all seemed to think Clemmie should drive around in an Austin Cambridge, painted in rainbow colours and affectionately known as Peggy.

She was just opening the Peugeot's door, deciding to drive to the *Winterbrook Advertiser*'s offices on the trading estate and demand that the sits vac department should check on the credentials of their clients before accepting their adverts and wasting the time of desperate job-seekers, when a dark red 4×4 bucketed to a halt beside her.

"Sorry!" A slender, exquisitely made-up blonde woman cooed huskily through the open window. "So very sorry! Are you Miss Coddle? Have you been waiting long? Buggering roadworks! Hang on a sec."

Clemmie hung. The blonde woman slithered from the driving seat and swayed across the parking area. Clemmie blinked. She was tallish, but this woman towered over her. She must be six feet at least. With her fashion-shoot make-up and platinum blonde artfully tousled hair, and showing a little too much cleavage in a tightly fitting wool dress, under an open squashy fun-fur coat and high boots, all of which screamed designer, she was as far removed from chunky Bunty Darrington and the sensible shoe brigade as it was possible to get. It was like suddenly coming face to face with Gwen Stefani.

"Miss Coddle!" The woman smiled, displaying perfect cosmetic dentistry, and reached out an elegant, crimson-nailed, much-jewelled hand. A waft of expensive and exclusive scent enveloped her. "My apologies again. Thank you so much for waiting. Super earrings! Cabochon?"

"Butler and Wilson," Clemmie said in surprise, shaking the slim hand and wondering how anyone grew their fingernails that long and didn't chip their nail polish opening jars or doing the washing up. "One of my weaknesses."

"Ah, yes! Mine too! I've always loved B&W baubles. I'm very much a trinket girl, too. Oh, sorry — mustn't keep you hanging around out here. I do hope you're not too cold?"

"No, I'm fine," said Clemmie, trying not to let her chattering teeth give the game away. "I just wasn't sure I was in the right place."

The blonde woman sashayed Monroe-style towards the deserted unit and unlocked the blue door. "I should have explained on the phone — but then I'd assumed I'd be here before you. Sodding roadworks always catch me out, come along in, please."

Clemmie followed her inside, thinking that to get a voice that smokily sexy the woman must gargle gin and ground glass, and then stopped. Some sixth sense

34

kicked in as she realised that the cream-painted interior of number 19 was like no office she'd ever worked in — and given Clemmie's employment track record she considered herself some sort of expert — as there were no desks, no computers, no phones and no co-workers.

All number 19 contained was two wing-backed chairs, a chaise longue which had seen better days, a filing cabinet, a white board covered in hieroglyphics, a much-written-on Views of Berkshire calendar still open at August, a small window with what looked like a blackout blind pulled shut and a camcorder on a tripod.

"Er . . ." Clemmie hovered in the doorway. "Maybe I've made a mistake here."

The blonde woman looked concerned. "I do hope not — at first sight I'd say you were exactly what we're looking for. Oh, do you mean the office? Don't let this put you off. We mainly use this for our postal address. We live and work at home, so it's useful to have an outside office space to keep everything . . . well, above board. We just keep a few bits and bobs here, do a bit of planning, that sort of thing. We don't use it much." She scooped a small mountain of envelopes from the floor to illustrate the point. "Our main business goes on elsewhere, but we do like to meet potential staff here initially. And of course, a bolt-hole is always useful when we need to run through some ideas quietly — hence the video set-up."

Clemmie frowned. There was still something not quite right here. She caught a glimpse of the pile of mail the blonde woman had hurled carelessly on to the scruffy chaise longue. Several of the brightly coloured envelopes had pictures of long boots and leather gloves and other weird fetishy things and — no way! — were they PVC *corsets?* Clemmie squinted some more. Yes! She sucked in her breath.

At least half number 19's junk mail was clearly targeting a certain kind of industry.

Ker-ching! Like the final turn of a tumble lock, everything fell neatly into place.

Clemmie shook her head. "Look, I'm no prude, and I may be badly in need of a job, and what other people choose to do to earn a living is up to them — but I'm not going down this route."

The blonde woman, who had settled into one of the armchairs and was indicating that Clemmie should also sit down, frowned. "Excuse me? Which route?"

"Whatever this set-up is. However you describe it. You know: glamour shoots . . . adult films . . . escorts . . . After all, the video equipment — and those brochures . . ."

The blonde woman gurgled with throaty laughter. "Oh, bless you! How sweet! What a breath of fresh air! I'm so sorry to disappoint you . . ." she composed herself with difficulty, re-crossing her endless legs, "and I know it must all seem a bit odd, but this isn't a sleaze outfit. Far from it. You won't find a single naked body on that camera. Sadly we do seem to get some rather odd mail — doesn't everyone these days? But please sit down, Miss Coddle, and let me explain. Oh, and the Miss Coddle is far too formal — I'm sorry, it was remiss of me, but I didn't make a note of your first name."

"Clemmie," Clemmie said, still rooted to the spot.

"Lovely! Very pretty. It suits you. Short for Clementine?"

"Yes."

"After the small orange or the Australian ditty?"

"After Winston Churchill's wife. My dad proposed to my mum in the grounds of Blenheim Palace."

"Really?" The blonde woman raised perfectly sketched eyebrows. "How romantic. Now, Clemmie, please sit down and let me explain . . ."

Clemmie, making sure that the blue door hadn't been locked behind her, perched tentatively on the edge of the second chair. Every instinct warned her that she should still just say thanks but no thanks and be heading back to the Peugeot. However, her curiosity was certainly aroused, and the blonde woman seemed friendly enough, and she did so need a job.

"Do you have any objections to me smoking?" The blonde woman paused in rifling through a small handbag which exactly matched the glossy boots. "I'll quite understand if you do."

Clemmie shook her head "Please go ahead. I'm not a member of the anti-smoking brigade. I have one sometimes myself in moments of drunken revelry. Not that I have many moments of drunken revelry, you understand," she added quickly, as this was possibly not the best thing to admit during an interview. "Oh no, I don't want one now thank you. But please, go ahead."

The blonde woman removed a tiny enamelled flip-top ashtray, a gold lighter and a packet of cigarettes with a foreign brand name from her bag, arranged them in front of her, then lit a long tipped cigarette and inhaled with relish.

"Lovely." She batted huge eyelashes towards Clemmie. "And just help yourself if you feel the need. So — where were we? Oh, yes — the business."

She settled back in her chair and explained in the husky, throaty voice that they were a Winterbrook-based company, and were looking for someone reasonably computer literate who could help keep records, input data, cover secretarial duties, book appointments, deal with correspondence, answer the phone and generally help out where and when needed.

"In the good old days," the blonde woman chuckled, flicking ash into the ashtray, "I believe we'd have been allowed to advertise for a Girl Friday, but now with everything being so sickeningly PC we had to make the vacancy sound more bland and unilateral, but you get the drift?"

Clemmie nodded. A Girl Friday sounded OK to her. A Girl Monday to Friday was possibly even better from a fiscal point of view. As long as she remained upright and fully clothed.

Conveniently leaving out the details of her degree — she'd quickly learned that most would-be employers considered her to be woefully overqualified for the sort of jobs she applied for and rejected her on those grounds — she confirmed that she'd had wide experience in all the clerical fields mentioned and didn't think she'd find any of it problematical.

"We need someone straight away; we've been very badly let down by the last person we employed to cover our regular lady's maternity leave. Are you available now?"

"I am." Clemmie nodded. "I — er — left my last job yesterday."

"And you have references?"

Clemmie fiddled with the sleeves of her velvet jacket. "Some, yes. Not all of them are very recent. But," she looked up defiantly, "the ones I've got all say I'm honest and trustworthy and a pleasure to have around. And some even say I worked hard. Which I did. I just wasn't suited to most of the jobs I've had. When I'm happy I'll give a job a hundred per cent and more."

"And no one could ask for more than that, could they? Clemmie, if we choose to employ you, and if you choose to join us, then I'm sure we'll be able to make up our own minds about you without worrying too much about references. We're quite a liberal company — as I hope you'll find out."

Clemmie beamed. So far so good. "And what exactly do you do?"

"Me personally? Or the company?"

"Well, the company really."

"We're in the entertainment industry. Sort of party planners. Leisure and pleasure. That sort of thing, but absolutely nothing tacky, I can assure you. My role is . . ." she smiled sweetly, stowing away her smoking paraphernalia in her handbag, "mainly as a PA, I suppose you'd say. But I also have my own little business on the side which is why we need someone else in the office to cover for me when I'm busy elsewhere, and help me out when I'm in situ. Does it sound as if it would interest you?"

Party planning? Wasn't that more or less what Amber did at Mitzi Blessing's Hubble Bubble? And Amber said it was the best job ever and she absolutely loved it. This one probably wouldn't involve knocking up mind-altering herbal recipes for pensioners parties or anything like that, but a job in the leisure industry would surely be a breeze after the Dovecote Surgery, wouldn't it? And the blonde woman seemed pleasant enough so working with her would be a great deal better than working with Bunty the Bitch Woman. And it should fill the gap nicely until she'd made up her mind about the teaching thing.

Clemmie took a deep breath. "Actually it sounds very interesting indeed. Not that I'm exactly clear what it is you do, but it certainly doesn't sound humdrum or routine."

"No one would ever call it that!" The woman laughed throatily. "Now, Clemmie, I'm a great believer in first impressions and I like you, and I think we'd work well together. So, why don't you come along to the main premises and have a look a round and get a feel for the whole thing? We can chat more, have a question-and-answer session on site, then you can make up your mind."

Why not? Clemmie thought. Well, of course, there were a million reasons why not. She could hear Phoebe listing them inside her head.

"I'd love to. Thank you."

"It's not very far. Do you want to leave your car here and hop in with me?"

Lightning reflexes kicked in. She still had some sense of self-preservation and a few niggling doubts. Clemmie shook her head. "Maybe I should just follow you, is that OK?"

"Fine by me. Let's go."

So, five minutes later, Clemmie was following the 4×4 away from the trading estate and along Winterbrook's busy main street. They'd negotiated the roadworks, various sets of traffic lights and the normal mayhem of the busy market town's new one-way system. It had given Clemmie plenty of time to realise that she'd missed out several vital parts of the rather odd interview.

Things like the name of the company, the name of the blonde woman, the location of the main office, the number of employees, the salary . . .

Clemmie frowned as the 4×4 indicated left at the next roundabout. Following suit, she tailed the blonde woman away from Winterbrook's main shopping and office area, driving alongside the municipal park and out towards the new housing estates and the river. The trees in the park, a riot of autumnal colour, looked muted under their swathe of damp mist. The proximity of the river always made this part of Winterbrook clammy in winter and tropical in summer. Clemmie smiled to herself. How lovely if her new workplace — always assuming it *was* to be her new workplace — had a river view.

Yes, it looked hopeful. The 4×4 was turning away from the housing estates now, and picking up speed along narrow roads with high hedges and overhanging tangled branches. It was isolated and rural here, as Clemmie knew well from years of picnics on hot days. Very close to the river. Surely there were no offices of any sort on the outskirts of Winterbrook? It was all green belt. No one would be allowed to build anything industrial out here, would they?

Clemmie stopped humming along with Kasabian on the radio. What if the blonde woman wasn't as pleasant as she pretended to be? The siren had said it wasn't sleazy but still, maybe she was waiting to spring on her the true nature of the business. What if number 19 really was a front for the porn industry? Or what if it was even worse? Clemmie's overactive imagination was running riot. What if she was being lured to some deserted spot to be drugged and bound and gagged and shipped off for the white slave trade? What if . . .

The 4×4 had disappeared round a sharp bend and, unable to reverse, Clemmie followed, pretty sure now she'd turn and run as soon as the opportunity presented itself.

"Oh — wow!"

The 4×4 had pulled up on a gravel drive in front of a sprawling mellow brick two-storey boathouse, lovingly renovated into a home, standing on what appeared to be a small isthmus. Mullioned windows, overhung with

42

centuries-old gnarled wisteria, reflected the river as it curled and rushed around three sides of the boathouse, disappearing over a small foaming weir on the left, dancing up loamy banks and swirling the trailing branches of willow trees to the right. The back of the original building, Clemmie guessed, must have total river-access, possibly with slipways and sloping lawns and — whatever their business was — there was clearly a lot of money to be made in it.

"Here we are!" The blonde woman had erupted from the 4×4 and was beaming at Clemmie. "What do you think?"

Struggling from the Peugeot, Clemmie decided not to mention her earlier thoughts about sex traders at this point. However, she kept a firm grip on her car keys and her mobile phone, just in case.

"I think it's absolutely gorgeous. Is this really where the offices are?"

"Offices in the house, workshops and storage sheds over there." With a flourish of her fur-coated arm the blonde woman indicated the red tiled roofs of several other equally pretty outbuildings fleetingly visible through the dancing willow branches. "Heavenly, isn't it?"

It certainly was. Clemmie thought she'd never seen anything quite so beautiful. If it looked this gorgeous now on a cold and grey October day, it must be positively stunning in summer.

"Come along in." The woman teetered away on her high-heeled boots across the gravel, brandishing a front-door key. "You can get a real feel for the place inside." She unlocked the door and stood back. "After you."

Clemmie stepped into a wide hallway, wonderfully snug and warm after the chill outside. All gleaming real wooden floors and walls, with an ancient coat stand, a sideboard almost buried beneath newspapers, old letters, and the general detritus of living, and dominated by a large crimson vase of mixed autumnal leaves, it was cosy, comfortable and very homely. As were the other rooms she managed to see through several open doors as the blonde woman ushered her through to the back of the house. Vague images of big mismatched chairs, lots of colourful cushions and a much-polished hotchpotch of old furniture flitted past her eyes.

"This is where you'll be working." The blonde woman opened a panelled oak door. "Always assuming you like the look of us of course. It's a nice little office, with river views — well, you'd be hard pressed not to find river views here of course — all the latest office equipment and everything else on tap. I'll show you the kitchen and the cloakroom and things in a mo. Look, why don't you take a seat, Clemmie, and I'll just pop upstairs and get rid of my coat and boots, then we can have a proper chat." She paused. "First impressions OK?"

Clemmie shook her head, gazing out of the long office window at the width of the river and the misty fields stretching away on the other side. It was like being on a boat. "Far, far more than OK. I don't know what to say — it's amazing . . . but how many other people work here?"

"Daily, just the three of us — then we have a regular team of a dozen or so who come in when we have a special event on. You'll meet them all soon, no doubt. This office will be your domain — I hope you'll be all right working on your own when I'm away, although someone'll always be popping in and out. As I mentioned, we live here too so there's always someone on hand to answer those awkward little questions. Look, you nose around while I get changed then we'll have a proper chat."

"Fine — thank you." Clemmie was still mesmerised by the view and the sheer splendour of the high-tech office, and bewildered by the scatter gun volley of additional information. "Er — yes, of course — um, I don't know your name."

"Oh, sorry — I think the blonde is going to my head." She paused in the doorway and gave a theatrical wink. "I'm YaYa, love. YaYa Bordello."

CHAPTER
FOUR

Clemmie stared at the shut door, open-mouthed. What sort of name was *YaYa Bordello*?

Unless YaYa was some cute diminutive for Yvonne, and Bordello was as common a surname as Brown in some Mediterranean countries, it was pretty obvious, wasn't it? It was a porn star name if ever she'd heard one.

Which meant, Clemmie thought angrily, that this really could be some sleaze set-up! And YaYa might be recruiting! Had she lured Clemmie here to change her name to FiFi or Mimosa and writhe — writhe! — in front of the video camera with some bloke with a Village People moustache and leather underwear while really, really bad seventies music played in the background?

As her experience of blue movies was fairly limited — she'd only ever seen one, and that had been by accident at a drunken university party — she assumed this was what the entire adult film industry involved.

Right, she thought crossly, each to their own and all that, but it won't involve me! No way! I'm off!

Seething at her simplicity, at being suckered in by YaYa's plausibility, she yanked the door open. And screamed.

A long, furry streak shot past her feet.

Clemmie clutched her skirt against her legs as the huge rat — it had to be a water rat, being so close to the river — circled the office area, standing up on its hind legs and sniffing at things.

Jesus! she thought, can things get any worse? Let me get out of here — now!

Keeping one eye on the massive rat, she sidled through the door and collided heavily with someone coming in the other way.

"Shit!"

"Thanks," Clemmie said, muffled against the newcomer's chest. "I was thinking much the same thing. If you'll just let me get past, I'll — ohmigod!"

"Almost. But not quite." Guy Devlin stepped back and grinned down at her. "I'm Guy. And you are?"

"Leaving."

"Nice to meet you, Leaving."

Clemmie didn't trust herself to say anything else. She'd gibber the moment she opened her mouth. Her brain was gibbering. Her whole body was gibbering.

Was she dreaming this? Had she fantasised so much about Guy Devlin that her brain had exploded and produced a mirage? Or, for some weird and wonderful reason, was this real and were she and Guy Devlin actually breathing the same air?

Clemmie closed her eyes, took a deep breath and opened her eyes again. Guy Devlin was still there. He hadn't dissolved or disintegrated, so he must be real . . . and twenty million times more sensational in the flesh than he'd ever been in her fantasies.

While the tall, dark and devastating remained the same, the fantasy really hadn't accommodated the deep, warm voice, or the huge eyes which surely had to be embellished by eyeliner and mascara to get that effect . . . nor the skinny black jeans, or the sloppy black sweater, or the thin circle of ebony beads circling his throat, or the single small gold hoop earring, or the longish black hair which fell in silky layers over his collar and into those sensational eyes . . . or the sulky-sexy mouth, or the cheekbones, or the smile, or . . .

Aware that her mouth was open, Clemmie shut it with a snap.

"I don't believe you're called Leaving," Guy was still smiling, "unless your parents were hippies and your surname is OnaJetPlane. Mind you, I had friends at school called Midsummer and Rhapsody. Harsh for boys."

"I'm Clemmie Coddle," Clemmie said, horribly aware that it sounded as if she were chewing a tissue. "And I am leaving."

"Shame." Guy shrugged. "Just when we were getting on so well. Are you a customer? I'm sorry, Steve usually keeps me abreast of bookings."

Steve? Steve must be the third member of the team. YaYa had said there were three of them working here — and "customer" and "bookings" only compounded the flesh-films in Clemmie's brain. Blimey! Of course! Steve was probably going to turn out to be the one with the droopy moustache and the leather underpants. Her co-star!

But what the hell was Guy Devlin doing mixed up in this? Surely he wasn't in the porn industry too, was he? Unless it was a lucrative sideline. She didn't know what the truth was but it all seemed very fishy indeed and she was obviously better off out of this crazy environment. Oh, God — Phoebe would definitely not believe any of this.

Fortunately Guy didn't wait for her to answer. "Oh no, stupid of me. You must be the new — ah! Brilliant! There he is!" Guy suddenly spotted the rat over Clemmie's shoulder and made strange cooing noises. "Thank God — I thought he'd got out of the house again. Come on baby."

The rat, whiskers quivering, tail erect and twitching in delight, scampered across the office and stood on his hind legs again, his tiny paws scraping at Guy Devlin's jeans, leaping up and down in excitement.

Still cooing, Guy scooped him up, and the rat draped himself round Guy's shoulders, staring triumphantly at Clemmie from beady bright eyes deep-set in a creamy face with a dark-fur bandit's mask.

"This is Suggs," Guy Devlin said, tickling the dark brown animal under the chin. "Suggs, this is Clemmie. Sadly, I don't think Clemmie likes you."

"Not true — he startled me, that's all. Actually," Clemmie bridled, "I love all animals. Even rats."

"Rats! *Rats?*" Guy and Suggs looked askance. "Suggs isn't a rat! He doesn't even look like a rat! He's not a *rodent*. He's a mustelid."

"A what?"

"Mustelid. The same family as otters and raccoons. Suggs is a ferret. A polecat-class ferret. A domesticated house ferret. A much-adored ferret. A cherished ferret. Say sorry to him."

"Sorry, Suggs," Clemmie laughed. Even to her it didn't sound like her normal laugh but hey, what was normal in this situation? "And is he an extra in the films?"

Suggs bridled slightly.

"Now you've lost me." Guy's brow furrowed. "Films?"

Just as Clemmie was about to burst into her tirade about the exploitation of women and being duped into being here at all, and why did someone with a superbly successful firework display business need to be involved with blue movies, YaYa — minus the fur coat and the boots but plus a pink cashmere cardigan and a pair of ridiculously high-heeled pink shoes — shimmied back into the room.

"Ah, lovely. You've all met," she gushed, batting the eyelashes that were on a par with Guy's. "That'll save me doing the honours. So, Clemmie, are you happy to be The Gunpowder Plot's new assistant?"

Now it really had turned into *Alice in Wonderland* — or was it *Through the Looking Glass*? Whichever, Clemmie thought, none of this made any sense at all. She really had to be dreaming.

"Clemmie looks pretty baffled," Guy said kindly. "And I'm guessing," he grinned at YaYa, "that you've carried the cloak and dagger bit just a touch too far. As usual. You haven't told her anything at all about us or this job, have you?"

YaYa chuckled, lighting another long cigarette. "I might have kept a few of the more pertinent details secret — you know what you're like about privacy."

Guy indicated one of the chairs, while Suggs snuffled happily in his hair. "Clemmie — I'm so sorry. Please sit down. Shall we start from the beginning?"

"It might help," Clemmie said as they all sat down and Suggs curled on Guy's lap, hardly daring to allow herself to believe that she might, might, just have walked into a job at The Gunpowder Plot — and suppressing the shudder which rose at the thought how easily she could have walked out of it. "But first, please assure me that it's nothing to do with the porn industry?"

Guy and YaYa laughed a lot. Suggs wrinkled his nose in disdain.

Talking together, like some sort of manic double act, Guy and YaYa eventually managed to convince Clemmie that yes, they really did need a temporary secretarial assistant at The Gunpowder Plot; the cameras and camcorders and videos were all for things like research, planning and filming displays, checking on the musical choreography, seeing how different colours worked together, and that the advert's careful wording, the anonymity of the trading estate unit, and YaYa's initial secrecy had been because they always had to be careful about rival companies planting moles. They had just been badly let down by the last temporary PA who had lasted a week, after YaYa had discovered him going through the company accounts on behalf of a competitor.

Clemmie, truly in seventh heaven, sat and listened, tried not to drool over Guy who simply grew more gorgeous with every second, and just about managed not to leap up and punch the air and tear round the office with her jacket over her head screaming YESSSSSS!

". . . so," Guy finished. "That's about it. If you still want to work in this madhouse, I'll take you through the basics of what we do and what your duties will involve. OK?"

"OK," Clemmie attempted to sound nonchalant. "That all sounds wonderful. And I do apologise for thinking —"

"My fault," YaYa giggled throatily, leaning across Guy and idly stroking Suggs' tail. "I do tend to be a bit, well, protective."

Ping! Clemmie had another tumble-lock moment.

Oh, sod it! YaYa was not only an employee, but obviously Guy's Significant Other. Of course, she'd said, "we live here" earlier, hadn't she? And popped upstairs to change her coat and boots? YaYa must have ousted the Mrs Peel-type *Avengers* woman who had been glued to his side on May Day. Which meant that Guy had a penchant for extremely glam — dare she say, *a tad obvious* — women, but if YaYa had moved in, then the relationship must be serious.

Bugger. Clemmie's heart plummeted. So much for telling Phoebe that fated destiny would bring her and Guy together. Obviously no one had pointed out to damn fated destiny that a live-in lover was a bit of a stumbling block to any embryo relationship.

And could she bear to work alongside Guy every day, knowing that she could look but never, ever touch?

She was aware of Suggs surveying her with a knowing expression in the sharp brown eyes. Was he reading her mind? Surely ferrets weren't psychic, were they? She stared back at him. He winked, wrinkled his nose again and carefully slid to the floor, heading for the door.

"Suggs wants lunch," Guy said. "Which isn't a bad idea. Shall we get the rest of the tour out of the way first?"

As they filed out of the office, and Clemmie pinched herself very hard to prove that she wasn't dreaming, YaYa touched her arm. "Clemmie, love, sorry if you got the wrong end of the stick earlier. Everything's clear now, I hope?"

"Oh, yes, crystal," Clemmie said breezily. "I just got a little bit confused. No, this is exactly the sort of job I've always dreamed about." She thought it was politic to not mention that for the last five months she'd also dreamed about its owner and YaYa's lover with an even deeper and more intimate intensity.

Suggs peeled off towards the kitchen as Guy opened a side door leading from the hall, and led the way out of the house through the chilly mist, across a courtyard and into the first of the outbuildings.

"This bit is my library." Guy looked at Clemmie over his shoulder. "I reckon I've got a copy of every history of fireworks book ever written since — well — since books were written."

Excitedly, Clemmie skimmed the titles crammed onto the floor to ceiling shelves. Some of the books graced her own bookcase in Bill and Molly's shed. Others were titles she'd borrowed from the library and some were so obscure that even internet searches had proved futile. Guy's collection was absolutely wonderful. If she got any free moments she'd have to sneak across here and catch up on her reading.

"Don't look at me, love." YaYa dismissed the bookshelves. "If it ain't a Mills and Boon I don't want to know. This is all double Dutch to me."

Clemmie laughed, still hungrily devouring the library. "It's more ancient Chinese I'd guess, as they discovered and used fireworks first, didn't they? Oh, wow! You've got a copy of Allbard's *Magikal Medieval Alchemy*! I didn't think anyone could get hold of that. Isn't that the one with ancient pyro recipes that link compounds with magical spells that no one has ever managed to master?"

Guy frowned. "Yes — not that I've ever understood enough of it to try any of them. It's just one of those titles that every pyrotechnician covets. But how do you know about it?"

"Oh — it was something we did at school," Clemmie improvised wildly, convinced that if she now mentioned the depth of her lifelong obsession with fireworks they'd suspect she was another mole and she'd be straight out on her ear.

54

"Um . . . in English. We had to choose a subject and try to find out about all the books ever written on it. I was never great at the arts but I liked science lessons, so I picked fireworks because I've always loved them." She stopped. Would Guy believe that? Did it sound truly feeble?

"How enlightened of you — and your school." Guy's expression was slightly quizzical. "And what a wonderfully retentive memory you have. Do you remember any of these other titles?"

"Oh, well, yes — I've always thought that Berkstein Hillyard's version of historical European fireworks was the best. Really concise. Doesn't he credit Marco Polo with bringing gunpowder into Europe sometime in the thirteenth century? And you've got a copy of *The Elizabethan Firemasters*, too! I was always bored by Shakespeare, but dead impressed that he featured fireworks in his plays — oh, and finding out that Queen Elizabeth the First actually employed a Firemaster! And James the Second knighted his and —"

"You know an awful lot about the history of fireworks," Guy interrupted, still frowning. "Even given your enthusiasm for your school topic, which must have been at least ten years ago. Is there something I should know?"

"Apart from the fact that she's as sad as you are?" YaYa interrupted, chuckling throatily. "Back off, Guy. Don't be so paranoid. The poor girl's only trying to impress you. And if you're not impressed, then I sure as shit am. Well done, love."

Blushing, realising that she'd allowed her enthusiasm to run away with her and that if she wasn't careful she'd blow this job before she even started, Clemmie pulled a face. "Sorry — YaYa's right. I was showing off a bit. I do tend to store up trivia and unleash it at inappropriate moments. I've lost several jobs by pretending to know more than I do."

Fortunately Guy seemed to accept this explanation as he'd moved away from the marvellous library and ducked through an adjoining archway.

He grinned at her. "As fireworks is a marriage of art and science, this is our technical room. No doubt you'll have loads of interesting snippets of retained information about this too?"

"Ooh." Clemmie gratefully grasped at the straw he threw her and gazed around at the banks of screens, mixing decks, keyboards and high-tech paraphernalia. "Nope. Nothing at all. Although it looks like a recording studio. Or, at least, what I imagine a recording studio looks like. Is it?"

"Almost right." Guy flicked a few switches. "It's where we — that's me the amateur, plus the really talented techno boffins I employ — choreograph the computerised displays. All the music is listed here and when we select a piece it runs through here, see, then it shows up on these screens, with split-second accurate timings, and we can co-ordinate the fireworks accordingly. So, if say we were going to have a purely aerial display lasting five minutes themed to something — for example the Northern Lights — we'd select the right category, there," he scrolled through dozens of titles, "and we could try Berwald's *Fourth Symphony* which lasts for five minutes and twenty-four seconds — et voilà!"

The music soared and whirled around them, and as Guy moved the desktop sliders, tiny coloured columns danced on the screen. Clemmie, fighting the urge to hurl herself into his arms, focused her attention on the music instead and imagined the spectacular firework display which would accompany it.

Guy switched off Berwald and ran through the list again. "Or we could marry Sibelius's *Karelia Suite* — four minutes — with three minutes of Grieg's *Holberg Suite* — and blend them together like this . . ." Again, the music played, and the screens danced. He turned and smiled at Clemmie. "Is this making sense?"

She really, really wished he wouldn't smile at her like that. It was such a kissable smile. And a girl was only human. With a huge effort, she reined in her rampant thoughts and nodded. "And when you go to displays, all this information, the music and the exact timings of the fireworks, and the order of the firing, is saved and stored on a sort of massive computer which you take with you? And you set the fireworks up in order, with delayed action fuses, and fire them by remote control to the timings dictated by the computer? And then if all goes according to plan — the music plays and the fireworks — um — fire, and it all meshes spectacularly together."

"Bloody hell." Guy peered suspiciously at her over the top of the bank of screens. "That's it exactly. Sorry if I'm being a bit paranoid here, but I'm beginning to smell a bit of a rat. Come on, Clemmie. Time to be honest, I think. How on earth do you know all this stuff?"

CHAPTER
FIVE

"Oh, it's just things I've picked up. Like I said, I've got a stupid retentive memory for scientific bits and pieces — and I've always loved fireworks as I told you." Clemmie kept smiling. Oops. Now he'd really think she was some sort of snooper at worst or an anorak at best and chuck her out before she'd even started.

She pulled what she hoped was a keen-amateur expression and launched into nerd-mode. "To be honest, I watch ever such a lot of the pyro programmes on the Discovery Channel and I've always been fascinated by display fireworks, how they function, what makes them work the way they do, that sort of thing. So, as you can imagine, being here is bliss for me."

"Cool," YaYa sighed in Clemmie's ear. "He might look pissed off, but secretly he'll adore you for knowing all the techno gumph, love. You'll be a whiz on the phones when people ring up and ask awkward questions."

"I think," Guy said slowly, "that if Clemmie's telling the truth then she was heaven-sent. And that if she's a bit of a closet firework-fancier and a fact-gatherer and nothing more sinister, then clearly we were made for each other."

Oooh . . . Clemmie thought, if only you knew. At least he seemed to have been fooled by the firework-fan gushing. She smiled brightly. "Seems so, doesn't it? What a lucky coincidence me answering your ad."

Guy nodded. "Wasn't it? So, do you want to have a go at some mixing — just for fun? Say we're doing a display for Valentine's Day. Ten minutes of starburst pyrotechnic hearts and flowers, mostly reds and pinks with some silver and gold — I'll have already taken care of that side of things. What music would you choose from the play list? It's made a bit easier because we've arranged them in the most popular categories for specific displays."

Clemmie moved closer beside him, hoping that he wouldn't hear her heart thundering or notice that her hands were shaking, and skimmed through the titles listed under "Romance". Classical music wasn't her forte, but at least some of the titles were reasonably familiar.

She took a deep breath. "Definitely Tchaikovsky's *Romeo and Juliet* — three minutes and twenty-one seconds . . . and let's see — ah yes — Mozart, *Marriage of Figaro*, just under three minutes — which leaves . . . three and a bit minutes which means we've just got time for — Elgar's *Salut D'Amour*?"

"The lady's a star!" YaYa clapped her hands. "C'mon Guy, you've got to admit that's pretty bloody impressive."

Guy nodded, grinning. "Not my first choice — but yes, it would work really well. You're quite sure you haven't been sent to suss us out by one of our rivals?"

"Of course she hasn't." YaYa laughed throatily. "She didn't even know who we were or what we did when she replied to the advert, did she? Anyway, crack on, because I'm starving. Suggs isn't the only one who wants lunch — and I've got work to do this afternoon, remember?"

"How could I forget." Guy switched off the computers and screens. "Right, the next shed is where we store the fireworks: so absolutely no smoking."

YaYa pulled a yeah-yeah-OK face. "We're not stupid. Anyway Clemmie only smokes when she's drunk. She told me so at the interview."

"That must have been a pretty in-depth interview." Guy looked at Clemmie in surprise. "How many other secrets did she drag out of you?"

"Only that one. And that just slipped out because I was nervous."

"Actually," YaYa chuckled, "didn't you also tell me that you were conceived in the grounds of Blenheim Palace?"

"Really?" Guy tried not to laugh. "That was very daring of Clemmie's parents."

"Not true!" Clemmie blushed. "I didn't say anything of the sort! I was not conceived there! Mum and Dad got engaged there, that's all."

"Oh, yes." YaYa chuckled again. "I knew it was something like that. Sorry, love. So it was just the smoking-when-bladdered thing you confessed to, wasn't it?"

"Yes, but I don't often get drunk, so I don't really smoke at all, and —"

"It's OK," Guy cut in. "YaYa's great at wind-ups, and I never trust anyone who says they're whiter than white. I like people who admit they're human. And we've all got our little vices. Including me, believe it or not."

YaYa snorted.

"I really didn't mean to say anything about the smoking to YaYa," Clemmie said, anxious that Guy shouldn't think she was a habitual binge drinker with a fag hanging out of her mouth as she lay in the gutter clutching her seventy-eighth alcopop with her skirt round her neck every weekend. "I'm usually far more discreet about my personal life."

"Discreet?" Guy headed across another chilly courtyard, towards a chunky building constructed of breeze blocks. "Well, that's a plus in this set-up. YaYa wouldn't recognise discreet if it introduced itself and was wearing a name badge. Indiscretion is her stock-in-trade. Right — back to business. The storage sheds are our highest security area; but as you'll never need to come in here without me being there, don't let it worry you."

Clemmie, trying to keep up with Guy's long strides, shivered as the cold mist swept up from the river. A grey, winding ribbon, it disappeared round the side of the outbuildings and disappeared over the unseen weir with an echoing roar.

"Health and Safety check us out all the time," Guy said as they reached the next shed and he unlocked several Yales and mortises. "You'll get used to their visits. There are more stringent safety regs for pyro companies than practically any other in this country. It's why I choose to live and work miles from any built-up areas — just in case there's an accident. As you can see, these storage sheds have the regulation solidly built thick walls and very thin roofs."

Clemmie looked puzzled.

"If the worst happens," YaYa explained, "and there's an explosion or some maniac breaks in and sets fire to the stock or something, then the fireworks will all go off upwards and take the roof with them. The solid walls make sure they don't explode outwards and the flimsy roof will blow off with the first blast, so it won't turn the whole place into a huge fireball bomb."

Clemmie nodded. It made perfect sense.

"Fantastic!" she gazed at the floor-to-ceiling boxes in absolute delight. "This is better than being let loose in a chocolate factory!"

She was aware of Guy and YaYa watching her with affectionate amusement, like proud parents admiring their offspring's joy when encountering snow for the first time.

Rockets, multishots, shell bursts, cakes, batteries, candles, wheels, mines — hundreds and hundreds of different versions of the basic display fireworks were stored floor to ceiling in gloriously coloured containers.

"We sometimes sell separate fireworks or boxes of smaller candles and rockets direct to the public," Guy said, "but these sets here are mostly our stock-in-trade for our commissioned parties. One of your jobs will be making sure there are always enough of all of them at all times. I hate having to turn down a gig because we haven't got what the customer needs."

YaYa gave a shiver. "I don't know about you two but I'm freezing. And I reckon Clemmie's going into information overload. There'll be plenty of time for her to learn more about the nuts and bolts once she's working here."

Guy nodded. "OK. Maybe we ought to have some lunch — I know you're off up north this afternoon and there really isn't much else to see here."

"What's that bit through there?" Clemmie asked, suddenly torn between staying in this Aladdin's Cave of pyrotechnic delights and sticking as close to Guy for as long as possible.

"That's his holy of holies," YaYa gurgled. "Enter on pain of death."

"It's my lab," Guy explained as they all moved towards the outer door again. "I guess I really want to be a sort of present-day medieval alchemist. It'll probably interest you, but YaYa finds it very sad that my business is also my one and only hobby."

"Excuse me?" YaYa adopted a very camp voice. "One and only hobby? I don't think so. What about the laydees? You've had more than your share of those over the years."

"Can't help being irresistible, can I?" Guy grinned. "Anyway, thanks to you, that's all behind me, isn't it? Now where were we?"

"Er — chemicals as a hobby?" Clemmie suggested, really not wanting to hear any scurrilous details of Guy's myriad sexual conquests, past or present.

64

"Oh, yes." Guy nodded. "I love to try out different chemical mixtures just to see what happens. I'm actually licensed to develop my own fireworks — for my own use, definitely not for sale — but I'd never use them in displays, they're simply not up to the standard the punters demand these days."

"You actually make your own fireworks?" Clemmie tried to sound über-girlie and not at all scientific. She was now sure the casual mention of her chemistry degree added to her previous indiscretions would lose her this job quicker than you could say Whoopa-Doopa Rocket. "How fantastic."

Guy smiled at the girlie gush. "Of course there's no need for me to invent anything because my Chinese suppliers provide everything I'll ever need ready-assembled, but that doesn't stop me having a bit of a dabble every now and then. I'd love to discover and build some sort of pyrotechnic holy grail."

Clemmie wanted to caper on the spot. She clamped her teeth together really, really tightly in case the fateful words. "Oh me too!" escaped without warning.

Reluctantly, she followed Guy out of the shed and back towards the house. YaYa had linked her arm through Clemmie's in a chummy way. Clemmie groaned inwardly. Damn and bugger. By some miraculous set of circumstances she'd landed the only job she'd ever wanted, working with the only man she'd ever want, and the package included YaYa. And YaYa was lovely. Sod it.

"You'll stay for lunch?" Guy asked as they walked into the cosy warmth of the kitchen. "I'm sorry that we kept you so long — I hope you haven't been bored?"

"I've loved every minute of it, thank you. And I won't stay to lunch if you don't mind; I promised my aunt I'd work in the shop this afternoon. I've got to earn my keep."

Of course Clemmie would have loved to sit at the big untidy farmhouse table, pulling up one of the many mismatched chairs, leaning her elbows amidst the papers and magazines and the blue and white crockery, spending as much time with the delicious Guy as possible. But she couldn't. Because of YaYa, and also because she was terrified she'd appear greedy, or make some sort of mess with her food and alienate Guy completely.

YaYa had swept out of the kitchen, muttering about getting ready for her trip up north. This must be for the little business on the side she'd mentioned, Clemmie thought. It must be as some sort of researcher for future firework displays. Maybe she sussed out sites, drummed up new customers, dished out promotional material and generally carried out the PR side of things. Probably having conquered Berkshire and the neighbouring counties, The Gunpowder Plot was eager to go global.

Guy bent down to coo at Suggs, who was curled on a sort of miniature sofa beside the stove. Suggs preened and twisted his ferrety head round to give Clemmie a hard stare from behind the bandit-mask markings.

Clemmie stared back at him. She was still pretty sure he could read her mind.

"OK," Guy said, standing up and reaching for a loaf of bread. "If YaYa told you how bad a cook I am I'm not surprised you've turned down lunch. But I make a better than average sarnie."

Longing to tell him that as far as she was concerned nothing he did could be described as average, Clemmie simply smiled. "Your culinary skills weren't mentioned at the interview — and thank you for taking the time to make this introduction so comprehensive. I'm sorry I babbled on back there, but I do love fireworks so much. I can't wait to start. Actually, when do you want me to start?"

"Monday will be great if that's OK with you. It'll give us both time to get all the official bits sorted out. Contracts, references, P forty-five — that sort of boring stuff. Nine thirty on Monday morning sound all right?"

"Perfect, thank you so much. Oh — are they pictures of your displays?"

Guy looked across the kitchen to the wall of photographs beside the larder. "Some of them. They're the more personal ones; we keep others on the website and in our brochures too. Have you ever seen one of The Gunpowder Plot's shows?"

"Yes, loads. They're simply the best ever. Can I look at the photos?"

"Of course." Guy was hacking at an iceberg lettuce. "Some of them are quite funny."

Clemmie walked across the uneven flagged floor and gazed at the ranks of pictures. The majority of them were of brilliantly hued perfect pyrotechnic explosions against black velvet skies, but dotted in amongst the starbursts were some more personal group pictures. Guy, she noticed, had much shorter hair in some of the older photos. He still looked unbelievably desirable, although, she decided, she preferred his hair long.

"I was there!" Clemmie pointed at a recent shot of a long-haired Guy with Fern and Timmy Pluckrose at their Fiddlesticks wedding reception, remembering just in time not to mention that it was the first time she'd seen him in the flesh and the effect he'd had on her. "It was a fantastic night — and a brilliant display."

"Thanks." Guy paused in buttering bread. "We enjoyed it, even if the whole village is insane. Oh, God — sorry. You don't live there though, do you? Yours is the next village along, isn't it? Small world."

"Mmm." Clemmie continued to stare at the wedding reception pictures. There was one of Guy, looking amazingly sexy, with several Fiddlestickers and the Mrs Peel Avenger woman. Clemmie squinted at it. Surely, she looked exactly like YaYa. Black hair instead of blonde, and a different style of clothes but, yes it had to be YaYa. Her heart sank. It meant YaYa had been with Guy for ages.

"Is that YaYa?"

"Yes, in her all-black boots and catsuit persona." Guy laughed. "She's got more personalities than a multiple schizophrenic. Tonight she's being a showgirl I believe. All feathers and spangles and fishnet tights."

Clemmie shook her head. "Sorry? I thought —"

"Thought what, love?" YaYa, freshly made up and with the fun fur draped over one arm, swept into the kitchen, dumping a pile of luxury bags on the floor. "Oh — the pics. Yes, that's me — and that one — and that one. A wig and an outfit for every occasion. I told you that I played several roles here, didn't I? The least onerous is as Guy's constant public companion whether I actually want to be with him or not. He's so bloody gorgeous that he can't go anywhere without some sad cow throwing herself at him and they can be a real pain in the butt. God! See that one? Tarnia Snepps in Hazy Hassocks! Remember her, Guy? She was a devil to get rid of!"

"Don't remind me," Guy groaned. "I thought she was going to eat me alive. And she's booked us again this year so please don't let her anywhere near me."

"I'll do my best, sweetie, as always." YaYa winked at him, then smiled at Clemmie. "Guy swore to me that he's never going to look at a woman again but they keep throwing themselves at him, so we decided it was easier for me to be anchored firmly to his side at all public appearances."

Clemmie held her breath. Was she being warned off? Had she given any hint during the induction that she fancied the pants off Guy Devlin? Was she in danger of being labelled a sad cow?

"How long have you been working together?" she asked slowly.

Guy and YaYa smiled at each other companionably.

"We've been together for more years than most married couples. But there's a lot more to it than meets the eye — which I guess you'll find out about." He looked at YaYa. "Go on. She's going to have to know."

YaYa gave a theatrical bow and suddenly yanked off the blonde wig, revealing a perfectly shaven head.

"No way!" Clemmie simply couldn't believe it. "You're a —"

"Bloke, yes, love." YaYa chuckled. "I'm Steve. When I said there were three of us working here full-time I wasn't alluding to a split personality — I meant you, me and Guy."

Guy slapped slices of bread on top of his massive salad sandwiches. "The YaYa thing has been going on for ages, so even I think of her as YaYa now. But Steve was my best mate at school and sometimes I still forget and call her that."

"I'm still your best friend, darling," YaYa cooed, pouting provocatively.

"You are," Guy confirmed, grinning as he hacked manfully through the sandwiches. "I can honestly say no other woman can compare with you."

YaYa fluttered her outrageous eyelashes. "Just you remember that, love."

"As if you'd ever let me forget it."

Clemmie truly didn't know what to say. She was absolutely stunned. Nothing in the world could have prepared her for this ultimate death-blow to her romantic dreams.

Guy was gay. Just when she was congratulating herself on everything going so brilliantly.

She swallowed and looked at YaYa. "And your other job? Up north? The — um — showgirl thing?"

"I'm a drag queen, love." YaYa flicked the sassy blonde wig back into place. "YaYa Bordello — ace drag queen. One of the best in the business, though I do say so myself."

CHAPTER
SIX

Clemmie was in her second week at The Gunpowder Plot. October was drawing to a close with a spell of cold, wet and very windy weather, and the river hurled itself past the office windows in a foamy roar.

She had almost, but not quite, got over the shock of the Guy — YaYa thing. Happy they might be, but from her perspective it was a wicked waste of such a gorgeous man, she thought, and such a cruel end to her wild, romantic dreams.

Although neither Guy nor YaYa had asked her to keep the nature of their relationship a secret, she'd not breathed a word. If Guy Devlin wanted to open the closet door, he'd do it in his own time. If having the glamorous YaYa accompanying him to every public appearance gave credence to the lie that he was a red-blooded heterosexual Lothario — and that's what he wanted — then so be it.

It was almost enough simply to work with him, to laugh with him, to share his enthusiasm for all things pyrotechnic. Almost.

Molly and Bill had been delighted at her good fortune in securing this job. They both agreed that it was a miracle she should fall on her feet so wonderfully, and one of those odd quirks of fate that no one could ever explain.

However, Phoebe, who alone knew about Clemmie's feelings for Guy, had been a little more intrusive in her questioning.

"Are you sure you didn't set it up?" she'd shouted above the drum'n'bass disco echo of the Friday night live entertainment in Winterbrook's one and only yoof pub. "It still seems far too much of a coincidence to me."

And Clemmie had insisted for the umpteenth time that it had been just that — a heaven-sent coincidence — and one of those things that goes to prove fact really is stranger than fiction.

"So has this put paid to the sometime teaching career?" Phoebe had queried, screaming over a particularly loud drumming solo. "Are you going to stay at The Gunpowder Plot for ever and ever?"

"Hopefully, unless the previous incumbent decides to come back after her maternity leave — which at the moment looks doubtful apparently as she's in her forties and loves being a stay-at-home first-time mum," Clemmie had yelled back. "I'm keeping my fingers crossed and my options open."

She'd already told Phoebe about Guy and YaYa being a fully paid-up couple without mentioning the fact that YaYa was a drag queen who began life as Steve. Some things were best left unsaid, she felt. Just letting Phoebe know that YaYa was the Mrs Peel *Avengers* woman from Fern and Timmy's reception night was enough to put a stop to any heavy hints that Clemmie was only keen to make a career of The Gunpowder Plot because of her lust-filled dreams about Guy Devlin. It also meant she wouldn't have to field any further awkward questions about him, or Phoebe's teasing queries about how far her fated destiny scheme had got.

"They've been together for ages," she'd said, breaking her own heart. "Known each other since school, apparently."

"A bit of a bugger for you, but really romantic if they were childhood sweethearts." Phoebe had gone all gooey. "Just like me and my Ben."

Exactly like you and your Ben, Clemmie had thought sadly, with just one teensy but rather vital difference.

And then Ben had turned up and not looked too pleased at Clemmie playing gooseberry, which had put an end to any more deep questioning on Phoebe's part. Leaving them to bill and coo, Clemmie had fled the yoof pub with a headache, realising sadly that at nearly thirty she was no longer a yoof, was far too old for drum'n'bass nights, and was destined to spend her life in sad spinsterdom yearning for a man whose predilections were never, ever going to include a boho wannabe pyrotechnician who just happened to be female.

Phoebe had, however, been an angel in getting Clemmie organised for proper full-time work. No longer did she fall out of bed each morning and fight her way through messy heaps of clothes and jewellery and make-up, trying to find something that went together, usually failing and always, always turning up late and scruffy.

74

Phoebe had spent a whole Sunday with Clemmie in the tiny bedroom above the Post Office Stores, colour-co-ordinating her dozens of long skirts and hippie tops and boots, and arranging them in her wardrobe. Molly and Bill had chipped in with a trendy headless lady jewellery tidy — all black net, beads and sequins and looking exactly like a decapitated YaYa, Clemmie had thought privately — for her dressing table, and Phoebe had disentangled Clemmie's huge flamboyant earring collection and hung them neatly in pairs on the hooks.

It meant, Clemmie thought now, staring through the office window at the river's tearing torrent outside, that for the first time in her life she arrived at work each morning on time, fully made-up, and with an outfit and earrings that matched.

It had everything to do with Phoebe's organisational skills, she told herself, and absolutely nothing to do with pointlessly wanting to look her best for the unattainable Guy Devlin.

Today her skirt was a floor-length circle of electric blue crushed velvet with a red and blue patterned Kaftan top and mock sapphire and ruby earrings sparkling through her tumbling curls. YaYa, who was a redhead today and wearing black leather trousers and a Bardot top in lemon, had pursed her glossy, pouting lips in appreciation. Guy hadn't.

"Clemmie!" YaYa, clutching a phone to each ear, shouted across the office. "Wake up, love! You were miles away."

"Sorry. Did you ask me something?"

"I just wondered if you'd got Guy's diary — not the computer one, his paper one. I've got a couple of enquiries here and want to make sure he hasn't already agreed to do displays on certain dates without telling us. I don't want to double book him."

Clemmie shook her head. "I haven't seen it. I know he took it with him yesterday when he went to Steeple Fritton. He hasn't left it here. Is he in today?"

"Mmmm, playing in the lab I think. I know some of the firing crew are over this morning to run through the booking for November the fifth. Guy's probably over there, still chasing the holy grail."

"Do you want me to give him a ring?" Clemmie tried not to sound too hopeful. It was OK-ish to know that Guy was never going to be hers as such, but she still loved looking at him, talking to him, being with him. "Has he got his mobile?"

"Probably not." YaYa covered both phones and stretched noisily. "He's a bit of a useless sod for things like that, as you've no doubt discovered."

Clemmie had. She'd discovered an awful lot about Guy Devlin's likes and dislikes and foibles in the ten days she'd been at The Gunpowder Plot. None of the discoveries, sadly, had made him any less desirable in her eyes.

YaYa waved an elegant hand across the office. "You wouldn't like to be a proper poppet and nip over to the lab to grab his diary off him would you? And take Suggs with you. He needs a walk."

Clemmie frowned. She and Suggs still had issues.

"OK — tell me when your enquiries are for. I've got some letters here asking about dates too, and several emails enquiring about bookings. I'll scribble yours down and take the lot. He must have to turn down loads of work." Clemmie grabbed the sheaf of papers. "Has he never thought about expanding?"

"Never." YaYa was whispering huskily into both phones, promising them she'd ring them back with confirmations in the next hour. "He's always being approached by the big boys in the business for a takeover or a merger, but Guy wants to run his own show. He's happy to leave the Olympics and the London New Year celebration displays to the large conglomerate companies. He's achieved what he wanted, being a huge fish in the little localish pyro pool, and he'd hate it if he wasn't in control of everything."

Clemmie could understand this. Knowing Guy was as obsessive as she was about fireworks, and how justifiably proud he was of his skill as an artistic pyrotechnician, she could see that he wouldn't want to take orders from anyone else.

Hurrying into the kitchen which was as warm and untidy as usual, she frowned. Suggs was nowhere to be seen. She called his name and took his tiny harness and lead from its hook and rattled it hopefully. It still amused her that Suggs was perfectly house-trained, having the run of the house, using a cat-flap to reach his litter tray in the lean-to when necessary, and answering to his name.

A muffled scrabbling was coming from the far side of the kitchen.

"Oh!" She looked at the larder cupboard in exasperation. "Oh, Suggs!"

Someone had left the larder door open. Suggs had niftily clambered onto the shelves, recklessly discarding things that didn't interest him, and was sitting amongst the debris happily slurping on a double-pawful of fish paste.

Quickly removing him from the shards of glass from the shattered jar and picking up the mess, Clemmie wiped Suggs' paws with a piece of kitchen roll, and strapped him into his harness. He wriggled a lot, eager to get back to his impromptu breakfast, and dribbled fish paste down Clemmie's sleeve.

"Cheers." She grinned at him. "Now I'll stink to high heaven too. And don't look at me like that — I'm still not your biggest fan."

Suggs bounced around a lot, flicking his bottle-brush tail, and giving her coquettish looks from behind the bandit's mask.

"Oh, OK," she scooped him up and kissed his nose, "maybe I'm just a little bit smitten. Now, please behave and walk nicely."

Once he'd accepted that Clemmie was in charge, and that he was being taken out, Suggs abandoned all ideas of reclaiming the fish paste and scrabbled excitedly towards the back door.

"No way," Clemmie told him, grabbing an umbrella from the stand by the door and tugging at Suggs' lead.

"We're going across the yard — not out for a riverside walk. Far too wet and windy. We're going to see Guy."

There. She'd said it. Aloud. Because she could. She said it over and over in her head. Like a besotted teenager, repeating his name gave her a thrill of pleasure. She'd just about managed not to scrawl it all over her pencil case.

Suggs shot her another knowing look, then gave in, and trotted happily across the courtyard beside her, his little legs working like pistons to keep up and fight off the worst gusts of wind that howled up from the river at the same time.

"Guy's through there in the lab," Syd, one of the firing crew, told her, looking up from the music-mixing as she reached the computer room. "You'll have to knock on the door and shout. His mobile's here so you can't use that — said he wanted to be alone. His head is away in the stratosphere this morning."

They all laughed. Clemmie smiled too. She'd been introduced to The Gunpowder Plot's vital support crew in her first week. This dedicated bunch of men and women — engineers, computer buffs, explosive experts, pyrotechnicians all — had welcomed her with metaphorical open arms.

"Tell him I'll need him in a moment." Syd was fiddling with the sliders on the music deck. "I can't quite work out what he intends to do with this finale. I've got more firework than music according to his notes so ask him if he wants me to add something else, will you, please, Clemmie?"

Saying she would, of course, Clemmie darted across the next chilly outdoors bit and hurried through the delightfully tempting storage shed, managing not to linger among the rainbow coloured containers.

"Guy!" she yelled, closing the umbrella and thundering against the lab's door. "Guy! It's me — Clemmie! Can I come in?"

The door opened. Guy, all in skinny black, looked sensational. He grinned. "Hello, baby. Lovely to see you."

For a split second Clemmie's heart went into overdrive. She was just turning mental somersaults when she realised that Guy was talking to Suggs.

How embarrassing could that have been? Quickly concentrating on her dripping umbrella and praying that Guy hadn't seen her smiling soppily, Clemmie felt her heart subside like a pricked soufflé.

Suggs scampered and cavorted and leaped up Guy's black jeans to be cuddled.

Lucky, lucky Suggs, she thought enviously, using the moment to try to pat her wind-dishevelled hair into some sort of order.

"Sorry to disturb you, but you haven't got your mobile and we've got loads of enquiries and we need to check your diary and —"

"Christ! He stinks of fish!" Guy pulled a face. "What have you been feeding him?"

"Nothing." Clemmie bridled. "He went on a self-service mission. Someone had left the larder door open."

"Ah — that'd probably be me, yes, sorry." Guy managed to look apologetic. "I was searching for a new packet of cornflakes this morning and must have forgotten to latch it properly. Ferrets are notorious thieves and Suggs is up amongst the best of them. Did he make much of a mess and did you have to clear it up?"

"Yes to both but it wasn't a problem. He didn't really want to be parted from the paste though."

"No, he's got a bit of a thing about his fish paste." Guy grinned. "And chicken paste and beef paste and crab paste. We buy them specially in bulk for him to mix in with his proper healthy ferret food which he finds very boring unless it contains additives and E numbers. He's never happier than when he's eating junk and he always makes a terrible mess."

Sounds a lot like me, Clemmie thought, watching Suggs nuzzling round Guy's neck and wishing like billy-o that she could take his place. Quickly changing mental tack, she passed on Syd's message and then explained about the sudden surge of possible bookings she and YaYa had taken and spread the lists on Guy's workbench.

"Sorry, I should have left my diary in the office." Guy put Suggs down and walked over to the bench. "Let's have a look."

While he checked the lists against his diary, Clemmie eyed the chemical mixtures greedily. Her first instinct was to eye Guy of course, but as that was pretty pointless, she was weaning herself off that. Slowly.

There were shelves of containers all labelled with the magical names that had fired Clemmie's imagination for as long as she could remember: strontium salts, lithium, calcium, sodium compounds, copper, titanium, magnesium. And discarded firing tubes and fuses and huge sacks of charcoal — the essential black powder without which no firework would do anything at all.

"Are you concocting something at the moment?" She longed to pick up the tiny scoops and measure a mixture onto the scales. She looked at the phials beside the open copy of Allbard's *Magikal Medieval Alchemy* on the bench. Was Guy trying to build some ancient and mysterious firework? "You are! Is it from the book? Oh no, too modern — there's strontium and lithium to make red — and calcium for orange — ah, and sodium for yellow. What a fantastic combination! It'll be like a supernova!"

Guy stopped checking the lists and looked at her, his eyes steely. "Go on."

"Er . . ." Clemmie back-pedalled mentally. "Well, no — I mean I *guess* that's what they are, it is, will look like, um, I mean —"

"Too late." Guy tapped his pen against his diary. "If you weren't already involved in pyrotechnics there's no way on earth you'd even recognise the names of the compounds, let alone know which combinations produce which colours. I know you said you liked fireworks and science at school but this goes way beyond that. I think you owe me some sort of explanation — like which company you work for? Who sent you here? How much information about my business you've passed on to them? And how long it'll take you to clear off."

Clemmie groaned. "It's nothing like that. Honestly. I certainly don't work for another pyro company. Please don't think I'm another spy. It's just —"

"Just what?" Guy's voice was as steely as the stormy October sky. "Just what, Clemmie?"

She shrugged. This would probably lose her the job anyway, but she couldn't bear it if Guy thought she was some sort of mole. "Look, YaYa wasn't the only one who held stuff back at the interview — but I promise you, I honestly didn't know I was being interviewed for a job here. I had no idea what your business was. She said you were party planners and I just didn't want to tell her everything in case she thought I was overqualified."

Guy's face was impassive. Suggs scrambled onto one of the charcoal sacks and curled up, watching her from one mocking eye.

"Really?" Guy's voice was still cold. "And how overqualified would that be exactly?"

Clemmie swallowed. She couldn't lie any more. "I've got a chemistry degree. I've also experimented with making my own fireworks since I was old enough to light a match. That's how I knew about the books in your library, and how displays worked, and of course, about the chemistry stuff. I've had umpteen boring jobs because the only job I ever wanted was — well — this one."

Guy turned away from the bench and stood looking out of the window. His back looked pretty unfriendly. "Where did you study?" he asked suspiciously.

"Cambridge."

"And exactly how good is your chemistry degree?"

"I — I got a First."

He turned round. "Bugger. Better degree than mine. Better uni than mine."

"Really?"

"Yes, really. I got a two one. But I'd rather you forgot that bit of information."

"Which bit of information?"

"I'm so glad we understand each other." He looked as if he were trying very hard not to laugh. "So, when did you intend to let us know that you were more than just a pretty face?"

Did he mean that? Clemmie thought wildly. Was that a compliment? Or simply a jaded expression? Not that it mattered of course, with Guy being gay, but even so . . .

"I hoped it wouldn't be necessary. Look, I'm sorry: I wasn't being devious but I so wanted this job and now, well, I simply love it, and I knew if you knew about the degree and my amateur explosives stuff you'd just think I wanted to muscle in on the pyro bits or ask for more money or something. And that's not what I want at all." She took a deep breath. "All I want is to carry on working here, as a general office dogsbody and —"

"I really don't think that'll be possible now, do you?"

CHAPTER
SEVEN

"Oh, God!" Clemmie shook her head. "You can't sack me now! I'm really happy here."

"Sack you? I'm not going to sack you." Guy was scribbling notes from his diary on the sheets of paper. "Why on earth would I want to sack you? I always knew there was more to you than a pleasant phone manner and an efficient way with emails. I never really bought all that guff about you mugging up on fireworks for a school project or watching pyro programmes on the telly."

"You didn't?"

Guy shook his head. His black hair fell silkily across his face. Clemmie itched to touch it. He looked up. "No. Oh, I'm sure you watch the programmes — we all do — but once a pyro-obsessive always a pyro-obsessive, and I always recognise a fellow explosives anorak."

Clemmie grinned. "I really should have fessed up, as my mate Chelsea says, earlier, but I was so worried that you'd think — well, what you did think, actually — that I was a spy. Especially given your experience with your last employee."

"Well, we've cleared that up, haven't we? And you've already proved to be a real asset in the office and YaYa loves you; and now I know about your chemistry degree, you'll be an even bigger asset to the business. So, if I review your salary, would you like the job permanently — with a few additions? And one proviso?"

Clemmie mentally capered on the spot. Don't look too needy, she told herself. Don't appear desperate. Don't accept it too quickly. Don't —

"Would I? You bet! Thank you so much! Oh, but what about the lady on maternity leave? And what sort of extra duties? And the proviso?"

"Jacky phoned me last night. She's more than happy to be a full-time mum and doesn't want to come back. I was going to offer you the office job permanently today anyway — and the extras — well, you'll be more than useful here of course, but I think we could use you out on the displays from time to time. Would you fancy that?"

"Fancy it?" Clemmie tried hard to stop the full-moon beaming and failed. "Fancy it? That's like asking a groupie if she'd fancy an Access All Areas pass to every major gig at Wembley Stadium!"

"I'll take that as a yes, then," Guy said, grinning. "But there's still the proviso."

Clemmie stopped beaming. This could be the bummer moment. "Oh, right. What is it?"

"That you never tell YaYa your education and your degree are better than mine."

"Never. Scout's honour. Cross my heart."

"Great." Laughing, Guy handed her back the diary and the sheets of paper. "Right, if you and YaYa can just cross-check these dates, because I can already see a couple of clashes, we'll sort everything else out later. Welcome to the team — I'm sure we're going to have a lot of fun together."

Fun? Together? Clemmie exhaled. He'd never know the sort of together-fun she'd fantasised about them having. No, fun wasn't quite the word she'd have chosen. Frustration was probably nearer the mark. Now, if Guy and YaYa weren't an item it might have been different, of course; but as it was, she'd simply have to be content with the fireworks.

She smiled. "Oh, I'm sure we will. This is like a dream come true. You have no idea how much I've wanted this —" Sadly, Clemmie caught Suggs' eye at that point. The bandit mask was raised in a mocking manner. OK, she thought, staring him out, you know and I know the truth here: just let's keep it between us. "Sorry — I won't keep babbling. I know you're busy."

"It's not really work. I'm experimenting," Guy indicated the ancient Allbard's alchemy book and the collection of chemicals on the bench. "After you waxed lyrical about Allbard, I thought I'd have a go at translating him into twenty-first century compounds — so far without success. I'm still chasing the impossible dream."

"A firework that no one has yet managed to build? Oh, yes: me too." The bliss of being able to say it at last! "That is, not on this scale of course, but I've always had this dream that I'll one day make my own ground-breaking firework — to preserve my immortality, I suppose. But I'm very much a hit-and-miss type of chemist. I'm a sort of Jamie Oliver type of pyrotechnician. A pinch of this and a dash of that."

"Amazing that you haven't blown Bagley-cum-Russet to kingdom come," Guy laughed. "And do you use Allbard for reference too?"

"God, no — I've tried to get hold of a copy of that for years even though, like you, I'd probably find translating it impossible. Not that I'm sure about the magical element, of course." She looked quickly at Guy. "As you know, there are far too many people in the local villages dabbling in magic; and science and magic simply don't mix in my book."

"Allbard wouldn't agree with you. He reckons that blending chemicals is exactly the same as mixing herbs to produce a magical formula. That the inexplicable can happen when you have the right combination. Look what happened to Mitzi Blessing in Hazy Hassocks. She's cornered the market in earthy magical recipes and people swear they work. And what about that girl who does massages? YaYa was desperate to try one of her love potions last year."

"Does YaYa really need one?" Clemmie asked, striving for levity. "Actually Sukie Ambrose has been my friend since school — and yeah, OK, she did somehow discover that strange things happened with her lotions when she used her godmother's recipes — but I still don't buy it. I'm too practical."

"So, Allbard aside, what's your trademark firework going to be? I'm not going to pinch your ideas; I'm just curious."

Clemmie hugged the diary to her. "I've been trying to devise a staged multishot. I call it — don't laugh — Seventh Heaven. It's based on the old religious theory about there being seven different heavens all with their own colours."

Guy simply stared at her. Clemmie sighed. He'd think she was crazy, of course. Maybe she was, spending years playing with mad ideas in the Coddles' shed.

"Go on." He leaned against the workbench. "I'm intrigued. It sounds far more exciting than my research. I thought I'd use Allbard to try and find a firework colour which so far hasn't been discovered."

"Green!" Clemmie grinned at him. "A really deep forest green or the deepest green of a tropical ocean? The kind of green that has sent pyrotechnicians scatty for years?"

"You do know your stuff," Guy laughed. "That's it exactly. And believe me, I've tried every combination of blue and yellow known to man and it still comes out wrong — too pale or too bright . . . But tell me about the seven heavens. I've never heard of them."

"We had a great RE teacher who told us all sorts of interesting things about various religions and beliefs but as I was only interested in colours and explosives, I only listened to the bits that I thought I might be able to use." Clemmie fiddled with her earrings. "Apparently, the first heaven is filled with silver stars on golden chains, the second is blazing with pure gold, three is pearly, the fourth is tears of white gold and silver, five is silver and all orange and red fire, the sixth is rich ruby and garnet — red jewels, and then you reach Seventh Heaven . . ."

Guy was staring at her. "Christ — don't stop now."

"Yeah, well, this is the problem. According to the ancient scriptures, the colour of the seventh heaven is an indescribable divine light, a glorious colour never seen before. Which is where, in firework terms, the magical deepest green comes in, I reckon."

Guy didn't speak. Suggs sat up on his charcoal sack and watched them both closely.

Clemmie shrugged. "Sorry — you must think it's pretty sad. I mean, you're at the top of your profession and I'm just an amateur dabbler with a crazy dream."

"I think," Guy said, unpeeling himself from the workbench, "that your Seventh Heaven sounds totally amazing and I can't believe that none of the big pyro companies have ever thought of it. I can see it now as a mind-blowing magical finale: one sensational lingering burst of colour cascading down on top of the other as the shots explode, eventually culminating in that amazing as-yet-unseen deep green."

Clemmie could see it too. They stood in silence for a moment, both lost in the same dream.

Guy frowned. "What I can't understand though, is why you've never joined one of the national firework companies. Surely they'd have snapped you up? Why on earth are you still living in Bagley and taking office jobs you mostly hate?"

"The truth?"

"It'd make a nice change."

They looked at one another and smiled. Oh, lordy, Clemmie thought, looking quickly away again — he is just sooo achingly gorgeous.

She took a deep breath. "You'll probably think this sounds very sad, but I love living round here. I was desperately homesick at uni. I couldn't wait to come home. My friends, my aunt and uncle, all the familiar things, have always been here and I really had no desire to leave them again. Fireworks were just a private passion, my hobby; I wanted to have both. I just wanted to be happy, and I wasn't happy anywhere but back here, in Bagley and the surrounding villages."

"You could have applied to The Gunpowder Plot for a job."

"Believe me I thought about it." Clemmie avoided Suggs' eyes at this point. "I scanned the job pages all the time to see if you were ever advertising a vacancy, but I guessed you'd have a waiting list of eager wannabe pyros a mile long." She fiddled with the earrings again. "I'm not that confident about my skills so I'd never have had the nerve to approach you on spec."

"Thank goodness you answered our office ad, then," Guy said. "Mind you, YaYa won't believe it was just a happy coincidence. She'll believe it was the collusion of some astral forces or heavenly intervention or something."

Clemmie laughed. "She should talk to my friend Phoebe, she's mad on all things astrological. But seriously, I don't care how it happened, I'm just delighted that it did."

Suggs sat up and gave a derisory snort.

"Me, too." Guy lifted Suggs from his charcoal sack and gently stroked his head. "And like I said, I have no intention of pinching your ideas, but if you'd like, have a free run of the lab to see if you can develop your Seventh Heaven further."

"Really?" Clemmie longed to kiss him. "Wow! Thank you — that would be unbelievable. But I couldn't do it without you. That's my problem. I just play at pyrotechnics because I simply don't have enough knowledge. I don't suppose you'd have time to help me? No, of course you wouldn't."

"Believe me, I'd like nothing better. How do you feel about setting aside some time one evening when I'm not out on a gig to see what we can come up with?"

How she felt, Clemmie thought, would probably make a sinner blush.

"That sounds fantastic. I'd absolutely love to. You have no idea —"

A thundering on the door fortunately prevented the gushing getting out of control.

"Guy!" Syd's voice echoed. "Sorry to bother you, mate, but we can't go any further with the Snepps' display until you come and sort out these bloody timings!"

"Sorry," Guy told Clemmie. "We'll concentrate on Seventh Heaven later." He handed Suggs' lead to her and pulled open the door. "Right, Syd — on my way."

92

Clemmie made sure she'd got all the sheets of paper and the diary and, ignoring the rain and with Suggs trotting beside her, floated back across the yard to the house.

YaYa was in the kitchen, sitting at the untidy table with an opened newspaper, smoking a long cigarette and nursing a mug of black coffee. Suggs immediately scrambled up onto her lap.

"Oh, yuk! You're both drenched!" She looked up from her newspaper, reached across the cluttered table and grabbed a handy piece of kitchen roll to wipe the excess rain from Suggs' fur. "Didn't you take an umbrella?"

"Yes, I think so," Clemmie said dreamily. "I must have left it behind."

"Sweetheart," YaYa gurgled as Suggs briefly groomed himself before curling up on her lap. "You look like you've been poleaxed. What happened? Oh, he wasn't a bastard to you, was he? Sometimes he can get quite ratty when he's playing with his whizbangs."

"No, nothing like that," Clemmie sighed. "Quite the opposite in fact. He offered me a full-time job and said I can go to some displays and —"

She stopped, deciding that it would be possibly straying a touch too close to the proviso if she mentioned Seventh Heaven to YaYa.

"That's bloody great news, love." YaYa winked. "I'm so pleased. And excellent timing as I've just had a bit of news of my own. Grab a coffee, pull up a chair, and we'll go through the dates for those bookings and enquiries."

Clemmie grabbed and pulled and still couldn't stop smiling.

"What star sign are you?" YaYa studied her newspaper.

"Don't bother reading it out. I don't believe in astrology. My best friend Phoebe is mad on all that stuff, though. I was just telling Guy about her. She does tarot readings and plans astral charts."

"No way!" YaYa's batwing eyelashes fluttered into overdrive. "You must introduce me, Clemmie, love! I adore all that hocus pocus! Would she do me a reading some time?"

"Course she would." Clemmie sipped her coffee. "She's always looking for new victims — er — subjects."

"Fantastic. I'll hold you to that. And, come on, join in — what sign are you?"

"Gemini. But there's no point."

YaYa fluttered her long scarlet-tipped fingers excitedly, scattering ash across the table. "Gemini! There you are — it all makes sense! I'm Libra and Guy is Aquarius! We're all air signs, love, don't you see? Bound together by an astral bond! We'll make a superb team, working in planetary harmony. No wonder we all get on so well. And you know loads of firework stuff too. You really were heaven sent."

"All bollocks," Clemmie giggled. "Hokum and tosh! Anyway, you said you had some news."

Suggs sat up, stretched, looked at Clemmie through narrowed eyes and shook his head. Clemmie winked at him. He wrinkled his nose dismissively and re-curled himself on YaYa's lap.

"Oh, yes: my news . . ." YaYa wriggled the Bardot top further off her slender, tanned shoulders. "Well, I've been offered a little tour. Only a week — but it's with the Dancing Queens. They were doing a show in Melton Mowbray and one of the girls got into a bit of a fracas with an off-duty policeman. She's in hospital in traction."

"Oh, dear." Clemmie quickly swallowed a mouthful of coffee. "And the policeman?"

"Just a bruised truncheon. But the vital thing is this is such an honour to be asked. The Dancing Queens are simply the best." She looked across the table. "Have you heard of them?"

"No, sorry. I don't know anything at all about drag acts."

"We'll have to remedy that," YaYa said happily. "When some of my mates do a localish gig I'll take you along."

"I'll look forward to it," Clemmie said faintly. "I think."

"You'll love it. I'll make sure it's not a tacky one. We do stag nights and hen nights and all sorts of clubs — rugby clubs are biggies — and of course, the gay bars." YaYa chuckled. "Anyway, point being, the Dancing Queens want me for the first week in November, which means I'll be away for the Snepps' firework party in Hazy Hassocks on November the fifth. You'll have to go along in my place, love."

"In your place?"

"As Guy's other half, yes. Mind, it won't be an easy night. You'll have your work cut out. That Tarnia Snepps is rampant, love. Rampant. And Guy can't be as rude as he'd like to be because she's a good client."

Absolutely itching to scamper round the kitchen punching the air and screaming, Clemmie managed to look mildly interested. "OK — I'll try my very best to keep him safe for you."

"Good girl." YaYa lit another cigarette. "Guy probably won't be best pleased, but he's always pretty cool about my work. After all we don't live in one another's pockets."

Just in the same house, the same bed, Clemmie thought, reining in the absurd thoughts that she'd had about spending an entire evening as Guy's woman-in-situ. He's gay, you daft bat. Remember that.

"So, that's the Snepps shenanigans sorted — now let's have a look at what other bookings we can tie up." YaYa reached for the diary. "Mmmm, we'll have to rejig a couple and update the wallcharts. I always try to see if we can offer alternative dates before we have to say we're already booked. But the rest of these look OK. I'll ring some and confirm, you can email the others. Right — now these two are a bit odd."

Clemmie peered at Guy's huge scrawly writing. "Steeple Fritton — isn't that where he went yesterday?"

YaYa nodded. "A wedding enquiry. For Valentine's Day next year. Sweet. And, if you promise not to say I told you, also Guy's birthday."

"No way!" Clemmie was entranced. "How perfect! Guy being born on Valentine's Day! Er . . . I mean —"

"I know exactly what you mean. He had sacksful of cards for both when we were at school! Poor postman nearly got a hernia." YaYa laughed, her cigarette dancing between her pouting glossy lips. "However, there are complications with this particular wedding, and the bloke Guy needed to see yesterday had to cry off at the last minute. Apparently it's all a bit cloak and dagger. We need to make another visit, soon as, to find out exactly what he wants. Do you want to do that one?"

Clemmie nodded. "I know where Steeple Fritton is." "Somewhere towards Ufton Nervet — one of those really quaint little Berkshire villages. But I don't think I know anywhere near enough about The Gunpowder Plot to be able to do it on my own."

"We'd do it together," YaYa said, flicking through the diary. "You and me. Guy can look after the office while we're out. It'll be an interesting one for you to get to grips with."

"I'd love to. But why is it so complicated?"

"Because it's a secret wedding, love. The groom is arranging it without the bride knowing. Guy says he's going to pretend they're going to someone else's wedding at the registry office and spring it on the lucky lady when they get there."

"Blimey! What if she doesn't want to marry him?"

"A risk he's obviously prepared to take. Brave boy. So — I'll pop him in for next week, shall I? Tuesday if it suits him. Now, what's his name? Ah, yes, Ellis Blissit, and we've got a mobile number so I'll call him this afternoon. Right — now the other one we need to go and suss out is another wedding. I so love weddings, don't you, love?"

As she was obviously never going to have one of her own Clemmie wasn't sure she did, but she nodded anyway. "And where's this one?"

"Milton St John. For Charlie Somerset and Jemima Carlisle. Early December. She phoned last week."

"Milton St John's the horse-racing village isn't it? Near Newbury? And even I've heard of Charlie Somerset. My Uncle Bill won a fortune on him when he was a jockey — Charlie Somerset that is, not my Uncle Bill."

"Dead sexy chap," YaYa said approvingly. "Really fit. Charlie Somerset that is, not your Uncle Bill — although never having met your Uncle Bill maybe that's not true."

"It's true."

"Pity. Anyhow, we'll need to make a couple of visits for this one as Jemima and Charlie want a quiet firework display because of the horses, so we'll need to take them some video clips and work out something pretty, celebratory, but non-noisy to suit. Shall I pop you in with Guy for that one? Say the end of next week?"

"Sounds great," Clemmie sighed happily. "Yes, I'd love it."

"However," YaYa flicked through the diary, "Jemima has also asked us to make a prelim visit so that she can work out our timings to fit in with her other reception entertainments. She did say we may have to meet her away from the village as she's so busy with the last-minute wedding arrangements. Poor girl sounded completely frazzled. So, if you and Guy do the second meeting, how about you doing the first on your own now Guy has made you a permanent staff member? We'll just have to ring Jemima and sort out a convenient time and place for you to meet. OK with you?"

"Wonderful! I'm sure I can cope with that. Shall I get on with sorting all this out straight away?"

"Oh, let's have another cup of coffee first," YaYa said, picking Suggs up and heading towards his tiny sofa. "And a sticky bun. Nothing like a sticky bun at lunchtime. I'll do the coffee and you get the buns. They're on the cold shelf in the larder."

As Clemmie had managed not to eat anything disgusting for at least twenty-four hours, and as today had been so sensational, she felt no guilt at all in indulging in a ton of calories and cream before resuming work.

She lifted the box carefully out of the larder, remembering to bolt the door against Suggs' scavenging, and stared again at the wall of photos. Tarnia Snepps certainly looked predatory. It would be fun living out her fantasy though, pretending that she and the gorgeous Guy Devlin were together — even if it was simply a charade for one night only.

"Oh — she's stunning!" Clemmie pointed at a photograph of a classically beautiful blonde woman and four angelic children, sitting round a wooden table in a massive and perfectly manicured summer garden. "And those children! All four of them — blonde and so cute.

They all look like something from a telly advert. Are they customers of The Gunpowder Plot, too? Did you do a display for them?"

YaYa had shimmied across the kitchen and was looking over Clemmie's shoulder.

"Oh, that." Her voice was dismissive. "Guy keeps taking that one down and I keep putting it back so that I can spit at it when I'm feeling particularly venomous."

"Why?" Clemmie laughed. "Who are they?"

"The blonde's Helen — as in the face that's tucked a thousand nips — and the sprogs are the bug-eyed spawn of Satan: Crap, Puke, Snot and Mungo."

"You're such a bitch," Clemmie giggled.

"Thanks. I try my best."

"But what on earth did this Helen and her children do to you?"

"To me, love, not a lot. To Guy — far, far too much."

"Why?" Clemmie asked, puzzled, as YaYa carried the box of sticky buns towards the table. "What did they do? Not pay their display bill? Criticise the fireworks? Who on earth are they?"

"Oh, you'll meet 'em soon enough." YaYa sucked in her breath. "They're Guy's wife and kids."

CHAPTER
EIGHT

A few days later, driving towards Newbury through the late autumnal sunshine to meet up with Jemima Carlisle, Clemmie tried to marshal her thoughts. As this was her first official outing as a Gunpowder Plot employee, she knew she had to concentrate and get everything right. She simply couldn't dwell on the more personal issues which crowded her working life at the boathouse. Not today. Today she really, really had to be professional.

It was going to be tricky.

Having just got used to the dream-busting news about Guy and YaYa, suddenly finding out that he also had a wife and four children had been a really confusing sideswipe.

A million questions had tumbled through her brain that day. She'd clenched her teeth to prevent them spilling out as words that could damn her forever, and tried valiantly to keep her face steady and her reactions muted.

"His wife? Really? I had no idea he was married."

"*Was* married being the operative words." YaYa had plonked the box of buns on the table and dished them onto two plates. "Helen's officially his ex. Not that you'd notice. She still can't keep away from him. Oh, she says she doesn't want to pop into his bed any more, but she sure loves his bank account. He pays her guilt-money every time she asks."

An ex-wife was still a bit of a bummer, Clemmie had thought, biting into a bun, not caring about the squish of sugary syrup that dripped down her chin or the spray of fruit that immediately splashed onto her fingers. And even more so as Guy was gay? Or was he bisexual? Or had he now decided to give up women completely now he and YaYa were together?

Oh, dear. This was all very confusing foreign territory to her. And a bit much that the biggest glimmer of hope she had in her love live was that the man of her dreams would turn out to be bisexual rather than gay.

"So, she still visits him here, does she?"

"Whenever she needs a new pair of designer shoes or a holiday or a new car or fresh cosmetic surgery or when the brats want a skiing lesson or —"

Clemmie had washed down the bun with a mouthful of coffee. "She must hate you."

"Loathes me, love," YaYa had said happily. "Hates the whole Steve/YaYa thing. The cow is always very rude to me and about me. I, of course, respond in kind."

Much as Clemmie had come to like YaYa, she had a certain amount of sympathy with the exquisite Helen on that point. How galling must it be to discover that your husband has always been secretly in love with his best mate from school and dumps you in favour of an over-the-top drag queen who used to be called Steve?

"And the children? Guy must have been very young when they had them, surely? He can't be more than thirty now . . ."

"Thirty-one next Feb." YaYa had reached for another bun. "And the brats aren't actually his. Not biologically. They're his stepkids. The foul Helen started her marrying-for-money career straight from school. She'd already despatched a couple of husbands when she got her talons into Guy. Already had Crap, Puke, Snot and Mungo in tow when she snaffled him. He loves kids, always said he wanted to adopt a football team of them, but that lot were little shits to him right from the start. Sadly, he's such a gentleman that he took them on without a murmur."

"But if she — and her children — were so unpleasant, why on earth did he marry her, especially if —" Clemmie stopped. It possibly wasn't the best time to mention Guy's sexual preferences.

"Lust, loneliness and falling prey to a very clever predator," YaYa sniffed. "Helen is, as you noticed, exceptionally beautiful in a pale ice-maideny sort of way. She turned up at a time when Guy was pretty vulnerable. He'd had girls — and boys — hurling themselves at him from puberty. He was always spoiled for choice. His reputation is pretty awesome. But he'd just split up with someone who really mattered to him, and Helen, being a bit of a stunner and also presenting him with a ready-made family, pushed all the right buttons at the time. She played such a clever game, made him think that she wasn't particularly interested. He wasn't used to that, so he pursued her relentlessly

— then wham! She sprang her trap and the poor bloke was up the aisle before you could say Lily Savage."

Realising that she'd just polished off three buns, Clemmie had removed the worst of the residue from her sleeves and swept crumbs off the table for Suggs who had scampered from his basket and was hoovering up the debris at the speed of light. Could she even dare hope that if Guy had once loved women enough to marry one, that she might still be in with a chance?

And how could she even think about that if it meant breaking YaYa's heart?

"So, when they divorced, you moved in with him?"

"Blimey, love — no! I was here before, during and after Helen. That's why she loathes me so much. I knew him, you see. Really knew him. Better than she ever would. And I always loved him more than she ever could. He's my best friend. He was never hers."

And then Clemmie had cleared away the plates and the coffee mugs, and she and YaYa had trekked back to the office, and Clemmie had tried really, really hard not to think that the more meaty details of the Guy — YaYa — Helen ménage-à-trois would keep the tabloids in copy for weeks.

Shaking herself back to the present and realising that she really had to push all the Guy stuff out of her head for the time being, Clemmie found a car park, and checked the address Jemima Carlisle had given her.

"I'm really sorry," Jemima had said on the phone, "but I'm frantically busy with last minute arrangements, so would you mind meeting me at the wedding dress shop in Newbury? We can sort out the initial display details there, while I'm in wedding mode, which should make it easier when you come to meet me with Charlie to finalise things. Is that OK?"

And Clemmie had said it sounded fine — not to mention fun — and she'd be delighted to fit in with whatever Jemima wanted.

So now, locking the Peugeot, she headed off into Newbury's bustling High Street.

At precisely that moment, Jemima was devouring the atmosphere of ankle-deep cream carpets, crystal chandeliers, acres of silks, satins, chiffon and net, and Lionel Richie playing softly on a constant loop in one of Newbury's wedding boutiques.

"I can't wear white!" Jemima groaned. "I've been living in sin for eight years!"

"Living in sin?" Maddy Fitzgerald, Jemima's matron-of-honour, paused in stroking armfuls of dazzling satin. "Hark at you. Cohabiting, you mean. No one lives in sin these days."

Suzy, Maddy's younger sister, paused in trying on a diamanté tiara and surveyed them both through the mirror. "Holy hell — she lives with Charlie Somerset, Mad. *Anything* to do with Charlie Somerset involves sin."

They all giggled. Charlie Somerset, one time champion jump-jockey and lady-killer, was sex on legs. Since falling madly in love with Jemima, who ran the village bookshop in Milton St John, he was a reformed character. Charlie, still drop-dead gorgeous but now strictly a one-woman man, worked as assistant trainer for Maddy's husband, Drew, at Peapods, their racing yard where he and Jemima shared the beautiful stable flat.

"Grab my mobile." Jemima passed the phone to Suzy. "In case the girl from The Gunpowder Plot rings for directions while I'm in my underwear or something."

"Stop panicking." Suzy continued to plonk tiaras on her spiky blonde hair, discarding them almost immediately. "It'll all be fine. If she turns up while you're trying something on, I'm sure she won't mind waiting."

It was sweet of Jemima to have asked her to be a bridesmaid, Suzy knew, but she'd never been a froufrou girl and the dress was bound to be a meringue. Still, it'd hide her foreshortened, twisted leg from a church full of wedding guests who weren't used to seeing it displayed round Milton St John beneath her cut-off shorts or miniskirts.

Not that she cared much about her leg any more. She'd almost forgotten about it, after all the accident had been seven years ago now, just before her twenty first birthday. But she was still aware of strangers trying not to stare as she limped past them. Maybe they thought it tragic that a young, slender, very trendy woman should be afflicted with such an obvious disability. Maybe they thought she should have had something done about it.

Suzy shrugged. She'd had everything the best orthopaedic surgeons could manage. They'd been brilliant. She'd never be able to thank them enough. They couldn't save her career as an up and coming jockey, anymore than they could save her relationship with the only man she'd ever loved, but they'd saved her life and her leg. She was more than happy with that.

"So," Maddy said to Jemima, "we've established you don't want to wear white. What about choice of material? Silk or satin or what?"

"Velvet is very effective for a winter wedding," the owner of the boutique's voice echoed spookily from behind a curtained-off cubicle. She gave each word seven strangulated syllables and sounded as if she was being sick. "With swansdown. I trust madam is having a winter wedding?"

"Who's a madame?" Jemima frowned, gazing round the shop.

"She means you." Suzy poked Jemima in the ribs. "She's talking in posh-frock-shop speak."

"Oh, um, yes." Jemima nodded in the direction of the cubicle. "The wedding's the first weekend in December. But I'm quite tall and — well — a bit on the scraggy side. I think velvet and swansdown will make me look like a stork."

The hernia-voice behind the curtain tutted and sighed but offered no further advice.

"I also think," Jemima muttered, "that maybe I need to choose a colour before I get to grips with style or fabric. Oh, I'm useless at all this. You know me, I'm perennially happy in hippy grunge."

"Hippy grunge is definitely out," Maddy said shortly. "As is your penchant for black, grey and all shades muted. So, what about ivory for a colour?"

"Ivory is very popular." The wedding boutique's assistant popped her head round a second curtained-off cubicle where several largish women were trying to squeeze themselves into bridesmaid's dresses of zebra-print satin. "Very flattering for the older bride."

Jemima giggled as the assistant disappeared behind the curtain to wrestle with her herd. "Ivory it is then. Which one's ivory, Mad?"

"The one between white and cream I think." Maddy sighed. "They're all so gorgeous — and of course, with you being tall and slim, you could wear anything. You're spoilt for choice here, but surely you've got some preference?"

"Well . . . seriously, I want everything to be really traditional. Charlie's proposed nearly every day for the last eight years but it's taken me this long to convince myself he means it and won't regret it."

"Of course he means it," Suzy snorted. "And he'll never regret it. He adores you, Jemima. Loves you truly, madly, deeply. He's been totally faithful to you for eight years and he's deliriously happy. With his past reputation, and the fact that every woman with a pulse fancies him rotten, he couldn't make it more obvious that he loves you and wants you — and only you — for the rest of his life."

Jemima blushed. "I do know that, and I love him to death, too. I wouldn't be marrying him otherwise. So, yes, I want the whole shebang. Proper gown, top hats, matching bridesmaids . . ."

"I wonder if they do a range for the chubby older bridesmaid?" Maddy grinned. "As I'm now clearly never going to be less than a good size fourteen and was an awfully ancient thirty-seven last birthday."

"Me too." Jemima lifted out a dress of pale ivory satin, the strapless bodice encrusted with glowing three-coloured seed pearls. "Where on earth has the time gone? Oh, this is beautiful — but do you think it'll make me look too mutton?"

"Madam!" The boutique's owner, her work behind the curtain clearly done, sashayed towards them, her approach silenced by the depth of the carpet. "That will suit you perfectly. Could have been made for you. Why don't you try it on, maybe with this veil — you do want full length? And perhaps a matching wrap for the chilly bits — the photos and what-have-you? And maybe a pearl coronet? Then we could perhaps find something in a complementary shade for your bridesmaids? Are these two ladies your only attendants?"

"My daughters are going to be flower girls," Maddy said. "And my son is a page boy. But we thought it would be better to get ourselves sorted first before letting them loose in here."

Suzy stroked the rows and rows of fabulous gowns and grinned to herself. Her nieces, nine-year-old Poppy Scarlet and four-year-old Iris Blue, and her seven-year-old nephew, Daragh, were actually all extremely well behaved, but growing up in the mucky male-dominated world of horse racing at home in Milton St John,

Daragh had never been seen less than slightly grubby, and the girls lived in jeans and boots. The thought of Daragh in a kilt and Poppy Scarlet and Iris Blue looking demure in crinolines was practically impossible.

"Very wise." The boutique's owner was sweeping both the ivory and pearl dress and Jemima towards a cubicle. "You wouldn't believe the tantrums some angel-faced moppets have thrown in here when their dresses don't make them look exactly like Britney Spears. Now, let's see how this suits, shall we? Then maybe your older bridesmaids could aim for tonal ensembles?"

Maddy and Suzy exchanged amused glances, trying hard not to giggle again at the murdered vowels, and parked themselves on spindly gold and cream mock Queen Anne chairs outside the cubicle.

"This makes me really nostalgic," Maddy murmured. "It only seems five minutes ago that I married Drew. It was the most wonderful day of my life. Time flies so quickly."

Suzy nodded. Maddy and Drew were still totally besotted with one another. Still living in lovely sprawling Peapods where Drew was now one of the country's top racehorse trainers. For Maddy and Drew the last eight years had been blissful: they had each other, a thriving business they adored, their menagerie of much-loved animals, three gorgeous children . . .

And what did she have? Not a lot, to be honest. How much had her life changed since Drew and Maddy had married? Of course the accident — a crashing fall in the first race at Ascot in which her horse had stumbled, thrown her leaving her right foot dangling in the stirrup, staggered into the rails and finally rolled on top of her — had changed everything.

But it had been her fault, hadn't it? Not the fall, but the fact that she'd been so arrogant about her ambitions: overconfident, hard-nosed, driven, determined to be the best female jockey in the country: not just as good as the men, but better. She'd left Milton St John and Maddy and Drew and all her friends for her ambitions. She'd left Luke for the same reasons. She'd chosen her career above Luke Delaney — and paid the price.

Suzy swallowed. Still now she remembered not the pain when her leg was crushed by half a ton of panicking animal but only her terror in case the horse was not OK. She'd known her leg was definitely broken in several places, but human limbs always healed. Equine ones rarely did.

But the horse had been fine. He was still racing. She'd never ridden a horse professionally since that day. She worked for Drew now, as his secretary, efficiently organising the day-to-day running of the Peapods yard and booking his horses and jockeys into meetings, and trying, really trying, not to mind that she wasn't the one riding at Epsom or Haydock or Doncaster or Cheltenham.

"Suze?" Maddy leaned across. "Are you all right?"

"Fine — just thinking . . . about your wedding, and everyone being so happy, and how lucky you are. And now Jemima and Charlie will be like a mirror image of you and Drew."

Maddy hugged her. "Yes, they will. And so will you. One day. You're still very young. And how many blokes have you turned down since —"

"Loads," Suzy sighed. "Because they weren't the right one."

Mad was right, of course. She was young. One day maybe she'd be in a shop like this with her own mum, choosing a dress for her wedding. She could almost see it. And Poppy Scarlet and Iris Blue as bridesmaids, and her dad, uncomfortable in his suit, proudly taking her arm and walking slowly down the aisle because of her leg . . . Oh, yes, she could practically see it all. Funny though, she simply couldn't see the face of her bridegroom. Because, she had to admit it, the only man she'd ever wanted to marry was Luke Delaney. And that was impossible.

They both sat silently again, and Maddy flicked through a sheaf of bridal magazines, strategically placed, probably in the hope of finding something Poppy and Iris wouldn't totally object to.

"Oh, look at this pearl choker and the matching earrings — wouldn't that look lovely with Jemima's frock? I'll just go and show her."

As Maddy waded through the carpet towards the cubicle, the boutique's door opened, and a tall, slender girl in a long black coat, with a mass of dark red hair, peered across the shop.

"Excuse me — I'm looking for Jemima Carlisle?"

"She's being fitted." Suzy smiled. "Are you the fireworks person she's arranged to meet here?"

"That's me, yes. Clemmie Coddle."

"Suzy Beckett. One quarter of Jemima's and Charlie's bridesmaids. Please, sit down and keep me company. She shouldn't be long."

"Thanks." Clemmie perched on the edge of the spindly chair which Maddy had vacated and looked around. "Oh, this is lovely, isn't it? Even if you're not getting married, it sort of sucks you into the mindset straight away, doesn't it?"

Suzy nodded. "I was almost planning my wedding just now — and I'm not going to have one."

Clemmie grinned. "Me neither. But I know what you mean. I could easily run amok amongst those dresses."

"Exactly! And I don't even like frocks! It must be bridal brainwashing."

Before they could say anything else, another pre-wedding party pushed their way into the boutique, the mother-of-the-bride clearly in charge, a list of requirements already being flourished in her hand. Her daughter, a pale mousy girl, hung back, looking embarrassed. Another assistant swooped down on them, looking at the list, then nodding and smiling and whisking them in the direction of a row of pink Cinderella-type ballgowns.

"If it were good enough for that Jordan," the mother-of-the-bride was saying, "it's good enough for my Natalie. We wants the whole lot — pink crown, pink wand, pink doves, pink horses, pink coach, pink everything."

Suzy, catching Clemmie's eye, tried not to giggle.

Clemmie smothered a snigger. "Sorry — I really shouldn't laugh — but I can somehow imagine my

113

mum being a bit like that, too. She's the sweetest person in the world, but I guess your daughter's wedding turns you into some sort of overbearing monster."

"Probably." Suzy nodded. "When my sister, Maddy, got married, my mum nearly ran herself into the ground making sure it was the wedding of the year. Fortunately for Jemima, her mother's staying well out of it."

They smiled at one another again, then lapsed into a dreamy silence.

Luke had been to see Suzy after the accident. Every day. They'd told her at the hospital. And she'd refused to see him. She hadn't wanted his pity. She'd broken his heart and left him. She'd thought she'd wanted fame and fortune more than she'd wanted him. He'd only come back because he felt sorry for her.

And he'd written and phoned and emailed and texted, but she'd ignored those too, and eventually he'd given up. She hadn't heard from Luke Delaney for six years; although she'd followed his career, of course. He almost out-Frankie'd Frankie Dettori all those years ago: the youngest, sexiest, most charismatic and talented jockey on the circuit. Then he'd left Berkshire and ridden equally successfully in Hong Kong and America, where he'd settled, and had married his Kentucky trainer's daughter four years ago.

"Oh, wow!" Clemmie nudged Suzy, snapping her back to the present, as the cubicle curtains swished open. "Is that Jemima? She looks like a supermodel!"

Suzy swallowed the lump in her throat as Jemima emerged from the swathe of curtains. The column of ivory satin moulded to her glorious figure, lustrous pearls glimmered in her dark, shaggy hair, the heavy train sweeping on the floor around her, the veil, a mere froth of cream lace, like a pale, shimmering aura.

"Holy hell!" Suzy grinned. "Charlie won't be able to keep his hands off you."

"He never can." Maddy laughed, emerging from behind Jemima.

The boutique's owner stood beside a rather shell-shocked Jemima, hands clasped, preening. "This is The One, ladies, I'm sure you'll agree. Madam looks as beautiful as every bride should. Now, while we're on a roll, what about your dresses? I think something similar in style but maybe in a more peachy colour, to complement the seed pearls? Come along. Choppy-chop."

"Actually," Clemmie said as she found herself propelled with Suzy and Maddy towards the rows of bridesmaids' frocks, "I'm not a bridesmaid. I'm here to see Jemima, the bride . . ."

"Whatever." The shop owner almost flicked her aside. "But please don't get in the way — and right now I only need the attendants."

Suzy looked over her shoulder. "'Bye Clemmie. Nice to meet you."

"You too."

Alone now with Jemima, Clemmie smiled. "I'm Clemmie from The Gunpowder Plot — but honestly, before we talk about fireworks, I must say you look absolutely amazing."

"Thanks." Jemima stared rather dazedly at herself in one of the many spotlighted mirrors. "But it's like looking at a total stranger. Sorry — I know you're busy — and I do apologise for doing this here but," she swished across the boutique in her sensually rustling frock and picked up a briefcase, "I can only take the odd day away from my business, and there's so much to do."

Clemmie peered over Jemima's shoulder as she produced several folders from the briefcase and started to flick through them. "Oh, that's clever — you are so efficient! Everything cross-referenced and colour-coded."

"I'm the epitome of anal retention, as Suzy has probably already delighted in telling you," Jemima sighed happily, stroking the veil away from her face. "But I do so need this wedding to be perfect."

"Of course you do." Clemmie nodded. "Look, shall we spread everything out over there on that desk, then you tell me what you've got arranged and what you want from us and I'll leave you the literature I've brought with me. Then when I go back to the office I can cost things out, then we'll come and see you and — um — Charlie nearer the wedding to finalise everything."

"That sounds wonderful." Jemima, catching up the hem of her dress, sashayed across the shop with catwalk elegance. "Right: now this is what we've got, and these are the times. And what I'd like you to do is to provide

116

a sensationally colourful display without any noise. Is that possible?"

"Absolutely." Clemmie produced the brochures Guy had given her that morning, and the price lists. "Now these are all geared to quiet displays. Down here are the timings of each of the fireworks, and this is our price list."

As Jemima ran a slender finger down the list, scribbling things in her folder and occasionally tapping details into an electronic organiser, Clemmie glanced at the other items on the reception agenda.

"Oh, how lovely — a live band and a disco, and a chocolate fountain, and The Bradley-Morland Memory Lane Fair . . . it all sounds fantastic. Who are Solomon and Bonne Nuit? Some sort of music hall act or something?"

Jemima stopped writing. "Don't laugh — they're the oldest horses in the stableyard where Charlie and I live. They mean so much to everyone in the village, so the old boys are coming to the wedding with flowers in their manes. I've written down absolutely everything in case it slips my mind."

"It's a lovely idea to have the horses there."

"Well, yes, and of course, it's because of all the horses we can't have a loud firework display." Jemima resumed her notes. "But everything you've got here sounds perfect. Thank you so much for this. OK — I've written down what I'd like, and how it should fit in, and I'd love to see some film clips of what I've chosen, if that's possible?"

"Absolutely." Clemmie pushed Jemima's notes into her bag. "We'll do that when we come to see you."

"Thank you." Jemima smiled and peered at herself in the mirror again. "I suppose we really could have done this by phone and post or even email."

Clemmie nodded. "We could. But Guy Devlin," she savoured the words, "who owns The Gunpowder Plot, always says that the personal touch is very important in this business. He always makes sure he meets all his customers face-to-face."

"A man after my own heart," Jemima said, packing the folders into her briefcase again. "And wonderfully refreshing in this age of on-line communications and faceless business."

"Right." Clemmie beamed at Jemima. "I'll get back to Winterbrook and we'll work out a display for you, then we'll be in touch again. And — oh . . ." she sighed. "You really do look sensational."

Jemima swirled round and gave a little curtsey. "Actually, I do love it. I don't think I'll ever want to take it off. Thank you, Clemmie — and I'll look forward to seeing you again soon."

And saying goodbye and beaming at her first out-of-office success, Clemmie almost skipped out of the rarefied atmosphere of the boutique and back into the noisy, busy reality of Newbury High Street.

An hour later, heads spinning, Jemima, Suzy and Maddy, arrived back in Milton St John — gowns chosen and left for slight alterations and further fittings

— with a promise that they'd return with the more youthful members of the bridal party next time.

"Coffee," Jemima said weakly, as Suzy steered her car through Milton St John's narrow main street. "Before I go back to work I need caffeine. Loads and loads of caffeine."

"I think we all do," Suzy agreed, pulling up outside her cottage. "I haven't been pushed around so much since my days in physiotherapy. That woman must have been a bodybuilder in a previous life. And I can't believe I was actually enthusiastic about wearing something almost skintight in glimmery peach."

"You looked a dream," Maddy said, struggling from the rear seat. "I thought glimmery peach was the least flattering thing anyone could pick for someone my shape but, strangely, I loved it too."

"We all looked very glam," Jemima giggled. "If totally unrecognisable."

Suzy unlocked her cottage, wrestling slightly with the door, and kicked at the hall rug as she went in.

Across the road from Peapods, this had been Maddy's cottage first. Then Suzy and Maddy had shared it, and when Mad had moved in with Drew, Suzy and Luke had made it their home. And after the accident, returning to Milton St John, with the cottage still empty, Suzy had simply moved in and rented it again. Single storey, it had made coping with her injuries easy in those early days. It was her shell, her sanctuary, the only place she now ever wanted to be.

Maddy and Jemima had flopped into the armchairs on either side of the fireplace while Suzy made coffee in

119

the cottage's oddly shaped kitchen. When she returned to the living room, they'd got the contents of Jemima's wedding folders spread over most of the floor.

"Such organisation!" Suzy mocked, putting the tray on a small side table. "Have you got a tick-list for everything?"

"Yep," Jemima said contentedly. "Ooh lovely, Suze, thank you. Biscuits too. So, that's the dresses sorted — and the flowers, and the photographer and the cars. And Clemmie was really efficient, so that's the fireworks sorted, too."

"I liked her," Suzy said. "Shame she'd left before I got to show off in my glimmery peach frock. Hopefully she'll be at the wedding with the firework people."

"I'll make sure she is." Jemima shuffled her files. "And she's going to bring us some DVDs nearer the date so you can be there then, too. Now, how are we doing on the guest list?"

"I know the whole village will be there, but are Kit and Rosa and their brood coming over from Jersey?" Maddy was already dunking a biscuit. "And Georgia and Rory and their boys from Upton Poges?"

"Yes to both — although I did have a bit of a problem with Georgia's grandmother. We wanted her to come, but she's such a flirt no one knew which man she'd be with, so we just sent her a plus-one."

"Good old Cecilia," Suzy chuckled. "Still pulling at the age of — God — what must she be now? Eighty-odd?"

"At least." Jemima nodded over her coffee mug. "She's amazing."

"The whole thing is going to be amazing," Maddy said, selecting another biscuit. "It'll be the most wonderful day Milton St John has ever seen — well, at least since my wedding day. It'll be just perfect."

It would, Suzy thought. Well, almost. Only one thing would be missing from her perfect day. Or rather, one person. But it wasn't going to happen, was it? It would take magic or a miracle or both for Luke Delaney to be there, alone, and wanting her. But Luke was thousands of miles away with his new life and his wife.

And she only had herself to blame. Still, she really couldn't rain on Jemima's parade. It *would* be a truly wonderful day, even if Luke couldn't see her in her elegant dress, showing that she'd moved on, come to terms with everything, was coping with and enjoying her new life. She gave herself a severe mental shake. Onwards and upwards.

CHAPTER
NINE

Ellis Blissit stood behind the bar of Steeple Fritton's only pub, the Crooked Sixpence, which he ran with his partner and live-in-lover, Lola Wentworth, constantly glancing at the clock over the fireplace. Bloody hell — ten past eleven already. If The Gunpowder Plot people didn't come soon, he'd have to open up for the lunchtime trade and Lola would be back from Reading and all his plans would be shot to pieces.

Posy had promised to delay Lola's return to Steeple Fritton for as long as possible, but surely Lola was going to suspect something was going on? She was scarily intelligent, not to mention perceptive, and had already asked more than a few awkward questions. And she simply couldn't understand why Posy Malone, seven months pregnant, had asked her, Lola, to accompany her to this morning's antenatal appointment even if they were best friends.

"Why can't Flynn go?" Lola had queried. "Surely he wants to be there?"

"Normally, yes — but this one's just a routine appointment, not a vital one for husbands to attend, and Flynn's too busy to come with me," Posy had said blithely. "I can go to the hospital session on my own of course, but I'd like to have someone with me just in case they suddenly tell me I'm expecting quads."

And naturally Lola had agreed to go, although she'd been pretty harsh about Flynn's defection, because she'd never forgive herself if anything happened to Posy.

Ellis smiled to himself. Poor Flynn. Desperate to be with Posy at every appointment, he'd only very reluctantly agreed to bow out to leave the coast clear for Ellis. And Lola would go mad if she knew what Ellis was doing, but what other way was there? He wanted to marry her so much, and she'd always refused because . . .

"Ellis! Ain't you open yet?" Neddy Pink, one of the Crooked Sixpence's elderly regulars, bellowed as he rattled the door. "Me and Martha and Mary are fair shrammed! Oi! Ellis! Can you hear me? This blame door's stuck again! I can't get in!"

"That's because we're closed!" Ellis yelled. "It's not twelve yet! Go and sit on the bench — I'll open up when it's time." And when someone arrives to stand behind the damn bar, he thought, while I discuss the firework display with The Gunpowder Plot — if they ever turn up.

"It's October, not flamin' June! It's blame nippy out 'ere for the gels. They ain't no spring chickens, you know."

"Don't try and make me feel guilty," Ellis shouted. "It's quite mild today and your sisters are as tough as you are. Sit on the bench in the sun — you'll be fine."

123

"It's damn daft if you asks me," Neddy grumbled at full volume. "You should be open twenty-seven-four like them proper pubs in Reading."

Ellis grinned to himself. Since flexible licensing hours had been introduced, he and Lola had tried out all sorts of opening times in the Crooked Sixpence but had quickly settled back into the old routine of three hours at lunchtime and five hours each evening, with late opening only for special events.

Their brief sortie into being open all hours had resulted in mayhem and chaos. Oh, not that there had been violent glass fights outside, and a lot of projectile vomiting just before dawn. No, it had meant that by midnight the majority of Steeple Fritton's older punters, happily sozzled, were sound asleep in the cosy chairs by the fire and he and Lola had had to tuck them in, and provide them with breakfast in the mornings.

"Ellis — sorry, I got held up," Flynn Malone opened the pub's back door. "Am I late?"

"Not really." Ellis smiled at Posy's husband and his closest friend. "But I'm really glad you're here. God knows where The Gunpowder Plot people have got to. I've tried ringing the mobile number I was given for today and keep getting a very strange message. Sounds more like a massage parlour than a fireworks company. And the Pinks are giving me a hard time because they think they should be let in early."

"Yeah." Flynn nodded. "I saw them perched on the bench outside looking mad as hell. That's why I came round the back. They still scare the shit out of me. Anyway, I'm here now and Posy'll keep Lola out of the way for as long as possible, so it'll be all systems go when the firework guys arrive and that'll be the last thing on your list done."

Ellis sincerely hoped so. He'd arranged everything else for this Valentine's Day wedding with military precision. Posy and Flynn were the only other people who knew what he was planning, and even they'd voiced very real concerns to start with. Still, he thought, they'd been stars ever since — and hopefully Lola still had no idea at all that on February fourteenth of next year she'd be whisked off to Fritton Magna Registry Office to become Mrs Ellis Blissit. At long last.

He'd booked the flowers and the limousine and the photographer from Reading so that no one in the village could get wind of what was going on, and Posy's parents, who ran the local B&B, were going to supply the wedding breakfast back here in the pub although Posy hadn't let them in on the secret yet, while Flynn was going to provide the traditional village evening entertainment with his superb showman's traction engine and fairground organ outside the Crooked Sixpence. So far, so good.

Even the registrar, in the tiny village office which served as a legal jack-of-all-trades building for Fritton Magna, Steeple Fritton and Lesser Fritton, had been great in dealing with the necessary paperwork. Ellis had become very James Bond and whizzed off with Lola's birth certificate on the pretext of renewing both their passports — which he had to allay suspicion — and the ceremony had been booked.

"I understand you want a late afternoon wedding. I'm happy to offer five o'clock: OK? Good. And neither of you have been married before," the registrar had said, handing him back the documents. "No impediments of any kind. All nice and straightforward."

Straightforward? Well, yes, of course, it should be — if only Lola wanted to marry him.

"Where the hell are we?" Clemmie peered through the 4×4's windscreen at the tumble of trees and overgrown hedgerows. "Is this a road or a path?"

"Sat nav says it's the Lesser Fritton road," YaYa, a blonde today and wearing a tight lime-green woollen frock with bottle-green accessories, sang out loudly above one of Dusty Springfield's greatest hits. "Which means we must be near Steeple Fritton. Which, as I recall, you said you knew like the back of your hand."

"Don't start on me," Clemmie giggled. "I know where it is, yes. I never said I knew how to get there once we left civilisation. Shall I ring Ellis Blissit and ask for directions?"

"Let's see if we can find it on our own first, shall we, love? It always looks so amateurish admitting to being lost."

"Better to look amateurish than to lose the booking by being inefficient."

"Oooh, get you!" YaYa plunged the 4×4 into a narrow tunnel of gorgeously glowing autumn leaves. "Little Miss Perfect Secretary! Just because you handled the Jemima Carlisle prelim meeting so well, you think you're infallible don't you?"

"Yep. And I also think we're lost."

YaYa chuckled. "How spooky is that? Listen, love. Dusty's singing 'In The Middle of Nowhere'! One of my faves."

"I still think we should ring." Clemmie picked up YaYa's mobile from the dashboard. "There are a couple of messages on here already . . . let's see — yes, it's Ellis Blissit wondering where we are. And he's not the only one."

"Bugger," YaYa shrieked above Dusty now singing 'Son of a Preacher Man'. "I'd left the mobile primed for a couple of my chums to call re the Dancing Queens tour. I didn't expect young Mr Blissit to ring. He must think he's got the wrong number."

"Why?" Clemmie peered suspiciously across the cream leather interior. "What does the message say?"

"Nothing to worry your pretty little head about, love," YaYa said blithely. "Although I do hope he enjoyed the Dancing Queen ringtone. Ah — what's this?"

This, Clemmie reckoned, as they suddenly emerged from the fiery splendour into the misty autumnal sunlight, might just be Steeple Fritton.

"Oh — it's lovely — now we just need to find the pub."

White cottages and mellow brick houses circled a common of short scrubby grass criss-crossed by foot-wide pathways, glossy mounds of brambles and drooping hazel trees. There was a small row of bow-fronted shops and — yes! — a tiny creeper-covered pub squatting in an oasis of golden gravel with further tiny roads and paths shooting away from it in a starburst.

"That must be it." Clemmie pointed at the Crooked Sixpence. "Isn't it gorgeous? How late are we?"

"Only about ten minutes," YaYa said cheerfully, dispensing with her cigarette out of the window and roaring the 4×4 onto the gravel, clearly terrifying a benchful of elderly people who appeared to be dressed in the entire contents of a jumble sale stall. "Grab the stuff, love, and let's get the show on the road."

Ignoring the stares of the three septuagenarians on the bench — Clemmie had become very used to YaYa's outlandish appearance but was still aware she must come as something of a shock to strangers, not to mention her own long black and red skirt and floppy crimson blouse business outfit of choice — Clemmie grabbed, and they hurried towards the Crooked Sixpence's door.

It was opened by a fairly young, very good-looking, man who looked delighted to see them and ushered them into the cosy warmth of a gorgeous, sparkling, beams-and-brasses country pub.

"So sorry we're late," YaYa said breathily, giving him the full eyelash-flutter. "I do hope we haven't inconvenienced you."

"I was getting a little worried. I'm Ellis Blissit." He shook their hands, looking slightly perplexed. "And no, as long as you're here now, it's fine. Sorry, I didn't catch your name?"

"YaYa Bordello," YaYa beamed, still holding Ellis's hand.

128

"Right." Ellis looked as if he was trying not to laugh. He smiled at Clemmie. "And you must be Honey Bunch? Or are you Foxy?"

"Clemmie Coddle. Who the hell are Honey and Foxy?"

YaYa let go of Ellis's hand, and giggled. "Ooh, sorry! You got the wrong answerphone message! Honey and Foxy are chums of mine in another little business venture. No, this is Clemmie."

Ellis still looked confused as well he might, Clemmie thought.

"As long as you're from The Gunpowder Plot," he said, "I'm just grateful you're here, especially as I had to cancel my previous appointment at such short notice, but I was expecting someone else. Guy . . .?"

"Guy Devlin," Clemmie put in quickly. "Yes, he's The Gunpowder Plot's owner, and the person your original appointment was with — but we're his assistants and fully conversant with your requirements."

YaYa shot her a "way-over-the-top-convoluted-management-speak, love" look.

"Thank the Lord someone is," a second tall dark and handsome man said from behind the bar. "Hi, ladies — I'm Flynn."

"Hi," they chorused in unison.

"American . . ." YaYa breathed in Clemmie's ear. "Oooh — how sexy is that accent? Fancy there being two of them, and such pretty boys. I wonder which one's the bride."

"It's a wedding," Clemmie hissed back. "Not a civil partnership. Please don't ask them about frocks."

"Spoilsport." YaYa giggled, then turned her attention to Ellis. "So, Mr Blissit, how can we help you?"

"Ellis, please." Ellis still looked slightly shell-shocked at YaYa's full-on glamour. "Well, what I want is — sorry, can I get you something to drink? Oh — bugger . . ."

Neddy Pink, and his two equally disreputable sisters, had stormed in through the unlocked door.

"We're still closed!" Ellis snapped. "These ladies are — er — brewery reps."

"And I'm Edwina Currie," Neddy spluttered. "Give us a drink, Flynn, lad and we'll say no more about it. While the girls are away, eh?"

"It's nothing like that!" Ellis snapped. "Oh, for God's sake, Flynn, give them three pints of Old Duckpond on the house. He turned again to the trio of Pinks. "But you'll have to drink it outside. This is business."

"Monkey business," Neddy snuffled. "Whatever, Ellis . . . three pints'll keep us quiet. No bother. Nuff said?"

"Bugger off!" Ellis roared.

Once the pints and the Pinks had been despatched and the door locked behind them and Clemmie and YaYa had declined refreshments, Ellis quickly outlined what he had in mind.

"I didn't know if I'd have to book a full display because that's not what I wanted. What I want is an archway of fireworks for when we — me and Lola — come out of the register office. That's why I booked the wedding for as late as possible, so that it'd be dark."

"Sounds a great idea, and something we can supply to spectacular effect." Crossing her stupendous legs, YaYa flicked the laptop into life. "Right — now this is one we did last year . . . at a church, but we can do it at any venue. We set several rows of large Roman candles into the ground on either side of the path, angle them to create an arch, fire them by remote control at the appropriate moment — they'll reach a height of about fifty feet, so no fear of anyone being burned — and give you and your bride a stunning, lasting, tumbling pergola of light and colour as you leave the ceremony. Breathtaking, I think you'll agree, and far more impressive than a handful of confetti."

Clemmie sat back and watched Ellis's face as he peered at the screen. From slightly sceptical, to intrigued, to amazed and delighted, the expressions said it all. Fireworks truly worked their magic on everyone, Clemmie thought. No one is ever immune.

"Superb," Ellis said, beaming. "Absolutely amazing. Exactly what I was thinking of. Lola will adore it. Flynn — come over here and have a look at this."

YaYa ran through the display on the laptop again, and then flipped through several alternatives on the same theme, offering colour combinations, timings, and costs. Then, ever the business-woman, she suggested that even if Ellis didn't want a full display back in the village, a small personal barrage added to the arc of light might be suitable.

Clemmie, sitting snugly in one of the cushiony armchairs, listened intently. With luck, one day she'd be doing this on her own: working as an ambassador for

The Gunpowder Plot. Almost everything she'd always wanted.

Dreamily, infected by the sheer romance of all these weddings, she allowed herself to drift off into a fantasy of her and Guy and . . .

"Clemmie!" YaYa was leaning across the burnished pub table. "Wake up, love. God knows where it is you go to in those daydreams. Which lucky fella makes you go all faraway like that, love? Remind me to ask you about your love life sometime — he must be really something."

Oh, he is, Clemmie thought. And totally, absolutely, out of reach.

During Clemmie's brief reverie, Flynn had obviously opened the Crooked Sixpence's doors and the Pinks, followed by a further clutch of villagers, were trooping into the pub.

"Let's escape to the kitchen," Ellis said, gathering up The Gunpowder Plot's paperwork. "I don't want the village jungle drums getting wind of any of this."

Under close scrutiny from the Steeple Fritton inmates, Clemmie grabbed the laptop and followed YaYa and Ellis behind the bar and into a tiny gleaming kitchen.

"Flynn'll tell 'em all you're brewery reps," Ellis said as they all sat round a white-scrubbed table. "It should keep them quiet. Right: so where were we?"

"I think we'd definitely decided on the candle arch fountains, hadn't we?" YaYa flicked the computer into life. "In silver and blue. And a couple of multishots, fairly quiet, with silver hearts and blue raindrops to run

132

simultaneously. And did you want to think about the lancework and let us know later?"

"The sort of illuminated sign thing?" Ellis shook his head. "No, I'll go with that now too. I need to get everything sorted while she's out of the way. Can you do that in a silver and blue heart as well? Silver and blue have a really special significance for us — I'm not sure we'd even be together if it hadn't been for some blue and silver underwear years ago . . ."

"Wow," YaYa chuckled throatily. "Care to expand on that?"

"Definitely not," Ellis laughed softly. "But Lola'll understand."

"Spoilsport . . . but you can have whatever you want, love. No probs. I'll get Guy to OK it, and the team will have to come out to the site nearer the day to suss things out, and then of course set it all up before the wedding — all with the maximum of discretion, natch — but I think if we're sticking with the silver and blue theme, we can do one large heart with Ellis and Lola inscribed inside, and an arrow through the middle of course."

"Perfect! She'll love that!" Ellis nodded enthusiastically. "And sorry for being such a pedant, but how exactly does it work?"

"We'll fire the lancework remotely as you come out of the register office. We'll probably place it at the end of the path so that as you and your Lola — lovely name, by the way — walk towards it, it'll light up at the same time as the candle arch. The lancework fires on a single ignition — the heart and words will all ignite in about four seconds and burn for at least a minute — so, the explosion of blue and silver barrages, the candle arch and the heart will give you a superb ending to your ceremony."

Ellis nodded again and Clemmie sighed happily. It all sounded perfectly lovely. She could just picture it in her mind's eye. How fantastic it would be to have a man adore you so much that he'd plan something as wonderful as this.

"I'm sure Lola will love it," she said dreamily. "And a secret wedding is sooo romantic."

"If fraught with problems." Ellis looked suddenly exhausted. "And all for nothing if she says no."

"Blimey, love." YaYa looked horrified. "Surely she won't do that?"

"Who knows?" Ellis shrugged. "She's turned me down every time I've mentioned it so far in the conventional way. And as our relationship is far from conventional, I thought this might just work."

Clemmie frowned. "How exactly do you plan to get her to the registry office without her sussing out what's going on?"

Ellis leaned his elbows on the table. "I'm telling her that an old school friend of mine is having a small local Valentine's Day wedding. And that Posy — she's Flynn's wife — and Flynn, who are going to be our witnesses but she won't know that of course, are coming along with us to swell the numbers and we've hired a limo because of it being such a romantic day. All our other close friends will already be there, the flowers and photographer will be waiting and the rest of the village will be back here in the pub for the reception as soon as we've left. The registrar knows what's happening — and now you're on board, everything's arranged to the letter. It'll all depend on Lola."

"But why on earth do you think she might not want to marry you?" Clemmie insisted. "I'd marry you like a shot — that is, I mean —"

YaYa and Ellis laughed together.

"She thinks I'm too young to marry her," Ellis said. "We've been together for five years, she's the most beautiful woman in the world, I'll never, ever want anyone else and I love her more than life. And she loves me, I'm not in any doubt about that. And we're really happy. But she still thinks that at twenty-nine I should be settling for someone of my own age."

"Ah." Clemmie nodded. "She's older than you. But surely, no one worries about a few years these days?"

"Lola does," Ellis said softly. "And those 'few years' are pretty crucial to her. She thinks that one day I'll want children and I'll regret marrying her. And I don't and won't, believe me."

"I believe you." Clemmie smiled at him. "But even if you changed your mind about kids, loads of women are having babies in their forties now."

"They may well be — but that won't work for us."

"Why, love?" YaYa frowned. "How old is your Lola, then?"

Ellis grinned. "She's fifty-five."

CHAPTER
TEN

"Pass the barium chloride," Guy muttered, shaking his black hair away from his eyes. "Please. Sorry — this is getting tricky and I don't want to stop stirring."

Clemmie passed the requisite jar across the workbench, being very careful not to let her fingers touch his. "I still think it'll come out too bright. We've already got too much of the chlorine producer in the Petri dish, I reckon."

"Maybe . . ." Guy frowned in concentration. "We'll soon know, won't we?"

They were side by side in the lab, jointly striving for that elusive deep green, the final Seventh Heaven colour. Outside, the late October evening was closing in in a flurry of gusty wind and heavy rain. The radio sang softly in the corner and Suggs was curled sleeping on his favourite charcoal sacks.

Clemmie couldn't remember ever being happier.

These brief moments when she and Guy played with chemicals in the lab were the simply the best at The Gunpowder Plot. She loved everything about her job, but these times were special; not only because they were so rare and involved messing around with fireworks, but also because it meant she and Guy were alone and she could forget all about YaYa and Helen-the-ex, and indulge in dangerously heartbreaking fantasies.

"There . . ." Guy finished mixing. "Right, let's pop it into a tube, pack in the black powder, find a fuse — and see what we've got this time."

Clemmie watched him, admiring his skill. Like cookery, getting the ingredients exactly right were imperative. A thousand different people could use the same recipe and achieve a thousand different results. Guy's expertise meant that there was never too much smoke or chemical residue to mask the effects of his fireworks.

Together they went through the building ritual, the same method used for tiny experiments like this one and in manufacturing huge multishot fireworks: packing the combined chemicals into the separate chambers inside the tube, adding a layer of black powder between each, making sure the fuse ran all the way down the inside of the tube.

As soon as the fuse was lit, either manually or by remote control, the first layer of black powder would detonate, creating the gas which would shoot the first explosive chemical cocktail into the sky, followed by the next layer and the next, until all the packed shots had whooshed heavenwards.

They'd already tried out one mix of copper carbonate and cryolite — Clemmie's concoction — that evening which had produced a fabulous shower of neon-bright green stars over the courtyard. But,

137

Clemmie sighed, as they shuddered outside again, neon bright wasn't what they were seeking.

The wind screamed through her long denim skirt and chunky black jumper, tangling her jet earrings with her wayward hair.

"Christ." Guy shivered inside his leather jacket, setting the tube inside a firing cylinder on the flagged yard. "It's bloody freezing out here. Whatever happened to global warming? OK — I've lit the portfire . . . so, as they say in all the best books, let's light the blue touch paper and stand well back."

The fuse glowed, then ignited, and the embryo firework sizzled excitingly. Clemmie inhaled the familiar smell of cordite, then held her breath. It didn't matter how many times she did this, it still filled her with a frisson of exhilaration.

With a crackle and a swoosh, their creation came to life. As the firework streaked skywards like a green meteor, she and Guy grinned at one another, co-conspirators chasing the same dream. They gazed upwards, watching the blazing trail twisting into the dark clouds, hovering for a breathless moment, then showering earthwards again in a cascade of twinkling green stars.

"Beautiful . . ." Clemmie breathed. "Very beautiful. But wrong."

"Yep. Far too bright," Guy agreed. "As you so correctly predicted, Miss Clever Cambridge First Clogs. Ah well, back to the metaphorical drawing board — although sadly not tonight. I've got the final planning meeting with the team for the Snepps fiasco."

Clemmie nodded. The Bonfire Night party at Tarnia Snepps' footballer's-dream mansion on the outskirts of Hazy Hassocks was less than a week away. She couldn't wait — because it meant she'd be representing The Gunpowder Plot, of course; it had absolutely nothing to do with the fact that she'd be accompanying Guy as his pretend-lover in YaYa's absence.

"Next time," Clemmie said, as they quickly cleared up the debris and headed back into the lab, "why don't we really go with Allbard's *Magikal Medieval Alchemy*? I know you've already tried translating his medieval stuff into modern compounds, but what if we stuck exactly to one of his recipes? It might turn out that he has some ancient prescription for a dark green that we've missed?"

"He might have," Guy agreed, closing the door and catching Suggs as he scampered joyously towards his knees. "I've never really delved into translating some of his more obscure formulas. Yeah, OK. We'll try him out to the letter if we can get hold of his potions these days — and if you're prepared for the magical outcome should we be successful."

Clemmie wrinkled her nose. "What magical outcome? I told you I don't believe in magic. There's no way some ancient chemical combination will solve the problems of the world, or make star-crossed lovers fall for each other, or any of that rubbish. What I do believe, is that the old-time alchemists probably knew things that we no longer consider relevant. I'd love to source some of his original substances and just see what happens."

"Yes, sure, I'm up for that." Guy fastened Suggs' lead to his harness and they all hurried across the courtyard in the bitter wind. "It'll have to wait for a while though, because we've got that meeting in Milton St John tomorrow, haven't we? Then I'm booked for displays all over the weekend, followed by the dreaded Snepps. Jesus, it's cold tonight! Come on, Suggs — run!"

"Sweeties!" YaYa, all raven hair, scarlet fun-fur coat and crimson thigh boots, shimmied towards them as they came puffing into the gloriously warm kitchen. "I was just going to send out a search party! Oooh, look at you two! All dark and dishevelled and grinning like a matching pair of wicked kids." She studied them, her head on one side. "D'you know, if Guy had a touch more eye make-up and Clemmie could grow a shade of designer stubble it'd be like looking at the love twins of Russell Brand and Amy Winehouse. You really do make a lovely couple."

Clemmie was relieved her tangled hair hid her blushing face.

"YaYa — pack it in," Guy said cheerfully. "Christ! What's all this?"

YaYa smiled. "Slight change of plan, love. And I'm so glad you're back now. I didn't want to go without saying goodbye."

The kitchen floor was piled high with cases, holdalls, bags, suitcarriers and wig boxes.

"I didn't realise you were off tonight," Guy said, removing Suggs from his harness and pouring boring

140

ferret pellets into his dinner dish. "I thought it was tomorrow morning?"

"It was, love. Like I said, change of plan. We were going to kick off tomorrow night, me, Foxy and Honey Bunch — it being Halloween — with our Wicked Witch revue at the Rinky-Dink before I went off to join the Dancing Queens for the week. However, Martinique — she's that big management noise in the troupe, who had the bad transsexual realignment done cut-price from that bloke off the internet, remember? — has just called me, and the Dancing Queens' PR company has set up a mass-media interview session in London tonight — all the major telly and radio news shows and some of the glossies and the listings mags are lined up — and I don't want to miss it." She paused for breath, pouted and fluttered her eyelashes. "I'm sure you'll manage for an extra night without me, love, won't you?"

"The silence will be heaven and it'll be blissful not to fall over the wigs and the frocks," Guy said. "And I've got Clemmie to keep me company, haven't I?"

He grinned across the kitchen and Clemmie felt her knees wobble. He really shouldn't be allowed to smile at anyone like that.

"I'll try and help out as much as possible," she muttered.

But both YaYa and Guy laughed. Suggs paused in munching his pellets, lifted his head, and gave her a derisive stare.

"With the business, of course," Clemmie added quickly. "I didn't mean —"

"Keep digging that hole, love," YaYa gurgled. "Anyway, you know the score and Guy knows he's safe from you turning into yet another sad deluded stalker. I told him you keep going off into daydreams about some cute boy or other."

Clemmie joined in the laughter.

"I'd better be off, anyway," Clemmie said, grabbing the lifeline. "I'm meeting someone at eight."

It was only Phoebe, Sukie and Chelsea, minus Ben, Derry and Nicky, for a quick girlie drink with Fern and Amber, minus Timmy and Lewis, in the Weasel and Bucket in Fiddlesticks, but she was never going to let on. Not now. Not ever.

"Lucky sod," YaYa gushed. "Think of me when you're all snuggled up, won't you? I'll be battling with the panstick and the eyelash glue and the magic knickers and trying not to hate the size zeros. See you when I get back, love."

Clemmie nodded. "I hope it goes really well — and I'd love to see your show sometime."

"Oh, God, you'll probably live to regret that," Guy murmured as he added minced chicken to Suggs' dinner.

"We've already agreed that Clemmie's going to come to a gig one night," YaYa sniffed. "In fact, the Rinky-Dink would be ideal. It's a super little club and not too far away. We must arrange it."

"That'll be great," Clemmie said, meaning it. Well, it would be a new experience, wouldn't it? And life was supposed to be a mesh of new experiences, wasn't it? Like loving a gay — possibly bisexual — pyrotechnician?

142

Like sharing your working life with a drag queen and a ferret? "Now, I must dash."

"Have a nice date and I'll see you in the morning." Guy looked across the kitchen. "And we'll get off to Milton St John by about eleven. And thanks for your help this evening."

"Any time," Clemmie said glibly, trying not to grin like an idiot as she grabbed her coat and bag and hurried towards her Peugeot.

The next morning, Clemmie was at her desk by nine. She'd been up since six, trying on and discarding clothes for this first business trip with Guy. With Molly's help she'd settled on a long black velvet skirt, a black T-shirt and a multi-coloured velvet jacket with her rainbow-glitter waterfall earrings. Her hair stubbornly refused to behave itself in a barrette, so she'd left it loose and compensated by adding several extra layers of eye-make-up.

"Gorgeous," Molly had said while Bill made the breakfast which Clemmie knew she'd never be able to eat. "Mind you, them earrings aren't sparkling half as much as your eyes, Clemmie. It's wonderful to see you so happy."

Happy? she thought now, sifting through the early morning emails. Of course she was happy, but this feeling that bubbled away inside her was far more than just happiness, surely? It was like Christmas morning and her birthday and seeing the sea for the first time all rolled into one.

She rested her elbows on the desk and stared at the river. The previous night's storm had blown itself out and Halloween had dawned sunny, cold, and cloudless. The flaming leaves whirled into the tumbling froth of the river, sweeping under the office window in a multicoloured torrent.

She beamed to herself. Even her working conditions were heavenly. And as for Guy . . .

"Hi." Right on cue he appeared in the doorway. Again, dressed in skinny black, his hair still damp from the shower, he looked sensational. "You're early — have you had breakfast?"

"Yes — no — well, just coffee."

"Come and join us, then. You're just in time. Me and Suggs are doing the full English while YaYa's out of the way. She thinks that eating a healthy breakfast makes up for the amount of junk and nicotine she absorbs during the rest of the day, so she insists on yoghurts, crispbreads, juice, fruit and muesli — and I do love saturated fat, sugar, and a mountain of carbs first thing, don't you?"

"Well, now you come to mention it . . ."

Clemmie followed him out of the office. Oh God, please don't let her slurp or spill things or appear greedy.

"We're in here." Guy turned away from the kitchen from where wonderful cooked breakfast scents were wafting. "Another treat. To fit the healthy-eating image, YaYa insists on sitting at the kitchen table for breakfast and it's easier just to go along with it. But the news is on the telly and I thought if we had breakfast on our knees we might catch the Dancing Queens thing."

"Here" was a big square sitting room, one of the rooms Clemmie had only previously glimpsed. With nubbly white plastered walls and black beams and one massive picture window framing the river and the weir, the room was like something out of a style supplement.

The style supplement came to an abrupt halt with the décor and furnishings, though. They, Clemmie thought cheerfully, were pure Guy. Several large elderly sofas and big mismatched armchairs were grouped round a marble fireplace, standing solidly on the original dark floorboards. Haphazard rugs and cushions in a mass of colours and patterns gave the room an air of cosy comfort. Floor-to-ceiling bookshelves filled the inglenooks, the walls were vibrantly splashed with blown-up pictures of firework displays, and in one corner stood a wide-screen television and all the accoutrements of home entertainment, while in the other a gloriously retro red and chrome Wurlitzer jukebox took pride of place.

It was a room simply asking for snuggles and cuddles and carefree relaxation.

"It's fantastic," Clemmie said. "Did you do this yourself?"

"The bastardisation? Desecration of what the design police reckon should be a waterside room in neutral shades with minimal furniture? Yep, all my own work, I'm proud to say. It was the antidote to a brief and unhappy period of living with cream and beige and white and sodding magnolia and no colour and no softness and no books or ornaments or pictures and no bloody personality."

Clemmie stared at him. She'd become used to his equanimity. She'd never heard him sound so bitter.

"Sorry." He shrugged. "A bit of a bugbear of mine. I shouldn't sound off at you. Now, please make yourself comfortable and I'll go and retrieve what I can from the kitchen. I warned you my culinary skills aren't up to much, although I'm usually OK with a fry-up, so if you're feeling brave . . ."

"Brave and starving," Clemmie said honestly.

"Great — oh, shove Suggs up a bit."

Suggs was ensconced on one of the long, squashy sofas, surrounded by several huge tapestry cushions and a large bowl of what looked like eggs and bacon.

"Sit down then," Guy indicated the sofa, "and I'll be mother. What would you like?"

"Whatever's going," Clemmie said, praying that her stomach wouldn't rumble. "I'm easy. That is —"

Fortunately Guy had already disappeared into the kitchen, so it was only Suggs who had noticed her faux pas. He made full use of it, lifting his head from his breakfast, a piece of bacon hanging from the corner of his mouth as he gave her his best "sad cow" stare.

"He didn't hear me," she said, settling herself into a corner of the sofa, "so you carry on having your ferrety breakfast and leave me alone."

Suggs snuffled a bit, spat the dangling bacon back into his bowl, winked at her, then continued eating.

Guy returned carrying a large tray piled with plates of fried breakfast, two mugs, and a coffee pot. "I just

146

dished you up with everything," he said, setting the tray on the sofa, handing her a plate and pushing Suggs out of the way. "Leave what you don't want."

"It all looks great, thank you." Clemmie picked up her knife and fork. "Oh, and brown sauce — I love brown sauce."

"Me too." Guy grinned, sitting beside her, balancing his own plate and flicking on the television set. "Another of my vices."

They ate in companionable silence, with Clemmie miraculously managing not to spill anything, while the male presenter on the breakfast news programme warned them sternly about the latest on global warming, terrorism, feral children on sink estates and avian flu.

The cameras then moved on to the very pretty female newsreader, who dimpled and giggled and announced that they were now going to have something completely different.

A blast of Abba's 'Dancing Queen' roared into the room, and the screen was filled with a dozen oh-so-glamorous women dressed in feathers and spangles and tight costumes executing a sort of 1950s Tiller Girl routine.

Still chewing, Guy, Clemmie and Suggs stared.

The Tiller Girls changed into the Spice Girls, then into something altogether more raunchy.

". . . and that's enough for this time of the morning," the newsreader dimpled some more. "It's my pleasure to welcome the hottest drag act in the UK — the Dancing Queens — into the studio."

"There she is!" Clemmie almost choked on a piece of fried bread. "Oh, doesn't she look fab!"

YaYa, in her black wig and dressed in short, tight electric blue, was batting her eyelashes at the camera. She was surrounded by a crowd of equally slender, fabulously turned-out drag queens, all pouting and posing and blowing kisses.

"Is that Martinique?" Clemmie asked, as a severe looking woman in a Dolly Parton wig, black minidress and tarty boots appeared to be the spokesperson. "The one whose op went awry? Yes, I guess it must be. She seems to be in charge. Crikey, she looks scary."

After Martinique had explained about dates and venues and stressed the adult content of the shows, the newsreader went on to ask further questions about the troupe and the upcoming tour, and was almost drowned out by a dozen raucous and robust replies. There seemed to be an awful lot of preening and hair tossing. The Dancing Queens didn't miss a promotional trick. It was sensational.

The item faded out on a clip of the Dancing Queens' opening number — an amazing Busby Berkeley tribute — and Clemmie realised that she'd eaten every bit of food on her plate without making a mess.

"You must be so proud of her." Clemmie pushed her plate back on the tray. "And that was the best breakfast I've ever eaten — but don't tell my Uncle Bill that I said so."

"Wouldn't dream of it." Guy added his plate to hers and poured coffee. "And yes, I am proud of YaYa. Always have been. That's why I'd never stand in the way of her performing. She's an amazing asset to The Gunpowder Plot — at school, she — er, he was Steve then, of course — was an absolute magician at maths, and although she'd probably hate me for telling you this, she is a qualified accountant."

"No way!" Clemmie spluttered through her coffee. Damn! And the eating bit had gone so well. She mopped at her lap with a tissue. "YaYa an accountant? She can't be — aren't accountants all grey and suited and deadly dull?"

"A common misconception," Guy concurred, "but clearly you've mingled with the wrong sort of accountants. No, YaYa's brilliant and I'd never allow anyone else to do my books. As for selling, she's a natural. And the most loyal person I've ever met. I'd trust her with my life. All in all we make a good team."

"And you were always friends?"

"Right from day one. Oh, we weren't the two oddballs thrown together or anything like that. Me the nerdy chemistry swot and Steve the effeminate one. No, we were both normal kids with tons of mates, but we just clicked on so many levels. Believe me, no one would have dared to take the piss out of Steve then for liking make-up and nice clothes. He was, and she still is, as tough as old boots. Mind you, back then there were still a lot of Goths, which suited me — being long-haired and dark and skinny, and one or two left-over dedicated New Romantics — so there was an awful lot of eyeliner and pretty costumes doing the rounds."

"And when did the YaYa thing take off?"

"In the sixth form." Guy drained his coffee. "He became she just before he sat his second maths paper. Oh, not the full transition, but the name change and the wigs and stuff. The staff didn't know what to make of it, but as he was the only boy in the class who was guaranteed straight A stars — and remember this was in the days when you got the grades you studied hard for and deserved, not those awarded simply to bump up government targets — they didn't dare say anything."

"And you've been together ever since?"

"Yes." Guy gathered all the crockery together on the tray. "And always will be. Now, can you take Suggs out for a quick pee before we go, please — and make sure he's got food and water, and I'll chuck this lot in the dishwasher? Then it'll be Milton St John here we come."

CHAPTER
ELEVEN

"Are you doing anything tonight? For Halloween?" Guy asked twenty minutes later as they drove away from Winterbrook and out towards Newbury. "Any wild scary parties lined up?"

Was he going to ask her out? Nah, course not. No chance of that, was there? Shame. Clemmie wriggled comfortably in the passenger seat of Guy's large elderly BMW and wondered fleetingly if she should flesh out YaYa's imagined "cute boy" as some sort of insurance policy, just in case Guy might twig how she felt, and instantly brand her one of the dreaded predatory women who seemed to gravitate towards him with monotonous regularity. No, it wasn't a good idea; she already had enough complications in her life.

"No, nothing." She shook her head. "I'm probably far too old to don a black bin liner and smother myself in white face paint."

"Bin liners and white face paint would be a big no-no these days, surely?" Guy laughed. "From what I've seen recently, today's Halloween costumes are on a par with anything you'd find on the set of a Freddie Krueger movie. Home-made simply doesn't cut it any more for twenty-first-century kids."

"Sad, that." Clemmie nodded. "But you're right, it does seem a pity that even dressing up is commercially competitive for children. I was in Woolworths the other day and there were racks of mini off-the-peg costumes for every occasion. So no, I won't be prancing around Bagley-cum-Russet tonight with flashing fangs and a pointy hat and fighting the local couture-clad kiddies for a lucky bag. Hopefully they'll all be in Hazy Hassocks anyway."

Guy chuckled. "Hazy Hassocks being a hotbed of witchery, haunting and home of choice for the pre-pubescent living dead?"

"Well — it has been rumoured — but no, actually Mitzi Blessing organises a fancy dress pumpkin contest in Hassocks village hall for the kids from all the surrounding villages. She reckons it keeps the little sods from terrifying the life out of the residents with trick or treat menaces."

"Good idea," Guy said, negotiating the single track roads with ease. "I've met Mitzi at several local events. She's certainly a force to be reckoned with. So, if you're not otherwise engaged tonight, shall we have another go at discovering Seventh Heaven?"

Oh, if only . . .

"Love to," Clemmie said happily. "And we'll try to work out what Allbard says, shall we?"

"Definitely. Although I did have a quick sneaky look last night after you'd gone and before the Snepps run-through, and he still doesn't make much sense to me. And I wasn't prying about your party plans just now, by the way; I only asked because I really don't know very much about your life away from work other than what you've told me."

"Not a lot more to know," Clemmie said airily. "You know I live with my aunt and uncle, that I've got lots of friends who I meet up with all the time, and that I play with explosives — which, I suppose, looking at it, is a pretty sad tally for someone of nearly thirty."

"Not if you're happy." Guy steered the BMW onto the main Lambourn road. "Happiness is, I've discovered, the only thing that counts. Settling for the what's here rather than the what's-over-the-horizon works for me. Why beat yourself up chasing something you can never have? So, no Mr Right in the offing?"

Hah! One question she could answer — and one that was asked simply out of curiosity, not as in a checking out the opposition way. In some senses, she thought, sneaking a lustful look at Guy across the car, being in love with a beautiful gay man was, if frustrating, rather restful. At least a girl knew exactly where she was.

"Dozens of contenders," Clemmie lied cheerfully, definitely deciding not to flesh out the "cute boy". "I'm spoiled for choice — but no one special. Actually, being honest, my relationships have been a bit like my employment record: loads of great starts, masses of disappointing middles, and plenty of not-too-unhappy partings." She smiled across the car. "However, now I've got the job thing sorted out maybe the lurve bit will follow suit. After all, you're a pretty good role model."

"Me?" Guy squinted at yet another skew-whiff signpost with all the directions obliterated by years of wind and rain. "Did that say Upton Poges? Where the hell is Upton Poges? Oh, well, let's give it a try. I wouldn't use me as a role model for good relationships, if I were you. Christ — I've made some real screaming mistakes in my past, believe me. Too much too young. Quantity rather than quality. Sometimes I'm surprised I survived some of them. Oh, and no doubt YaYa delighted in telling you about my biggest mistake of all? Helen from the Dark Side?"

Clemmie nodded casually. "She mentioned you'd been married."

"Vegas wedding, quickie divorce," Guy laughed. "Blink and you'd miss it. Still, as we're on the way to pick a pretty wedding firework display for a presumably happy couple, maybe I shouldn't allow my matrimonial bitterness to show."

"Probably not." Clemmie smiled at him. "And at least we know both the bride and groom will show up at this one. Did YaYa fill you in on that odd set-up in Steeple Fritton?"

Guy nodded. "That Ellis Blissit sounds like a true romantic. I do hope his Lola realises that she's a very lucky lady. And I don't buy the age difference thing anyway. If they've been together happily for five years, and love each other, why the hell should the age gap matter?"

"No idea," Clemmie said honestly. "I know it's a pretty huge difference, but as you say, they must be well suited or they wouldn't still be together. And he loves her so much it was almost tangible."

"That's what YaYa said too. Let's hope it doesn't all go tits up on the day when she realises what he's done. Now — which way do you reckon we should go from here? Left or right?"

"Right. My Uncle Bill always says if you're lost, if you keep turning right you'll eventually end up in the right place."

"Really? OK — right it is."

Ten minutes later, having turned right about twenty times, they were back where they started.

Guy grinned at her. "Any more bright ideas?"

"None, sorry. Maybe I should have also said my Uncle Bill is an inveterate liar."

"Great. Let's try left, this time, shall we?"

They did and found Milton St John less than five minutes later.

It was another exceptionally pretty Berkshire village, Clemmie thought, staring through the windscreen at the twisting main road with its mix of picturesque cottages and mellow brick houses, banked on either side by a fat brown stream gushing with crystal clarity over its peaty bed, and a wash of late-autumnal colour spreading upwards towards the Downs from the orchards and spinneys which cushioned the village from the worst of the weather.

"I was expecting it to be gridlocked with racehorses," Guy said, peering disappointedly at the deserted street. "And I guess all these really big houses are the racing stables. Which one are we looking for?"

"Peapods. On a bend — on the left — before the shops and the pub — which must be — here! Ooops, sorry — was that a bit late?"

"No, I'm getting used to your methods of navigation. And at least we didn't have to turn right."

Clemmie poked out her tongue.

Guy drove the BMW into a pristine cobbled stable yard, with half-doored boxes on three sides where horses observed them with curious liquid velvet eyes.

"Aren't they beautiful? I wonder if we can look at them properly later? Er — we need the stable flat." Clemmie glanced at the sheet of paper on her lap. "Through the clock arch, past the main house — oh, isn't it gorgeous? All that fabulous creeper! — and over there on the right."

"Your navigational skills seem to have improved," Guy told her as he brought the BMW to a halt. "Have you got all the stuff we need?"

"Yep." Clemmie unfastened her seat belt and grabbed The Gunpowder Plot's display folders, brochures and price lists, leaving Guy with the laptop. "And it looks as though Jemima is waiting for us."

Jemima, wearing a long floral Laura Ashley dress in muted colours, her glossy hair tucked behind her ears, was peering short-sightedly out from the stable flat's ground-floor door.

"Clemmie!" She waved at them. "Lovely to see you again!"

"Jemima Carlisle?" Guy asked, holding out his hand. "I'm Guy Devlin from The Gunpowder Plot. Lovely to meet you."

"And you. Thank you so much for putting all this together so quickly. Clemmie was really efficient."

"I'm sure she was. She's a real asset." Guy and Clemmie followed Jemima up the polished wooden staircase to the stable flat.

"Sorry I was squinting at you," she said over her shoulder. "I really should wear my glasses but I've been trying out contacts for the wedding and I've lost them . . . again. Through here."

The flat, which stretched along one side of the second smaller yard and had clearly been built over a previous stable block, was open-plan, light, airy and very untidy. Clemmie loved it. There were sensational views of the Downs from one side, Peapods yard from another, and the sprawl of Milton St John from a third.

"Charlie should be with us in a minute," Jemima said, putting her spectacles on and looking much happier. "He's got a bruised fetlock in the hot pool at the moment."

"Oh dear." Clemmie turned away from the window. "I hope he'll be OK in time for the wedding."

"It's not *his* fetlock," Jemima said quickly. "It's a horsy one. And before you ask, the pool is sadly not for humans either: only the horses here get the seven-star treatment."

"Oh, right." Clemmie knew that Guy was laughing and managed not to meet his eyes in case she giggled out loud. "Sorry, I don't know anything technical about horses."

"Nor did I when I first came here," Jemima said. "But you soon learn. Sorry again — I'm rambling and you're probably really busy. What do you need me to do?"

"Nothing," Guy said gently. "At least not yet. Let me set up the computer then I can show you what I had in mind, how we've tailored the details you gave Clemmie into a display, and then you can ask whatever questions you need."

"Lovely — and I haven't completely forgotten my manners. My friend Suzy is in the kitchen making coffee," Jemima said. "Clemmie met her in Newbury. She's also one of my bridesmaids, so I thought she might be useful if you have any questions." She smiled dreamily at them. "I'm so blown away by this wedding that I can't even remember my name some days. Oh, Lord — sorry — please sit down."

Jemima cleared a space on the long low sofa and they all sat in a row. Guy flicked the laptop into life and started showing Jemima various earlier displays where quieter fireworks had been required.

"You see," he explained. "The quiet showpieces and aerial repeaters can be just as stunning as the louder explosive ones. We wouldn't skimp on spectacle. We can provide exactly what you want, the length of the display, the types of fireworks, the colours — and all quiet enough not to disturb any of the horses. Now this one is something I've put together for you as an example: an ongoing aerial mixture of fountains and candles and florals — still visually stunning, but virtually silent."

Jemima peered at the images and smiled wistfully. "They're really, really beautiful. So clever, and just what I had in mind. Thank you — you're brilliant. I'm such a kid over fireworks and they'll make the reception so special. I'm not really fussy about colours — I'll leave that to you — and I thought maybe if we could have about a display of about fifteen or twenty minutes. Oh, and can you do music?"

Guy assured her that, yes, The Gunpowder Plot could certainly provide whatever musical accompaniment was required. Jemima sighed happily, said Charlie was tone deaf to all but heavy metal and wouldn't care a jot, but she'd particularly like some Prokoviev and maybe Rossini? Guy said they'd both work beautifully and that they were both included in The Gunpowder Plot's musical pyrotechnic display DVD which he'd leave with her.

Jemima beamed some more and went on to say that the reception was being held in a field on the outskirts of the village.

"It belongs to Diana and Gareth James-Jordan and it's as far away from all the horses as possible," she added. "And as it's been used for music festivals and things in the past, we know that the access is OK. You'll need to give it the once over, I suppose?"

"As soon as we've decided on the display, I'll get my crew over here to work out how we're going to do the ground plan. I guess you're having a marquee?"

"Two. One for food and drink and sitting and talking. The other for drink and food and dancing. Heated, of course, because it'll be a December wedding. December is the best time for the racing fraternity as it won't interrupt too many training schedules."

"Jemima!" Suzy called from the kitchen. "Where are the biscuits?"

"Top cupboard! Top shelf! Blue tin!"

"Right — oh, holy hell! Can't reach! Just because you're a giant, doesn't mean the rest of us are!"

Jemima pulled a face. "Suze — don't try climbing — with your leg. I mean —" She turned to Guy and Clem and confided, "She had a really bad fall from a horse years ago, her leg's badly damaged."

"Shall I go and help?" Clemmie stood up. "While you and Guy run through the details of your display?"

"Would you mind?" Jemima smiled. "Thanks so much. Kitchen's just through that first arch."

Clemmie hurried across the room and through the archway.

"Hi again — great to see you, and here," she said to Suzy, who in jeans and a blue rugby shirt was limping heavily as she dragged a chair across the kitchen, "let me. I wasn't needed in there — they've got it sorted without me. Blue tin, was it? There!"

"Cheers. Jemima fusses too much about my leg."

"She just told us that you had an accident," Clemmie tried not to stare at Suzy's leg. "I'm really sorry, I didn't even notice it in Newbury."

"Probably because that assistant practically carried me into the cubicle!" Suzy remembered. "And because I try not to stomp about like Long John Silver in public."

They smiled at one another.

160

"So did the bridal brainwashing work? Did you get your dress sorted out?" Clemmie asked. "Is it as gorgeous as Jemima's?"

Suzy opened the tin and tipped a pile of biscuits onto a plate. "Almost. Glimmery peach. Very girlie. My sister, Maddy, and my two nieces have got similar dresses, too, so we're all going to look very swish. Fortunately they couldn't make it today. They're all a bit OTT and would have caused mayhem."

"So you're here to keep her feet on the ground?"

Suzy smiled. "Yeah, that and because Jemima said you'd be coming over today. I sort of sensed a kindred spirit? Not that we had much chance to chat in the frock shop, did we?"

Clemmie shook her head. "That might have been a good thing — if we'd laughed at any more of the customers we might have been asked to leave."

"I know." Suzy giggled and lifted the tray. "Which would have had Jemima tearing her hair out. Bless her, but she's so besotted with Charlie and such a control freak and so determined that this is going to go without a hitch that she does need someone with a grip on reality, which is where I come in. I reckon it's because she's such a competent, calm, organised, unflappable person normally, that this has knocked her totally for six. Not that I blame her — Charlie Somerset is absolutely —"

She paused in the archway and turned round to look at Clemmie open-mouthed.

"What?" Clemmie frowned.

"Holy hell! You lucky cow! He is *gorgeous*."

"Oh, right — Guy. Yes, he is — but he isn't mine. Just my boss."

"You mean — you and he aren't —"

"Nope. And never will be. He's — um — very much attached elsewhere."

"Bummer." Suzy walked slightly unsteadily towards the sofa. "Here we are then, coffee and biscuits."

"Thanks a million, Suze." Jemima looked up. "This is Guy Devlin. Suzy Beckett."

They shook hands solemnly. Then Suzy took two mugs of coffee across to one of the wide window seats. "You come over here with me, Clemmie. We'll let the grown-ups get on with the business stuff and we can have a chat."

Settled on the window seat with coffee, and refusing a biscuit as Guy's full English had satisfied even her rapacious appetite, Clemmie grinned at Suzy. "Stop staring at him."

"Bloody difficult," Suzy giggled, dragging her eyes away from Guy. "He's so beautiful. I bet every woman he meets flirts with him even if she's been happily involved forever. He's that sort of man — like Jemima's Charlie — too damn sexy for his own good. Ooh, talk of the devil . . ."

"Blimey." Clemmie chewed the rim of her coffee mug. "I see what you mean."

Charlie Somerset, heart-stoppingly handsome, his dark red hair dishevelled, his faded jeans and T-shirt sprayed on, tornadoed into the flat, grinning broadly. After kissing Jemima thoroughly, shaking hands with Guy and winking at Suzy and Clemmie, he squeezed

162

onto the sofa, managing to stroke Jemima's thigh as Guy ran through their chosen firework display on the laptop.

"Oh, yes," Clemmie breathed. "He truly is sensational. Sex on legs. But he's absolutely mad about Jemima, isn't he? Lucky Jemima."

Suzy snorted. "Yeah, she is. But so's he. Jemima's a star. And Charlie had been through most of the women in this village and for miles around before he settled down, so she knows he really, really wants her and no one else."

"*Most* of the women?" Clemmie raised her eyebrows. "You included?"

"Me, my sister, all my friends, all Maddy's friends, the vicar's wife, the entire local sixth form, several totally unsuitable quite *old* women, millions across the country while he was race-riding that we never even met, divorcées, widows, unhappily marrieds, even a few happily marrieds — Charlie test-drove the lot. And then finally fell head over heels for Jemima and hasn't strayed for a nanosecond since."

"Aaah," Clemmie whispered. "That's so sweet. I do love a happy ending. They make a lovely couple. Berkshire seems to breed gorgeous blokes, doesn't it?"

Suzy smiled knowingly, casting another covetous look at Guy and Charlie. "Too right, if those two on the sofa are anything to go by. And my sister Maddy is married to this super-looking bloke called Drew and he makes everyone go weak at the knees too. Mind you, don't you find that no matter how sensational-looking a man is, if he isn't the one that presses all your buttons, there's still something missing?"

Clemmie nodded. "Oh, yes." For some reason she found sad-eyed Suzy very easy to talk too. "Actually, Guy does it for me — and there's nothing I can do about it. What about you? Is your bloke drop-dead-gorgeous too?"

"Oh yeah," Suzy sighed wistfully. "Out of this world. And living in America. And married. He really loved me, and I was a complete prat because I let him get away. No, worse than that. I *drove* him away because I thought I wanted a career more than I wanted him. Then when this happened," she tapped her be-jeaned leg, "I didn't have either. My fault and something I have to live with."

They sat in united silence for a moment, each understanding the other's dilemma.

"Still," Suzy brightened, "I'm not a completely self-obsessed bitch, you know. I'm thrilled to bits for Jemima and Charlie, and I've resigned myself to becoming a sad old spinster surrounded by other people's kids and a lot of animals."

Clemmie nodded in empathy. Except, she thought, substitute fireworks for the children.

"But," Suzy looked fiercely at Clemmie, "if there was any way — any way at all — that I could get him back, I would. There'll never be anyone else for me. I'd sell my soul to turn the clock back and spend the rest of my life with Luke Delaney."

CHAPTER
TWELVE

It was growing rapidly dark: a proper cold Halloween night, with a bruised brooding sky and a howling wind sending black clouds scudding across a misty moon.

In the remote boathouse's lab, surrounded by nothing but isolated fields and tossing skeletal trees, Clemmie could just imagine the lost souls of ancient Winterbrook skulking beside the shadowy, relentless river, seeking salvation. And ghouls and ghosts moaning in the hostile gloom. And witches cackling as they crept through the night, hunting down unsuspecting victims on whom to practise their evil spells.

"Get a grip," Clemmie muttered to herself. "You don't believe in any of that rubbish. Stop being fanciful and focus on what you're doing. Focus, woman, bloody well focus."

Since their return from Milton St John, Clemmie and Guy had checked phone messages and emails, booked several more displays including one huge three-day corporate event at Kenilworth in two weeks' time, and an open-air rock concert in Hampshire for January, had a makeshift meal of a sort of cobbled-together ploughman's shared with Suggs in the kitchen — and had spent the rest of the time in the lab.

As a result of the short-notice Kenilworth display, where The Gunpowder Plot was to replace another company which had pulled out at the eleventh hour, Guy had called an impromptu meeting with Syd and various other members of the pyro crew.

"Sorry, Clemmie but I'm going to have to fly into Winterbrook," he'd said, pulling on his leather jacket. "We're getting together in the bar at the Masonic Hall to see if we can supply what Kenilworth needs in the time available. I've already told them we'll do it — so we'll have to wing it one way or another. Sorry to have to dash out — I'll only be a couple of hours. Do you want to go home and call a halt to Allbard for tonight?"

As Clemmie knew that Uncle Bill and Auntie Molly were going to be out at the Berkeley Boys Witches' Whist Drive at the Barmy Cow, Phoebe was viewing a potential love-nest with Ben in Hazy Hassocks, and everyone else would be at Mitzi Blessings' pumpkin party, the thought of being home alone certainly didn't appeal.

"No," Clemmie had said. "If you'll trust me with the lab and Suggs on my own, I'd like to carry on."

"Great — and good luck. I've spent forever trying to sort out where the alchemy ends and the magic begins or vice versa. I reckon he was away with the fairies most of the time — or wrote the damn book back to front."

Clemmie had laughed. "It should keep me entertained, then."

"Don't drive yourself mad." Guy had grabbed the car keys. "Oh, and you know where everything is in the lab, don't you? Kettle, coffee, small fridge? I've left a few bits and pieces in there for you and Suggs should either of you feel you're going to die of starvation. I should be back by eight, or nine at the latest. You've got my mobile number if there's an emergency." He'd paused. "And I'll expect the magical green to be in the bag when I come back."

And they'd laughed together, and he'd kissed Suggs but not her, and roared away in the BMW.

So, completely alone and trying not to let her imagination run away with her, Clemmie had tried to get to grips with Allbard's *Magikal Medieval Alchemy*. Somehow her attention kept wandering back to Milton St John.

While she'd been delighted to meet Jemima and Charlie and help to plan their wedding fireworks — and couldn't wait to tell Uncle Bill all about actually talking to the man who'd won him a fortune in reckless gambles on break-neck finishes in the Grand National — it was Suzy Becket who stayed uppermost in her mind.

Poor girl, Clemmie thought. Hopelessly in love with her absent Luke Delaney. Never wanting to look at another man because she knew they wouldn't measure up to the one she'd lost. And how much more galling to know it was all her fault.

Whatever Clemmie had expected from working at The Gunpowder Plot it hadn't included these emotional challenges. Not only was there her own romantic problem with Guy and YaYa and the unknown predatory Helen, now there was also the sad-eyed Suzy to add to her worries along with her concerns for the ever-optimistic Ellis Blissit.

"Blimey," she muttered. "This way madness definitely lies. Stop thinking about ghosts and lost lovers and get on with it!"

With Suggs on her lap, and the radio turned up against the scream of the witching wind outside, Clemmie sat at Guy's workbench and trailed her finger down Allbard's index trying to concentrate on nice logical scientific problems.

Once she'd worked out that all those *fff*s were actually the letter *s*, and that the elaborate flowery writing needed to be pared and translated, she was still no further forward. No wonder Guy hadn't been able to make head or tail of it. Everything was higgledy-piggledy, there was no order to any of the concoctions or the compounds or even the magical spells. It was all frustratingly illogical to someone geared to the spectacular technical and editorial advances of the last fifty years.

"Green," Clemmie muttered. "Let's try it this way, then. Let's not work out chemicals — let's try it by looking up the colour."

Suggs sat up and stared at her, then gently licked her chin and cuddled down again.

"What?" She looked down at him. "You think it's the way to go, too, do you? Fine, let's give it a whirl. Right, let's look at the table of contents again — oh, bugger!"

Green didn't exist. At least, not in the sparse index. God, it was so annoying to be stymied at every turn.

And no doubt Guy had already explored all these avenues a trillion times.

As the wind crashed branches against the side of the lab, Clemmie flicked through Allbard's flimsy yellowing pages. What was this? She'd spotted the word "green" somewhere among the closely-printed script. Ah yes, here . . . oh, sod it.

The Green Man?

She sighed. Wasn't that a pub? Surely Allbard had better things to do than throw his favourite hostelries into the mix? Still, at least it was green.

The Green Man, she read on slowly, deciphering the words with difficulty, was, among many other things, a fire-bearer. A magical fire-bearer. The most magical fire-bearer in the history of conflagration.

Clemmie's scalp prickled. She squinted at the page again.

In medieval times, it appeared the Green Man — who represented New Hopes and New Beginnings — would lead parades and ceremonies carrying a blazing Club of Fire, spraying sparks and flames onto the crowd, and chanting his magical verses. These verses when mixed with the sparks from his green fire, apparently, made new life possible and dreams and wishes come true.

A trickle of excitement shivered down her spine as she pulled the *Magikal Medieval Alchemy* closer.

Allbard, roughly translated, concluded that the Green Man represented the magic of fireworks: slightly mysterious, a little dangerous, always exciting and always new.

169

Wow! It sounded exactly like Guy. Clemmie blinked away from the almost-indecipherable words, and looked triumphantly at Suggs. This was a huge step nearer.

She picked up the book again, her hands shaking in her impatience.

Allbard, making reference to Gawain and the Green Knight, suggested that absolute belief in the powers of The Green Man and his magic green fire blend would *tranfform the difbeliever into a believer; the unhappy knight into a joyful lionheart; the lonefome fad foul into a merryman.*

The green fire waf — Allbard continued — *only efficaciouf on little wifhef of the heart.*

Clemmie frowned. So, sorting out the *fff*s and roughly translating it all into twenty-first-century speak, did that mean this Green Man mix and magic would make good things happen, then? Wishes come true? Unlikely, she thought! And clearly only on very localised wishes only — sort of one-to-ones, then — no point in imagining it could be used for world peace or global prosperity or anything huge.

And what was the magic potion anyway?

A handful of pureft fun-bleffed chlorophyll and two of powdered copper falts and a cup filled with the juice of yellow jaundy-afh . . .

Clemmie stopped and frowned. Chlorophyll and copper salts she understood, but what the hell was jaundy-ash? She blinked some more and continued reading.

170

According to the scrawly script, this recipe, when mixed with saltpetre, would produce the perfect green fire — and when ignited at the same time as the Green Man New Life verse was chanted, could make all impossible small-scale dreams possible.

Clemmie snorted in derision. She might have worked out the green-fire ingredients and translated the spell, but it didn't mean she believed in the wishes-come-true nonsense, did it? She was a scientist through and through; and unless there was a provable method and a tangible result it was all airy-fairy rubbish as far as she was concerned.

However, the making of the green fire was something else. That was pure chemistry, wasn't it? Medieval alchemy . . . Something she could make and try out and prove.

"Jesus!" Clemmie sat up. "So — does that really mean that, if I've read this properly, this is Allbard's 'magikal' bit for the colour green explosive then? Yay!!!"

Suggs opened his eyes and met her excited stare. She picked him up and kissed him and danced round the lab, hugging him and smiling. He made happy snuffling noises and smiled back.

Realising that dancing with a ferret was possibly one of the most stupid things she'd ever done, she sat down again. Quickly.

"Right." She took a deep breath. "So this mumbo-jumbo at the foot of the page must be the 'magikal spell' nonsense — now, do we want that? Or just the green fire recipe?"

Suggs snuffled some more and nodded.

"Both? Sucker. Magic doesn't exist. No way is that a magic spell — but OK, I'll assume we have to have both to make it work." She dragged a notebook and pen across the bench and started to copy down the centuries-old words.

> When the Green Man danceth with fire
> Ember and flame overcometh ire
> Light the jaundy-afh and falty mix
> Fayeth the wordf to wifhef fix
> "Verdigrif and verture pure
> Fparketh with naturef verdanture
> Maketh wifhef fore'er endure"
> And what the fadden heart defireth
> Will be gifted e're by Green Man firef

Quickly transposing the f's for s's Clemmie tried the three-line spell out loud.

"'Verdigris and verture pure, Sparks with nature's verdanture, Makes wishes forever endure.'" She looked at Suggs. "Hardly Lennon and McCartney, is it? Still, it's easy enough to remember — not that I believe in this hocus pocus of course — worth a try when and if we can work out how the green flame is made. Oh," she glanced at her watch, "I wish Guy would hurry up. I can't wait to tell him about this. So, if I scribble down what we've already worked out for building the first six stages of the Seventh Heaven multishot, then add Allbard's final little gem."

She started scribbling again.

172

One — silver stars on golden chains: easy — antimony, aluminium, and lampblack. Two — pure gold, waxing and waning: lampblack mixed with sodium compounds and a touch of calcium. Three — pink opalescence: OK, strontium carbonate, magnesium and a dash of copper carbonate. Four — white gold and silver tears: simple, aluminium, titanium, and magnesium flakes. Five — ice and fire: white hot barium oxide and strontium carbonate. Six — the red jewels — ruby and garnet: so yes, strontium again, and an equal amount of lithium. And now we have the makings of Seven.

And if Allbard was right, all they had to do was concoct his chemical mix and they just might have made the discovery that had eluded pyrotechnicians for years.

"Holy shit!" She stopped writing. "What was that?"

Suggs sat bolt upright, his eyes bright, his whiskers quivering.

Clemmie felt suddenly icy cold. Was that someone outside? A voice? A footstep?

She turned down the radio and listened again. Now she could hear nothing but the howling of the wind, the rush of the swollen river and the tapping of the bare branches against the window.

"Get a grip," she muttered, her voice sounding unnaturally loud in the lab's echoing silence. "You don't believe in magic and you certainly don't believe in ghouls and ghosts and things that go bump in the night. Shit!"

Suggs jumped to the floor and ran towards the door. Holding her breath, Clemmie could swear there were footsteps outside on the cobbles.

What if it wasn't a supernatural footstep at all? What if it was a flesh and blood intruder? Realising just how isolated she was here in the outhouse, not only from civilisation generally but also from the relative safety of the main boathouse, she began to panic. Suppose someone was prowling around outside? The doors were locked, but that surely wouldn't stop anyone who was determined to get in?

Should she call the police? Most likely they'd just issue her with an incident number and tell her to ring again if she was murdered. What about Guy? No — not a good idea. He was too busy to be disturbed and he'd think she was being fanciful, and certainly wouldn't want to be dragged back from planning what could be The Gunpowder Plot's most lucrative deal of the year.

Listening again, she could hear nothing unusual now. Suggs had trotted away from the door and subsided once more into a ball on the charcoal sacks.

"Good boy. Nothing to worry about. It was probably just the wind," she said cheerfully to him in an attempt at reassuring herself. "Right, so let's have a cup of coffee and see what treats we've got in the fridge, shall we? I'm pretty hungry and I bet you wouldn't say no, would you?"

Turning the radio up and wishing the DJ hadn't had the bright idea to play Michael Jackson's 'Thriller', Clemmie switched on the kettle, spooned coffee and sugar into a mug and opened the fridge for the milk.

"Oh, Guy Devlin! You angel!" She clapped her hands. "Cream slices! I love cream slices!"

All the night-terrors were forgotten as she carried the coffee and the delicious piles of cream, jam, choux pastry and icing to the workbench. There were five cakes and not even Clemmie could eat all five. However, she thought, sipping the scalding coffee, two should be easy. Which would leave two for Guy when he came home — and one for Suggs, who had slithered from the sack as soon as he'd smelled the cream and was dancing round her on his hind legs.

"There you go." She broke off a chunk and placed it carefully in his front paws. "Oh, now you've got it all over your whiskers, which," she chuckled as she squished into a gooey mouthful, "probably makes two of us."

Ooh, bliss, she thought, licking cream from her fingers. Cream slices, hot coffee, and the solution to the Seventh Heaven conundrum.

"Jesus Christ!"

The scream outside echoed above the wind and the rush of the river. It even drowned out Michael Jackson's spectral singing.

As the scream increased in pitch, someone was thundering on the lab door.

Suggs, still cream-covered, shot behind the charcoal sacks.

Clemmie's heart felt as if it was going to explode and her sticky hands were clammy.

Jesus — now what should she do? Stay put and hope the maniac outside shuffled away to haunt someone else? Open the door and risk being massacred?

"Help me!" a thin voice trebled. "Help me! Open this door!"

Oh God. Clemmie slid tentatively from her stool. Was it a wounded soul seeking solace? Or some madman wielding an axe? If only Guy was here. If only YaYa wasn't away. If only she wasn't so bloody terrified.

"Let me in!" the voice screeched again. "Please!"

Grabbing her mobile, dry-mouthed, shaking from head to foot, Clemmie moved slowly towards the door, slid back the bolt and turned the key.

Then she pulled the door open slightly and screamed.

"What you screaming for?" A small glowing skeleton glared at her. "I were the one screaming. I fell over. Look — I'm bleeding. Where's Guy? And what's that mess on your hands? Is it blood? Have you killed someone?"

Mightily relieved that the small skeleton was at least human, and wondering why on earth any responsible parent had allowed a junior trick-or-treater to stray so far off the beaten track, Clemmie realised that she was still clutching her cream slice and it had oozed gorily through her fingers.

"Oh, no — mine's just a cake." Her voice was till trembling. "Is yours real blood?"

"On my knee. I need it cleaned up. Now."

"Well, look, don't you think that's something your parents should do? Where do you live — hey!"

176

The small skeleton had pushed past her, injured knee completely forgotten, and was gazing round the lab. "Oh cake! Scrumpty! Get me a drink."

"What?" Clemmie frowned at the small intruder who was forcing a cream slice through its skeletal mask. "Sorry, you can't stay here. I don't know how you got here —"

"In the Jag," the child mumbled disdainfully. "And it's last year's."

Shame, Clemmie thought. Clearly some yummy mummy from one of the more select Winterbrook estates had decided to go upmarket trick or treating this Halloween. "Now, seriously, let me take you home and — dear God!"

Two small witches and a Dracula stormed into the lab and immediately punched the skeleton until it dropped the cake.

"Stop it!" Clemmie yelled above the screaming. "Stop it at once! What the hell do you think you're doing?"

Not relenting in their fist fight, the four children scuffled perilously near the lab's workbench.

Clemmie grabbed Dracula's cloak and tugged the bundle of biting, punching mini humanity towards the door. "Out! Now! God knows what your mother is thinking of —"

"Their mother," a plummy voice drawled from the darkness, "is thinking this place is truly the pits, and wondering why on earth the house is in darkness, and why we've been wandering round this Godforsaken tip for what seems like hours trying to find someone to let us in. Where's Guy?"

"Out," Clemmie said sharply, awfully aware that the drawling voice belonged to the face on the kitchen wall.

Helen from the Dark Side. And Crap, Puke, Snot and Mungo.

Dear God.

"Who are you?" Helen stepped into the lab and peered at Clemmie. "Are you another one of Guy's lost causes? Care in the community or something?"

The children had resumed their bloodbath on the floor. Helen ignored them.

Helen was even more exquisitely beautiful in the flesh than she was in the photograph, Clemmie thought miserably. And whatever YaYa had hinted about the nips and tucks, they certainly didn't show. Helen was a fashion-plate of perfectly groomed sleek blonde hair, perfectly made-up angel's face, perfect body perfectly dressed in country-casual designer clothes.

Helen, Clemmie realised, could only see a dishevelled, scruffy, bohemian wreck with big earrings and more cream cake on her face and fingers than had ever made it into her mouth.

"I'm Guy's assistant." She tried to lick dried cream from her lips. "He's out at a business meeting. And yes, before you introduce yourself, there's no need. I do know who you are, I've seen your photograph — but was he expecting you tonight?"

"No, of course not." Helen shook her head. "God forbid that we'd actually drive from London and choose to spend more time here than necessary.

178

However, needs must, and I do need to speak to him. Urgently. Now."

"He shouldn't be long. Why don't you wait in the main house? Do you have a key?"

"If I had a key, you stupid girl, I wouldn't have been wandering around outside in this freezing weather, with my poor kiddies in tow, trying to get in, would I?"

"No, I suppose not. Have you tried his mobile?"

"Yes." Helen's voice was aching with anger. "It's switched off. And I've tried the house phone and got that — that *thing*'s voice — inviting me to leave a message. No doubt *it* is out with Guy, too?"

"YaYa's away," Clemmie said shortly, itching to fly at Helen and beat her to a pulp. "And if Guy wasn't expecting you and you don't have a key, then I don't think I should let you into the house. So why don't you and the — the — children go and wait in your car until he comes back?"

"Just who do you think you are?" Helen sneered. "You give me the key and I'll let myself in."

"No."

"What the fuck is going on here?" Guy suddenly appeared across the courtyard. "Helen — I saw the car. Have you driven down from London tonight? What on earth do you want? And get the kids away from the chemicals!" He turned quickly and roared at the children. "You four! Stop fighting! Now!"

Crap, Puke, Snot and Mungo stopped fighting and glared mutinously at Guy.

He was more angry than Clemmie could ever have imagined him. His eyes glittered in her direction. "Are you OK? And Suggs?"

Before Clemmie could answer, Suggs shot out from his hideaway and hurled himself into Guy's arms.

The children screamed in unison.

"Jesus!" Helen sneered. "I'd hoped that disgusting creature was dead by now."

"I'm fine," Clemmie said softly. "So's Suggs. Thanks for the cakes, by the way, they were gorgeous. I'm afraid I've made a bit of a mess — both with the cakes and the chemicals. Look, I think I'll just get my stuff and —"

"We're moving in here with Guy," the largest of the witches interrupted her. "We haven't got a house any more."

"Bloody electrics," the second tiny witch spat. "Mummy says electricians are tossers."

"The house caught fire this afternoon," Dracula whined. "Just when we were going to Jeremy Pointing-Meyer's Spooky Party. And he was having real dead bodies and now we've missed them."

"Give me a few moments to find a sharp instrument," Guy muttered, "and I'll soon remedy that."

"Can we see our rooms?" The skeleton jangled a few loose bones. "I'm knackered."

Guy looked hopelessly at Helen. "What the hell are they talking about?"

"The new conservatory extension," Helen said dismissively. "And cowboy electricians. A bit of faulty

180

wiring they said. Quite a lot of damage though and no power at all until they've resolved the problem. Just a temporary blip. But we do need shelter for a week or two. And don't suggest I try chums — for some reason they've all said they can't take us, and Mummy and Daddy are already away for the winter and the house barred and bolted of course."

"Oh, of course," Guy said icily. "And can't either of your other exes help out? They are the children's fathers after all."

Helen didn't meet his eyes. "Sadly, no. They're both otherwise engaged."

Guy sighed. "What about a hotel if it's only short-term?"

"Good lord, no! Not with the children. Not when you have at least four bedrooms standing empty here. And Winterbrook, being so close to the motorway network, is so convenient for running the kiddies to school and for their extra-curriculars." Helen made a moue with her perfect lips. "Don't be a meanie, Guy, darling. You won't even know we're here. And we'll be gone in a week."

"It'll be a bloody long week," Guy groaned. "But if you really don't have anywhere else to go . . ."

Clemmie moved towards the doorway. "I'll leave you to it," she said quietly to Guy. "I'll see you tomorrow."

"What? Oh, yeah — whatever," Guy said, distract-edly stroking a quivering Suggs. "'Bye, Clemmie."

Feeling more miserable than she could ever remember, Clemmie hurried shivering through the biting wind, negotiated a sleek peppermint green Jaguar piled to the roof with designer bags, and unlocked the Peugeot.

"Oh, buggering bloody sod it!" she spat as she steered away from the boathouse. "And I never even got to tell him about discovering Seventh Heaven."

CHAPTER
THIRTEEN

Hopefully, November the fifth was going to be perfect for Tarnia Snepps' firework party. If the perfect clear frosty day turned, as it was forecast to do, into an equally perfect cold frosty evening with no clouds and a sickle moon, tonight's firework display would be sensational.

At least something was perfect, Clemmie thought irritably, as she worked her way through the emails and letters at her desk. Life at the boathouse had been simply awful since Helen and the children had arrived. The woman was a nightmare, her dreadfulness only eclipsed by the appalling behaviour of her offspring. And Clemmie really missed YaYa with her flamboyant friendship and constant chatter. Even Suggs had taken refuge in the office, spending his days with Clemmie on his little sofa by the window, staring out at the river.

And Guy had been out more than in, and when he was in he was short-tempered and distracted.

"Sorry, Clemmie," he'd said each morning when he'd popped into the office to check the post and leave her his day's itinerary. "Nothing personal — it's just easier for me to be out of the way on planning trips and stuff. Thank God this invasion will soon be over."

As there hadn't been any opportunity to tell him about her Green Man discovery since Halloween, Clemmie had taken the scribbled notes home and spent her evenings concocting her own version of Allbard's recipe in her shed at the Post Office Stores.

The chlorophyll had been easy — after the recent heavy autumnal rain, there was still plenty of lush green grass in Bagley-cum-Russet — and Clemmie was well used to extracting compounds from dried raw materials with the aid of her small oven, laboratory flasks and tiny Bunsen burner. The powdered copper salts had also been easily translated and obtained — even if the villagers had watched her with grave doubts as she scraped verdigris from the railings round the village's Celtic cross and from several ancient urns in the churchyard.

The jaundy-ash, however, had still proved a mind-bending problem until, over supper the previous Friday evening, she'd mentioned it to her aunt and uncle.

"Ah! That takes me back, Clemmie, love! Jaundy-ash is what we used to call willow trees when we was kids. It's an old Berkshire name I think — totally wrong of course, Alan Titchmarsh would have a horticultural fit," Uncle Bill had said, sprinkling vinegar liberally on his chips. "I suppose the juice would be the sap you get when you scrape the bark away."

Auntie Molly had nodded. "The willow tree had lots of names, and lots of uses. My grandma used to get us to chew chunks of it when we had a headache.

184

Jaundy-ash worked a treat. A right magical tree, the willow."

And Clemmie had kissed them, and with her fish and chips left uncharacteristically half-eaten, had belted out in the blustery darkness to the sad, neglected willows behind the Barmy Cow and carved discreet lumps from several trunks.

Back in the shed, once the three ingredients had been dried and crushed and mixed, Clemmie had excitedly decanted the powdered blend into several Kilner jars pinched from the shop. Triumphantly surveying the results, Clemmie reckoned she knew exactly how Louis Pasteur had felt.

Of course, the proof of the pudding would be in the eating, so to speak, but as soon as Helen and Crap, Puke, Snot and Mungo had departed, she'd have time to explain it all to Guy, and they could carry out a controlled explosion — and who knew what might happen.

To that end, she'd taken a single jar of home-made Allbard's Magik Green Powder into work with her, waiting for an opportunity to try it out with Guy. It was currently burning a metaphorical hole in her desk drawer.

November the fifth was dragging. Fortunately, according to the activities wallchart which Helen had annoyingly pinned to the office wall, it was the day the children had their after-school skiing lesson and then were going out to their own fireworks party somewhere non-local, so with any luck they'd all be out of the way for the rest of the day. And then, tonight . . . Clemmie

185

sighed in anticipation. Tonight she'd be with Guy for the entire evening, at his side as YaYa's substitute stand-in lover, to repel the predatory advances of Tarnia Snepps.

She simply couldn't wait.

Suggs clambered up onto her lap and head-butted her gently under the chin.

"I know." She kissed him. "It's all been hideous, hasn't it? Never mind, they'll be gone soon."

"You," Helen sneered as she swept unannounced into the office, "must be mad. Talking to that thing — and cuddling it! I'd drown it if I could get my hands on it."

Suggs whimpered and snuggled closer to Clemmie.

"Did you want something?" Clemmie asked icily, tucking Suggs firmly under her arm. "Guy isn't here."

Helen flicked back her elegant blonde bob, and flicked non-existent fluff from her immaculate cashmere cardigan. "I know. I saw him leave at first light — again. But I need to speak to him. Why does he never have his mobile switched on?"

"Because he's out with the pyro crew setting up the tubes and the firing wires for a really important display tonight and can't be disturbed," Clemmie said, not adding that he'd told her to ring Syd's mobile in an emergency because his was switched off "in case *she* tries to contact me, OK?".

Helen sighed. "Always playing with bloody fireworks. Like a child. Anyway, I've got a disaster looming."

Oh, goody, Clemmie thought. She said nothing.

"If he should ring in," Helen continued, "could you tell him I'm going to need him tonight."

"He's doing a display tonight," Clemmie repeated, glaring at her. "As you well know."

"That's as maybe, but we — the children and I — are attending Serena Kauffman's children's bonfire night party, and that — as you clearly won't know — means the kiddies are being invited to join the junior A-list."

"Nice for you," Clemmie muttered. "I hope you all enjoy it. So, where does Guy come in?"

"I need him to collect the children from school and take them for their skiing lesson first then drop them off at Serena's."

"Out of the question. He's going to be tied up all day. Why on earth can't you take Cr — er — the children to the snow-dome and on to the party as planned?"

"Because," Helen wrinkled her pert nose, "if it's any of your business, they need to be taken to our usual ski place in South Ken. I've just been informed that your local dry-snow ski place is very near a council estate. I'm sorry, but I simply can't allow the kiddies to come into contact with common children. They might catch something."

"I wouldn't worry too much. I'm sure common children are pretty hardy." Clemmie smiled sweetly. "There's probably nothing yours can infect them with."

"Are you being deliberately insulting?"

"Me? Oh, I'll leave you to figure that out yourself. And I still don't see why Guy has to take them?"

"Because I'm booked in for a full facial and manicure in Reading during their lesson, which is an absolute must. I simply can't face the Kauffman's crowd looking like this tonight. The glossies will be there. And the children can't possibly miss their skiing lesson. It would traumatise them. So, while I'm being pampered, someone will have to take the kiddies to London and then drive them on to Serena's in Surrey."

"Well it won't be Guy," Clemmie said calmly, clenching her fists under the desk. "Even if he wanted to, he simply won't have time. So, you'll either have to brave the common hordes or cancel your facial, or maybe ask one of your other ex-husbands, won't you?"

Helen snorted. It was a harshly unfeminine sound, totally at odds with her appearance. Clemmie almost expected to see fire roaring from her perfect nostrils.

"Oh, Clemmie, dear — how gallant you are, rushing to Guy's defence. And how painfully transparent you are. So smitten. So sad. Surely you've been here long enough, know him well enough, to realise he would never look at you?"

That was a pretty close barb. Clemmie prayed she wasn't blushing. She fiddled with her earrings and decided silence was better than any reply.

Helen sighed heavily. "You really are a particularly stupid girl, aren't you?"

"I'm neither a girl nor stupid." Clemmie felt this was a safe one to answer. She stretched her lips into a smile. "And — just a thought — if you take the — um — kiddies skiing in London, can't you cancel your

Reading appointment and book a facial in a London beauty salon while they're on the pretend-piste?"

"Dear me — just how provincial are you? You can't just walk into a salon of any standing, straight from the street, in town you know. The decent places are booked months in advance."

"Are they? Really? You can pop into our local one in Hazy Hassocks at any time. Jennifer Blessing will have a go at anyone's wrinkles. She's not fussy — no job too big for our Jennifer. I can't imagine why a London salon would be booked so far in advance, although urban living clearly takes it's toll on the face."

"Is that an insult?"

"Just an observation."

Helen, clearly not sure whether or not she'd been outsmarted, faltered slightly. "Don't argue with me. Don't try and outdo me. Don't even try to be clever. Just pass the message on to Guy."

"No," Clemmie said. "One, I don't take orders from anyone. Two, Guy can't do it. Three, Guy isn't coming back here today. Four —"

She wasn't sure she could think of a four. It might be better to stop now before she ruined the effect.

"Oh, for heaven's sake!" Helen turned round and headed for the door. "You really are pathetic!" Very well, I shall have to tell the children they can't have their skiing lesson tonight — and I hope you realise they'll bear the scars for the rest of their lives."

"You could always cancel your titivating." Clemmie, on a roll, was determined to have the final barrage. "That way it'll only be your scars on show, won't it?"

Helen gave a feral roar and hurtled out of the office. Suggs gave a little gurgle of delight and drummed his tiny paws on Clemmie's lap.

"I think I might have made an enemy there." Clemmie grinned down at him. "What a shame."

The episode, when Clemmie repeated it to Guy on their way to Hazy Hassocks much later that evening, lost nothing in the retelling. It was an amazingly exciting journey, not just because she was alone with him in the BMW heading for Tarnia Snepps' party and pretending to be his lover, or because he looked more darkly, devastatingly sexy than ever, but also because every person in the entire world was letting off fireworks and the sky was a constant explosion of noisy colour.

". . . so," Clemmie finished, twisting round in her seat to admire a particularly clever blue and pink chrysanthemum effect with whistles and firecrackers, "sorry about being rude to her. I'm not usually that offensive to people, but honestly, she deserved it."

"I'm sure she did. There's no need to apologise to me." Guy chuckled in the darkness, as he steered the BMW away from Hazy Hassocks village and along the narrow lanes towards the Sneppses' bad-taste mansion. "Helen would manage to antagonise a saint. I just wish I'd been there to see it. YaYa would have been far, far more brutal, believe me. It was brave of you to take Helen on — she's a total cow — and those kids are even worse now than they were when we lived together.

190

Anyway, your firm stand seems to have worked. There wasn't a sign of any of them when I got home."

"She was forced to cancel the skiing and had to promise the brats — er — children double junior master chef lessons or something instead. She left at about three, complete with luggage, to collect them from school and break the bad news as they headed for this posh party. Presumably, once they've all had post-traumatic-stress counselling, she'll be sleeping over at this A-list shindig?"

"I don't think Helen does sleepovers," Guy said. "Far too lower-middle-class. But yes, she'd left a note on the bloody wallchart to say she'd be back tomorrow night — like I care — so I guess she's foisted herself on some other poor sap for the night. Possibly not the A-list Serena Kauffman, though. Not with the children in tow."

"Then they'll be going home to London soon, surely? It was only a tiny bit of fire damage, wasn't it?"

"So she says." Guy sighed. "God, I hope they're gone before YaYa gets back. It'll be like Armageddon."

"I really miss YaYa." Clemmie pleated the hem of her very best long scarlet coat, worn especially with her best long black boots and long red wool dress for this evening. She'd added the Butler and Wilson jet and ruby earrings and taken forever with her hair and make-up. Guy had told her she looked beautiful. She'd taken it as a style compliment — gay men were always so clever about clothes and design, she felt — rather than anything remotely personal. "She's texted me several times. It sounds like she's having a great time. You must really miss her being around."

"Mmm." Guy nodded. "We've been living together so long, it's always strange when she goes away. She rings most nights before the show. It'll take her ages to come down to earth after this one — sometimes I think she'd like to do it full-time. And I wouldn't stand in her way, of course, but —"

"You'd miss her if she did?"

"When you've been as close as me and YaYa for over twenty years, being apart seems like I've lost part of me. God, hark at me. No, seriously, I just can't wait to get back to normal."

Clemmie nodded agreement in the darkness, not even finding it slightly odd that normal to her now involved Guy, YaYa and Suggs — a trio that would be far from normal for most people. "And once Helen's gone and YaYa's back and you've got a bit of spare time and are feeling more — um — relaxed, maybe we can get on with developing Seventh Heaven."

"Yeah — I can't wait. I was so looking forward to that on Halloween — then Helen arrived and made it impossible. Christ, that woman's buggered up everything. I wish I'd never clapped eyes on her. YaYa warned me that she'd be trouble right from the start, but I wouldn't listen because . . . Oh, well — all water under the proverbial bridge now. I don't suppose you've got any further with Allbard on your own, have you?"

"Well, actually, now you come to mention it . . ."

Clemmie quickly gave Guy the abridged version of her discovery on Halloween and her subsequent attempt at recreating the Magik Green in her shed.

Guy stood on the brakes just as they reached the Snepps mansion, making the BMW slew against the high bank. "What? And you never thought to tell me?"

"There hasn't been a moment." Clemmie frowned as the car came to a halt. "Has there? Look, sorry if you think I shouldn't have dabbled without you, but you have been a bit busy and preoccupied and —"

"Tell me what you've discovered again." He looked at her in the car's darkness. "Right from the beginning."

So she did. She told him everything, including the fact that the green-fire was linked to the Green Man medieval folklore and the magic spell seemed to be inextricably linked to the concoction, adding that she still didn't believe in magic, but didn't want to risk the whole experiment failing because she'd chosen to only use certain bits of it.

The only interruptions came when they were distracted by an occasional breathtaking starburst of colour or deafening crescendo of noise from the direction of Hazy Hassocks village green where the residents were clearly enjoying their own Bonfire Night celebrations.

"And you've actually got a jar of this green chemical mixture back at the boathouse?" Guy said when she'd finished.

"No, not exactly."

"Sorry? I thought you said you'd decanted it, and saved all but one of the samples in your shed."

"Oh, yes. I have. And I brought one into work. But I didn't leave it at the boathouse — in case it fell into the wrong hands. I get a bit paranoid over my experiments. I've got it with me tonight. It's in the carrier bag on the back seat. Just in case."

"Clemmie Coddle!" Guy leaned across and took her face between his hands. "I think I love you!"

CHAPTER
FOURTEEN

Clemmie stared at Guy for a moment, allowing herself a brief and blissful fantasy that he really meant it. He was so close in that intimate darkness: so close that she could see the navy flecks in his cornflower-blue eyes, see the freckles smudged beneath the tanned skin on his face, feel the warmth of his breath on her skin. How deliciously easy it would be to kiss that sexy, sulky mouth. How deliciously easy — and how terminally stupid.

She pulled away, gently, reluctantly. "Maybe, if there's a lull in tonight's proceedings, we could give the Magik Green a trial run? Tarnia Snepps' place is huge and I'm sure we could find a quiet spot so no one would notice. You'll have loads of spare tubes and fuses and black powder on site, won't you?"

"Too right." Guy's eyes gleamed. "It'll be the highlight of my night."

"Don't get too enthusiastic." Clemmie pulled a face. "It might not work — after all, so many pyrotechnicians must have read Allbard over the years, and some of them are bound to have translated it like I did. This has probably been done hundreds of times before — and failed."

"And maybe it hasn't." Guy restarted the car and turned towards the wrought-iron gates at the foot of the Sneppses' mile-long drive. "But we'll soon know. I'm sure we can find time to manage a little private experiment. Oh, Lord, I hate this place! Are you ready for this?"

Clemmie stared ahead in trepidation, first through the hideous filigreed gates at the multi-coloured gravel drive, then at Tarnia's self-designed South Fork mansion shimmering in the distance. Massive floodlights, which wouldn't have looked out of place on an international airport's runway, illuminated a sprawl of pink stucco, gilded lions rampant, fairytale crenellations, curlicues, cornices and cherubs puking blue water.

"Ready as I'll ever be."

A towering figure wearing a floral headscarf and a floor-length tweed coat suddenly appeared from the gloom, ducked as a low-flying Skyline Screama howled off-course from the village, plonked itself four-square in front of the car, and indicated with extravagant arm movements that Guy should open the BMW's window.

Guy obeyed, allowing gusts of freezing November night air to rush into the car.

"Invite, duck?" Big Ida Tomms from Fiddlesticks, six feet tall, broad-shouldered, somewhere in her eighties and scarily aggressive, stuck her head inside the car. "We've got a party on 'ere tonight. Fireworks in the Big Meadow. No one can come in without an invite."

"I'm Guy Devlin," Guy said politely. "From The Gunpowder Plot."

"I don't care if you're bloody Noddy from bloody Toyland." Big Ida sniffed. "If you ain't got an invite you ain't coming in."

"Hello, Ida." Clemmie leaned across the car. "It's me — Clemmie Coddle. Amber's friend? Amber who lives next door to you and Gwyneth? Is Gwyneth doing security here, too?"

Big Ida peered at Clemmie. "Oh, hello duck. You're Molly and Bill's young niece, aren't you? The scruffy one who can't keep a man or hold down a job. Yes, Gwyneth's around somewhere. But you'll still need an invite for the bonfire. Mr and Mrs Snepps have a hand-picked guestlist. It ain't for the hoi polloi. The hoi polloi's all down the village green. We can't let all and sundry in 'ere, you know."

"I work with Guy — at The Gunpowder Plot. We're the fireworks crew, Ida. If you don't let Guy in there won't be a party."

Fortunately Gwyneth Wilkins, also in her eighties, about four feet tall and the same wide, waddled across at that moment blowing heavily on her mittens.

"Hello ducks." She beamed up at Guy and Clemmie from beneath the brim of a rather perky bowler hat. "Going to do us some pretty sparklers for tonight, are you?"

"Er — yes," Guy said, clearly relieved that someone recognised him, "if you could just get your friend to let us in."

"Oh, has she gorn all Stalin on you, duck?" Gwyneth shook her head sorrowfully at Big Ida who was now looking slightly crestfallen. "Sorry about that. Big Ida's usually involved in car-parking at these do's. She gets a bit Third Reich when she's on security. Let's just press the right buttons on this 'ere gate — and in you goes!"

The gates swished open to a disconcertingly discordant blast of 'Big Spender', and, waving cheerfully, Gwyneth and Big Ida stood back as the BMW finally passed.

"Barking," Guy observed as they swept up the acres of drive and came to a halt in front of large white wedding-cake pillars and a flight of pink and gold steps. "But very sweet. Now, the pyro crew are all in the Big Meadow so do you want me to drop you off there, or do you want to get the introductions with the terrifying Tarnia out of the way first?"

Clemmie shrugged. "Escaping to be with Syd and the rest is very tempting, but I did promise Ya Ya that I'd stay glued to your side and keep you safe from the marauding Ms Snepps, didn't I?"

"You did," Guy chuckled. "Right, so we hold hands and giggle a lot and whisper sweet nothings. OK?"

"Blimey — that's going to be a tough one."

"I know, but someone's got to do it."

The front door was slightly open. Clemmie, holding Guy's hand and absolutely relishing the intimate contact while trying to remember not to stroke it, or squeeze it, or massage it in any sort of seductive way, stared into the entrance hall's bad-taste opulence.

A soaring riot of pink, gold and white, it had statues at the foot of the stairs, fondant-pink picture frames, marabou-trimmed floor-to-ceiling mirrors, and a stained-glass window dominating the stairwell.

198

"Bloody hell!" Clemmie muttered as they stepped into the hall's delicious tropical warmth after the sub-zero temperatures outside. "I've heard about this place, but even so . . ."

"I know," Guy whispered back. "Nothing, but nothing, can actually prepare you for the reality. And don't ask about the stained glass window."

"Why not?" Clemmie peered at it. "Who is it? Stevie Wonder?"

"Originally it was the Beckhams, then it got damaged while they were trying to add little Cruz to Brooklyn and Romeo, so the designers mutated it into this. For ages Tarnia insisted it was Martin Luther King, but recently she's been saying she was years ahead of the pack and it's Barack Obama. As I said, it's probably best not to mention it at all."

"OK. Hard not to, though, really. Oh — look at that! I've never seen an indoor fountain before! Jeeze. Is that really a little boy standing on a *dolphin*? *Peeing*?"

Guy laughed. "Mmm, possibly best not to mention that one either."

"Guy! Angel!" Tarnia Snepps, a size eight vision in a very short pale pink leather dress, gold stilt-heels, with coal-black razored hair, the tips frosted in pink and gold, suddenly swept into the hall and teetered towards them. "How wonderful to see you! And — oh . . ."

"Lovely to see you too, Tarnia," Guy said manfully. "And allow me to introduce you to my best girl Clemmie. Clemmie, this is Tarnia Snepps."

Tarnia looked disapprovingly at Clemmie. "Hello."

"Hello, Mrs Snepps." Clemmie looked back. Surely if Tarnia intended wearing that outfit for the firework display she'd freeze her assets before the first rainbow explosion had waned across Hassocks. She'd seen Tarnia Snepps many times at various village functions when she'd been doing her Lady of the Manor act, but never this close before. Tarnia must have been more lifted and Botoxed than Helen. She had to be in her fifties; yet there wasn't a line or wrinkle to be seen on the extremely orange face. It was very impressive. "How nice to meet you."

"Likewise, I'm sure." Tarnia smiled stiffly at Guy. "Whatever happened to that glamorous woman you had with you last time? Yvonne?"

"Ya Ya," Guy said, his lips twitching. "Ah, well Ya Ya and I are on a break."

"Naughty boy!" Tarnia's face didn't move although it looked as if it very much wanted to. "Well, I must say, young Clemmie is a complete change."

"You know what they say? A change is as good as a rest."

"I bet you don't do much resting!" Tarnia screamed coquettishly. "You are so wicked, Guy! Oh, come here."

Wrenching him away from Clemmie, Tarnia hugged him fiercely and slapped Mwah! Mwah! air kisses on both cheeks.

Guy quickly disentangled himself and fixed his professional smile. "Right — lovely — er, sorry to have to cut this short, but I just thought we'd pop in to let you know we've arrived. We'll shoot off up to the Big

Meadow now and start getting things organised. Still OK to start at eleven, is it?"

"Perfectly," Tarnia dimpled coyly. "You're the boss. My guests are having a little soiree in the stables at the moment. A few nibbles: foie gras, pak-choi fondue, caviar from the most remote part of Uzbekistan, washed down with several slugs of Cristal, naturally."

"Oh, naturally." Guy nodded. "I do hope you'll provide some leftovers for the workers."

Clemmie shuddered. She really hoped not. A jacket potato and a hot dog would do her fine.

Tarnia giggled girlishly. "You, my angel man, can have whatever you like, you know that. Now — what were we talking about? Oh, yes. The guests. Marquis and I will bring them up to the Big Meadow bang on time. And I do hope you and I will manage to have a little moment alone later."

"I'm sure we will," Guy murmured, gripping Clemmie's hand. "If Clemmie will let me out of her sight."

"No chance of that," Clemmie said, not entirely untruthfully, snuggling closer to Guy's black leather jacket. "I'm very possessive."

Tarnia tried to frown. "That's a rather juvenile attitude to a man like Guy if I may say so, Clemmie. A man like Guy needs a very, very long leash."

Guy laughed bravely. Clemmie joined in, moving even closer. God, she thought, if I cosy up much more we'll be sharing the same skin.

"Much as I'd love to stay," Guy sounded as if he really meant it, "duty calls. Tarnia, I'll see you at

201

eleven." He glanced at his watch. "Which isn't that long away now. I must go and make sure the display is set up properly. Till eleven, then."

Somehow managing to worm herself between them, Tarnia elbowed Clemmie sharply aside, and kissed Guy again. Guy, to give him his due, didn't even flinch.

"Oh, dear, Tarnia." He smiled sadly at her. "You do make it difficult for a man. But I really must go and do some work. It's what you're paying me for."

"I'd pay you for much more than that," Tarnia trilled lasciviously, clenching pink frosted talons into his sleeve. "If only you'd let me."

Remembering her part in this charade and itching to stamp on Tarnia's toes, Clemmie started to pull Guy towards the door. "Come on, darling — we really must be going."

Tarnia reluctantly let go and like a cork popping from a bottle, Guy staggered backwards.

"Jesus!" he laughed as they stumbled out of the hall and onto the glittery top step. "I thought she was going to eat me alive."

"It's your own fault," Clemmie said as they hurled themselves back across the multi-coloured gravel and into the BMW. "You positively encouraged her."

"She's one of my best customers," Guy said with a shudder as he drove the car away from the house and towards the distant Big Meadow. "She's paying thousands for tonight's display. I simply can't afford to upset her. Just," he looked across at Clemmie, "don't let her get me alone."

"I'll try," Clemmie said. "But it clearly won't be easy. Of course you could put an end to it yourself."

"How? I told you, I can't offend her."

"By telling her you're gay."

"What?" Guy laughed. "I couldn't do that! Why on earth would I do that? I'd never get another gig here again. That's half my appeal to Tarnia. The fact that I might one day become a notch on her gilded four-poster. Sadly, ladies like Tarnia need to think they're in with a chance. And you did very well back there — YaYa would have been delighted with your performance. Even I thought you were a typical possessive lover."

"Oh, I've had my moments," Clemmie said wistfully, peering at the activity ahead of them as the car bumped across a rutted field. "I vaguely remember the moves."

The Gunpowder Plot's pyro crew were bustling about on the Big Meadow under several spotlights. It was fascinating, Clemmie thought, to see a firework display from the other side for the first time. The scientist in her suddenly kicked in, and she felt her skin prickle with that frisson of anticipation that occurred whenever she was close to explosive chemicals.

She knew that the tubes had already been buried deep in the ground; that the fireworks, transported safely to the Sneppses' field in several of The Gunpowder Plot's solid security vans, would have been placed inside them by Syd and the rest according to Guy's display plan; that the fuses and igniters had been attached, the wires all snaking invisibly across the field; and that the order of firing by remote control — all set up along with Tarnia's music of choice — was ready and waiting on the computer which was also housed in one of the vans.

The crew, all dressed in black, moved around like animated shadows, and welcomed Guy's arrival with their usual bawdy greetings, and the next half an hour passed quickly in a flurry of final checking, and double-checking, and checking again.

"She's booked a thirty-minute display," Syd told Clemmie, "which is mega-huge in pyrotechnic terms — not to mention financial ones. The New Year one in London only lasts for ten minutes, but Mrs Snepps was determined she'd outdo them. And some of the music she's chosen is excruciating to work into a choreographed display."

"Really? How bad?"

"Chris de Burgh. Celine Dion. Need I go on?"

Clemmie grinned. "I get the picture. Still, the fireworks will be sensational even if the music isn't to everyone's taste. I'm sure her guests'll love it."

"Doubt it," Guy said, appearing suddenly out of the darkness. "These are just people that Tarnia and her Marquis want to impress. Business cronies, nouveau-riche hangers-on, media wannabes and the like. They've probably been bored to tears by firework displays at every corporate event going. It always pisses me off that my art is wasted on people who have no interest in the magic of pyrotechnics at all."

"Think of the money, then," Clemmie said, shivering. "And I'll appreciate the fireworks anyway."

204

"Yeah," Guy said with a grin. "I know you will. Oh, bugger. It looks like the rich and famous are on their way."

Tarnia and her husband Marquis — a pseudonym Tarnia had used for years, Clemmie knew, but who was known locally as Snotty Mark — were marching towards the viewing enclosure.

Tarnia appeared to have wrapped herself in a large pink teddy bear and replaced the stilt-heels with golden Wellingtons far more suitable for the freezing weather. Marquis looked like a hit man in an overlarge Crombie, and the guests were muffled in a mixture of furs, Jaeger wool, and old school scarves.

"Fortunately they all have to stay on the viewing platform," Guy hissed, "so we should avoid any silly questions."

Clemmie watched as Tarnia and her guests fussily sorted themselves on the neat little raised benches supplied by The Gunpowder Plot, and pulled their gloves tighter onto numb fingers and wrapped the provided car rugs round their knees, oohing and aahing over the tiny flasks in front of them. It seemed odd to her that anyone could sit down while watching fireworks. She spent her whole time hopping from foot to foot, spinning round, staring upwards, jigging about with excitement.

"They've got my wife's home-made hot cider-punch in those flasks," Syd told her. "And it's lethal. So at least they won't be cold — just bladdered. Right, Guy — are we ready?"

Guy nodded, tense now, his face darkly immobile. Clemmie ached to kiss him, to tell him he was wonderful, to tell him it would all go like a dream because he was the most brilliant pyrotechnician in the world. Instead, because any one of those things would let him know precisely how she felt about him, she just winked at him.

"Stick with me, baby," he said, winking back at her. "And let's get this show on the road."

CHAPTER
FIFTEEN

As if by magic, following their well-rehearsed routine, the entire crew melted to their display positions. Following Guy to the back of the largest van where the control panels, computers and remote firers were set out like something from NASA, Clemmie held her breath.

The local displays had all but died away, and the frosty night was clear, dark, silent. Tarnia had chosen her time well. There'd be no aerial competition.

As the first strains of Mariah Carey echoed into the field, a non-stop fountain of colour erupted into the sky accompanied by whistles and screams.

"Oh," Clemmie breathed. "Candle bundles . . . Ah! That's clever — all pinks and whites and golds — specially for Tarnia. Nice touch."

One after the other, without time to draw breath, the fireworks ignited, and the display went perfectly, each massive barrage longer, brighter, noisier, more spectacular than its predecessor until the whole world seemed to be filled with reflected incandescence.

To 'Lady in Red' a mass of scarlet and ruby chrysanthemums erupted in a series of wide arcs all around the field, and hung teasingly in the sky as further cushions of colour whistled, expanded, exploded and finished in a tumbling cascade of stars.

Then a salvo of rockets screamed skywards, dozens and dozens of them fired at the same time, criss-crossing the sky, leaving rainbow meteors plummeting in their wake.

It was as if the heavens had detonated, splintering the planets and sending the galaxies crashing to earth.

Guy was a master, Clemmie thought, shivering with excitement. It was without doubt the most extravagantly expert display she'd ever seen.

"Multishots next," he said, his lips close to her ear, his voice hoarse.

Syd, his fingers working miracles on the computer keyboard, grinned. "Shame they're going to drown out Sir Elton."

The multishots were even more spectacular — sending a thousand time-delayed comets hurtling heavenwards, each one changing colour in the blink of an eye, until the dizzying, dazzling effect formed a ceiling of stars.

Clemmie had long since given up listening to Tarnia's choice of elevator-musak. It simply didn't matter. She cast a quick glance across to the viewing platform and smiled. Despite Guy's gloomy predictions, the entire party was staring upwards, open-mouthed.

The time flew. Clemmie would have happily stayed there, close to Guy, watching his brilliance come to life, for the rest of her days.

"Finale," Guy nodded towards the crew. "And so far so good."

The finale, designed to fit exactly to Tarnia's selected George Michael compilation, was five minutes long, a non-stop deafening grand slam of squirming, spinning white-hot serpents tearing towards the half-moon, spiralling into the ether, then each one separating, then tantalisingly slowly bursting into enormous coloured peonies which hung in the sky for ever before melting into an earthbound firestorm of glittering sequins.

And then, as suddenly as it had begun, it was over. All that remained was a swirling cloud of smoke and the smell of gunpowder.

The silence was awesome.

Clemmie was trembling. Her ears were filled with the noise, her eyes with reflected luminescence, her whole body infused with the gut-tingling scent of cordite.

"Oh my God."

Dazedly, the viewing platform rose to its feet as one, and whooped and hollered and applauded their delight. The Gunpowder Plot's crew all grinned and jigged and did high-fives.

Guy, Clemmie noticed, looked relieved, totally drained, and ecstatically happy.

She took a deep breath. "That was simply amazing."

He gave her a wearily triumphant smile. "It went well, didn't it?"

"Understatement." Clemmie met his eyes, deciding that the truth was needed now however he chose to interpret it. "And you know it. It was inch-perfect. Superb. You are very, very talented."

He grinned. "Thank you. Coming from someone with a better degree than me and who has possibly just cracked the biggest pyro puzzle in the world, that's some compliment. I haven't forgotten the Magik Green thing. We'll have a go as soon as we're cleared away."

"Great — I'll go and rescue it from the back of the car. Do you want me to help with the clearing up?"

"No thanks, we've got a pretty good routine. You just stay here and keep warm. I won't be long."

Then, with the rest of the pyrotechnicians, Guy dissolved silently and efficiently into the darkness to start the after-show safety-checking and clearing up and packing away.

Clemmie, still stunned, huddled at the back of the van, and smiled dreamily.

Tarnia and Snotty Mark and their guests had all trampled across the field and were enthusiastically congratulating whichever crew member they could get closest to.

"Drinks for all of you chaps and chapesses back at the stables!" Snotty Mark guffawed, slapping the pyrotechnicians' backs. "Wonderful show! First class! Well done!"

For someone she'd heard had been brought up on the Bath Road council estate in Hazy Hassocks, Clemmie reckoned Snotty Mark had taken reinvention to a whole new level. She'd almost expected him to cry "Top hole!".

As the guests staggered dazedly away towards the stables and more gosling on toast or whatever latest culinary must-have the Sneppses had been duped into providing, led by a clearly delighted Snotty Mark, Tarnia seemed to have disappeared. She'd probably gone on ahead to pour the après-display champagne, Clemmie thought. Even if she was having a predatory skulk in the darkness, at least with the rest of the pyro crew around, Guy should stay safe.

He was back in a remarkably short time. The residue of smoke still hung over the Big Meadow in a gauzy haze, but all other traces of The Gunpowder Plot's display had now completely disappeared.

"Syd and the others are nipping back to the stables to join in the posh nosh," Guy said. "Which will give us a perfect opportunity to try out your Allbard's thing. I'll grab a tube and fuse and some powder, you go and get your mix, and let's see what we've got."

Having retrieved the makings of the final stage of Seventh Heaven, they smiled at each other, co-conspirators in a twenty-first century gunpowder plot.

As always when trying out some new chemical recipe, Clemmie felt the anticipation bubbling inside her. She skidded across the frosty grass, her breath hovering in smoky plumes in the freezing air.

Working by torchlight, Guy had set up one of the cardboard tubes in the back of the largest van. "I've fixed the fuse inside and packed the first layer of black powder." He looked up as Clemmie clambered in beside him, hoiking her long red coat up round her knees. "We're not going to be able to use a binder on the compound — but that won't matter as this is only going to be a trial run — and we don't need a regulator or anything tricky."

"Right." Clemmie unscrewed her Kilner jar and, with shaking hands, ladled her chlorophyll-verdigris-jaundy-ash mixture carefully into the tube. "There — that should be enough to give us some sort of idea of the colour. If we just pack it down a bit . . ."

"I'll make another one, just in case the fuse fails, and it'll be good to have a control anyway. We don't want to claim success on a one-off, do we?"

"No way," Clemmie laughed softly. "That would be sooo unscientific. Right . . . You take the torch and the spades for digging, and I'll take both the fireworks. If we set up over there, that should be far enough away."

Totally absorbed in their joint venture, they grinned at one another again, scrambled out of the van and now, ignoring the sub-zero temperatures, hacked deep into the grass and eventually managed to sink the first tube firmly into the solid ground.

Clemmie straightened up. "Phew! That's my exercise done for the next ten years. Right — have you got the light?"

"Yes, but you do the honours," Guy said, also out of breath, handing her the glowing portfire. "This is your baby."

"OK . . . One, two three — here goes!"

Shivering, Clemmie lit the fuse and they both retreated rapidly to the safety of the van.

The fuse could just be seen, glowing feebly in the pitch dark. Clemmie was holding her breath. Oh, God, oh God, oh God . . . don't let it fail. Don't let it flicker and die. Don't let it —

"It's going," Guy whispered. "Right — now we'll see — Jesus!"

With a swoosh and whoosh that made them both jump, their home-made firework exploded, illuminating the Big Meadow in a brief shimmering diaphanous green cloud.

A deep, dark green; a true forest green with fathomless green-blue undertones; the allegedly unobtainable ocean green. It looked unspeakably beautiful, so ethereal that even Clemmie felt she could believe — just a little — in the magic of Seventh Heaven.

"Bloody hell!" Clemmie gulped as the verdant colour gently ebbed away. "Oh, my God!"

"You are a star! A genius!" Guy exclaimed, hugging her. "Jesus Christ, Clemmie — what have you done?"

"We," she said, loving being held so tightly in his arms. "This is very much a joint venture. Oh, I feel sick."

Guy let her go. "Yeah, I have that effect on some people."

She punched him gently. "You know what I mean — but, oh, wow!"

"Oh, wow! just about sums it up. I think you — OK, we — we might have hit on something pretty remarkable," Guy's voice was faint, "but let's try out the second one, just to make sure."

They slithered across the crisp glittering grass again, feeling like conspiratorial children.

"You light this one." Clemmie handed him the portfire. "It's only fair."

"Right — there — that's it — now stand well back."

"Guy! You naughty, naughty boy!" Tarnia appeared suddenly from the darkness just as the fuse started to glow. "What on earth are you doing here still playing with your fireworks? I've been waiting for you back at the house. I've got something much more exciting for you to play with."

Oh, shit!

Clemmie shot a frantic look at Tarnia, who had changed into a totally unsuitable, considering the rapidly plummeting temperature, seduction outfit of short pink miniskirt and sparkly gold vest-top, and who was positively vibrating with lust.

"Guy . . ." Tarnia pouted, elbowing Clemmie out of the way. "Come along, you gorgeously sexy man, you. I've got a little extra special treat waiting for you while Marquis is otherwise engaged."

The second Magik Green firework ignited exactly the same as the first.

Guy looked frantically at Tarnia, then pleadingly at Clemmie. "Oh bloody hell — I wish there was some way she'd fancy the pants off her bloody husband and think I'm the most gruesome nerd she's ever clapped eyes on — while retaining me to fire her future pyro displays, of course."

Clemmie, mentally dredging up the words that she'd repeated over and over ever since Halloween, knew it was now or never to prove the true worth of Allbard's Magik Green.

She looked at Guy. "Maybe there is a way. It's worth a try. Remember what the book said about wishes coming true? Why don't we try it now? There's nothing to lose." Clemmie stared defiantly at Tarnia as the Big Meadow was once more suffused in the glorious deep-green glow. She cleared her throat.

> "*Verdigris and verture pure*
> *Sparks with nature's verdanture*
> *Makes wishes forever endure.*"

"What?" Tarnia blinked her long eyelashes at Clemmie in surprise. "Did you say something, Clemmie? Goodness me — it's freezing out here — what am I doing here anyway? Where's my Marquis? I want my Marquis.

And totally ignoring Guy, she teetered bemusedly away in the direction of the stables.

Clemmie clapped her hands to her mouth in stunned delight. The scientist in her wanted to say it was coincidence but Tarnia's change in manner — and prey — had been so sudden that there was only one real explanation for what had happened. She and Guy had made it happen; he had made the wish and she had said the spell that made it come true.

Guy caught on quicker than she would have credited. "Absolutely bloody fantastic!" He swept Clemmie up in his arms and swung her round. "All that talk about magic we thought was tosh but it works, Clem! It bloody works! Not only have we discovered the holy grail of fireworks — making a colour no one else can — but we've just made a wish come true, haven't we? I tell you, we've discovered the holy grail!"

215

CHAPTER
SIXTEEN

"Well." Constance Motion, her face puckered angrily beneath her flamboyant hairdo of lacquer-stiff curls and whorls, peered at her cousins across the oak-lined office of the Motions Funeral Parlour in a Hazy Hassocks back street. "I call it a damnable cheek. It's apparently all laid out in here — we don't get a chance to add any of our personal touches. We just have to follow the instructions."

It was three days after Bonfire Night. The weather had remained bitterly cold and frosty, and the *Daily Express* was already forecasting snow.

The Motions, Constance, Perpetua and Slo, unmarried elderly cousins thrown together in the undertaking business by inheriting a third share each from their respective sibling fathers, hoped very much that the *Daily Express* was right. An early winter was always good for business.

However the weather wasn't their main topic of conversation this morning.

They'd had a letter. From America.

"I've never heard of him," Perpetua sniffed, folding her thin grey hands into her thin grey lap. "Have you, Slo?"

Slo — christened, whether by accident or design no one really knew, Sidney Lawrence Oliver — shook his head. "Nope. Max Angel don't ring no bells with me."

"That was his stage name," Constance snapped, her mean red-slashed lips turning inwards, "according to this letter. He was one of them pop singers in the sixties. Guitarist with the Burning Banshees. Probably died of sex and drugs and rock'n'roll."

"Lucky bastard," Slo muttered.

Constance glared at him. "He was born and raised here in Hassocks and was called . . ." she traced the words with a podgy much-ringed finger, "James Lesney."

"Lesney . . . Lesney . . ." Slo's elderly brow furrowed in concentration. "Ah . . . There was them Lesneys what lived out on the Bath Road, our Con. Remember 'em? Big family. About ten kiddies. One of them might have been a James."

"Little Jimmy Lesney!" Perpetua suddenly piped up. "Yes, I remember him. Lovely boy. I bought all his records."

"That was Little Jimmy Osmond," Constance said coldly.

They stared again at the letter. It had caused a bit of a commotion, arriving as it had by airmail with a lot of foreign stamps. And if the outside of the bulky envelope had caused the Motions consternation, its contents had been even more disturbing.

Max Angel, the artist formerly known as James Lesney, had sadly departed this life during his sixtieth year, on stage in a small town in America's Midwest during an energetic rendition of one of his greatest hits.

It was, the letter from Max's American agent told them, the way he'd have wanted to go, and also his final wish that his funeral service should take place in his home village, Hazy Hassocks. An internet search had shown that the Motions were the only funeral parlour in said village, and therefore Max's mortal remains were to be handled by the Motions, the funeral to be organised To The Letter of his last requests.

"The agent says Max never married, and there are no relatives in America, but a service of remembrance has been arranged in the States for his many friends and fans at a later date. Oh, and none of Max's family are still living here in Hazy Hassocks, nor have been in touch with him for years — although they've all been informed of his sad passing." Constance used the voice she usually saved for breaking the bad news of funeral fees to the nearest and dearest. "None of them want anything to do with the funeral. He was considered the black sheep."

"Probably kept all his money to himself." Slo fidgeted with his knitted waistcoat. "And never sent any home to his kin. Them Lesneys were allus tight buggers. Doubt he left 'em anything in his will either. They wouldn't like that."

Perpetua nodded sagely. "They don't. Families. They like to get their hands on as much as possible. So, go on, our Connie, what sort of service does this pop star want? All glitter and guitars and dancing girls? It could be quite exciting."

218

"For heaven's sake!" Constance patted her rigid hair. "I'm getting to that. Slo! Where are you going?"

"Lav." Slo had stood up and was shuffling from foot to foot. "That 'erbal tea you makes us for breakfast allus goes straight through me."

Constance narrowed her gimlet eyes. "Just make sure that's all it is. I don't want you sneaking off for a crafty fag. You're supposed to have given up that filthy habit years ago. You know what the doctor said about your chest."

"Dr Avebury said my chest were fine," Slo wheezed as he edged through the door. "He said I had the lungs of a bloke half my age. He said I were a miracle of medical science considering all that formaldehyde I've digested over the years. Don't you diss my chest, our Connie."

"I do wish he wouldn't watch *Pimp My Ride*," Constance sighed as Slo disappeared. "Now, Perpetua — shall we see what else Max Angel has in store for us?"

"Yes, please!" Perpetua said eagerly. "You know I don't get out much. This is better than Fern and Phillip."

Constance rattled the pages. "Right, now this part is from the firm of American solicitors who have handled Mr Angel's will. Well, your hoped-for rock'n'roll funeral couldn't be further from the truth. Oh, dear me, no. Once the mortal remains arrive, by air, which is due to be . . . let me see, oh yes, at the end of November, he's requested a private cremation in Newbury. Very low-key. Two hymns, a couple of readings from the

New Testament, the Lord's Prayer. No flowers. No mourners. Just us and the vicar. Well! How damnably boring is that?"

"Disappointing." Perpetua pleated her grey cardigan wistfully. "Can't see the point of his body being flown all the way from America for that. Such a waste of money."

"Hardly." Constance wore her caring face. "It's what he wanted at the end that's important. And we're being paid very well to see that he gets it."

Perpetua slumped back into grey silence. Slo sidled back into the office reeking of tobacco and flapping his hands in a studiedly casual manner.

"You've been smoking!" Constance barked. "Haven't you?"

"No." Slo sat down, looking innocently indignant. "It's that downstairs lav. You know it don't flush proper."

Constance snorted and read through the closely typed pages again. "Right, ah — now this is where it gets interesting. The other members of the Burning Banshees now also live in America and they've said their final farewells so they won't be flying over for the funeral, but Mr Angel has made a list of people he wants to be present at the scattering of his ashes. Let me see . . . goodness, they're all ladies. Local ladies. Ladies we all know. Ladies of a certain age."

"Am I on there?" Perpetua leaned forward excitedly.

"No," Constance snapped, "but you'll be there anyway, won't you, our Perpetua? Seeing as you're part of the damnable undertaking set-up."

220

Perpetua smiled happily. "Oh, yes — silly me. That's lovely; I would have hated to be left out."

"Hmmm." Constance read through the list. "Interesting. Very interesting. These ladies, apparently, all made Max Angel Very Happy back in nineteen sixty-nine. He remembers them all very, very fondly. Max Angel, it seems, sowed a good few youthful wild oats in Hazy Hassocks during the summer of sixty-nine."

"We could blackmail 'em," Slo said eagerly. "You're always saying we must diversify, our Con."

"By using the limousines for weddings and baptisms and hen nights and the hearse for furniture removals, yes." Constance's beady eyes glittered. "Not by blackmailing the bloody mourners."

"Who's on the list, then?" Slo frowned. "And where're his ashes being scattered?"

"I think the whole list should be kept private for the time being, until we've had time to send out the letters — nicely worded, with condolences, and maybe not mentioning why these particular ladies have been invited — we don't want to cause marital strife in Certain Quarters, do we?"

"I do," Slo chuckled wheezily. "No, go on then. What're we doing with the urn of ashes when we've got 'em back from the crem?"

"Well not using them as a damnable ashtray in the chapel of rest like you did with Gertie Bickersdyke, that's for sure. Oh — my sweet Lord!"

"What, our Constance?" Perpetua looked concerned. "What's the matter?"

"Max Angel," Constance spoke with grave concern, "wants to go out with a bang. He's requested a firework funeral. He wants his ashes to be fired into eternity in a bloody rocket."

"Good morning. The Gunpowder Plot. How may I help you?"

Clemmie smiled into the telephone. She'd smiled non-stop since the Snepps party. "No, sorry, Mr Devlin isn't here today, but I'm sure I can help you — what? Really? Heavens. OK, but I'll need to ask my colleague. Hold on one moment, please."

Biting her lip, her hand over the mouthpiece, Clemmie waved across the office to YaYa.

"Oooh, leave me alone," YaYa, blonde again, and dressed-down in a deep-purple wool frock and black boots to suit today's persona of office-crone instead of showgirl, yawned lazily. "It's my first day back. I'm having withdrawal symptoms. I should still be in bed — and I would be if bastard Crap, Puke, Snot and Mungo hadn't made more noise than a Cup Final crowd at bloody dawn. I could kill that bitch Helen! She never hangs around when I'm here. I simply don't believe her sodding electrics aren't sorted yet. I think she just enjoys leeching on Guy — the Bank of Devlin clearly still has its attractions."

"I know," Clemmie said with sympathy, "and it must be chronic for you, but I do need your help on this call. Please."

"My brain is full of frocks and footlights." YaYa winked and tossed her head. "I can't be bothered with the mundane, darling — I'm a star. Oh, look love, if it's something tricky, just take the details and say we'll be in touch in a couple of days when Guy and the crew are back from Kenilworth."

"Can't," Clemmie hissed. "They need to have an answer today. They need to see us. It's the Motions."

YaYa frowned. "The Motions? Who the hell are — oh, do you mean those mad old coots who run the undertakers in Hazy Hassocks? What on earth do they want?"

"They want us to arrange a firework funeral."

Half an hour later, with The Gunpowder Plot's office phones diverted to YaYa's mobile, Clemmie, YaYa and Suggs in his harness and lead scrambled into the 4×4. Clemmie, who had expected YaYa to make this trip alone, was delighted to be included. With Guy away in Kenilworth, she really didn't want to be left alone in the boathouse with Helen for a minute longer than necessary.

As they were fastening their seat belts, Helen, just returned from the lengthy school run, slid elegantly from her Jag, pulled her camel coat more closely round her, and frowned. "You're not both leaving the office unattended, are you?"

"None of your business, love," YaYa sang from the 4×4's window. "Not The Gunpowder Plot, not us, not Guy, not this house. Why don't you take your mewling brats and piss off! 'Bye!"

With gravel ricocheting from the tyres, the 4×4 roared away from the boathouse.

"Christ," YaYa spluttered round one of her long cigarettes, "I hate that cow. Why the hell did Guy let her stay? It wouldn't have happened if I'd been here. I know he's a nice man who wouldn't see anyone homeless — but in this case he's been too soft by half."

"I don't think she gave him much choice, to be honest." Clemmie arranged Suggs on her lap so that he could put his front paws on the dashboard and look at the frosty scenery.

YaYa had been incandescent when she'd arrived home from the Dancing Queens the previous day and found Helen in situ. Clemmie, for once, had been glad to scuttle off home to Bagleycum-Russet.

"Honestly, I was there and she just steam-rollered him into it. It was bedlam that night." She looked across the car at YaYa. "But it must be pretty awkward for you."

Clemmie actually hadn't dared to think about the more intimate problems caused by Helen and the kiddies being in the boathouse now that YaYa was home.

"Awkward doesn't even come bloody close." YaYa squealed the 4×4 to a halt at the roadworks on the outskirts of Winterbrook. "If she's not gone by the weekend, I'll kill her."

"And I'll help you."

"Good girl." YaYa flicked ash out of the window. "Christ — it's cold today. You look nice and snug in that black get-up." She chuckled. "Black and purple — we look just right for visiting a funeral parlour, don't we?"

224

Relieved that Helen was no longer the main topic of conversation, Clemmie nodded and settled back in her seat and smiled soppily at the slowly passing scenery. It was such a shame the three-day display at Kenilworth had come so close after the success with the Magik Green. Both she and Guy were itching to build a real multi-layered Seventh Heaven prototype and see how it fired.

Tarnia's reaction to the green fire incantation, they'd agreed, might have simply been coincidence. They'd need to try out several more controlled experiments to be able to prove scientifically that the magic worked — a dichotomy of the first water — but despite that, the euphoria at discovering that fabulous green colour and possibly solving one of the pyro world's biggest conundrums, hadn't been even slightly dented.

They'd decided to still keep the whole Magik Green thing secret, even from YaYa who, lovely as she was, wasn't the most discreet person in the world — just in case it never happened again. Not that YaYa, buoyant on an adrenalin high, would have even listened. In between her burst of invective over Helen's arrival, she'd talked non-stop about her success with the Dancing Queens, showed them hundreds of digital photographs of the tour, and regaled them a dozen times with stories of what really went on at the television studios.

"Have you ever done a firework funeral before?" Clemmie asked as they turned away from Winterbrook and headed onto the Hazy Hassocks road. "It sounds fascinating — if a bit off the wall."

"It's not something I've ever been involved with, no."
YaYa turned down Dusty Springfield who had been
bemoaning that she just didn't know what to do with
herself at full-volume. "And I can't remember Guy ever
mentioning one, either. So we'll just have to fly by the
seat of our pants on this one, Clemmie, love. Right:
now do we go straight ahead into the High Street or
what?"

"Turn off here," Clemmie said. "The funeral parlour
is in Winchester Road, round the back of Big Sava. God
— I hope they won't have, well, bodies."

"Me, too," YaYa shuddered. "Too macabre for words.
Look, I think the best way to play this is to get as much
info as possible, fit in what they want with what we
know we can do, give them some idea of cost, then we'll
leave the fine-tuning details to Guy. Oh, this must be
it."

Leaving Suggs curled on the front seat of the 4×4
with a chewy ferret treat, Clemmie and YaYa shuddered
in the icy blast of the north-east wind, took deep
steadying breaths and rang the Motions' doorbell.

Constance opened the door and, after a quick double
take at their appearance, ushered them into the office,
which fortunately was much the same as any other
small office, and not, as Clemmie had envisaged, full of
coffins and wreaths and candles and bereaved people
crying.

"My cousins have been called away to an emergency
embalming," Constance said, ushering them towards
two uncomfortable-looking upright chairs. "But as the

226

senior partner, I'll be able to deal with this. Now, this is the information I have . . .."

Listening to the story of Max Angel and his final wishes, Clemmie felt suddenly very sad. Nineteen sixty-nine hadn't been that long ago. Max Angel must have thought then, as Clemmie did now, that he'd live forever. And wanting all his old flames to be there to see his final send-off into the heavens was immensely touching. There'd be an awful lot of tears, Clemmie, thought. And possibly some long-broken hearts: all those old ladies who had been young and pretty girls then, and in love with the youthful Max Angel, and hadn't given a thought to their own fragile mortality, and only remembered kissing him and laughing with him and loving him in that long hot summer.

She shuddered. God, she couldn't do an undertaker's job. How on earth did they cope?

". . . and," Constance finished, "as far as I can gather, we collect his ashes from the crematorium the day after his funeral service, you collect them from us here, and then pack them into a rocket built to the specifications included in this letter from his solicitor, return them to us . . . and then he wants his final countdown, so to speak, to be at midnight from the crest of Hassocks Hill."

YaYa paused in scribbling down notes. "That all sounds perfectly clear, Ms Motion. And, with the dates you've given me, if we collect the ashes early on November the twenty-ninth, we can build his rocket exactly as stipulated, and send the late lamented Max into orbit on the night of the thirtieth."

"Excuse me? Are you mocking the deceased's funeral choices?" Constance frowned at such levity. "Because if you are, let me tell you that death is not a matter for damnable flippancy, you know."

"Sorry — I wasn't being flippant or irreverent." YaYa looked suitably chastened. "Just throwing in a bit of gallows humour to lighten the funereal mood. After all, having your ashes launched into space isn't normal, is it?"

"No, it isn't," Constance conceded, patting the coils of stiff hair. "Oh, and we, the funeral directors, have to be present at the — er — send-off. The solicitor has given us full instructions on the legal side of things. There's a separate letter from him here too, about exactly how things are to proceed on the night of the firing. You'd better take it with you."

Constance and YaYa talked a little longer about the cost, the logistics, and the timing, leaving Clemmie to indulge in a pleasant if pointless fantasy about her and Guy and a fur rug in front of a roaring log fire.

"Thank you, Ms Motion." YaYa stood up, shimmying slightly inside her tight purple wool and shaking hands with a slightly shocked-looking Constance. "We'll take all these details back to the office, speak to Mr Devlin, and get back to you as soon as everything's organised. Come on Clem, love. Time to go."

Clemmie's fantasy faded. She smiled dreamily and stood up.

"Ooh!" YaYa shuddered as the door of the funeral parlour closed behind them and they hurried through the cold to greet an ecstatic Suggs in the 4×4.

"Someone's just walked over my grave. That was too spooky for words. And so sad."

"I know," Clemmie agreed, cuddling Suggs closely. "I could have cried in there. Thank goodness we work in a business that brings happiness and is connected with life and jollity and parties and celebrations and weddings."

"And now funerals," YaYa reminded her, heading out into the main thrust of Hazy Hassocks. "I think we deserve a little treat after that, don't you?"

"Definitely," Clemmie said, immediately picturing the trays of squishy cream cakes in Patsy's Pantry just round the corner on the High Street. "What did you have in mind?"

"While Guy's away and Helen From the Dark Side and Crap, Puke, Snot and Mungo aren't, why don't we cheer ourselves up a bit? Are you free tomorrow night?"

"Yes, I think so." The cream cakes faded. "Why?"

"Because," YaYa lit a cigarette, "some of my girlfriends are putting on a little show at the Rinky-Dink. You did say you'd never seen a proper drag act, didn't you? Are you up for it? Just you and me?"

Oh, Lordy . . .

Suggs surveyed her seriously, then nodded his head, nibbling her chin.

"OK," Clemmie agreed. "Yes, definitely. I'd love to. I can't wait."

CHAPTER
SEVENTEEN

"You're going *where*?" Phoebe, perched on Clemmie's bed at the Post Office Stores the following evening, frowned. "Where on earth is the Rinky-Dink?"

"Somewhere out in the wilds between Reading and Newbury, I think." Clemmie carefully drew another black line round her eyes. "There! What does that look like?"

"Very glamorous if a little tarty."

"Great — just the effect I was aiming for." Clemmie swirled round in the tiny room, happily admiring her recently acquired-from-eBay long vintage sequinned frock in the mirror. "And it's lovely to have an opportunity to wear this. It's so long since I went clubbing. I sort of thought I'd have to wear a crop top and miniskirt."

Phoebe laughed. "Not unless you're fourteen, or very overweight, or have a limited vocabulary and an addiction to bad tattoos."

Clemmie pulled a face. "You sound like the *Daily Mail* — all sensible and grown-up."

"That's because I am. But honestly, you look lovely. Peacock blue is really good on you and the earrings match wonderfully. So, who is he?"

"Steve?" Clemmie giggled. "Oh, just some bloke I work with."

"Right . . ." Phoebe made the word sound nineteen letters long. "So, what happened to the promise to love Guy Devlin until the day you died?"

"Oh, I'll still do that," Clemmie said truthfully, "but as I've told you, he's seriously attached and definitely off-limits so I'll just have to settle for us being mates and work colleagues — more's the pity. Anyway, when Steve asked me out I said yes. We're just mates, too."

"Aha! Do I sense an embryo workplace romance on the cards?"

"No you definitely don't. Not a chance. And, while it's great to see you, why aren't you with Ben tonight?"

"I will be. When I leave here. He's getting the keys."

"To what?"

Phoebe dimpled with delight. "That's what I came to tell you. We've got a flat! We're moving in together! At last!"

"Oh, wow! That's great!" Clemmie hugged her. "Where is it?"

"Hazy Hassocks. Winchester Road."

"Really? What a coincidence. I was there yesterday — for work." She decided not to mention the Motions just in case Phoebe wasn't yet aware she'd have a funeral parlour as a near neighbour. "They're lovely old houses — I didn't see any sold signs though."

"We're renting." Phoebe shrugged. "It's a ground-floor flat. Quite spacious, with two bedrooms and a nice little garden. We couldn't wait any longer to buy. The prices are going up and up and our savings won't get us a deposit on a shoebox. Don't tell me it's dead money because we know that — but we so want to be together."

"I'm the last one to criticise anyone. Look at me: never owned any property in my life. Scuttled back here after uni. I'm hardly an intrepid investor in bricks and mortar." Clemmie stopped and grinned. "But I bet it didn't just depend on the two bedrooms and the nice little garden, did it? I bet you did your Madame Zuleika bit and consulted the tarots and the tea leaves and your crystal ball?"

"The tarots gave it very good vibes, actually."

"Oh, don't get sniffy — I'm only kidding. I'm just thrilled for you. So, when's the house-warming party?"

"As soon as we're in and settled. Probably not until after Christmas, though." Phoebe raised her perfectly plucked eyebrows. "Shall I put Steve on your invite?"

"No way! I'll come alone, thanks."

"Clemmie!" Molly Coddle shouted up the stairs. "Your young man's outside! Are you ready, or shall I ask him in?"

"Nooo!" Clemmie grabbed her bag. "I'm on my way!"

And with Phoebe close behind, she hurtled down the stairs.

"Thanks," she kissed her aunt and uncle. "I've got my key. 'Bye — 'bye, Phoebes!"

"Er — 'bye." Phoebe, joining Bill and Molly in the doorway, looked puzzled. "But why the rush — aren't you going to introduce him?"

232

Clemmie flew out of the Post Office Stores and hurled herself into the 4×4. "Drive!" she hissed at a skimpily gold-clad YaYa. "No — don't wave at them! I've just told them you're a bloke called Steve. Just bloody drive!"

The Rinky-Dink was, as Clemmie had thought, way off the Berkshire beaten track.

"It makes it more exclusive," YaYa said, parking the 4×4. "Gives it more of a country club feel, you know? Retro but very glam. Think Revue Bar meets Skindles-goes-country."

"Sorry?" Clemmie peered at the long, low building with wooden steps, veranda and a lot of fairy lights. "You've lost me already. This looks just like a big ranch-house in old Western films. And what's Skindles?"

"Before my time, too, love, but apparently *the* Berkshire nightclub to be seen in in the sixties — outrageously glamorous and filled with all the big names from every walk of life. It had an indoor swimming pool when they were as rare as rubies. You weren't in with the in-crowd unless you got chucked in fully clothed. Everyone who was anyone poured out of London just to be seen there, back then. Of course, they were celebrities when the handle really meant something."

"Sounds wonderful." Clemmie looked at the expensive cars parked alongside the 4×4. "So will I be able to celeb-spot tonight? And actually, when you first talked about this place, I thought it was a gay club."

"Just let me have a quick fag before we go in — I can't be doing with standing outside on a night like this." YaYa lit another of her long cigarettes. "This bloody smoking ban will be the death of me. Pneumonia not emphysema. What did you say? Oh, yes, is it a gay club? Not solely, not at all, really. In fact the Rinky-Dink is popular with gays and straights, minor celebs, locals, anyone in the know — everyone who just wants a good night out without getting beaten up or puked on by a shaven-headed lout in a cheap shirt."

"Sounds like it'll suit me fine, then."

"I'm sure you'll love it. Hold my fag for a sec." YaYa flicked at her ash-blonde layered hair in the driving mirror and applied another layer of lip-gloss then reclaimed her cigarette. "OK — I'll do, and so will you, love. You look super tonight. Let's just make sure Suggs is all right in the back."

"Suggs? You've brought Suggs?"

"Not for a night of bopping, love. But yes, I've popped his little sofa on the back seat — and packed his food and drink and litter tray. You didn't think I'd leave him alone with hellish Helen and the brats, did you?"

"God, no." Clemmie shook her head as YaYa sorted out a sleepy Suggs. "She hates him — oh, I do wish she'd go home."

"You and me both." YaYa grimaced. "Right, let's not think about the old bat any more tonight — let's go and meet the girls."

And, linking arms, they hurried through the biting November night.

234

Inside, YaYa warmly greeted everyone they passed and introduced Clemmie, who said hello and smiled until her lips ached, and simply couldn't help staring.

The Rinky-Dink was everything Clemmie had dreamed it might be.

A long stage filled one wall, a long bar matched it exactly on the opposite side. A DJ, in a discreet corner of the stage, was playing smoky jazz. Small tables and chairs were dotted on a raised platform which encircled the dance floor, and the lighting was plentiful but muted: simply millions of tiny star-specks sunk into the low, wooden ceiling and studded into every other surface including the floor, giving the impression of being inside a huge, bejewelled Fabergé egg.

And the people! Clemmie looked around her in delight. Everyone was scandalously stunning. Not a crop top to be seen!

"I'll get the drinks, love," YaYa said, extricating herself from yet another clutch of similarly dressed friends, "and you grab a table with a good view of the stage, then later I'll introduce you to a few more people. What would you like?"

"White wine will be lovely, thank you." Clemmie nudged her way through smooching couples on the dance floor, and up the steps to the seating area. Finding a vacant table overlooking the stage, she sat back and relaxed.

How lovely it would be if she and Guy could come somewhere like this. Have an evening out together in somewhere so unashamedly swish. She grinned. No, forget the swish — how wonderful it would be if she and Guy could go out together full-stop. Anywhere. If only he wasn't gay and with YaYa. Ah well, a girl couldn't have it all, could she? At least she had Guy — and YaYa — as friends.

The club was an absolute riot of colour: all the women wore elegant glittering frocks and amazing jewellery, and the pinpricks of light danced and reflected from every beautiful body. The men were sadly not quite so colourful, but pretty attractive, nonetheless. Although none of them could hold a candle to Guy. How superb he'd look here: dressed in his skinny black, with his long hair and smudgy eyes, all tall, lean, dark and dangerously, sexily androgynous, holding her close on the tiny dance floor, their bodies pressed together.

"There you go, love," YaYa said, breaking into this wildest of fantasies. "House white."

"It's champagne!" Clemmie exclaimed. "I love champagne! But —"

"It passes for house white here." YaYa settled herself easily into her chair and sipped at something blue and much-cherried in a cocktail glass. "And this is non-alcoholic — I never drink and drive so don't worry. They do a lovely selection of fruit cocktails that taste just like the real thing. So, sweetheart, what do you think of the place?"

"It's fantastic. Amazing. Thank you so much for bringing me here. I can't believe I've never heard of it before."

"As I said, it's fairly exclusive. But great for the drag scene. Whether they're straight or gay, the punters here love a glam act."

Clemmie stared at the throng in the club. She found it impossible to tell who was gay and who wasn't. Not that it mattered. The atmosphere was amazing, unlike that of any other club she'd ever been in.

YaYa smiled happily. "It's one of my best venues. Me and Honey Bunch and Foxy went down a storm a couple of weeks ago — and tonight — well, you'll see."

"You're not doing your act tonight, though, are you?"

"No, love, not me. I know I promised you could see my act, but maybe another time. At least tonight you get to see some of my other mates. Speaking of which —" YaYa stood up, waving. "Honey! Foxy! Yoo-hoo! Over here!"

Clemmie's jaw dropped. Two of the most alluring women she'd been watching on the dance floor, one in lime-green, the other in acid-yellow, all perfectly done hair and make-up and slender as reeds, looked up, gave little yelps of excitement, and shimmied towards them.

"They're *blokes*?" She shook her head. "No way!"

"You really couldn't tell?" YaYa looked surprised. "How odd — I always know. So does Guy. It must go with the territory."

Clemmie supposed it must. Like being qualified for some elite club to which she'd never be admitted as a member.

"I didn't guess about you, did I?"

"No, you didn't — and I promise you on my life that when the girls get here we won't talk Polari and exclude you."

"Polari?"

"It's an old form of gay slang that's making a bit of a revival. The verbal currency of the drag scene — oh, hi, loves. This is Clemmie. The lovely new girl at Guy's I told you about. Clemmie, meet Honey Bunch, she's the blonde, and Foxy is the redhead."

"Hi — oh!" Clemmie had been about to shake hands, but instead found herself being well hugged twice over, and enveloped in a twinning of the perfumiers' exotic best.

This was followed by a lot of delighted exclaiming over her antique frock and her earrings and a decision made over more drinks: "get loads of bottles, love — nicer than having to keep to-ing and fro-ing" — which Foxy was despatched to buy.

A kitty set up, drinks bought, YaYa, Foxy and Honey Bunch then dissolved into a flurry of gossip and scandal. Clemmie, sipping her champagne, relishing the way the bubbles popped on her tongue, simply loved every ground-breaking minute of it.

YaYa leaned forward. "I was just telling Honey that you can't tell the drags from the hags, love. She says it's because we're all class acts here. You should see some of the sights in the more downmarket clubs. Sad or what — so slutty, more like clowns than queens."

"It's a whole new world," Clemmie admitted. "And I suppose I always thought that drag queens only, well, dragged when they were on stage."

"'Dragged'," replied YaYa in mock disgust. "Never say 'dragged'. We reveal our inner fabulousness. I just enjoy being a girl. For others it's showbusiness."

Just then, as Clemmie's third glass of champagne was taking effect, the DJ broke into Ella Fitzgerald to say he'd be back in half an hour and that the first show was about to begin, so clearly YaYa's confession was going to have to wait.

Honey, Foxy and YaYa raised their single-track eyebrows in excitement.

"This'll be good," YaYa hissed. "These girls are mates and the real McCoy. No bad miming to Gloria Gaynor or trying to get off on crap blue jokes from these two. You'll love 'em, Clemmie. Love 'em."

Feeling slightly woozy and warmly euphoric, Clemmie was sure she would.

The first drag act, Halo and Aura — the Heavenly Twins — pale faced, panda-eyed, long white-blonde hair cascading to their waist, teetering on silver stilettos, undulated onto the stage in gloriously froufrou angelic costumes which they proceeded to remove with graceful, tantalising movements while singing a sultry version of Robbie Williams' 'Angels'.

To deafening applause, and following a lightning costume change, they reappeared in nothing but diaphanous bras and tutus and silver thigh boots and rocked the Rinky-Dink with a raunchily burlesque version of Wizzard's 'Angel Fingers'.

Clemmie was up on her feet, waving her arms and clapping her hands, along with everyone else, and the dance floor was packed as Halo and Aura belted out their own version of 'Heaven Must Be Missing an Angel'. Finally, the Heavenly Twins, changing into a third divine outfit at the speed of light, ended their act with a wistful deep-soul version of Louis Armstrong's 'Heavenly Music' and the club erupted as they left the stage.

Blimey, Clemmie thought dizzily, I didn't know what I was missing.

The DJ returned, this time with a more up-tempo disco selection, and the dance floor was packed again. Despite her earlier assertions, YaYa had sneaked off outside for another cigarette and "to check on Suggs".

"Come on." Honey Bunch grabbed Clemmie's hand. "Let's boogie."

Phoebe will never believe this, Clemmie thought, as she found herself gyrating wildly to a blast of Kylie between Honey and Foxy.

They were suddenly joined by two more extravagantly dressed drag queens. Or at least Clemmie presumed they were drag queens; they were equally gorgeous. Clemmie, beaming at them, thought they looked superb in their identical pink and lilac lacy outfits, chosen as a matching pair she hoped, and not that awful she's-wearing-the-same-dress thing that she and Phoebe had had in the past.

"Campari and Cinnamon," Honey introduced them, yelling in Clemmie's ear as they all stomped riotously to 'Uptown Girl' complete with flouncing and pouting and posing and full arm movements. "From the Dancing Queens."

240

Clemmie beamed some more. Conversation was impossible. Then YaYa returned and kissed Campari and Cinnamon and they all formed a circle and shimmied together, high-kicking along to 'I Should Be So Lucky'.

Just as Clemmie was sure her legs were going to give way, the DJ announced Midnight — the next stage act, Clemmie realised, and not a time-check — and, in a tidal wave of Spandex and sequins, the dance floor emptied.

"Come and join us," YaYa yelled to Campari and Cinnamon. "We can squeeze two more in round our table."

Yet more drinks appeared, as the girls, loudly, laughingly bitchy by now, crowded round the table.

"You'll be knocked out by this one," YaYa said in Clemmie's ear. "Midnight's an absolute star. We're lucky to have her here tonight."

The Rinky-Dink erupted as Midnight, who was six feet tall, black, beautiful, with a waterfall of ebony curls, sashayed onto the stage and belted out nearly an hour of an absolutely sensational Diana Ross tribute act.

Clemmie was spellbound.

"I can't believe she's not a woman," she whispered to YaYa as Midnight eventually shimmied off the stage in her stilt-heels after three curtain calls and a five-minute standing ovation. "She must be!"

YaYa, the only sober one round the table, giggled. "Clemmie, love — you have so much to learn. Listen, Midnight is called George and in her day job she's —

he's — a bus driver. He's also a totally heterosexual man and is happily married — straight married — and has three kids."

"No way!" Clemmie's lips were by now champagne fizzy and she was aware her words were slightly slurred. "You're kidding?"

"I kid you not," YaYa assured her. "Before we hit the dance floor again, let me give you a quick masterclass, love. First, most transvestites are straight. Straight men who occasionally enjoy dressing like women for their own pleasure: think Eddie Izzard. Transvestite comes from the word traviste or travesty, and that's obvious when you look at some of the poor dears, not a sequin or beaded eyelash between them. Secondly, transvestites are not drag queens, anyone can put on a frock and heels, but to become royalty, you need that extra special sparkle. Thirdly, not all drag queens are gay, some aren't even male, but let's not even go there. Fourthly, some people are just born in the wrong body and so go on to have transsexual realignment — think Dana International. With me so far?"

Clemmie nodded in a happy haze.

"Right, now round this table Campari and Cinnamon are a couple. Campari always knew she liked men — she thought she was gay but then realised she was transgender. Now she's had the full works and is going out with Cinnamon who is totally straight but likes to dress up. The complete transsexual realignment treatment — you do know what that means, love, don't you?"

242

Clemmie nodded again and wished the Rinky-Dink wouldn't sway quite so much.

"A few nips and tucks and a caterpillar becomes a butterfly. OK. Then, Foxy and Honey Bunch here are gay and still boys under their dresses. They're also friends who don't fancy each other so they're always out on the pull together. And bloody competitive. With me so far?"

Clemmie just smiled. She didn't trust the nodding any more. "Yep. With you all the way. And you're gay and with Guy — only you're the transvestite drag queen girlie one and he plays the straight boy role? Are you transgender too?"

"Yes." YaYa nodded, then stopped. "What? No — wrong. Very wrong. Very, very wrong. Oh, I've had a bit of surgery, a facelift, and a few tucks here and there though nowhere near as much as the vile Helen, I might add, and of course the hormones and the electrolysis. I've even had breast implants but not the whole shebang. No, I just got in touch with my feminine side earlier than most and am more than happy with being what I am."

Clemmie stared at her. "But you and Guy? You're together. Guy's gay."

"Guy? Gay? Bloody hell! You couldn't be further from the truth! Guy's as red-blooded, heterosexual, alpha — whatever you like to call it — as they come. He's had more women than Cliff Richard's had Christmas hits, and that must be well over the two hundred mark."

Clemmie tried to think through the champagne fug. "But you and Guy live together."

"As mates, love. Because we've been bezzie mates since school. We get on well together, work brilliantly together, care about one another, love one another in a best-friends sort of way — but we ain't a couple. Not a bloody chance! I don't really do the icky stuff. And even if I did. I'm as likely to want to share your bed as Guy's. And that ain't at all likely in this lifetime. Frankly, I'd rather have some champers and a chinwag than get down and dirty. Hey — what are you doing with my handbag, and where are you going?"

"Outside." Clemmie beamed blissfully unsteadily, wondering hazily if a drunken handstand would be a celebratory step too far. "I need a cigarette."

CHAPTER
EIGHTEEN

Over the following days, as November plunged rapidly towards its sub-zero conclusion, Clemmie sang, 'I Should Be So Lucky' non-stop, and skipped, and smiled at everyone.

Guy had smiled a lot too, only obviously for entirely different reasons.

Kenilworth, he'd said, had been a stonking success, and the corporates who'd organised it, having been let down so badly by their previous pyrotechnicians, had signed up The Gunpowder Plot for regular work in the future.

Clemmie, who was still going over and over the things that YaYa had told her, had smiled hugely and told him she was delighted.

She was, of course, still even more delighted that he wasn't gay.

"I can't believe you thought YaYa and I were a couple," Guy had chuckled on the day he'd returned from his three-day corporate display. "Bloody hell!"

"She shouldn't have told you!" Clemmie had been crimson with embarrassment. "I'd had far too much to drink and —"

"YaYa, as I've said before, is wildly indiscreet. She tells me everything. She thought it was very funny. So did I. I always thought you understood our relationship. And as you knew I'd been married, it never occurred to me that you'd think ... maybe I should have explained."

"No you shouldn't." Clemmie had blushed even more. "It was none of my business."

"Well, if I was gay, YaYa certainly wouldn't be my choice of live-in lover," Guy had said, leaning sexily against the lab bench. "I'd rather shack up with Vlad the Impaler. No," he'd paused and grinned at her, "on second thoughts, I've already done that one. Helen could teach Count Drac a trick or two when it comes to blood sucking."

And then they'd dropped the subject and talked about work instead, and Clemmie had hoped they'd never have to mention it again.

Mind you, she'd still been swamped by acute embarrassment, remembering arriving home in the early hours from the Rinky-Dink and stomping round and round her bedroom trilling, "Guy isn't gay! Guy isn't gay!" as she struggled out of her antique frock, before collapsing in giggles on her bed.

And then there had been Molly and Bill's kind enquiries the next day about whether or not she'd had a nice time, and would she be seeing her young man again, and was he one of those hippie types as he'd seemed to have very long hair ...

The memories of the journey home from the Rinky-Dink were actually pretty hazy, but Clemmie

246

would never forget YaYa happily explaining the set up at the boathouse and her true role in Guy's life as "constant companion" to put off predators like Tarnia Snepps and their very separate bedrooms.

"When he met Helen," YaYa had said as Suggs bounced excitedly between them on the front seat of the 4×4, "he'd just split up with a girl he adored. She'd cheated on him big time and broken his heart. Helen was very much an on-the-rebound thing — and although I warned him about it being a big mistake, he wouldn't listen. His ego was dented. It was the first time he'd been the dumpee. He was really fragile, and had a sort of 'what a bastard I've been to women' epiphany. He suddenly needed to prove that he was loving and loveable and Helen, the cow was very beautiful and appeared vulnerable and he thought she really needed him — so it didn't matter what I said, he really was as low as it was possible to get."

"So he married Helen and it was a disaster — and that's when he gave up women?" Clemmie had given up trying to focus and found it was easier just to stare straight ahead at the glittery, frosty night. "I remember you saying that he'd put the laydees behind him."

"Exactly." YaYa had nodded, the ash from her umpteenth cigarette spilling onto her gold frock. "One badly broken heart and one crap marriage in quick succession — who can blame him for introducing me as his Significant Other to keep other females at bay? He's changed so much from the love-'em-and-leave-'em boy he used to be. I honestly can't see him ever looking at a woman seriously again. At least for a long time."

Hah! Clemmie had thought in her euphoric champagne haze. We'll see about that.

Of course later, in the cold light of day and sober, the idea that she could even remotely interest Guy had seemed as ludicrous as ever, but at the time it had made her laugh out loud with delight.

Even now, she was still happy to think that Guy wasn't quite so inaccessible as he had been.

She'd just have to handle things very, very carefully.

"So." Guy looked across the lab at her, three days after Kenilworth and the Rinky-Dink. "Are you up for it?"

"What? Oh, yes, definitely — er — up for what exactly?"

Guy laughed. "Your head seems to be as addled as mine these days. I warned you about going out with YaYa because that's enough to befuddle anyone. Although, according to her, you had a great time and took to the drag scene like a natural."

"I don't want to talk about that night ever again." Clemmie had paused in counting pipettes. "Can we please, please, please change the subject?"

"Still embarrassed?" Guy laughed. "There's no need, but OK, whatever you want. So, I know there's loads going on — the business, Helen, the wedding coming up in Milton St John, and that firework funeral in a few days, which I have to talk to you about — but surely you haven't forgotten we've still got to build the Seventh Heaven prototype? Unless," he pushed his hair from his eyes, "you've gone ahead without me on this too — like the Magik Green thing?"

"No, of course not. Have you got enough time at the moment, though?"

"The rest of the day," Guy said happily. "YaYa's manning the office. Syd and the crew have the day off. And — best of all — Helen's packing."

"No! Great! Oh, sorry . . . I mean, really?"

"Yeah, really. The fire-damage has been repaired, the electrics tried and tested, and the house is now habitable again, which means Helen and the brats will be out of our hair by tonight."

"That might be a good reason to celebrate," Clemmie said carefully. "I suppose . . ."

"The best." Guy reached for one of the largest square firework tubes from the storage shelves. "So, let's fill a tube with your extremely clever seven layers and go for a test run. We'll have to work out what to wish for. You have brought the other jars of Allbard's Magik Green from Bagley, haven't you?"

Clemmie nodded towards the padlocked chemicals cupboard. "And I've made up a lot more. They're all in there."

"Brilliant! I suppose, if this really works, we'll have to patent it — or rather, you will." He laughed. "Which will probably make you really, really rich and famous and you'll never speak to me again."

"I'd rather," Clemmie said, not looking at him in case he read her eyes, and concentrating on getting the right fuse length instead, "keep it our secret. I've never hankered after material stuff or the celeb lifestyle. I suppose we should register Seventh Heaven as The Gunpowder Plot's invention, just in case someone else works out the puzzle the same way as we did — but apart from that I think we should keep it low-key for the time being. Anyway, it might not work again."

"Let's find out, shall we? OK, the first heaven — silver stars on golden chains . . . right here goes — a measure of antimony, then the aluminium, and a dollop of lampblack . . ."

With the usual accompaniment of a softly playing radio and Suggs snuffling about in the charcoal sacks, they worked side by side, fitting the fuse, packing the seven separate compartments with the seven chemical concoctions, and adding the lift charge black powder between each layer.

They worked excellently as a team. Scientifically, they understood one another absolutely. Emotionally, well . . . Clemmie sighed. This was probably as good as it was ever going to get.

"Do you know," she said as they finally fastened the fully packed firework. "I was thinking about the magic bit . . . if it really *did* work on Tarnia, we could try it out again."

Guy looked at her. "And did you have a particular victim in mind?"

"Oh, no, not a victim as such — I thought we should use it for *good* reasons. You know, like when we do the wedding fireworks for Charlie and Jemima in a week or so? On that sad little Suzy Beckett. She so wants to get together with her Luke — and it all seems so hopeless. Why can't we make a quiet version of Seventh Heaven and take it along and well, just see what happens?"

250

"It can't do any harm, I suppose." Guy frowned. "But I can't see even Allbard being able to get this Luke bloke divorced and across the Atlantic at the speed of light, can you?"

"No, I suppose not," Clemmie conceded. "And if we ask if he's on the guest list it'll look suspect. There's no reason why he should be, is there? I mean, even if they're having the entire racing world there, they're still hardly likely to invite him after he and Suzy split up." She sighed again. "OK, not such a good idea. Forget it."

"I don't think we should discount it out of hand. We should bear it in mind. If not for reuniting Suzy and Luke, which does seem a remote possibility, then definitely for Ellis Blissit and his will-she-won't-she wedding next year. It might come in handy then." Guy laughed. "Hark at me — I sound like I really believe in this magic stuff."

"Well, you do — or did — at least more than I did." Clemmie chuckled. "And now I'm not sure at all either. Hardly being scientific, are we?"

Guy pulled on his leather jacket and wound a long black scarf round his neck. "Oh, I don't know. All science must have seemed like magic back in Allbard's day. And I've always thought every scientific discovery is magical in its own way. So we're probably not losing the plot completely. And all scientists should have open minds, surely, otherwise there'd be no experiments and no discoveries, would there? Right — do you feel virtuously vindicated now?"

"Absolutely." She smiled at him. "Thanks."

"So let's go and see if this particular blend of magical scientific discovery does what we think it will."

Leaving Suggs snoozing on the sacks, they hurried outside and headed towards the river bank. It was a particularly isolated spot, hidden from the house by the skeletal willows and not overlooked by anyone else, and far enough away from any farm animals or habitation not to cause a furore should things go wrong.

"Setting it up at night would be better for the full effect," Guy said, as they shivered inside their thick coats, clearing a safe space in the mass of soggy fallen leaves and digging a hole deep enough to bury two-thirds of the firework. "But as this is just to see if all seven layers work as we've predicted, and more importantly, fire in sequence, we'll have to forgo the visual effect this time. OK — got the portfire?"

Clemmie nodded, her teeth chattering as the river swirled past them, grey and unforgiving, roaring in a dirty foaming torrent over the weir in the distance.

"Yep. One, two, three . . . blast-off!"

They stood back, almost but not quite touching, as the first thrilling fizzle began.

Clemmie, her shoulders hunched against the cold, was holding her breath.

One after the other, the Seventh Heaven layers ignited and propelled their gigantic starbursts into the bleak grey sky. One after the other, in perfect synchronicity, gold and silver, pure gold, opalescent pink, white gold, orange fire and silver ice, and the deep red garnet and ruby jewel colours, exploded spectacularly upwards.

"Ohmigod." She turned to Guy. "It's beautiful — and it works!"

He pulled her against him. "Clemmie, it's absolutely sensational. I've never seen anything quite so fabulous. I don't know how you did it — but boy am I glad you did!"

Relishing being held against him — although the layers of coats and scarves and gloves prevented it being an erotic experience — Clemmie watched her creation come to life for the first time.

How spectacularly wonderful it would look, Clemmie thought dizzily, against a black-night backdrop.

Six heavens gone and now —

"What you doing?" One of the children — maybe Mungo? — suddenly appeared sulkily from between the willow trees. "I'm off school with a poorly tummy. I'm bored. What's that noise? Oh, fireworks — they're crap. Old-fashioned. I hate frigging fireworks. You're sad. This place is so bloody boring. You haven't even got wi-fi or high-def telly. It's like the dark ages in this hole. Mummy says —"

"Jesus!" Guy snapped. "I wish you'd learn some bloody manners!"

The final heavenly layer of Allbard's Magik Green exploded at that point, as breathtakingly pure and perfect as before.

Just as the deep forest-green sparks tumbled around them in a fiery emerald shower, Clemmie swallowed and whispered Allbard's magic words:

> "Verdigris and verture pure
> Sparks with nature's verdanture
> Makes wishes forever endure."

For a moment there was silence, then the child looked piteously at them.

"Sorry, Guy." The child scuffed at the ground. "Sorry Clemmie. I was being very rude. That was a very pretty firework. I enjoyed it very much. Thank you."

And then, turning on its designer-trainered heel, it sloped away, head down, between the willows.

Clemmie and Guy stared at one another.

"That wasn't magic," Guy said softly, "that was a bloody miracle."

"It works, doesn't it?" Clemmie's mouth was dry. "Not just the firework — which is more incredible than I'd ever dreamed — but Allbard's magic thing? I know I shouldn't believe it for a minute, but oh, Lordy. Suppose, just suppose, it really is magical?"

"Don't waste it," Guy urged. "Run and find the other three brats and bloody Helen and we'll magic them all at the same time. Oh — the joy! The power!"

Clemmie was still so stunned that the wind screaming across the fields, whipping the river's torrent into little muddy crests, seemed to have died away. The numbing air seemed to have become soft and balmy.

She looked at Guy. "Seriously, have we discovered the holy grail or have we opened Pandora's Box?"

Guy bit his lip. "Actually, I'm not sure — but it's obviously pretty powerful, scary stuff. Handle with care is clearly going to be an understatement. Are you sure you don't want to run a control test on the other three brats and my unbeloved ex-wife?"

"Don't tempt me," Clemmie giggled, hurrying over to the charred launch site beside Guy with sand buckets and a black bin liner. "Although abducting them, dragging them over here, and sprinkling them with green flames is more likely to get us arrested."

"Spoilsport. Clemmie Coddle, you are definitely no fun."

She poked out her tongue. "I told you, I only wanted to use the magic stuff for doing good."

"Making the brats human and Helen less of a snobby, pretentious, priggy, avaricious bitch *would* be doing good," Guy muttered, clearing away the Seventh Heaven debris. "It'd probably earn us a prize from the Royal Humanitarian Society. Jesus, it's cold. Race you back to the lab — last one back doesn't get a cream slice!"

Clemmie beat him by a hair's breadth.

During the following cream slice and hot chocolate interlude, which Suggs enthusiastically helped with, they mulled over the pros and cons of Seventh Heaven and decided, as they had a day free to play in the lab, they'd build several versions as a stockpile, just in case.

"If we try them out sort of sneakily at various Gunpowder Plot gigs," Guy said, licking cream from his fingers in a way which had Clemmie jigging with lust, "we can find out how much the magic really works, can't we?"

"OK." Clemmie beamed. Being with a non-gay Guy, building her own Seventh Heaven firework and eating cream cakes was almost as good as a girl could wish for. "Shall we make a start?"

"Yep, when we've shared the last cake. Oh, and I wondered if we should have two versions of the funeral rocket, too. What do you reckon? I've never done a firework funeral before, but I've asked around and I know how to construct it though I still think, as it's so important, that we should have a stand-by, just in case."

"Fine. It makes sense. Oh, I wish you'd been there at the funeral parlour. The whole thing, this Max Angel's final request, was so sad."

Guy nodded. "YaYa was pretty moved by it too. And the letter from his solicitor was poignant in the extreme. Max has detailed every single thing about his send-off: the colours of the firework, the choreography music, and of course, the list of specially invited mourners which the Motions are dealing with. Everything he's asked for has a special significance. He told his solicitor that his summer here in nineteen sixty-nine was the best of his life. That he wanted those who shared it with him to say goodbye to him remembering it — and him — too. We've just got to make it absolutely perfect."

They looked at one another in silence.

Clemmie swallowed the lump in her throat. "I'd like to be there, not just because it's part of my job and I've never seen anyone's ashes sent up in a rocket before, but because — well — because I want to say goodbye to him too. Mind you, I'll probably cry my eyes out."

"And I won't be far behind you. As for YaYa, she'll need a box of Kleenex all to herself. But we'll do the very best we can to make it special for him and — oh, sod it — what does she want now?"

Helen, pink-nosed with cold but still managing to look exquisitely gorgeous, and snuggled deeply into the camel coat, was hammering on the lab door.

"Yes?" Guy unlocked it, standing back as she swept in. "Oh, do come in. Have you come to say goodbye and thank you for having me — or not, in this case?"

"No, I damn well haven't!" Helen tossed the perfect blonde hair, dropped her big, squashy, eye-wateringly expensive, Chloe handbag onto the charcoal sacks, and placed her hands aggressively on her hips. "I've come to ask you what the hell you've done to Ivo?"

Hah, Clemmie thought, I got it wrong. The magicked child *hadn't* been Mungo, then. Easy mistake to make since they all looked much the same to her: sulky, scruffy and slightly threatening.

"Nothing, why?" Guy managed to look angelically innocent. "What's he said?"

"Nothing at all, that's the trouble. I think he's suffered some sort of trauma — and I think you're to blame."

"Why on earth would you think that? Helen, I know you'll happily accuse me of all the sins of mankind, but I swear —"

"Well, something happened to him." Helen glared at Guy. "The poor baby was ill with his tummy upset this morning, and after I'd taken the others to school and then come back to finish the packing — which," her

eyes blazed, "I'd hoped *someone* might help me with —
I suggested he took a little walk to get some fresh air. I
thought it would make him feel a little less nauseous."

Clemmie studied the floor very carefully.

"And it didn't?" Guy asked solicitously. "Shame."

"No, it bloody didn't!" Helen flared. "He went out a
normal ebullient child with a bit of a gippy tummy,
saying he was going to find you in the lab because being
bored by you was better than being bored in the house
— and came back like a terrified mouse. Silent,
subdued, hang-dog, cowed. Not like my little Ivo at all.
What did you do to him?"

"Nothing at all. Did I, Clemmie?"

"No. Absolutely not. Guy didn't say anything or do
anything. Neither of us touched him. He was only here
for less than five minutes. Maybe his stomach upset is
making him listless? Maybe he just needs to rest?"

"If I needed medical information," Helen snarled at
her, "I'd have contacted NHS Direct. I'm perfectly
capable of diagnosing my own children's maladies,
thank you very much."

"Well," Guy shrugged, "if he hasn't accused me of
doing anything then I can't imagine why you are. I'm
sure, as Clemmie says, it's just part of his bug and he'll
be right as rain in no time."

"When I asked him if he'd seen you, he vomited on
the jukebox."

"Christ. Not over YaYa's Dusty Springfield vinyls I
hope."

"How the hell would I know?" Helen screeched.
"God, Guy, you are so bloody irritating! I can't imagine

258

why I ever got involved with you in the first place! Why the hell I married you! Why —"

"Sex," Guy reminded her cheerfully. "Lust and sex. And more lust. And an awful lot of sex. Surely you can't have forgotten?"

Helen stamped her expensively shod foot. "I bloody hate you! Smug bastard! I will be so glad to go home. I can't bear to spend another minute in your company! Let me get out of here before I — ooooh nooo! I don't bloody believe it! That fucking ferret's just peed on my handbag!"

CHAPTER
NINETEEN

It was bitterly cold on top of Hassocks Hill. And darkly sinister. The highest point for miles around, with its copse of centuries-old oak trees and panoramic views, it was claimed, of the whole of Berkshire on a fine day, Hassocks Hill was a popular spot with dog walkers, ramblers, picnickers, and lovers alike.

Tonight, with the moon slithering in and out of purple-daubed clouds, and the wind whispering forlornly through the denuded trees, it looked a desolate place.

Clemmie, dressed entirely in black, complete with gloves and scarves, and with a layer of unflattering thermal underwear beneath her boho best, shivered under the tossing branches of the oaks.

"Spooky, isn't it, love?" YaYa, black-haired for the occasion, muttered from the cosy depths of her floor-length damson fun fur coat. "I don't like this one little bit. And I thought yesterday was bad."

Being present at the building of the funeral rocket the previous day had been a moving experience. Guy had collected the urn of ashes from the Motions and Clemmie had been surprised to see how large it was.

"Thank God I asked around the other pyro companies and designed a big enough chamber to take all of it," Guy, uncharacteristically sombre, had said in the lab. "He wanted purple and yellow stars, so that was easy enough — I've made two separate compartments on either side of the ashes one. The first with cryolite for the yellow and the second with a mix of copper and strontium carbonates to produce purple."

Clemmie and YaYa had watched as Guy carefully and reverently dispensed Max Angel's mortal remains in between these layers, and completed the rocket.

Truly ashes to ashes, Clemmie had thought dismally. Is this really what life is all about? Is this all there is?

"Now it has to go back to the chapel of rest to be brought to Hassocks Hill by the funeral directors," Guy had sighed heavily. "So far so good — but I'll have to make sure those mad old Motions realise they'll be housing a high-explosive device overnight."

The fact that Suggs had been richly rewarded with a whole chicken breast for his lavatorial misdemeanour, and that Helen, accompanied by Ivo, Puke, Snot and Mungo — three of them their normal obnoxious selves and one remaining subdued and rather sweet — had finally left the boathouse to return home, still couldn't lighten the mood and Clemmie had, for once, been glad to finish work.

She'd driven slowly back to Bagley-cum-Russet through Winterbrook's busy shopping centre, and even the Christmas decorations strung across the streets, the tall, twinkling Christmas tree outside the Masonic Hall, the gaudy shop windows, and the pre-festive hustle and bustle, failed to cheer her.

Today, feeling even more miserable about the coming funeral, they'd all finished work early, and Clemmie had explained to Bill and Molly that she'd be going back to The Gunpowder Plot at nine o'clock as they had a late display. She hated being so economical with the truth, but had sworn with everyone else at the boathouse to keep Max Angel's plans secret until the ceremony was over.

"It's just lovely to see you enjoying your job so much," Uncle Bill had said as Clemmie tucked into a fortifying meal of cheese omelette and chips. "This Gunpowder Plot thing has been the making of you."

"It doesn't even seem like work," Clemmie had mumbled, reaching for the tomato ketchup. "I'm having a ball. Thank goodness this opportunity came up when it did and I didn't go down the teaching route."

"Ah, that would never have been right for you." Bill had mopped his plate. "Don't I always say that fate'll sort everything out? You've found your niche all right, Clem. You're a lucky girl."

Hmmm, Clemmie had thought, I am. And if Guy could only see me as more than a fellow-scientist and pyro-freak, then I'd be the luckiest girl in the world.

Hah — I should be so lucky!

"I'm looking forward to having a bit of a blast of late-night telly," Bill continued. "All that stuff that

Molly considers unsuitable; with you both being out tonight."

"Oh, poor old you," Clemmie had sympathised, smiling. "Left home alone. I'd forgotten it was Auntie Molly's WI night tonight, too."

"They've got a 'make a miniature garden in a jam-jar lid' competition tonight," Bill said mournfully. "You know our Moll's none too deft with her fingers. Hers looks like a dead frog impaled on a twig."

"I hope you didn't say so."

"Lord, no. I told her it was the spit of a shrunken Sissinghurst."

"Good. Now once I've shoved this lot in the dishwasher, I'm going to have a bath and get ready. You enjoy your telly. I'll try not to disturb you when I come in."

Saying much the same to Molly and wishing her luck in the WI competition as they swapped places in the bathroom, Clemmie laughed when her aunt paused.

"Will that nice young man — Steve? — be there tonight?"

"Oh, yes, he'll be there." Clemmie had grabbed a clean bath towel. "But don't read anything into it, Auntie Moll. We're just good friends. And tonight is definitely work, not pleasure. Now I'll have to dash — I don't want to be late."

By eleven o'clock, Clemmie, YaYa, Guy and Syd, who made up tonight's small team of Gunpowder Plot personnel, had arrived for Max Angel's firework funeral.

So far, Guy had stored the spare funeral rocket — the one without the ashes, in case of emergencies — alongside another prototype solo Magik Green, just in case it might be needed to cheer up the mourners, and set up the firing site for the rocket containing Max's ashes, then he'd driven off to the Motions' to make sure everything went smoothly from their end.

Syd, helped by Clemmie and YaYa, had arranged the company ghetto-blaster, small generator and other electrical paraphernalia discreetly out of sight. Because the rocket was to be fired manually, they'd left the computer and equipment van on the lane at the base of the hill and made the several climbs on foot. After the last of these, a puffing YaYa had sworn to give up smoking — again.

A microphone had been linked to the stereo for the farewell address, and in accordance with Max's final requests, a CD would be provided to be synchronised with the dispersal of his ashes.

"No idea how it'll work, timing-wise," Syd had said. "Seeing as the whole thing has been kept so quiet. I've got no idea what music he's chosen. The undertakers are bringing that, along with his rocket, his eulogy, and presumably the mourners. If it's a long selection I'll just have to hope I can suss out the music timings to fit the firework at the eleventh hour."

"His solicitor's letter said he wanted it all cloak and dagger," YaYa lit a cigarette, carefully keeping well away from the fireworks, and the tip glowed eerily in the gloom, "to stop it turning into a media circus. He didn't want anyone cashing in on this last very private

264

moment. Apparently Max Angel's agent has slapped a press embargo on everything to do with his death until this is over, then there'll be a statement released."

Clemmie shivered some more. "Maybe he'll want to go out to a medley of his greatest hits?"

"God — I hope not!" Syd looked horrified. "Have you heard any of the Burning Banshees' stuff?"

Clemmie and YaYa shook their heads.

"Titles like 'You Oughta Slaughta Your Daughta's Daughta' and 'Visceral Love Of The Throat Slasher' and 'Ripping, Dripping, Living Heart Bleed' give you a clue?"

Clemmie winced.

"Bugger me." YaYa shuddered. "Give me a nice blast of Dolly Parton any day, love."

"To give Max Angel his due," Syd said, "apparently he didn't turn into a blood 'n' gore heavy metallist until he'd been in the States for a while and joined the Burning Banshees. When he was in Hazy Hassocks he was in a pretty long-haired close-harmony group called Love Child."

"Which is probably what he's got a lot of," YaYa sniggered, "if my experience of rock musicians is anything to go by."

Shivering on the top of Hassocks Hill, Clemmie was truly glad of YaYa's company and friendship tonight. She was still surprised at how unhappy she felt about this funeral. YaYa helped to keep the mood just the right side of suicidal.

YaYa peered at her watch. "Half-eleven. They should all be on their way now. And, although I have absolutely no intention of dying in this lifetime, should the unthinkable happen, this has certainly made me want to have my funeral in the height of summer, with sunshine and flowers and happy music and not a speck of bloody black in sight."

"With Honey Bunch and Foxy reading your shock-horror life-story eulogy and Campari and Cinnamon singing a selection of your favourite Dusty tracks?"

"Christ, no, love! I intend to outlive the lot of *them*! Oh, looks like something's happening down there: There are loads of cars pulling into the lane. We'd better light the lanterns."

True to Max's wishes, they'd set up a circle of candle lanterns on tall holders surrounding the firing site, and dozens of smaller lanterns were dotted around at ground level. At least when these were lit, Clemmie thought, Hassocks Hill might not look quite so depressing.

Even though the mass of dancing candles did somewhat lift the gloom and doom, Clemmie couldn't help feeling a tight knot of dread deep in her stomach as the torchlit funeral procession started to climb the hill towards them.

"Hold my hand, love," YaYa whispered. "I think I'm going to cry."

"Me too," Clemmie whispered back, sliding her black woolly mitten into YaYa's plum velvet. "Oh, dear this is awful."

The elderly Motion cousins, all dressed in black complete with top hats and veils, puffed slowly at the head of the cortége each of them carrying a case of champagne, followed by Guy carrying the rocket which he placed reverently in its allotted place and, finally, the privately invited mourners.

Clemmie peered at them appearing over the brow of the hill, and realised with something of a shock that they weren't all the elderly women she'd expected them to be. Of course, less than forty years ago, in 1969, the year that Max Angel wanted to celebrate with this send-off, most of his girlfriends would probably have been quite young teenagers. So now, they'd only be somewhere in their fifties.

Oh, poor things. Clemmie stared sadly at the procession — and so many of them! Max had certainly had a fair few flings. She wondered if they'd known about each other.

Well, they did now, she thought, watching the chain of women all dressed in purple and clutching a single yellow flower in one hand and a scrunched up hankie in the other, haul themselves, slightly out of breath and damp-eyed, to the summit of Hassocks Hill.

"Jesus!" She squeezed YaYa's hand. "I know her! And her! And — bloody hell!"

Oh heavens! There was Valerie Pridmore from Bagley, and Roo from Topsy-Turvey's village can-can troupe, and Mrs Hopkins, her friend Chelsea's mother, and Patsy from the Pantry, and Flo Spraggs who lived next door to Mitzi Blessing, and Pauline, Phoebe's boss from Cut'n'Curl, and Pam Peacock, the beigely boring practice manager from the Dovecote Surgery, and —

no way! — sturdy, mouthy, hateful Bunty Darrington. Clemmie's nemesis, and . . .

"Holy shit!"

"What, love?" YaYa had been silently staring as the mourners all grouped beneath the swaying lanterns in a ragged circle. "Who've you seen?"

"Far too many people I know," Clemmie gulped. "But particularly my Auntie Molly! She said she was going to the WI tonight. Probably that's the excuse they all used — although God knows how they were going to explain away the fact they didn't get home until after midnight. But it certainly explains away the frog on a twig."

"Sorry, love." YaYa frowned. "You lost me somewhere around the Auntie Molly bit. What frog?"

"Doesn't matter." Clemmie sniffed back a tear. "Poor Molly. I've never thought of her as anything but comfy and cosy and — well — old. I can't believe that before she married Uncle Bill she was once young and sexy and a Max Angel groupie." She huddled behind YaYa. "Don't let her see me — it'd break her heart if she knew I knew and she didn't want me to. And if she'd wanted anyone to know she'd have told me, and she wouldn't have lied to Uncle Bill about the miniature garden, would she?"

"Whatever you say, love. I think I'm with you," YaYa said slowly. "And don't worry, I won't let her see you. I doubt if she even knows you're here; no one can see anything in this light. Although, didn't you tell her you were doing a display tonight?"

Clemmie nodded. "But not where or what. She'd assume it was a birthday party or something. And I know she definitely didn't know that The Gunpowder Plot was doing this tonight. In fact, because of the secrecy, I doubt any of them knew what the funeral plans were, or even now thinks there's a professional firework company involved. They were probably just told to be here, and when, and to wear purple. I expect they all think whatever happens tonight is simply part of the Motions' all-in funeral service."

"Let's hope so, love. And you can rely on me to keep you hidden."

Guy, seriously solemn in a long black coat, the thin black scarf wound round his throat, his hair blown by the wind, his beautiful features dark in the candlelight, looked across at them and gave them a gentle lopsided smile of support and encouragement.

Oh, God, Clemmie realised suddenly, I love him. I really, truly love him. Not simply the fancying-the-pants-off-him bit of last May Day, or the liking-him bit of knowing him and working with him; but the sensational chemical mixture of lust and want and need and like and know and admire and care and understand and . . .

Oh, sod it.

"This has really got to Guy," YaYa whispered, sticking to her promise and dramatically shielding Clemmie from the shivering mourners like a towering damson modesty screen. "He hates seeing anyone cry. Please God we don't have to hang about up here more than necessary — oh, no — it looks as if we might be off. Pass me the Kleenex, love."

Perpetua had shakily handed each of the mourners a glass of champagne; Syd had got the mobile electrics working; and with a slight crackle, Guy picked up the microphone and a torch and read from a piece of paper pushed into his hands by Constance.

"Er — ladies . . . this is a brief eulogy for Max Angel, or maybe as some of you previously knew him, James Lesney. He's written his own farewell to you so these next words are his, not mine."

Guy paused, his voice not entirely steady, but still sounding deep and reassuring in the black, freezing night. Several women were already crying audibly. Clemmie didn't dare look to see if Auntie Molly was among them.

Guy cleared his throat. "This a very sad occasion, but also one for celebration. Sad, because I've come home to Hazy Hassocks for the final time to say goodbye. I'd always intended to return alive and well and healthy and revisit my youthful haunts and see my friends, but time passed so quickly, and sadly it wasn't to be. But it's also a celebration, because this is my final wish. In death I'm fulfilling the dream I couldn't complete in life. I've come home to say a final farewell to you, the girls I loved."

The weeping grew in volume.

"The girls who made me so happy, and who made my last summer in England simply the best of my life. I hope you remember me with not a little affection. I remember you all with far more than that. I also remember the fun we had here on Hassocks Hill on

270

warm summer nights and hot summer days. It was my summer of love. The best. So, to . . .”

Here Guy read out an incredibly lengthy list of female names. The sobs grew louder with each one. Clemmie, listening with growing surprise at the number of names she knew, had completely forgotten that before she unfortunately became a Coddle, Molly’s maiden name had been Millichip. Not a lot to pick from there, to be honest. Clemmie thought.

Guy continued. “. . . I’ve never forgotten you. I send you my deepest love and thanks and hope you’ll always remember me fondly. I hope you’ll also remember the significance of the purple, my favourite colour. I always wore something purple, didn’t I? And the yellow flowers — yellow, the colour of sunshine and summer and I was always good at remembering to give you flowers, wasn’t I?”

Audible moans echoed under the canopy of oaks. Someone blew their nose fiercely.

“And the fact that I’ve chosen midnight for my final countdown will hopefully rekindle some memories too, because that was the best time up here, wasn’t it? To be young and in love. With no one else around.”

There were a couple of grief-stricken shrieks and a little keening sob.

“However, because I may have been inconsiderate enough to die in winter and hopefully by now both you and I are about a hundred years old, I won’t drag this out any longer. I just wanted you to be here, with me, for one last time before my ashes are sent into the heavens. Girls — my girls — thank you from the bottom of my heart. I love you all. Still. I hope you'll remember me with love forever. So raise your glasses and drink one last toast to a million happy memories. Goodbye."

"Not a dry eye in the house," YaYa sobbed noisily. "Oh, blimey, love — that was a killer. Heartbreaking but dignified."

"As a funeral for a gigolo," Clemmie dashed away her tears on her mittens, "it's simply perfect."

The uncontrolled weeping from the candlelit mourners was ebbing and flowing unseen like a midnight ocean. Despite the champagne's happy bubbles, the grief was tangible.

The Motions, stately, and clearly chilled to the marrow, moved slowly with Guy towards the firing site. Syd, a dark shadow, crossed towards the ghetto blaster.

"Here we go," YaYa muttered. "Lights, music, action . . ."

"Shit!" Clemmie grabbed YaYa's arm. "YaYa! Look! He's *smoking*! That old undertaker bloke Slo has lit a cigarette! Stupid sod! Quick — tell Guy that —"

With a whoosh and a roar, the rocket ignited and screamed away through the oaks.

Misrouted, it meandered upwards and upwards into the midnight sky before trailing haphazardly away across the darkness of the Berkshire countryside.

Unprepared, the mourners shrieked, clutched at one another in shocked surprise, stared tearfully at one another in confusion, then looked perplexedly skywards.

Someone screamed. Everyone was crying loudly. One or two had fallen over.

272

"Slo!" Constance Motion's voice bellowed through the mayhem. "I'll damnable kill you!"

"What the hell?" Guy, incandescently furious, glared at Slo, his elderly face singed by the close-up explosion, the spattered remains of his cigarette and the rocket's igniter smouldering pungent holes in his frock coat. "Why did you do that? Jesus!"

Hoping that Auntie Molly was far too overcome by grief to notice her, Clemmie darted out from behind YaYa and stumbled across the frozen tussocks.

"Guy! It's the wrong one! It's OK . . . Well, sort of . . ."

"What?" Angrily, Guy pushed his hair out of his eyes. "Christ Almighty — what a balls-up! After all that careful planning, the poor bugger got heaven sent without any of the pomp and circumstance he'd intended. Bollocks! Sorry, Clemmie, I didn't catch —"

"Slo Motion dropped his cigarette on the *spare* rocket. He never got as far as the firing site did he? He must have tripped over the Magik Green in the darkness and set off the spare-in-case-of-emergencies-rocket."

"Are you sure?" Guy peered at her closely in the chill gloom. "Really sure?"

"Positive. Look, the ashes rocket is still there — Slo never got that far over. Quick, before this lot all have a multiple fit of the vapours." Clemmie eyed the crowd of helplessly sobbing women in horror. "Get back to the microphone and tell them something, anything — just let poor old Max Angel have his moment of glory."

"OK," Guy held her face between his hands. "And if this wasn't so awful it'd be funny and I might kiss you."

Clemmie, knowing he was joking, ducked away from him before he could see the longing in her eyes. "Oh, there'll be plenty of time for all that later. Just let's get this over."

Grabbing the microphone, Guy practically yelled across Hassocks Hill. The reverberation of his voice was enough to waken the dead.

"Ladies! Ladies! LADIES! I am so sorry — that little — er — hiatus wasn't part of Max Angel's plans, although I'm sure you who knew him best would agree he'd probably find it extremely amusing."

The sobs died slightly. Several of the women nodded.

Guy, who obviously had no idea of Max's sense of humour, simply hoped he'd hit the right note. "So, without any more delays, let's all join together and say goodbye to the man you all loved and who loved you. Raise your glasses and say: 'Goodbye to Max Angel'."

The chorus of "goodbye Max" was ragged and teary.

Taking no chances, Guy made sure Slo was held back by a simmeringly angry Constance on one side and Perpetua, who had been at the leftover champagne and was now bawling wildly through a nasal version of 'Long Haired Lover From Liverpool', on the other.

As Guy ignited the rocket's fuse, Syd pressed the start button on the ghetto blaster.

There was a deafening, thundering drum and guitar explosion.

"Oh, wow, love," YaYa shouted at Clemmie through her tears. " 'Summer of 'Sixty-nine'! Fabulous! One of

274

my faves! Such a clever choice of tune under the circs. Always makes me want to boogie."

Sadly, Clemmie found she was already irreverently clapping her hands, tapping her feet and swaying from side to side.

Hassocks Hill vibrated to the deafening raucous rock'n'roll strains of Bryan Adams' stupendous gyrating anthem as the mortal remains of Max Angel streaked skywards: a glorious profusion of purple and yellow stars, shooting higher and higher, then trailing, drifting, twisting, exploding again and again in huge cushions of coloured constellations.

Three and half minutes of breathtaking music perfectly matched three and a half minutes of astounding pyrotechnics.

"What a way to go . . ." Clemmie breathed, sniffing back her tears, unable to keep still as the superb rocking soundtrack continued to blast through the midnight air.

Max's mourners were all smiling through their tears now, reliving their own "Summer of '69" memories, clapping along, hands high above their heads. Several, including Bunty Darrington and Pam Peacock, were dancing. Valerie Pridmore was playing an extravagant air guitar. Perpetua Motion was head-banging.

On the downside, the surfeit of emotion meant that everyone's make-up had run and it looked like the final night of a particularly raddled Alice Cooper convention.

As Bryan came to the end of his perfect musical eulogy, the final notes ringing through the freezing air, and the last of The Gunpowder Plot's purple and yellow stars, mingled with Max's ashes, cascaded gently to earth, Guy walked across to Clemmie and YaYa.

"How bloody emotional was that?" He slid his arms round them both and hugged them close. "And I don't just mean the first little blip. God — I feel drained. I'm not sure I could handle many of these without needing counselling afterwards. Oh, who's that lady giving us a hard stare?"

"Bugger," Clemmie muttered frantically, "it's my Auntie Molly. Don't let her see me. She must have wanted to keep tonight secret. I couldn't bear it if she felt guilty about her past. I'd rather tonight was something neither of us ever had to share — oh, shit!"

Molly, emerging further from the sea of lined and make-up-streaked faces, was still peering across at them.

"Clemmie?" Her voice was hoarse with tears. "Clemmie? Is that you?"

Auntie Molly had come to a halt just by the firing site and was gazing into the candlelit darkness with all the intensity of a puzzled sheep.

Searching in her pockets for a handy portfire and failing to find one, Clemmie grabbed YaYa's fluffy damson arm. "Give me your lighter — quick. No, I don't want a fag, just the lighter — ta!"

And ducking between the oaks, keeping out of Molly's line of vision, Clemmie skittered across the crisped grass and after several futile flicks held the lighter's flame to the Magik Green's touchpaper.

"I wish," she whispered towards her aunt as the Magik Green started to crackle, "that you'd forget you thought you saw me here. I wish you'd forget everything about tonight that might involve me. And I wish you'd go home to Uncle Bill and tell him that you've had a lovely night out, that's all."

Too many wishes? Too late to know.

As everyone turned and stared at this impromptu colourful explosion, the Magik Green swooshed its fountain of emerald flame upwards with the merest whisper of propulsion, sending a shower of green sparks blowing across Hassocks Hill.

As they tumbled and shimmered around Molly, Clemmie took a deep breath.

"Verdigris and verture pure
Sparks with nature's verdanture
Makes wishes forever endure."

Molly suddenly shook her head, shrugged and, smiling in confusion, turned and walked back to be swallowed up by the crowd of mourners.

Clemmie, avoiding Ya Ya's quizzical gaze, exhaled and thanked the ancient Allbard with deep heartfelt but silent gratitude.

"Oooh, that was lovely!" Perpetua Motion clapped her hands. "Nice colour! Are we having more fireworks, Mr Devlin?"

"No," Guy said, grinning hugely at Clemmie. "That was another happy accident. I think we've all had enough of fireworks and everything else for tonight. It's very cold and we've all had a pretty emotional night. Shall we just call it a day and go home?"

The general consensus seemed to be that this was a highly sensible and desirable plan, and gradually the firework funeral party began to disperse.

"Go home, Clemmie," Guy said softly. "Don't stay to clear up. Disappear over there, behind the trees. If you leave now you'll be home and in bed before your Auntie Molly gets there. If Allbard's up to scratch, she won't remember any of it by the morning. Drive safely, and I'll see you tomorrow."

Clemmie nodded her thanks, and waving goodbye to YaYa and Syd, started to slither away down Hassocks Hill before the gaggle of mourners made their mass getaway.

"Oh, and Clemmie . . ." Guy called softly after her. "I haven't forgotten I still owe you a kiss."

Clemmie turned and smiled at him, then floated the rest of the way down Hassocks Hill, smiling soppily to herself and humming 'Summer of '69'.

CHAPTER
TWENTY

It seemed an indecently short time between the sadness of Max Angel's funeral and the joy of Jemima and Charlie's wedding. The last few frosty, sparkling days of November had turned sullenly into a sulky December, and the weather was now grey, still, and misty.

"At least it's not raining," YaYa said for the umpteenth time as she, Clemmie and Suggs headed away from Winterbrook through the Berkshire dusk for Milton St John in the 4×4. "I think I'd die if it rained on my wedding day."

Clemmie laughed. "As you've already said you're not going to die, and as you're unlikely to get married, I wouldn't lose too much sleep over that one if I were you."

"No, but you get my drift, love." YaYa flicked her cigarette ash out of the window. Her "I'm giving up" vow on Hassocks Hill had rapidly bitten the dust. "I mean, how awful for the bride, when she's invested everything she's got in looking the best she'll ever look, to have it ruined by a downpour."

"This being England, I'm sure trillions of brides have survived a rainy wedding day. Anyway, Jemima and Charlie will have been married for hours by now, won't they? We're only doing the evening reception. And it hasn't rained all day, and from what I saw of them, they were so mad about each other that they wouldn't even notice the weather."

"Do they make a cute couple?"

"Very." Clemmie shifted Suggs more comfortably on her lap. "And please God nothing will go wrong with this gig."

They had, as Guy predicted, eventually laughed over the funeral mayhem. Neither Clemmie nor Guy had mentioned the jokey kiss thing, though. And Auntie Molly hadn't mentioned anything about Clemmie or anyone else being on Hassocks Hill at all.

Uncle Bill had been gently sympathetic that Molly hadn't won a prize with her miniature garden at the WI, and had told Clemmie that her aunt had been ". . . real late home. Got in after you did — and you were late enough. Apparently she met up with some of her old chums she hadn't seen for ages. Got nattering. Talked until the cows come home and had a smashing time, bless her."

And if Molly had spent the last couple of days being quieter than usual and looking slightly wistful, no one commented on it. Neither did Clemmie mention the drooping yellow flower in a bud vase on the kitchen windowsill or the fact that a Bryan Adams CD had suddenly appeared in the Coddles' music collection.

Allbard's Magik Green, Clemmie concluded, had done the trick. Again.

Which had given her an idea. An idea which actually had been bubbling away for a long time, one idea she

280

knew she really shouldn't even consider. In fact, she'd spent the days since Max Angel's send-off planning the idea and — because she was a scientist — making sure there was a plan B should it all go horribly wrong.

The idea was, of course, to use the Magik Green to make Guy fall in love with her.

Easy enough to do, especially at a display when she and Guy were close together in the middle of multiple explosions, but, and here Clemmie had agonised through several sleepless nights, it wouldn't be *real*, would it? It probably would, she believed now, work, but it would be *interfering*, wouldn't it? She'd never be able to live with herself. But would she be able to live with herself if she didn't give it a try?

So, the dilemma: should she use artificial means to achieve her ends? Her heart said yes but her head was screaming no, no, NO! And then there was plan B: to use Magik Green on herself to wipe all stupid romantic notions about Guy Devlin out of her head and heart.

At the moment, plan B two was winning by a country mile.

"Sorry?" She peered across the 4×4 at YaYa. "I didn't catch that."

"You were away with the fairies again, love," YaYa chuckled throatily. "I really must meet this boy of yours. He sure has a strange effect on you. Anyway, I was just prattling — nothing important — and actually, I think we're here, aren't we?"

Clemmie nodded. Even though it was now pitch dark, it was easy to navigate their way to the field where the reception was taking place as a competition between sweeping criss-crossing lasers and the gaudy reflection of a fairground illuminated the sky.

"Nice village," YaYa said as they drove slowly along Milton St John's narrow, winding main road, past the Cat and Fiddle and Maureen's Munchy Bar and the tiny arcade of shops, towards the lights. "Classy. There must be loads of money in horse racing."

"As in all other businesses, probably a lot more at the top than at the bottom," Clemmie said tartly. "I wouldn't fancy being a stable lad. Up before dawn, working for peanuts seven days a week at the dirty-fingernail end of the sport, and sleeping in a hostel with at least thirty other people."

"Sounds like hell," YaYa observed with a shudder as they left the village behind and found themselves in the countryside again. "I think I'll stick to fireworks and drag queening. Here's the field and I can see The Gunpowder Plot vans parked over there, so we'll squeeze in between them. Blimey, love! Look at all those limos! Bentleys and Rollers! Dozens of 'em! And I thought this was going to be some small villagey affair tonight."

"I think the wedding was fairly quiet." Clemmie's voice was muffled as she leaned down and settled Suggs in his little sofa bed in the footwell. "Close friends and family only. The rest of the world was invited to the no-expense-spared reception — and it looks as if they've all turned up."

Oddly, despite only having seen Guy at the boathouse that morning, run through the digital

282

display with him, rehearsed the computerised choreography beside him, helped him double-check and finally pack the vans with the beautiful peaceful fireworks needed for the reception, Clemmie felt her heart give a strange little leap at the thought of seeing him again.

Completely mad, she told herself sternly. Yes, you know he likes you, probably admires your pyro skills, and enjoys flirting with you — but if he gets wind of how you really feel about him you'll be out of The Gunpowder Plot faster than a Whoopee-Doo Sky Screamer. The last thing he needs is yet another sad female drooling over him.

Which, of course, would be where the Magik Green would come in so handy.

"Oh, wow, Clemmie! Look at the fair!" YaYa shrieked as they bumped across the field. "I thought it would just be a coconut shy and swinging boats, but it's a proper full-on old-fashioned fairground! I love fairs! Christ, they must have spent a fortune on all this stuff."

The 4×4 pulled into a gap between the two vans and, having made sure Suggs was settled, Clemmie opened the door to be welcomed by a disco rendition of 'Oops Upside Your Head' echoing from the nearest enormous marquee.

Stunningly dressed people were skittering between the two tents, either of which could have housed an entire circus, and the dank December night was filled with laughter and a thousand splintered conversations, the tantalising wafting scents of rich food, the chink of bottles against glasses.

283

"Shall we find Guy and the crew first, or go and scrounge something to eat?" YaYa hesitated, inhaling greedily. "Smell that! Fantastic! Not a flaccid sausage roll or curly sandwich in sight, I bet. And I'm bloody starving."

"Me too." Clemmie sniffed the air, her stomach rumbling. "Although that's nothing new. But honestly, I think we should go and find Guy and co. We're not guests as such, are we? We may well be offered food after the display, but it would look sort of scroungy to barge in straight away and join the meal queue."

Although, she thought, it might well give her an opportunity to find Suzy Beckett and see how she'd survived the wedding day.

She and Guy had agreed to bring their specially built silent version of Seventh Heaven with them — just in case it might come in handy. Neither of them really expected to need it tonight, though. Poor Suzy . . .

YaYa reluctantly put a temporary hold on eating, so shoving their way though the beautiful people, they skirted the Bradley-Morland Memory Lane Fair, which was doing a roaring trade with all the rides packed, the lights and music throbbing into the night, and made their way to The Gunpowder Plot's firing site.

Guy, who was pacing out measurements beneath a spotlight with several of the pyro crew, stopped and smiled at them. Clemmie's knees turned to jelly. She smiled gamely back.

"You both look lovely," Guy said. "Did you co-ordinate the outfits?"

"No, love." YaYa tottered towards him on her high conker-brown boots, patting her multi-streaked hair. "We didn't check what we were wearing but we both seemed to come up with the autumnal colour palette for tonight. The long and short of it: me in the mini, Clem in the floor-length version. Tone nicely, don't we? Matching not clashing. However, Clemmie's earrings are a million times better than mine, the bitch. How's it going — need a hand?"

"Nearly finished." Guy stood up, pushing his hair out of his eyes, and stretched his shoulders inside his leather jacket.

Clemmie was practically gibbering with lust.

"Oh, goody. Actually, me and Clem are starving. We hoped we'd be able to go and blag some food."

"We've been given a free rein on everything," Guy reassured her. "So yeah, go and help yourselves. Better to eat now before we begin."

"What about you and the crew?" Clemmie asked. "Do you want a carry-out?"

"We've already eaten, thanks. Jemima and Charlie made sure we had heaps of everything going as soon as we arrived. But I'm sure Suggs would appreciate a takeaway for the journey home."

"OK — how long have we got?"

"We start in an hour. The JB Roadshow are just going to start their first set, then we're scheduled to take over the entertainment — and the band will come back and finish the evening off for another hour or so. So you've got plenty of time."

Clemmie smiled at him. "And have you seen Suzy?"

He nodded. "She looks lovely. But no sign of her being with anyone. Mind you, I wouldn't know what this Luke bloke looks like — but I reckon we'll draw a blank tonight."

"Shame."

"What's this?" YaYa frowned. "Have you two got a secret?"

I don't know about Guy, but I've got more than one, Clemmie thought. She shrugged. "Not really, it's just a little idea Guy and I had about matchmaking with someone we met — but it isn't going to come off. So forget it. Come on, let's go and find the food."

The reception marquees had been cleverly organised into one for eating and drinking, the other for dancing and drinking. Both were absolutely bursting at the seams.

"Oooh! Fab!" YaYa exclaimed, as they left their coats in a proper little cloakroom area at the entrance to the food tent. "Look at those flowers everywhere! All peaches and cream — how clever is that? It smells just like the Chelsea Flower Show, doesn't it? Isn't it lovely and warm in here? And look — they've got a row of chefs! Cooking! Real food! Oodles of it! If you carry the food, I'll grab the seats, love!"

Having queued behind a long line of designer-dressed guests, hopefully successfully fielded YaYa's questions about the matchmaking, and unsuccessfully scoured the crowds for a glimpse of Suzy, Clemmie heaped their plates with gourmet treats.

"People-watching is a great pastime, I always think," YaYa said once they were seated, crunching a glistening spare rib. "Oooh — I wouldn't have worn pink with that, would you? God, this food is to die for. And he's far too old for her! Sugar Daddy syndrome or what? Those shoes are fab — Jimmy Choos, do you reckon? And look at her . . ."

Clemmie, happily ploughing her way through a mountain of various delicious hot quiches and new potatoes and salads, hardly listened. YaYa's non-stop social observation commentary enveloped her, like a comfortable blanket.

There was Suzy's sister, she thought, the one she'd so briefly glimpsed in the frock shop, watching as the very pretty plumpish woman with masses of auburn curls and an absolutely gorgeous bridesmaid's dress in glimmery peach piled plates for three children. The children — two girls and a boy — all with dark curls and big smiles, were also dressed as bridal attendants. Unlike Helen's brood, the children seemed happy and well-behaved and normal.

Maybe she would have children after all, Clemmie decided dreamily. Then she'd have grandchildren and she'd be able to tell them all about the love of her life, a dangerously sexy pyrotechnician who . . . She sighed. There wouldn't be any children, would there? And no grandchildren to bore rigid with her stories — not unless the dangerously sexy pyrotechnician was their respective father and grandfather. Because, Clemmie admitted to herself, she would never, ever fall in love again.

It was Guy or no one. She speared a cherry tomato. And as she knew her insomnia-inspired magical plans were simply silly dreams and she'd never really dabble with Allbard's Magik Green, either on Guy or herself, it looked as if it would be no one then.

". . . and he's *very* hot, isn't he?" YaYa was still talking. "Fit or what? Looks just like Mel Gibson did in his *Lethal Weapon* days."

Clemmie, nodded, watching the very tall dark and handsome man join Suzy's sister — Maddy, wasn't it? — and the children. He touched Maddy's cheek gently with his forefinger and kissed her and their eyes locked.

Bloody hell, Clemmie thought, how much naked love was that?

Of course, he must be Maddy's husband who Suzy had said made women go weak at the knees. She could quite see why. And he and Maddy must have been married for ever; but they were still wildly and obviously deeply in love.

Clemmie watched as he reluctantly moved his hand from Maddy's face, then he grinned at the children, and they all laughed together, and disappeared happily into the crowd with their food.

No wonder Suzy missed her Luke so much if she was confronted with that sort of blissful devotion day after day.

". . . oh, no!" YaYa spluttered through the last knockings of a savoury roulade. "Not white with that skin tone! And her roots need touching up! And — crikey, love, can you hear that?"

"They can hear that in outer space," Clemmie agreed, as the JB Roadshow struck up 'Sock It To 'em JB', their signature opening number in the neighbouring marquee. "I love soul music."

"Me too." YaYa licked her fingers. "Come on, let's boogie! I want to get a glimpse of the bride and groom anyway — and they're not in here so they must be in the dance tent."

"Unless they're in bed."

"Oooh! Get you! Miss Sex on the Brain! That young man of yours has a lot to answer for. Oh, now they're playing 'Harlem Shuffle' — I do a really raunchy version of that in my act. Probably best not to go for the full showgirl thing tonight, though."

"Definitely," Clemmie said. "I don't expect Milton St John is quite ready for it."

"Possibly not," YaYa sighed. "So, how about it, love? Want to shake a tail feather or two?"

"In a minute." Clemmie looked at the superb food still temptingly arrayed on her plate. "When I've finished this."

YaYa sighed theatrically. "I really don't know why you're not the size of a house. Well, I'm off to strut my stuff, love — see you in there in a mo?"

"Yes, definitely. Won't be long."

YaYa shimmied away, a vision in skintight, very short, orange, gold and crimson, leaving everyone she passed staring open-mouthed behind her.

Clemmie picked up another slice of quiche. Next door, the JB Roadshow were playing 'Knock on Wood'. Clemmie's feet danced a little jig under the table. She hoped YaYa strutting her stuff hadn't brought the entire marquee to a standstill.

"Hi! I've been looking for you."

The voice made Clemmie jump. She turned her head and smiled in delight.

CHAPTER
TWENTY-ONE

"Hello — and blimey, don't you look fantastic?" Clemmie said to Suzy. What a gorgeous dress. Peach definitely suits you, and all those pearls are so beautiful. Oh, I'm really envious — I've always wanted to wear a tiara. No, seriously, you do look lovely."

"Thanks." Suzy placed her plate of chicken salad on the table and plonked herself in YaYa's recently vacated chair. "I really thought I'd feel like a right prat in a long frock and all the trimmings, but I've loved it. It's made me feel like a proper girl all day. Oh, it is OK if I join you, isn't it? I'm not playing gooseberry?"

"Yes, it is and no, you're not. How did it go? The wedding?"

"Brilliantly. And I was only a teeny bit jealous. It all went without a hitch. Jemima looked gorgeous, really nervous, but absolutely radiant. And Charlie — well, it was amazing. He couldn't stop grinning." Suzy nibbled a piece of chicken. "Couldn't keep his hands off her, either. They're just so happy. Mind you, we all cried when they made their vows. Charlie more than any of us. And everyone they invited tonight has turned up, as you can see. It's been the best day Jemima could have wished for."

"I'm really glad. This reception, with the fairground and the band and the fireworks is great, too. Truly, a day and night to remember. Everything a wedding should be."

"And not something that we'll ever know about unless we decide to settle for second best." Suzy raised her eyebrows. "Which I can't."

"Me neither."

Suzy smiled. "I saw your drop-dead-gorgeous Guy earlier and he wasn't with anyone. Well, he was with a lot of people dressed in black who looked like they might cause consternation if they turned up together in a bank, but no one who could be considered competition for you."

"Thanks. Well, things have changed quite a bit since we were last here — but not really in my favour. Not at all in my favour, actually. I've decided I'll really have to settle for being just good friends."

"Bummer . . . Mind you, I can't even do that with Luke. Difficult to be good friends when you haven't spoken for years and parted as enemies and there's thousands of miles between you."

Clemmie pushed the rest of her food to the side of her plate. That was that, then. Luke wasn't here and however magical the final stage of Seventh Heaven might be, it certainly couldn't work miracles.

The JB Roadshow plunged into a rousing version of 'Soul Finger' next door.

"They're really good, aren't they?" Suzy said. "I've been dancing with all the stable lads to the disco;

but I love a live band. And yes, before you ask, my leg still allows dancing. Maybe not quite as energetically as I used to, but I can still bop till I drop."

"Actually, I was wondering why, if Jemima and Charlie had booked a fair and a live soul band, both of which are wonderfully ear-splitting, they'd asked for a quiet firework display?"

"Because of the horses back in the village." Suzy pushed her plate away. "Horses can cope with solid, round, loud, constant noises like amplified music but, even at this distance, they spook at high-pitched screams and whistles and sudden sharp blasts of noise. Fireworks scare the shit out of most of them."

"Right — that's cleared that up," Clemmie laughed. "So are you going back into the dance tent now, or what?"

"Dancing, definitely. Then watching your fireworks, of course, and then some more dancing followed by some serious, serious drinking. It's really irritating — I've been knocking back champagne all day but I'm still boringly sober. What about you?"

"I'm sober and staying that way," Clemmie said as they stood up. "You can't play with fireworks when you're drunk. And as for the dancing — lead the way."

The wall of sound in the dance marquee nearly knocked Clemmie over.

The JB Roadshow, marvellously retro in their tight black velvet trousers and frilly satin shirts, were storming about on stage belting out an Otis Redding medley.

"Clemmie!" YaYa, bumping and grinding, waved wildly from the middle of an admiring crowd of dancers. "Over here!"

"Holy hell!" Suzy blinked.

"YaYa Bordello, my friend, we work together," Clemmie mouthed as, already dancing, they pushed through the gyrating mob towards YaYa. "YaYa meet Suzy."

They smiled cheerfully at one another, and continued dancing.

Otis Redding merged into Wilson Pickett and then into Eddie Floyd. Suzy, Clemmie and YaYa threw themselves into the dancing with wild abandon.

"There's the bride and groom! Over by the stage!" YaYa cupped her hand to Clemmie's ear. "They've slow-danced to every tune. Adorable, aren't they?"

Clemmie nodded. They certainly made a perfect couple. Jemima looked transformed, glowing with love, moving slowly to the music in Charlie's arms, as he gazed into her eyes. She was serene and beautiful in her classic wedding dress, every inch of her radiating love.

It brought a lump to Clemmie's throat.

She tapped YaYa on the arm. "I'm going to pop back to the site and see how they're doing. We've only got about ten minutes until the display starts. OK?"

YaYa nodded. "Me and Suzy will have another dance or two then I'll be up there to join you."

"Me too!" Suzy yelled above the chorus of 'Hold On, I'm Coming'. "I don't intend to miss a minute of it!"

Outside again, the drop in temperature was like plunging into an icy shower. Clemmie hurried through the laughing, noisy throng, pulling her deep-brown mohair cardigan round her, wishing she'd collected her coat from the cloakroom.

"I thought you'd forgotten all about me," Guy said as she arrived at the firing site. "Good meal?"

Clemmie, shivering, told him about the food, the music, and about meeting Suzy and their subsequent conversation.

"No chance of doing our magic act on her and Luke, then. Oh, well — it was a nice thought of yours. We'll just have to see if we'll need Seventh Heaven at Steeple Fritton, won't we? Although I'd still like to fire it tonight anyway, just to give Syd and the boys a thrill. Are you OK with that?"

"Perfectly. But what will you tell them?"

"Oh, nothing about the Magik Green — just that it's something you've developed as a private multishot firework, not for mass production, and wanted their opinion on. We'll keep it low-key — but they'll be blown away."

"Hopefully just by the colour of the final layer and not literally."

Guy laughed with her. "No, I couldn't cope with another incendiary accident like Slo Motion's little escapade. Clemmie — here — you're shivering. You must be freezing."

He wrapped his leather jacket round her shoulders.

"Thank you." Clemmie snuggled blissfully into the soft, worn leather, which smelled disconcertingly of

Guy. "Oh, that's lovely. I should have picked up my coat from the marquee. But what about you?"

"I'm fine. I'm wearing a T-shirt and another sweater under this." Guy plucked at his baggy black jumper. "And anyway I'm very hot-blooded."

She peered at him. Held her breath. Blushed at her thoughts.

"Guy!" Syd, accompanied by two more of the firing crew, marched across the field. "I've just started the countdown, and it looks as if the band's done what we asked and finished their set by telling everyone that the display's about to begin. There are about ten million people pouring out of the marquees and heading in this direction. You ready?"

"Ready." Guy nodded. "Clemmie, are you staying here to watch?"

She nodded, inhaling the aroma of his jacket, her fingers closing round the leather and stroking it in the darkness. "YaYa and Suzy will be able to find me here. Good luck."

"Cheers. I'll see you in about half an hour then."

As the first wedding guests arrived, laughing and chattering expectantly from the reception, Clemmie positioned herself behind the barrier and watched Guy walk away, absolutely itching to run after him and hurl herself into his arms.

More and more people appeared, their breath plumy in the chilly night air, their voices rising and falling above the fairground buzz, and Clemmie found herself squashed in between a large lady in a floral suit and ostrich-feather hat and a skinny boy in jeans and a padded jacket.

She smiled at the mixture: wealthy titled horse owner on one side and impoverished stable lad on the other. How very democratic. And so many people! Would YaYa and Suzy ever find her in this crush?

As always, The Gunpowder Plot had co-ordinated everything perfectly.

Guy led Charlie and Jemima, coats over their wedding finery, towards two golden chairs on a little raised dais in the centre. They looked like royalty. Everyone clapped and cheered.

"Ladies and gentlemen," Guy spoke into the microphone. "This display has been specially chosen by the bride and groom —" more cheers — "to delight and entertain you and help them celebrate their very special day." Huge whoops and catcalls. "But not to frighten the horses." More cheers and much laughter. "So, I hope you'll enjoy the spectacle that The Gunpowder Plot has prepared for you." Loud applause.

The boy beside Clemmie gave a shudder. She looked at him in concern. He was actually older than she'd first thought. Poor thing looked half-starved. So tiny and thin. It just went to prove what she was saying to YaYa earlier: the stable lads had a really hard life.

"Are you OK?"

He nodded. "Fine, yes. Thanks. Sorry, just too many ghosts here tonight."

Oh, Lord, Clemmie thought. Was he on drugs?

She gave him what she hoped was an encouraging smile. "Ghosts?"

"I used to live here, in Milton St John. It hasn't changed at all — oh, that's clever."

As Prokofiev's *Winter Bonfire* flooded the field, the pyro crew ignited the first quiet showpiece display firework, and everyone was gazing upwards as Silent Night sped softly into the sky, turning into tumbling glittering fish, then red and white falling leaves, followed by silver palms and multicoloured waxing and waning moons.

Clemmie felt a glow of pride on Guy's behalf. It was an absolutely beautiful combination.

"Used to live here?" she said to the boy, who she could see now was so emaciated that his cheekbones showed through his skin. "And are you on the groom's side or the bride's?"

"Neither," he told her with a grin. "I just gatecrashed."

"Oh, right . . ."

The display had moved on to a selection of huge comets which hung noiselessly in the sky, changing colour, twinkling and sparkling. The crowd adored it.

"I do know Charlie and Jemima. I knew them well years ago, but I only found out about the wedding two days ago and I thought it was now or never. It gave me a really good excuse to come back, you see. So, I arrived in the UK this afternoon. Arrived here about ten minutes ago. They don't know I'm here yet."

"I expect they'll be delighted to see you when they do," Clemmie said hopefully.

"Yeah — I — oh, great — that's cool."

298

The comets were replaced by silent volcanoes, hovering high above them, erupting into a dozen different colours.

Everyone clapped and whistled.

"I'm Clemmie," Clemmie said, deciding that this poor, skinny boy with the beautiful face deserved a show of friendship. "I'm part of the firework display team."

"Are you? Wow, what a brilliant job. Nice to meet you — I'm Luke Delaney."

Clemmie almost screamed in excitement. She almost missed the first sensational blast of Rossini's *La Danza Tarantella* and Guy's special silent Flower Power aerial floral display.

"Luke Delaney?" She stared at him. "Really? As in the Luke Delaney who used to go out with Suzy Beckett?"

He turned even more pale if that were possible and nodded. "Is she here? Do you know her? I looked and looked but there were so many people and I should have been in touch so many times, but I was always scared that she'd be — oh — she's not married is she? Or with someone? God, of course she will be by now."

Clemmie shook her head as everyone else was gasping at Silence is Golden exploding supernovas across the Berkshire sky.

"No, she's not married. Or with anyone. Yes, she's here." She took a deep breath. "Are you with your wife?"

"Haven't had one of those for nearly two years." Luke shrugged. "She ran off with someone older and richer. Luckily we didn't have kids. And anyway —"

"Anyway?" Clemmie managed to catch the end of Twinkle Twinkle Little Star as it cascaded down across the multitude of heads. "Anyway?"

"I never stopped loving Suzy. My wife knew it, even though I tried really, really hard not to show it or say anything. I tried so hard to be the husband she wanted me to be — but I don't blame her for leaving me."

"Nor do I. No woman wants to be second-best."

"Shit, I really shouldn't be talking to you like this and — oh, how lovely is that!"

Rossini's *Thieving Magpie* accompanied the final part of the display: three massive waterfalls of colour, covering three sides of the firing side, all glittering peaches and cream, changing walls of living colour. Then the lancework ignited — a huge heart with "Jemima and Charlie" picked out in dancing flames.

The crowd erupted with delight.

"Clemmie!" YaYa pushed her way through the throng, almost upending the large floral lady. "Blimey, love, what a crush! Why are you wearing Guy's jacket?"

"Where's Suzy?" Clemmie said urgently. "You haven't lost her?"

"No, she's right behind me somewhere. Why?"

"Doesn't matter — just grab her." Clemmie turned to Luke. "And you stay here — oh!"

Suzy had thrust her way through from the other side of the floral lady and was staring silently at Luke.

He stared silently back.

They were both pale, wide-eyed and looked as if they were going to faint.

"You weren't invited." Suzy shook her head. "You could have told me you were going to be here."

"Why?" Luke's voice was cold. "So you could ignore me again?"

"Well, given that you've been away from the village for years and you live in the States and you're married and —"

"Christ," Luke sighed. "Nothing's changed, has it?"

"Nothing in my life, no. One hell of a lot in yours."

"Suzy —"

"Forget it, Luke. Far too much water under far too many bridges."

"And whose fault is that?"

On the field, Guy was signalling to Clemmie that he was going to ignite Seventh Heaven.

"Come with me," Clemmie said, grabbing a stunned Suzy in one hand and a protesting Luke in the other, and practically dragging them under the barrier and into the middle of the firing site. "Quickly!"

"Stop it!" Suzy tried to drag her arm away. "Clemmie!"

"Don't argue with me, just do it. Trust me. Please."

"Clem!" YaYa screamed behind them. "Have you gone barking?"

"What the hell are you doing?" Guy asked as she reached him. "You can't bring members of the public in here, Clemmie, you know that."

"They're not members of the public. They're Luke and Suzy. And they're not exactly falling into one another's arms with rekindled joy. I think we need . . ."

Guy understood at once. "OK — yes we do."

Up on the podium, Jemima and Charlie were staring down at them, nudging each other, frowning in disbelief.

With a whoosh, Seventh Heaven exploded only feet away.

One by one, the fairy-tale layers burst into the sky, drawing screams of incredulity from the crowd, and stunned expressions from Syd and the pyro crew.

Suzy and Luke were still clearly completely confused, but, Clemmie noticed with a warm glow of satisfaction, he'd taken her hand during the scramble and she hadn't slapped him, bitten him or pulled away.

Sixth heaven — now . . .

She moved them gently towards the tumbling sparks.

"I wish that you, Suzy Beckett and Luke Delaney, would fall in love all over again and stay together forever and ever," Clemmie muttered. There was no time for thinking up words of great literary value. Time was of the essence. The Magik Green was already spurting emerald fire into the stratosphere. "Oh, and I wish that you'd get married and live happily ever after. There!"

As the first deep forest-green sparks trickled down around them, Clemmie looked at Guy.

He winked at her. "Go for it."

She went for it.

"Verdigris and verture pure
Sparks with nature's verdanture
Makes wishes forever endure."

"Luke . . ." Suzy dashed away her tears. "I'm so sorry. Can you ever forgive me?"

"Nothing to forgive." Luke pulled her into his arms. "Oh, God — I've missed you so much."

CHAPTER
TWENTY-TWO

"Suzy and Luke are getting married!" Clemmie sang, hurtling into The Gunpowder Plot's office on the cold, wet and windy Monday morning after Charlie and Jemima's wedding. "I can't wait to tell Guy! Suzy's just texted me!"

"Oh, cool! And bloody quick! Whirlwind, or what? They must have been red-hot for each other. Oh, and are we all going to be bridesmaids?" A back-to-blonde YaYa looked up from her computer. "I'd love to be a bridesmaid. I'd like to wear black net and a top hat and carry white lilies. Oh, but when is it? Not too soon, I hope? I've got so many drag gigs booked with the girls all round the festive period."

"No, we're not going to be bridesmaids." Clemmie thumped cheerfully down in her chair. "We're not even invited, so it won't interfere with your shows. They're just having both sets of parents, and Maddy and Drew as witnesses and their kids as sort of attendants. No one else. No fuss at all. Drinks for the entire village back at the Cat and Fiddle afterwards, and that's it. And it's next weekend. Special licence, Reading Registry Office." She sighed dreamily. "How romantic is that?"

"Five-star hearts and flowers romantic." YaYa leaned backwards on her chair. "But I'm still not sure I understand what was going on there."

Clemmie switched on her computer, playing for time. Neither she nor Guy had expanded on their part in the Suzy — Luke reunion, far less the massive part they both felt Allbard's Magik Green had played.

"Yes, you do. I told you. They were practically childhood sweethearts, lived together, split up years ago, stuff happened to them, but they never stopped loving one another and then —"

"I know all that," YaYa interrupted. "The bit I didn't get was you dragging them into the no-go zone and setting fire to that stupendous multishot at the same time. I quite expected Guy to kill you on the spot. That was madness."

"Hmmm, maybe . . ." Clemmie studied her emails. "I just got a bit carried away. Anyway, no harm done. Quite the opposite in fact."

"Yeah, I guess so. I really liked Suzy — great little mover — and she knew I was a bloke straight away but she didn't ask any daft questions. Just sensible ones. She'd never met a drag queen before."

"I wonder how she knew you were a man? I didn't, did I?"

YaYa shook her head. "She said it was my hands. She said they were too big."

"And you didn't mind?"

"No, love. It's always good to get feedback. As long as she didn't suss it from the face or the bod, I'm fine. I might have to start wearing lace mitts in public though." YaYa swirled round on her typist's chair. "You know the other thing that threw me about Jemima and Charlie's wedding bash?"

"What?"

"Guy saying you really designed that Seventh Heaven. All on your own. It was phenomenal. Syd's still going orgasmic over it."

Clemmie laughed. "I know. And yes, it's something I'd been dabbling with for a long time. But I wouldn't have been able to put it all together if Guy hadn't let me loose in the lab, though, so half the credit has to go to him. And we're never going to go commercial with it. We'll probably use it at suitable displays, but it's just for The Gunpowder Plot's private pleasure."

"Yeah, right." YaYa's eyebrows rocketed upwards. "You and Guy could make an absolute fortune with it if you went public."

"We don't want to. Truly. It was enough for me to know I could do it, and Guy's agreed to go with whatever I want to do with it. We've registered it as our invention, and applied for a pyro patent — just in case someone copies it — but that's as far as we're going."

"Daft bat," YaYa said kindly. "You could live in luxury for the rest of your life if you sold the idea to the Chinese."

"Not going to happen," Clemmie assured her happily. "So — what have we got planned for today?"

"Christmas decorations, love. We're already into December and this place badly needs a bit of seasonal tarting. And as Guy and the crew are away today, now's as good a time as any."

306

"Great," Clemmie enthused. "I suddenly feel all seasonal and filled with good cheer. I bet the boathouse looks fantastic decorated for Christmas. I can just see it with all the traditional trimmings in the living room, huge Christmas tree by the fire, the halls decked with boughs of holly."

"We just have the same cheap baubles and old tat as everyone else, love. Get a grip for heaven's sake. I know you're all bushy-tailed over Suzy and Luke getting hitched, but even so . . ."

Clemmie wrinkled her nose. "I'm just really pleased for them. We'll have to send them a card — oh, and talking of Christmas, do you have a works' Christmas party?"

YaYa shook her head. "Not something we've ever bothered with, mainly because the job itself is more-or-less partying all the time. We just turn up at other people's bashes all through the year — and get paid for it."

"Hmm, yes, I hadn't thought of it like that. So what do you do here about presents? Do you have a Secret Santa?"

YaYa looked at her pityingly. "Not a lot of point, love, seeing as it's usually just me and Guy. The Secret Santa concept would be a bit de trop in that situation, if you get my drift."

"Do we just buy each other presents then? It's always such a tricky area in a new job, knowing what to do."

"Guy'll whack a huge bonus in your pay packet, love, that's his way of saying Happy Christmas, and he certainly won't expect anything in return. But if you

307

want to buy me a little trinket, I wouldn't say no to a pair of Butler and Wilson earrings . . ."

"Only if you're a very good girl," Clemmie told her. "Now, where does Guy keep the dekkies?"

With Suggs' help, once Clemmie had phoned Guy with the Luke-Suzy-wedding news, she and YaYa spent the next couple of hours combining decorating every inch of the boathouse, residential and business, with answering the phone.

"We've got loads of bookings before and after the Christmas period." Clemmie looked at the diary. "Don't you ever have time off?"

"Oh, yes, love. Me and Guy both manage to snatch a few days. This year I'm performing with Honey and Foxy on a series of localish one-night stands right up to Christmas Eve, then I'm going home to Brighton for a couple of days with my mum and dad — What? What's so funny?"

"Nothing," Clemmie bit her lip, trying to disentangle an overexcited Suggs from a strand of tinsel. "I just suppose I didn't think about you having parents."

"God almighty, love. What did you think I had?"

"I don't know . . . sorry . . ."

"My dad's a welder and my mum works in Asda," YaYa said. "I've got four sisters and a brother, all straight and all still living at home. We have a great family Christmas, thank you very much."

"Sounds lovely. So does Guy stay here on his own?"

"Nah — he usually manages to get a few days with his folks as well. They live just along the coast from mine, more Hove way. A bit more snooty, love."

Clemmie shook her head. "I didn't think about him having parents either, actually. I never give anyone's parents much thought at all. I suppose it's because mine live so far away and haven't been part of my immediate life for the last fifteen years."

"Guy's parents are weird." YaYa gently removed a stray bauble from Suggs' inquisitive paws. "Posh. Not like him at all. They threw a fit when he turned Goth, I can tell you. Didn't go down at all well at the Tory shindigs. His dad works in a bank. Investment not high street. His mum's a teacher."

"Chemistry?"

"Children."

"Ha-ha-ha."

"She teaches domestic science as it was called in my day, love — God knows what PC name they have for it now — to posh kids. All I know is Guy blames it on his total inability to walk into a kitchen without wanting to scream and run amok and dirty things before stabbing someone with an entire set of Sabatier knives."

Clemmie laughed. "He did say he wasn't in the least domesticated, but not why. I guess that explains it. And does he have brothers and sisters, too?"

"He's an only child. Spoilt rotten. I think they intended him to become something big in the city. You have to admit, there's a delicious irony about calling your only son Guy — and he ends up running an outfit called The Gunpowder Plot. Ma and Pa Devlin sadly failed to see the funny side."

"Did they try to stop him becoming a pyrotechnician, then?"

"Not really. It was the same as with the way he dressed and used make-up when he was a kid. Even though they really loathed the Goth stuff, they put up with it rather than risk him leaving home. Indulged to the hilt, that boy. That's why he and I got on so well together at school: enough differences to make us interesting to one another but also enough in common to make us friends. The best basis for any relationship, really."

"And do you see Guy's parents much?"

"Once in a blue moon or less, love. They've never really liked me. Can't think why."

Clemmie giggled.

"Mind you," YaYa posed in front of the mirror wearing a tinsel tiara and two flashing angels as earrings, "they hate Suggs even more than they hate me. But they have to have him to stay for the festivities — no Suggs, no Guy. What about you, love? Do you ever go and see your parents at Christmas?"

"Not usually. I last went about four years ago and it was lovely. They have asked me to go this year — they always ask — but it's so far away and the flights are a nightmare, and I feel rotten leaving Auntie Molly and Uncle Bill on their own. Not that they are, because they have open house over Christmas for all the lost and lonely souls of Bagley. It usually looks like a Hollywood director's idea of a Dickensian soup kitchen."

Clemmie started to pack away the leftover decorations. She'd sort of hoped that Guy would be at home in Winterbrook over Christmas, and that she could pop in with a suitable small present and a humorous card and they'd have mulled wine by the fire and share mince pies and . . .

She really would have to get a grip on her fantasies.

"Guy shuts the office down for most of Christmas as all the bookings we're able to take are in by then," YaYa continued. "The Gunpowder Plot's got that small private party gig in Newbury tonight, and that's the last booking until New Year's Eve so Guy'll be heading off tomorrow for Christmas in the scrupulously clean minimalist hell that is Devlin Towers. Then we've got the Rotary Club's do on the thirty-first in Winterbrook, which both Guy and I will be back for, then there's the rock concert in Hampshire straight after, which he'll do with Syd and the entire pyro crew so won't need either of us. God knows who'll want to be at a rock concert in January, but clearly they think there's a market So, if you want to take time off, it shouldn't be a problem."

"Yes, I might." Clemmie finished packing away the last of the decorations. "It'd be nice to spend some time with Molly and Bill and have a couple of wild nights out with my friends — and my best mate, Phoebe, is having a flat-warming party early in the New Year, so I could give her a hand with that, too. Shall I ask Guy if it'd be OK to be off from say just before Christmas Eve for a couple of weeks?"

"Just put it in the diary, love. He'll be fine with it. You've worked your socks off over the last couple of months, nights and weekends, and put in more unpaid overtime than anyone should do. And as Christmas Eve is a Monday we'll be all but finished on the Friday before, so you might as well finish that day, too. You deserve a decent break."

Clemmie scribbled a note in the diary saying she'd be on leave from 21 December until 7 January but if it wasn't convenient, she'd be happy to cancel it.

She looked at the dates. Over two weeks. Over two weeks without seeing Guy. It was far, far too long.

The next almost-three weeks flew by in a flurry of Christmas preparations, which involved shopping both alone and with YaYa, who turned it into an eye-opening art form; cooking Christmas goodies with Auntie Molly; and working and playing hard in equal measure.

Clemmie spent an evening with Phoebe and Ben in their new flat, and a couple of pre-Christmas nights out clubbing with her girlfriends in Reading, drinking too many tequilas and regretting it the next day.

Her gifts to her parents were posted; all her deliver-by-hand presents were bought and wrapped, including YaYa's required earrings, a Christmas stocking of ferret treats for Suggs, and a present for Guy which she knew she probably ought not give him but simply couldn't resist.

Anyway, she consoled herself, it's only a jokey thing — nothing personal — even the most cynical man couldn't read anything into it. It was merely a gift from one science nerd to another, wasn't it?

The tiny solar-powered rainbow maker, she felt, would satisfy both Guy's love of colour and his scientific streak. The window-mounted demonstration model in the Winterbrook shop had fascinated her, and she'd watched for ages as the weak winter sun fired the rainbow maker's miniature solar panel-powered motor, which in turn rotated the attached Swarovski Crystals, and the whole shop had been flooded with moving, dancing, brilliantly coloured rainbow prisms.

Guy, she was sure, would be as mesmerised by it as she had been.

"It's a shame," Guy said on the Friday before Christmas when YaYa had left for the last of her shows with Foxy and Honey Bunch, and they were alone in the office, "that your friend's flat-warming party clashes with the rock concert. I'd have liked to have come along — so would YaYa."

"Mmmm." Clemmie was slowly tidying her desk. "They'd have liked to meet you, too." Understatement, especially as far as Phoebe was concerned. But a great get-out regarding the YaYa/Steve thing. "But there'll be other times, I'm sure. Right — that's me done here. What about the storage sheds and the lab? Do you want a final stock-check done before the New Year?"

"No, you've worked wonders in there. Even I can find things I didn't know I had, and the computerised cataloguing of the chemicals works a treat. Syd and the crew say they don't know how we managed without you — and I'm not sure, either." Guy leaned back in YaYa's chair, cuddling Suggs, and looked through the window at the lashing rain and the swollen, tearing river. "No signs of a white Christmas — just a dark, cold, grey one."

"It'll probably snow in March as usual." Clemmie packed her capacious boho handbag, remembering to include the gaudily wrapped present YaYa had left for her. She felt it might be politic to open it in private and not in the general family present-unwrapping at the Post Office Stores on Christmas morning. Just in case. "We'll probably have a white Easter instead. So, I'll see you next year, then. I've left presents for YaYa and Suggs under the Christmas tree." She'd still got the rainbow maker in her bag. She'd intended to hand it to him as she left so there could be no embarrassment. "Have a great Christmas — and thanks — for everything."

Guy shook his head. "It's me who should be thanking you. It's been great having you here. No, more than that. You've made such a difference to everything and everyone here and it's been —"

The phone interrupted what might have been.

"The Gunpowder Plot. Guy Devlin speaking. How may I help you?"

Clemmie stood up, stroked Suggs, and mouthed a silent goodbye to Guy.

"Hi — what? Bloody hell!" He frowned into the phone, running his fingers though his hair. "And you didn't think to tell me earlier? Right, I see, no — of course you couldn't . . . Sorry. No — no — you do whatever you think is right. Of course I'll be OK." His fingers twisted the slender ebony necklace in agitation. "In fact, I'll be more than OK — no, you have a good time. Yes, of course I can make alternative arrangements. Yes — and you . . . Cheers . . ."

Clemmie pulled a face. "Problems? Work?"

"Family." Guy swirled round in the chair. "That was my dad. He and Mum have just been offered an eleventh hour chance to join a winter cruise. Someone dropped out, the tickets are transferable and going begging. Three weeks in the Caribbean."

"Nice . . ."

"They leave Southampton tomorrow. Which means they won't be home over Christmas. Which means I'm at a bit of a loose end."

Clemmie said nothing. A million rather wickedly pleasant possibilities were squirming their way through her brain. She tried very hard to ignore them.

Guy shrugged. "In a way, it's a good thing. I'm always pleased to see them but also itching to leave within twenty-four hours. It's never, well, full of festive cheer and bursting with God rest ye, merry gentlemen at our house over the Christmas period. There's always far too much dressing for dinner, and obligatory church, and endless sherry with the neighbours."

"And you wouldn't just go home and stay in the house on your own?"

"No point." He shook his head. "And I'd hate it. So would Suggs. It's not like going home — it's like living in a white antiseptic box where you're scared to touch anything."

"Couldn't you stay with YaYa's family?"

"No way! Her sisters would eat me alive — and her mum's already had a go. More than once." Guy grinned. "Anyway, there are so many of them packed into that little house and they've got dogs and Suggs wouldn't be able to settle. No, I'll just have to go and do a bit of a last-minute shop in Winterbrook, then we'll be fine here with a frozen Christmas dinner and a microwaved Christmas pud and lovely trash on the telly. After all, it's only for a couple of days. I'm quite looking forward to it already."

"As long as you'll be OK."

"I'm a grown-up," Guy assured her. "Well, almost. No, I'll be absolutely fine. Anyway, I'm sure you've got loads of stuff to do at home, so I won't keep you."

"All right — take care — and thanks again. Oh, and do have a happy Christmas, and a lovely New Year."

"And you, Clemmie. 'Bye."

She'd just reached the office door when she remembered the rainbow maker. She stopped. "I've got something —"

Guy spoke at the same time. "Just a thought — say no if you've already got something planned . . . Sorry, I interrupted you. What were you saying?"

"Nothing at all." her fingers closed round the present in her bag. "Planned? For when?"

"Tomorrow evening. As I'm going to be here on my own now, and not doing the Driving Home For Christmas thing, I wondered if you'd like to come here and have a meal with me and Suggs. As my way of saying thank you for so many things, not least Seventh Heaven. Oh, it'll be nothing fancy — pick a takeaway menu sort of thing. I wouldn't inflict my cooking on you."

"Your fry-up was lovely." Clemmie tried to keep her tone neutral. Difficult when her entire body was skipping and shouting and doing cartwheels. "One of the best I've ever had."

"You're very kind, and maybe it's the only thing I can cook without setting fire to myself, but even I wouldn't offer a fry-up as an evening meal." Guy put Suggs on the floor and then shook his head. "God! Sorry, Clemmie — I'm being a complete prat here. Just because I'm a sad singleton by choice, I forget that other people have normal relationships. YaYa is still always telling me how dreamy you go over your 'cute boy'. Of course, you'll be going out with him tomorrow night and even if you weren't, he probably wouldn't be too happy about you coming here. With the hours we work, I'm sure he thinks I keep you away from him far too much as it is and —"

"I'd love to."

"Really? And he wouldn't mind?"

"Not at all. In fact YaYa shouldn't —" Clemmie stopped. It was definitely the wrong time to admit the "cute boy" existed purely in YaYa's imagination, and even gobsmackingly worse timing if she admitted now to Guy who the real "cute boy" was. "I'd love to come, thank you. About sevenish? Or is that too early?"

"That'd be great. Then we can decide whether it's to be Indian or Chinese or a pizza — or whatever else the more exotic carryouts can offer."

And I can give you the rainbow maker, Clemmie thought blissfully, and if the invite includes a fry-up for breakfast, then that will make this the best Christmas of my life.

She smiled. "It sounds fantastic — I'll see you tomorrow then. At seven."

CHAPTER
TWENTY-THREE

The next day passed agonisingly slowly. Clemmie, watching the clock, could almost swear the hands were turning backwards.

All day, her fantasies had raced out of control however hard she tried not to let them. What if . . . What if . . .

Guy had been hurt and disillusioned in his previous liaisons, particularly his short-lived marriage — but what had YaYa said? Something about close friendship being the best basis for any relationship?

And she and Guy were certainly friends, weren't they? And they already shared far more than that: their love of chemistry, the success of Seventh Heaven, the secret of Allbard's Magik Green . . .

Maybe, just maybe, tonight would move their relationship on from work-friendly to something altogether more exciting. After all, Guy wouldn't have invited her if he hadn't wanted to spend time with her, alone, would he?

Pushing away all these thoughts, and many more which were heading towards X-ratings, Clemmie tried to stay calm.

Unable to decide what to wear, she'd upended her entire wardrobe across her bedroom.

"Good heavens," Auntie Molly exclaimed as she peered in through the half-open door. "Are you having a pre-Christmas clear-out? Are you taking it all to Biff and Hedley Pippin's charity shop? If so, I'll sort out some bits and pieces too — and your Uncle Bill has dozens of shirts dating back to the nineteen-seventies which he'd still wear if I let him."

"I'm not clearing out," Clemmie laughed. "I'm trying to find something suitable to wear. Guy's asked me to have a meal with him tonight."

"Oooh!" Molly's eyes glistened. "Now that's exciting. Are you going to some swish restaurant? In town? But what about that nice long-haired chap — Steve — won't his nose be out of joint?"

"Steve won't care one way or the other," Clemmie said truthfully, "and Guy's just asked me for an informal supper at his place. We're not going out."

Auntie Molly's eyes gleamed a bit more. "Aha! Do I sense a bit of a romance here? A cosy dinner for two at home sounds pretty snug to me."

"Well, it isn't. Honestly. Guy's my boss, we're good friends, but there's no romance. None at all. I promise you."

At least, Clemmie thought with a delicious frisson of excitement, not yet . . .

Molly sighed. "How disappointing . . . First Steve and now Guy. Both 'just people I work with. Just good friends'. How very boring of you Clemmie! Oh, well, if that's really the case I don't suppose it matters what you wear really then, as long as you look clean and tidy."

Clean and tidy? Clemmie thought as her aunt disappeared. That was the last thing she had in mind for tonight. Vampish and sexy was what she hoped to achieve.

Would the Rinky-Dink antique frock look too over-the-top and desperate? Yes, definitely. What about the long black satin skirt, with the net underskirt and the silver top that slithered constantly from her shoulders? Far, far too obvious. OK, then, what about . . .

By half-past five, Floris-bathed, with her hair washed and dried in a snaking glossy cloud of dark red curls, and her make-up applied with theatrical precision, Clemmie had finally settled on her long purple crushed velvet frock and her best purple boots, and the purple and silver earrings that practically touched her shoulders.

"Oh, my!" Molly grinned. "You look lovely, Clemmie. Really lovely. Are you sure there's not a little bit of a twinkle in Guy Devlin's eye?"

"None at all." Clemmie pulled on her coat, pushed the rainbow maker into her boho bag, and picked up the bottle of champagne she'd bought from Big Sava. Not an own-label bottle, but Moët et Chandon. Of course, because she was driving she'd only be able to have one glass. However, if she was invited to stay for breakfast . . . "And there never will be. Or in mine, so don't go thinking in terms of a wedding outfit."

"As if . . ."

"I've got my key. No idea when I'll be home, but I'll try not to wake you."

"Drive safely," Uncle Bill cautioned as he kissed her. "It's a filthy night out there. Absolutely hissing down."

It was, but Clemmie didn't mind the screaming wind and torrential rain as, turning the windscreen wipers on to max, she drove blissfully through the darkness towards Winterbrook, singing along to Kasabian and trying to ignore the butterflies turning somersaults in her stomach. She was going to be very early, but that wouldn't matter, would it? It wasn't like this was a formal evening or a proper date or anything . . .

Parking outside the boathouse tonight was easy, with YaYa's 4×4 absent, and Guy's BMW obviously parked out of sight with The Gunpowder Plot vans at the far side of the gravel drive for the Christmas break, so Clemmie pulled up almost touching the steps. At least she'd be able to reach the front door from here without looking too much like a drowned rat.

There was a faint glow in the living room window — Christmas tree lights? Candles? Firelight?

Any of them hinted tantalisingly at cosy romance and a perfect setting for a getting-to-know-you-better evening, didn't they? She tried hard not to clap her hands in delighted anticipation.

Taking a deep breath, counting slowly to three and then exhaling, Clemmie unfastened her seat belt, grabbed her bag in one hand and the champagne in the other, and hurtled out of the Peugeot through the wind and rain.

322

Having rung the front doorbell she wondered if she should have gone round to the back of the boathouse and used what YaYa always referred to as the tradesman's entrance: the back door they all used every morning to make the shortcut between the office and the outhouses.

No, not tonight. Tonight was different. After tonight, maybe nothing would ever be the same again . . .

Shivering, she sheltered further into the porch. The wind tore at her hair and the rain, blowing horizontally across the invisible roar of the river, smacked irritating ice-cold splatters against her face. If Guy didn't open the door soon she'd look like the Wild Woman of Borneo's much scruffier sister.

She rang the bell again, her mouth dry with expectation, her heart doing a rather reckless whoopee-doo! tap-dance under her ribs.

At last the hall light flicked on and the door opened.

Clemmie held her breath. Her heart danced the salsa.

"Yes?" Helen, looking several million dollars in sprayed-on jeans tucked into immaculate stilt-heeled black boots and a tiny black cashmere sweater, flicked at her blonde hair. "Who is it? Oh, Clemmie — how nice . . ."

Clemmie was frozen to the spot. Words formed in her brain but never quite made it to her lips.

"Oh, champagne!" Helen removed the bottle from Clemmie's paralysed hand. "How thoughtful — not my usual brand, but scrummy nonetheless. What a nice gesture, a little festive gift. I'm sure Guy will be touched."

"Guy . . .?" Clemmie managed to co-ordinate her brain and tongue at last. "Is he here?"

"Busy . . ." Helen gurgled, giving the one word a full 18 certificate rating. "I'll tell him you called. I won't keep you."

Behind her in the dimly lit hallway, Crap, Puke, Snot and Mungo, suddenly erupted noisily from the living room and tore through towards the kitchen.

"Bet there's not a bloody Wii in any of those bloody presents!"

"If I've got a bastard book token I'll frigging spit!"

"Mum-mee! I'm sooo bored!"

"Hello, Clemmie. How nice to see you again. Merry Christmas. I hope you have a lovely time."

Ivo, Clemmie thought dazedly, still magicked.

"Poor Ivo is still in therapy. We haven't got to the bottom of his trauma yet."

Clemmie said nothing. What was there to say? Ivo's "trauma" reminded her of Guy. Every bloody thing reminded her of Guy. The rest of her life was going to be a relentless round of heart-breaking reminders.

"The children are sooo overexcited tonight," Helen explained. "And they're not the only ones — but for entirely different reasons, of course. Now, let me wish you season's greetings and send you on your way before the weather really closes in. I can see you've made a bit of an effort with your appearance so you must be going on somewhere nice and I wouldn't want to delay you. I'll let Guy know you called, of course."

324

Determined not to cry in public, or scream, or hurl herself to the ground and beat her fists into the wet gravel, Clemmie stretched her cold, stiff lips into a rictus smile. "Yes, do. And I wasn't expecting to see you here —"

"I couldn't leave him alone at Christmas, could I? As soon as he knew his folks were going to be away he was on the phone begging me to come and stay. Guy can be so persuasive. There's still a spark there, of course . . ."

Clemmie felt very sick.

Helen removed a strand of ash-blonde hair from her lip-gloss and peered over Clemmie's shoulder. "Oh, you've still got that old Peugeot. Did you see my car?"

"No! If I had, I'd —"

Shut up, Clemmie, she shouted at herself. Just shut up.

"Of course you were probably looking for the Jag, weren't you?"

Clemmie, who obviously hadn't been looking for anything, shook her head.

"I got rid of the old one last week," Helen purred. "It was too embarrassing to be seen on the school run with last year's model. The children were mortified and I was so afraid they might be bullied. The new one's parked over there. Nice, isn't it?"

Swallowing the mixture of bitter disappointment, agonising pain and tearing fury which was in danger of choking her, Clemmie turned round and flew through the storm, slamming into the relative sanctuary of the Peugeot.

Helen, she noticed, was smiling triumphantly as she closed the door.

"Noooo!" Clemmie screamed, thumping her fists against the steering wheel. "How could he do that — to me? The bastard! I hate him! And Helen! But mostly him — I bloody hate him!!!!"

And blindly crashing the gears, she kangaroo-hopped the Peugeot away from the boathouse.

Dashing away her angry tears, she stopped at the roadwork traffic lights on the outside of Winterbrook and wondered where on earth she could go. Not home. It was far too early, and also Molly and Bill would be sympathetic and kind which would make everything even worse.

The windscreen wipers slashed backwards and forwards, mocking her; the red light was faint and blurred by the teeming rain, the effect increased by her tears.

Driving around in this weather and this state of mind was lunacy, Clemmie realised. She was in no fit condition to drive anywhere. But where was there to go? All her friends were in couples and she simply couldn't face that sort of togetherness. Not tonight.

But Phoebe was different, wasn't she? She'd known Phoebe and Ben since childhood. They wouldn't mind her crashing in on them for an hour of shoulder-soaking. Not, Clemmie decided as the lights turned green and she drove away from the roadworks towards Hazy Hassocks, that she was ever going tell Phoebe the whole sad story.

No way.

Eventually managing to find a parking space in the dark and wet Winchester Road, Clemmie hurried up Phoebe's path and rang the bell. Maybe they were out. Maybe she should have phoned first.

Phoned . . . Why the hell hadn't Guy phoned her to tell her that he'd changed his plans and invited Helen to stay?

Why? Clemmie clenched her teeth. Because he wanted to make damn sure she knew where she stood, of course! That was it. He knew that Clemmie was stupidly in love with him, and had chosen this abominably cruel way to make sure she backed off and left him alone.

The cruel, evil, heartless bastard.

Phoebe opened the door. "Clemmie! God — you're soaking! Er, come in."

Clemmie shuffled into Phoebe's neat hall. In the few weeks she and Ben had lived here, they'd transformed it into a chic, immaculate home. It was very Phoebe, Clemmie thought, with clean pale colours, no knick-knacks, and absolutely nothing out of place. She couldn't have lived comfortably in it for more than ten minutes.

Seeming somewhat agitated, Phoebe ushered her into their living room, which was stylishly decorated for Christmas in various shades of designer cream and gold.

"Hi." Ben, as neat and blond and organised as Phoebe, looked up from the chair beside the modern white gas fire. "Oh, Clemmie — you're drowned. Er — were we expecting you?"

Clemmie stared at them, the rain dripping from her hair and trickling down her face. "Oh, Lord, I'm so sorry — I won't stop."

For the first time, she registered that both Phoebe and Ben were dressed for a black tie event. Phoebe looked wonderful in a floor-length black evening dress; Ben was equally impressive in his tux and bow tie.

"Sorry, Clem, but our cab'll be here at any minute. It's Ben's works' dinner and dance tonight. You should have phoned . . ."

"Yes . . . yes . . . I'm sorry. Stupid of me."

"Clem?" Phoebe peered at her. "Look, if there's something really wrong, Ben can go in the cab, I'll catch him up later."

Ben didn't look as though he was very thrilled with this idea.

"Don't be daft." Clemmie stretched a smile. "I'm fine — just at a bit of a loose end and I — I was going to see if you wanted to come out for a pre-Christmas drink. I should have phoned. Silly of me — I'll go now."

"Are you sure you're OK?" Phoebe looked concerned. "Has something happened? You've been crying, haven't you?"

"No! It's just the wind making my eyes water — and the rain — and —"

"That sounds like the taxi." Ben stood up, making little jerking motions with his head.

Clemmie sniffed and tried to smile. "Right, I'm off. You have a lovely time and I'll catch up with you over Christmas."

"Actually, we won't be here." Phoebe fumbled with her jacket and bag. "We're dividing ourselves between my parents and Ben's family. Still, you'll be at our flat-warming, won't you?"

"Yes — wouldn't miss it for the world." Clemmie headed miserably for the front door. "'Bye Ben, and Phoebes, have a lovely Christmas."

"You too, Clem. 'Bye."

Half an hour later, having driven aimlessly round and round a wet and windy Hazy Hassocks, with its deserted streets and bedraggled Christmas decorations, Clemmie knew she had to go back to Bagley.

She couldn't stay out like this, feeling as she did, looking so awful. On her own. And like Phoebe and Ben, all her friends would be with their respective partners, doing something wonderfully festive on this last Friday before Christmas.

She had never felt more alone in her life.

Praying that Molly and Bill would be out at the Barmy Cow, or hermetically sealed in the living room watching the television and wouldn't hear her come in, Clemmie headed back towards Bagley-cum-Russet.

Of course, she'd have to leave The Gunpowder Plot. She couldn't work with Guy now. Not with Helen and children in situ, her very presence mocking all Clemmie's hopes and dreams. Not knowing that Guy thought she was just another sad and needy and pathetic woman like Tarnia Snepps and all the others.

Sod him to hell! He'd not only broken her heart and destroyed all her foolish romantic daydreams, but he'd also made it impossible for her to continue working in the one job she'd wanted all her life.

In one stroke she'd lost not only the man she loved — loved? Hah! Been stupidly infatuated with, more like! — but also the best job in the world.

And then there were YaYa and Suggs.

Pulling up outside the Post Office Stores, Clemmie felt as desolate as the icy December weather.

Christmas . . .

She couldn't stay here and pretend everything was all right and join in all the joyous traditional things when her heart was breaking, could she? Couldn't face two weeks with her aunt and uncle who'd *know* however hard she tried to disguise her misery. Couldn't meet up with her friends, all glowing with love and blissfully happy in their relationships.

She simply couldn't.

She crept into the house, not disturbing Molly and Bill who thankfully were glued to something amusing on the television judging by the guffaws echoing from behind the living room door, and stumbled upstairs.

Quickly ripping off the purple dress and the boots and the earrings, and hurling her bag across the bedroom, Clemmie wrapped herself in her fluffy dressing gown, switched on the television, and lay on her bed, trying to get warm.

Flicking through the programmes, she winced at the seasonal laughter, the gaiety, the happiness. She snapped the television into silence and fumbled in her bag for her mobile.

330

Huh! Three missed messages — all from Guy. Clearly making sure that she'd got the only message that mattered to him.

She looked at the contents of her handbag strewn across the bed. Sad, sad cow!

The rainbow maker, in its carefully chosen multicoloured wrapping, lay in the middle of the chaotic heap of her foolishness: her make-up bag, her face wipes, her deodorant, her toothbrush, her moisturiser and her clean underwear. All the stuff she'd thrust into her bag in the expectation of staying overnight at the boathouse.

All tangible reminders of her blind stupidity.

She had to get away from all this.

Wiping her eyes on her dressing gown sleeve, Clemmie rolled from the bed and switched on her computer. Thank the Lord for Bill Gates and MasterCard.

Less than an hour later she'd booked a flight from Heathrow to Inverness the next day, sorted out regional transfers, and spoken to her mother, who'd been wildly excited and delightedly volunteered to drive down and collect her for the final stage of the tortuous journey to Thurso.

She was going home for Christmas.

CHAPTER
TWENTY-FOUR

January was simply the worst month of Clemmie's life. The cold, grey, wet and windy weather persisted. The only cheerful thing about the New Year was the clutch of photos which had arrived from Milton St John. Luke and Suzy, warmly dressed, gazing at one another, outside the registry office after their marriage ceremony; their smiles and eyes simply scorching with total happiness and mutual love.

Apart from that, everything was, Clemmie felt, unremittingly gloomy and hopeless.

She returned to The Gunpowder Plot on the morning of the seventh, her resignation letter in her handbag.

Guy wasn't there. Neither was Helen.

Suggs scampered excitedly from his sofa bed and scrabbled at her knees until she picked him up and cuddled him. His eyes, circled by his dark bandit's mask, were almost as sad as her own.

YaYa, coming into the office from the kitchen, greeted her with such an overwhelming enthusiasm that it made her want to cry all over again. Hugging, they thanked each other for their presents.

YaYa was wearing Clemmie's Christmas present earrings. Clemmie wasn't wearing YaYa's present of gorgeous but extremely scanty La Perla bra and knickers.

Fortunately, after the exchange of pleasantries, YaYa's non-stop résumé of her festive gigs with Honey Bunch and Foxy, and full details of her riotous family Christmas, meant that Clemmie didn't have to say much at all.

She briefly told YaYa about going to Scotland "on a whim" and said it was lovely. Which it had been, even if the travelling had been exhausting.

Her parents had been absolutely delighted to see her, and she them. They'd had a quiet family Christmas with all the trimmings, and she'd met their friends, and had been taken to every amazing beauty spot the Highlands had to offer within a thirty-mile radius. And it had snowed and she'd experienced the happy mayhem of a proper Scottish Hogmanay.

Most importantly, she'd almost been able to shut all the hideousness of her humiliation out of her mind for the entire duration of her stay. Almost, but not quite.

It was impossible to wipe Guy out of her heart and her head, and his face was the last thing she saw before going to sleep each night, and the first thing she thought of when she woke each morning.

And then she'd remembered the pain, and tried not to let her sorrow show.

Molly and Bill had been startled at her last-minute change of heart regarding her festive plans, but hadn't shown any real reluctance at her going. They always felt she should visit her parents more often.

"Bit of a dead time here, after Christmas," Ya Ya said, as they removed the decorations. "Might as well get shot of these — there's no point in waiting for Twelfth Night in my opinion. Damn silly when it's all over isn't it, love?"

Clemmie nodded. All over . . . Awful words.

"And there's no gigs, either firework or drag, because no one's got any money. We usually just spend the month tidying up and stock-taking and sending out the new season's flyers and catalogues and waiting for the slightly better weather and slightly less broke punters." Ya Ya pulled a face and lit a cigarette. "I hate bloody January. And I don't know about you, love, but my resolutions have already bitten the dust. As you can see. I stopped smoking for twenty-three hours. Yours doing any better?"

Clemmie, painfully reminded as she removed Suggs from the bauble box how blissfully happy she'd been just a few weeks previously when they'd excitedly enrobed the boathouse with glitz and glitter, muttered that she hadn't made any resolutions at all.

Ya Ya shrugged, blowing a plume of smoke across the room. "Probably the best way. Mind you," she paused in winding tinsel into a ball one-handed, "I sure as shit hope Guy's made at least one."

Clemmie didn't look up. "Why?"

"Because he's been as miserable as sin ever since I came back. I hope he's resolved to cheer up a bit. He

334

won't tell me what's up — and he always tells me everything. I know he couldn't go to his parents for Christmas, but I can't see that that would be any reason for him to be so bloody bad-tempered. Quite the opposite, in fact."

Clemmie said nothing at all.

"Did you two have a row, love?" YaYa peered at her. "When I wasn't here? Did anything happen?"

"No."

"Sure?"

"Positive."

"Right . . . So it isn't that," she sighed. "I really don't know what his problem is. And if you don't mind me saying so, you don't look as though your break has done you much good, either. You look like you haven't slept for a month."

"Probably jet lag," Clemmie tried to joke. "It's a long way to Caithness. And I was at Phoebe's party on Friday night, practically from stepping off the plane."

"Lucky you," YaYa said. "We were freezing our bits off at the rock concert — which was a virtual bloody wash-out. I got a backstage pass and didn't recognise any of the bands. It made me feel sooo old, love, you wouldn't believe. They were *children*. They weren't even speaking my language. And most of the audience went home at half-time and didn't even see the fireworks. And Guy — well! You'd think someone had given him a humour bypass."

Clemmie shrugged. She didn't care. If Guy was unhappy because Helen was making his life hell all over again, then it was all he deserved.

"Where is he today?"

"No idea, love. Work, I think. Sussing out a new site, probably. He's barely spoken two words to me since I came back from Brighton. I thought it was something I'd done, but he said no. So if it's not me and it's not you, God knows what or who it is."

Clemmie knew but she wasn't going to say so. No way. Guy would tell YaYa what a sad deluded cow Clemmie was in his own good time. Long after she'd left The Gunpowder Plot, she hoped.

The phone rang. They both dived for it. YaYa got there first.

"Who, love? Oh, right — yes, love. Hi. No, he's not here at the moment. Can I help you? No? Yes, I'll tell Guy as soon as he comes in and get him to ring you. Thanks, love. 'Bye."

"Who was that?" Clemmie asked listlessly. It didn't matter any more. She wouldn't be here much longer. Nothing that happened at The Gunpowder Plot would concern her.

"Ellis Blissit, the secret wedding bloke from Steeple Fritton. Wanted to speak to Guy. Didn't want to talk to me. Sounded OK though — wanted to tell Guy he'd changed his mind about the firework music if it wasn't too late, so the secret must still be a secret and the wedding must still be on."

"Good."

Clemmie picked up a stray drawing pin before Suggs could eat it. Her eyes hurt. They'd had such fun in Steeple Fritton, and she'd been so looking forward to seeing Ellis and Lola's wedding fireworks; and of course, because it was also Guy's birthday, hopefully sharing his celebration too.

Now she'd have left here long before then and would never know what happened. Never know if Lola became Mrs Blissit. Never know if Guy had a happy Valentine's Day birthday. All because . . .

She swallowed quickly. Oh, damn it — she had to know one thing more.

"How are you getting on with Helen?"

YaYa pulled a face. "Helen? *Helen*? Why would I be getting on with Helen? I haven't seen Helen, love. Not since she and the monsters left here at the back end of last year."

Clemmie couldn't even find any comfort in that. So Helen had left again — so what? What did it matter? Clearly Helen and Guy had an on-off relationship, and she'd been here for him when it mattered, hadn't she? And while they kept going back to one another there was no room in Guy's life for anyone else.

YaYa frowned. "What on earth gave you the idea that Helen was back here, love?"

"Because, well, because she was here on that last Friday before Christmas, when you'd gone off to do your gigs with Honey and Foxy — and I — well, I gathered that she was staying."

"Over my dead body," YaYa snapped. "Mind you, I'm not surprised she was here for a temporary visit if I wasn't. Although why Guy'd would want to spend any time with her baffles me. Always has. He seemed truly bloody delighted when she buggered off last time. But then, it seems Guy can never say no to her, love — as you know."

Yes, Clemmie thought sadly, she knew only too well.

"One good thing," YaYa went on, "is that she obviously didn't stay long this time; but that's not to say she won't be back. Especially now The Gunpowder Plot is raking in so much money. The gold-digging bitch will be rubbing her designer-labelled mitts with greedy glee," She growled. "I wonder why Guy hasn't mentioned her visit to me, though? I must ask him — we don't have secrets."

"Probably best not to," Clemmie put in quickly. "If he's not very happy. Maybe mentioning Helen wouldn't be the right thing to do at all."

"Maybe not . . . But if Helen went back to London straight after Christmas, and as he usually can't wait to see the back of her, I can't see that being what's making Guy so depressed and irritable now."

I can, Clemmie thought miserably as she pushed the lid back on the last box, if they'd spent the whole of Christmas upstairs in bed, rekindling their desire, while Crap, Puke, Snot and Mungo played downstairs with their Wiis.

She lifted Suggs away from the Sellotape. He gave her one of his best hard stares, then snuggled under her chin and snuffled comfortingly against her neck. Oh, God . . . the tears stung her eyes.

Suggs and YaYa — she'd miss them so much.

"Clemmie? Oh, love, what's the matter?"

"Nothing."

338

"Oh, I know! I've got it! It's your boyfriend, isn't it? You've split! He's dumped you! Over Christmas! While you were away! The bastard! Oh, you poor love . . . Come on, let's go and make coffee in the kitchen and have some cake and you can tell me all about it."

She'd got so used to not telling the whole truth, Clemmie thought, mechanically eating her third doughnut at the kitchen table, that letting YaYa think the break-up with the mythical cute boy was the reason for her despondency was surprisingly easy. In fact, she thought, you really didn't have to say anything at all. Just let other people make the assumptions.

As Phoebe had.

The flat-warming party had been a disaster. Never feeling less partyish, Clemmie had spent most of the evening huddled in a corner of the pristine flat, watching her friends — Phoebe, Amber, Sukie, Chelsea, Fern and Lulu — having a really great time. And watching their partners laughing with them, loving them.

She was the only unattached person there. Even Ben's friends and work colleagues and the girls from Pauline's Cut'n'Curl were all with *someone*.

And although her friends had included her, albeit half-heartedly on her part, in the evening's singing and the dancing and the drinking and the silly games, she knew she was alone. So did they.

Normally this wouldn't have mattered at all. Like her, they were all strong, independent women who had their own lives, and weren't simply ciphers. It was just, in a party situation, being the spare one was totally appalling. Especially when she'd had such hopes.

"Fortunately the Lancasters, the upstairs neighbours, aren't in," Phoebe had shrieked over an ear-splitting blast of Take That. "I did invite them so they couldn't complain about the noise, but they've been away most of the time since we moved in. Think they might work abroad or something."

And Clemmie had said that was probably a good thing, and resumed her skulking.

Then Phoebe had turned the music off and, blushing, announced she and Ben had become engaged on New Year's Eve — although it wasn't really official yet because they hadn't got a ring or anything — but they were definitely getting married in June next year.

Everyone had swamped them with hugs and shrieks and congratulations, and Clemmie had joined in and truly meant it when she'd said she hoped they'd have a brilliant life together.

Then, as soon as it was decently possible, she'd made her excuses — long journey, no sleep over Christmas — and left.

"We're just glad you came," Phoebe said, hugging her as she saw her off. "It must have been a really hectic time for you in Scotland, and really emotional leaving your mum and dad again. I miss mine all the time since moving in here and they're only living in Bagley, a few minutes away. Poor you."

"I'm really pleased you and Ben are getting married," Clemmie had sniffed. "Oh, sorry — I always get emotional about weddings."

340

"You'll be our chief bridesmaid, won't you?"

"Really? Oh — yes, yes of course. I'd love to. Thanks, and I'm really pleased for you, Phoebes. Sorry I'm such a party pooper, though."

"No probs," Phoebe had beamed, waving Clemmie goodbye. "No probs at all."

". . . plenty more fish in the sea," YaYa was saying, trying to remove jam and cream and chunks of doughnut from Suggs' paws. "Oh, I know you don't want to hear that now, but give it time, love. You'll meet someone a million times better, you'll see."

"Maybe," Clemmie said. "But somehow I doubt it. But thanks for being so understanding — and for the carbs."

"Nothing like a sugar-rush to lift the spirits," YaYa patted Clemmie's hand. "Oh, hell, love, look at me. I've used all the kitchen roll on Suggs and I've got jam practically up to my armpits."

"I've got a tissue." Clemmie lugged her bag onto the table. "Somewhere in here . . ."

"Ta, love — ooh, what's this? Love letters to Guy?"

Clemmie snatched at the envelope which had fallen from her bag. "It's private."

YaYa looked at her across the table. "Now call me a boring old cynic, but I know a resignation letter when I see one — and that's a resignation letter. You've had a better offer, haven't you? Because of that Seventh Heaven multishot? One of the Big Boys has found out about it and approached you? And you've said yes. That's why Guy's so angry —"

"Guy doesn't know anything about me resigning," Clemmie said quickly. "Yet. And I don't want you to tell him. Promise me you won't say anything. And, no, I haven't had a better offer. It's nothing like that."

"Then why, love? Because you've split up with your boyfriend? Because you want to get away, move somewhere else, start again?"

Clemmie shook her head.

"Then bloody why? You can't leave, Clemmie! You're my friend!"

"And you're mine." Clemmie sniffed. "And I love working here and I love Suggs and, well, everything — but I just have to go."

YaYa sighed heavily. "OK, if you have a really good reason." She looked fiercely at Clemmie. "But don't do it yet. Give it a bit longer. Please. I promise for the first time in my life not to mention a word of this to Guy, if you'll promise to think it over. And please don't say anything to him yet while he's so down. I can't imagine what it'll do to him."

I can, Clemmie thought sourly. He'll probably be swinging from the chandeliers with delight and throw the biggest hoolie Winterbrook's ever seen.

"Very well," she said slowly. "I'll leave it until the end of the month. But I will have to leave, YaYa. There are reasons which I can't tell you now, but you'll find out, then you'll understand."

"No I won't. And neither will Guy."

"Neither will Guy what?" Guy, dark and dishevelled, suddenly appeared in the kitchen doorway.

342

Clemmie froze at the sight of him. Oh, hell! Why didn't hating him stop her loving him? Why wasn't her stupid heart listening to her head? Why had she forgotten the effect he had on her? Why had she forgotten just how gorgeous he was?

"Neither will I what?" Guy repeated. Then he looked at Clemmie. His eyes were cold and disinterested. "Oh, hello — good Christmas?"

"Yes, thank you. You?"

"Fine, thanks. So," he turned back to YaYa, "what were you talking about?"

"Nothing much." YaYa smiled warily. "Just mulling over the crap that is January. We haven't got any decent gigs until Feb. Oh, that Ellis Blissit bloke from Steeple Fritton rang earlier — he needs to talk to you."

"And you couldn't deal with it? Neither of you?"

"Don't snap at me!" YaYa flared. "Whatever your problem is, it isn't my fault! And no, Ellis didn't want to speak to me. He's changed his mind about the music. He wanted to check with you if it was OK. OK?"

"Christ! I go out for a couple of hours and neither of you can cope with one simple enquiry? Yes, I'll phone him. I've got his number on my mobile — no, don't either of you move, you just sit there and stuff your faces."

And with a crash of the kitchen door behind him, Guy disappeared.

"See, love?" YaYa looked unhappily at Clemmie. "God knows what's going on there. He must be ill . . .

I haven't seen him like this since oh, God, since that girl broke his heart umpteen years back."

And after that little upset, Clemmie thought angrily, he'd gone off and married Helen, hadn't he? Well, as he was clearly so bloody smitten with the woman, he damn well ought to do it again and give them all a break.

YaYa shook her head. "You can't leave, not while he's in this sort of mood. It'll push him right over the edge. Promise me you'll stay for a while longer."

Clemmie sighed. "Yes, OK — I'll stay for a while longer."

CHAPTER
TWENTY-FIVE

As January blew bleakly into a freezing February, absolutely nothing had changed, and the temperature inside the boathouse was about on a par with that outside.

Guy and Clemmie were icily, briefly business-polite to one another when they met, which fortunately wasn't often. Guy seemed to find a million reasons not to be at home — most of them probably beginning with H, Clemmie thought dismally — and even spent ten days in Hong Kong meeting a new supplier. When he was in the boathouse for any length of time, the atmosphere on those rare occasions was both unnatural and uncomfortable.

He also seemed to make sure that they were never alone together, so there was never an opportunity for Clemmie to mention the Christmas Friday fiasco — not that she really wanted to — or tell him that she'd be leaving The Gunpowder Plot.

"If you wanted to, you'd find an opportunity and just do it," she told herself miserably. "You're just putting off the evil hour. This is the first time in your life that you haven't walked happily away from a job — and you can't handle it, can you? You really are pathetic."

To avoid any confrontation with Guy, Clemmie spent a lot of time in the storage sheds and the lab, just looking at the firework boxes, reading the names, running her fingers across the bottles of chemicals, ingesting all the basics of the pyrotechnician's trade; as if by doing so, she could make it part of her. As if, when she left the boathouse, it would linger deep inside her, like an organic thing. Something of Guy and her time here that she could keep for ever.

Syd and the pyro crew, also affected by Guy's mood, mooched around the storage sheds and the labs, tinkering with things and getting restive.

"It's probably the time of year," Syd had said as Clemmie did yet another routine stock-take. "We all get bored when there are no displays on. I can't wait for this Steeple Fritton gig, even if it's not the biggest one we've ever done. At least we'll be back on the road again — and then it'll be spring and the work'll start in earnest." He'd looked at Guy's diary. "See! Bookings galore right through the year from March, thank God. More than we can handle. Roll on the vernal equinox, I say!"

Clemmie, still loving Guy hopelessly and hating him intensely in equal measure, knew her days at The Gunpowder Plot were coming to an end. None of them could go on like this; it simply wasn't fair. Once she'd left, Guy would be back to normal, wouldn't he?

YaYa, visibly unhappy with the flat, downbeat mood, clearly frantic about Guy — who still, she said, maintained there was nothing wrong with him — and audibly concerned about Clemmie, smoked non-stop and started biting her nails.

"Look at them." She thrust her hand across the desk, on the morning of Valentine's Day. "Practically down to the quick! And they're acrylic . . ."

Clemmie had promised herself that she'd hand in her resignation properly after the Steeple Fritton wedding. She'd do it tomorrow. She wouldn't even work a month's notice. She'd just say the words, hand over the letter and go.

But not today.

She'd come this far and survived. However much it hurt, she wanted to be able to go to Steeple Fritton with the rest of them and see Ellis and Lola married. She wanted to see the carefully planned blue and silver display in all its glory. She wanted — oh, sod it! She just wanted to be with Guy and the fireworks for the last time.

"Right." Syd bustled into the office. "We're off on our mission to darkest Fritton Magna to set things out without the lovely Lola discovering what we're up to. Kelly's going to drive the second pyro van over later, and the wedding display fireworks are all numbered and ready in the shed, Clem, so you can load them whenever you like. And Ellis phoned Guy again with some special music which I think I've managed to work into the short time we've got. All bubblegum tunes! That's a first."

After Syd had gone, Clemmie felt a little surge of enthusiasm. They were planning a display again — and it was all she wanted to do. Even if that wasn't entirely true, she'd started working here thinking that Guy was off-limits because he belonged to YaYa, hadn't she? What was so different about working here with Guy being off-limits because he now belonged to Helen?

Well now. There were actually loads of differences, like him knowing how she felt, and despising her for it. Clemmie thumped her desk.

Should she stay or should she go?

"Would you like a fag, love?" YaYa squinted through the smoke. "To calm your nerves?"

"No thanks, I'm not drunk. Yet. And you do know the Nanny State says it's now illegal to smoke in confined working areas, don't you?"

"Bollocks to the Nanny State!" YaYa roared. "This is also my home and I'll smoke where I bloody well like! As long as you don't mind, of course."

"Oh, please don't dilute the rant." Clemmie smiled wistfully. "I was enjoying it. And I don't mind you smoking at all. So —" she took a deep breath, "has Guy had a nice birthday so far?"

"Search me, love." YaYa shrugged. "He was gone before I emerged. Probably pacing out the site at Fritton as we speak. I left him a card and a pressie outside his bedroom door like usual, and they're still there. Anyway, I was being tactful and not mentioning it being Valentine's Day because of, well, you know . . ."

Did she? Ah, yes: the break-up with the mythical cute boy.

"Oh, don't mind me. I'm OK. Honestly. So, are you coming to Steeple Fritton?"

348

"Wouldn't miss it for the world. It'll do us all good to be out of here and working. And what about you? Have you had second thoughts? About staying on?"

Clemmie shook her head. "I'm going to hand in my notice tomorrow. I've got to — look, I promise you, when I've gone, Guy'll be fine again. Trust me."

"No he won't!" YaYa stubbed her cigarette out with angry jerking movements so that the ash spilled across her desk. "And neither will I! And Suggs will pine away! It won't ever be the same without you here — oh, please . . ."

Clemmie stood up, determined not to cry again. "Stop it. I can't stay. Just can't. And now I'm going to load the van, and when I come back we'll settle Suggs down with some really special dinner, and we'll get ready and head off to Fritton after lunch, and make Lola's wedding day the best possible, and not mention that I'm leaving. OK?"

Clemmie hurtled out of the office and across the courtyard before she could hear YaYa's reply.

The wind had dropped, the rain had ceased, and the temperature had risen by a few degrees. It still couldn't be described as balmy, but at least they wouldn't all freeze to death outside the Fritton Magna registry office.

As she unlocked the storage shed and opened the rear doors of the pyro van in readiness for loading Ellis and Lola's wedding display, she thought: this will be the last time I'll do this. Really, the last time.

Sniffing, she carefully hauled the large display boxes, packing them securely into the van in the order that

Guy and the crew would need them for setting up. Then she stacked the spare fuses, the extra wiring, and all the other paraphernalia of the pyrotechnician's craft, in the side pockets. It had become routine to her, second nature, part of the only job she'd ever want to do.

She thought sadly that she probably could apply to one of the other fireworks companies now — especially with her creation of Seventh Heaven — and be snapped up. But she wouldn't and couldn't: she'd never work for a firework company again. Not if it wasn't The Gunpowder Plot.

She'd return to temporary boring office jobs. Bad jobs, a lonely lifestyle . . .

Bloody hell!

Clemmie third-checked the display sheet and was about to close the van's doors when she realised that Seventh Heaven was missing. A couple of lifetimes ago Guy had said that he'd take one to Steeple Fritton, hadn't he? Just in case Lola needed a bit of persuasion.

Clemmie grabbed one of their ready-made prototypes from the shelf and packed it carefully in the van. Then looked at the shelf of Seventh Heavens that she and Guy had produced with so much excitement and pleasure.

What should she do with the others? Leave them here? Take them? They were hers, really, of course, but she'd never have been able to produce them without Guy's help, and besides, they'd registered the design to The Gunpowder Plot.

She'd leave them behind, she decided. And the recipes for all seven layers. Guy could use them or not as he chose in future displays; it wouldn't matter to her any more.

But what about that seventh layer? The truly magical green? The seventh layer that had already worked in mysterious ways to make wishes and dreams come true; made the words Heaven Sent spring to mysterious magical life? Allbard's Magik Green . . .

Quickly, before she could talk herself out of it, she shoved a solo Magik Green into one of the van's security pockets and zipped the top shut.

Of course, she thought, slam-locking the van, she wasn't going to use it, was she? Not on Guy. That was a stupid idea she'd had once upon a time when life was slightly less complicated than it was now — but they might need it for Lola.

It would be dead easy to light it tonight and push Guy into the tumbling deep forest-green sparks and chant the Green Man words, and she truly believed now that Guy would forget all about Helen, and fall in love with her instead.

But she couldn't do it. Couldn't use any celestial forces to make him do something that was clearly so abhorrent to him.

With a groan of despair at the situation in general, and loving Guy in particular, Clemmie locked the van, punched out Kelly's number on her mobile and told her the fireworks were loaded and ready to go whenever she was.

Then, without allowing herself even a last lingering glance at the sheds and the lab, she hurried back to the office.

All the way to Fritton Magna, YaYa was in her mournful country mood, and blasted out Bobbie Gentry's 'I'll Never Fall in Love Again' repeatedly on the 4×4's CD player.

Clemmie miserably agreed with every single one of Bobbie's plaintive words.

By design this time, they'd colour-co-ordinated their outfits, and YaYa's short, tight crimson suit and thigh-high scarlet boots perfectly complemented Clemmie's long ruby wool dress, and cherry boots and jacket. They were also both wearing the same fabulous red and black Butler and Wilson crystal chandelier earrings. And YaYa had added a tousled dark red curly wig to ape Clemmie's hairstyle.

"We look like the entertainment, love," YaYa sighed as they hit the Steeple Fritton, Lower Fritton and Fritton Magna road. "For the last time . . . Oooh, sorry. Shouldn't say that, should I?"

"No, you shouldn't. Right — now we'd better go straight to Fritton Magna and spend the next hour keeping out of the way so that Lola doesn't get wind of what we're doing."

"Whatever, love," YaYa sighed. "But if I cry during this particular wedding it won't be for the usual reasons."

CHAPTER
TWENTY-SIX

"But I don't even know these people . . ." Lola Wentworth frowned in her bedroom above the Crooked Sixpence. "Never heard of them. And Valentine's Day's one of the busiest in the pub. Why on earth do we have to go to their wedding?"

"Because," Ellis said, hopping round the bed in his boxer shorts and with one leg in his dark grey trousers, "for the thousandth time, I was friends with them at school and they'd booked this very quiet wedding miles away from anyone who knew them — they're both divorced and didn't want any fuss. Then they found out I lived here and thought it'd be a good idea to meet up again. And it's really romantic, getting married on Valentine's Day, isn't it?"

"I suppose so . . ." Lola sighed, "but do we have to dress up like this?"

"Yes. And you look stunning in silver and navy — remember?"

She punched him playfully. "I'm not turning up at the registry office just in my knickers."

"Oh, go on . . ."

She punched him again, then resignedly pulled the dark blue and silver silk wrap-dress from her wardrobe.

Smoothing the dress down over her slim hips and sliding her feet into her navy blue high-heeled sandals, she said, "I still think this is way over the top for the wedding of someone I've never met. And who's running the pub while we're away? When I asked Flynn he said he couldn't."

"We'll only be an hour or so. Ritchie and Sonia have said they'll be pleased to do it. I — um — arranged it with them this morning. And Dilys and Norrie will be in to lay on a small buffet for David and Jane. It's all under control. Look, Lola: I know you're congenitally conjoined to this damn pub, but it will still be here when we get back. Trust me."

"I do. Implicitly. Always have. And what's Flynn doing, then? I know Posy will be tied up with Orla. My god-daughter has to take priority — but surely, Flynn could —?"

"We've been through all this a million times." Ellis fastened his dark-blue tie over his pale-grey shirt with shaking fingers, hoping Lola wouldn't notice, praying that he could remember the script. "Flynn's busy bringing Queen Mab and the fairground organ up here for a bit of a knees-up in the car park later. My friends hadn't booked any sort of reception at all, so I said it would be our wedding present to them."

"I know — and I know you've told me all this before. But it still sounds a bit odd to me. Still, it's sweet of you." Lola crossed the bedroom and kissed him. "As usual. And this . . ." she fingered the silver and diamond necklace round her slender throat, "was even sweeter. And far too expensive for a Valentine's Day present. I do love you."

"I love you, too." Ellis returned the kiss. "Whoa! Back off, Ms Wentworth! We've got a wedding to get to."

Grinning, Lola returned to the dressing table, and surveyed her immaculate short, layered multi-tonal blonde hair and her perfect make-up.

"So?" Ellis stood behind her. "Twenty more grey hairs and thirty-two more wrinkles since this morning?"

"Forget I said I loved you," Lola retorted to his reflection. "You're a thoroughly unpleasant man."

Ellis looked at his watch and took a deep breath. "We'd better get a move on. The wedding's at five and we don't want to be shuffling in when it's already started, do we?"

"No, absolutely not, but it's a funny time for a wedding." Lola frowned. "Why so late?"

"I've got no idea. I didn't ask. Now — here's your corsage." He handed her the tiny blue and silver spray of flowers which exactly matched his own buttonhole. "And don't spend any more time titivating in front of that mirror because you look absolutely perfect. Gorgeous. Good enough to eat. As always. Anyway — no one's going to be looking at you, are they? All eyes will be on the bride."

Finally, Lola shrugged, smiled and walked out of the bedroom.

Ellis, his mouth dry as he followed her downstairs to the Crooked Sixpence's bar, had never felt so nervous in his entire life. From the moment they first met he'd wanted to marry her but he knew that, even now, it could all still go disastrously wrong.

The rings! Where were the rings? Oh, yes, Flynn had them. If this worked, he vowed, he'd never do anything bad in his life again.

"Jesus!" Lola had paused in the doorway. "What's this?"

Ellis peered over her shoulder at the limousine parked outside the pub. "Another little Valentine's Day surprise. I thought we should travel in style."

"Oh, I love it!" Lola beamed. "Thank you! I'll feel like royalty." She smiled gratefully at the uniformed chauffeur as he held the door open for her. "But at this rate I'm going to out-swish the bride."

Ellis slid into the plush leather seat beside her and held her hand. He felt sick, excited, nervous, and absolutely elated all at the same time.

He nodded to the driver. "Let's go."

Out of sight, parked in the darkness beside Guy's BMW and The Gunpowder Plot's vans, and behind Fritton Magna's quaint little registry office, Clemmie and YaYa, sitting in the 4×4, were on the last lap of a countdown.

". . . four — three — two — one . . . It's now four fifty exactly! Go!"

Together, they slid from the car and crept quietly through the shrubbery, hidden in the early evening shadows. Everything had been timed to the nth degree. They'd arrived just as Guy and Syd had finished unpacking Kelly's van and discreetly placing the

356

fireworks where Lola wouldn't see them when she arrived. Deciding that staying out of Guy's way would be more useful than offering to help and being snapped at, they'd stayed in the 4×4 until ten to five.

Syd was busy connecting up all the wiring for the remote control firing, perfecting the timings, and running through the computerised musical playlist.

"Everything going to plan?" YaYa asked Guy.

He nodded.

Clemmie, standing behind YaYa, just stared at him. If she stared hard enough and for long enough, she thought, it would be like ingesting the fireworks earlier; some part of him would be hers for always.

As always, dressed in layers of skinny black, his hair falling into his eyes, he looked more beautiful than ever. Clemmie closed her eyes, imprinting the image eternally in her memory.

"You've added a Seventh Heaven," he said. "It wasn't on the list."

Clemmie opened her eyes. "No, but you did say it might be a good idea to put one in, didn't you?"

He shrugged. "Maybe. I don't think we'll use it, though. In fact I don't think we'll ever need it again. I've told Syd not to even think of wiring it up. It's not included in the display."

"Whatever." Clemmie swallowed any further words. Nothing she said would make any difference now. "Look, Guy —"

"What?" He frowned at her in the darkness. "Leave it, Clemmie. This is neither the time nor the place."

"Jesus!" YaYa hissed at him. "You can be a cruel bastard, can't you? Come on, Clem — leave the nasty boy alone."

They huddled back behind the registry office.

"Don't say a thing," Clemmie muttered. "Just let's leave it all as unsaid and read. Shall we people-watch?"

YaYa nodded unhappily and without conviction. "S'pose so — there are several guests coming up the path." She suddenly regained some enthusiasm. "Oooh, look: there's that stunning American boy, Flynn, and that must be his Posy — and she's got a really tiny baby! Ah, sweet! Don't they look the business? And those two look like proper hippies. And all those kids! Seven? Eight? No, nine! Nine kids! I wonder who they are."

"Tatty Spry and Baz and their assorted brood," Clemmie said. "Tatty does everyone's tattoos for miles around. She's well-known and quite a character."

Tatty was followed by a gaggle of elderly ladies wearing elaborate hats and thick coats, then a further stream of villagers and friends, all arriving at much the same time, giggling enthusiastically at their shared secret as they disappeared into the registry office.

"Oh — that's sweet," YaYa whispered, as dozens of tiny blue and silver fairy lights suddenly illuminated in the branches of the surrounding trees. "Doesn't it look pretty? Oh, blimey — is this them?"

"I think it is," Clemmie whispered, watching the long silver limousine purr to a halt, and Ellis help Lola step out. "Well, Ellis has got her this far . . . Oh, wow! She's stunning! No way is she fifty-five! No wonder he's so besotted!"

"She should be doing adverts for the over-fifties," YaYa agreed. "She looks young enough to be my daughter — the cow . . . Oh, hell! What's happening now?"

Lola and Ellis had come to an abrupt halt on the snaking path and she was shaking her head. YaYa and Clemmie looked at each other in alarm. Surely it wasn't all about to go wrong now?

Lola stopped walking.

"Come on," Ellis urged her, smiling "It's cold out here and we don't want to be late."

"No."

"What?"

"I'm not going in there." Lola looked at him. "I know what you're doing. And I'm not joining in."

Ellis looked at her in panic. "Lola — what are you talking about?"

"There's no David and Jane, Ellis, and there never has been, has there? I can't believe I was stupid enough to fall for it in the first place — it was all too far-fetched for words."

"Sorry, you've lost me."

"No I haven't. This isn't David and Jane's wedding, is it? It's ours."

"No! Why? How . . .?"

"Look . . ." Lola indicated the registry office. "The place is bursting at the seams. The doors are wedged open. I can see Tatty and Baz and the kids. And Glad, your grandmother, and Rose Lusty and Vi Bickeridge and all the Pinks and half the damn village. They wouldn't be at your friends' David and Jane's secret wedding, would they? But they'd be at ours."

"Oh, bugger it . . ." Ellis exhaled. "OK Lola, you've guessed it. But I so want to marry you. I so want you to be my wife. And we're always going to be together — and I knew you'd say no if I asked you to do this today in the conventional way. You've always said no."

"And I'm saying no now, too. Sorry, Ellis, nice try, lovely idea and very clever of you to keep it secret, given the power of the jungle drums in Steeple Fritton. And I do love you, more than life, but I can't marry you. You know that."

"Why? Because of your outdated ideas about the age difference? Because —"

"Because, if I'm lucky, I might live for another twenty, maybe twenty-five years. You'll still be in your forties. You'll be a widower — a childless widower — in your forties. Think it about it, Ellis. I can't do that to you. Not only that; because you should meet and marry someone who can give you children."

"I'll probably die long before you," Ellis said sharply. "Given the excesses of my misspent youth. And I wouldn't want to live without you anyway, and I don't want children. Not now. Not ever. I just want you."

"And you've got me. And always will have. We're happy as we are. Sorry to upset all your cleverly, carefully thought-out plans, but I'm not going through with this."

★   ★   ★

Clemmie, listening to the entire exchange, her mouth open with horror, belted out from behind the registry office, pushed through the shrubbery and yanked open the door of The Gunpowder Plot's van.

With her hands shaking, she ripped open the security pocket, and pulled out the solo Magik Green.

"Clemmie!" Guy stormed round the side of the van and glared at her. "What the hell are you doing?"

"No time — listen . . ." She gave him a brief précis of the overheard conversation. "And she's already heading back to the limo. Come on!"

"I'm not sure we should —"

"Should what?" She looked over her shoulder. "Dabble? Interfere? Too late! He loves her, she loves him. They should be married — and they bloody well will be! Grab a portfire and hurry!"

Still glaring, still muttering, Guy, however, lit the end of the portfire. It smouldered like a little airborne glow-worm.

Just as Lola was stalking back towards the limo, and Ellis, looking totally devastated and shattered, started to follow her, Clemmie, followed by Guy, pushed past him.

"Sorry — I'll explain later."

"She won't go through with it. She doesn't want to."

"She does. Trust me. She knows it's right for her. She's just scared it's wrong for *you*, and we all know it's the rightest thing in the world. Now please, just stay there." Clemmie puffed to a halt. "Lola — Lola — please, wait a minute."

Lola stopped and turned. Her beautiful face was desperately sad, not angry. "Sorry? I don't think I know you, do I?"

"No. I'm Clemmie, and you'll find out why I'm here later, hopefully."

"Don't waste your time," Lola said faintly. "If you're part of Ellis's lovely scheme, it's all very sweet. But it's not —"

Hurling the Magik Green on the path between Lola and the limo, Clemmie murmured urgently over her shoulder.

"Guy, light it — now! Please!"

Shaking his head, his eyes steely in the faint glow of the fairy lights, he stroked the lighted portfire against the touchpaper.

Again, with a hiss and a fizzle, the deep ocean green burst into verdant, glowing life.

"I wish," Clemmie muttered, clutching Lola's slender arm and holding it fast, "that Lola would realise that she loves Ellis and always will and that the natural culmination of this love will be to marry him. I wish that she'd forget her doubts, and realise her fears are unfounded, and enter into this marriage — today — now — with all the enthusiasm and love which she knows, deep down, she really, really wants to."

Christ, Clemmie winced. Terrible syntax — and again, probably far too many wishes — but hopefully the magic would sort it out.

"What on earth are you doing?" Lola shook her head and tried to free her arm. "Let me go — oh!"

Allbard's Magik Green softly exploded in all its glory, sending a shower of glittering emerald sparks drifting and dancing across the registry office path.

As the burning green fireflies tumbled around them, Clemmie swallowed.

"Verdigris and verture pure
Sparks with nature's verdanture
Makes wishes forever endure."

She let go of Lola's arm and stepped back. And waited.

"That was really pretty." Lola smiled at her. "Thank you. Now, where was I? Oh, yes!" She turned and hurried back up the path to Ellis and threw her arms around his neck. "Ellis Blissit! You are a star! Every time I think you can never surprise me again you come up with something new! A secret wedding! You are amazing — and I love you so much."

Ellis held her tightly. "You mean . . . you want to marry me?"

"Of course I do." Lola kissed him and pulled him towards the registry office. "I always have. I've been such a fool. You know, I've wanted to be Lola Blissit ever since we decided it sounded like a stripper — remember? The first night we spent together . . . oh, I can't wait! Come on, let's not keep our guests waiting."

CHAPTER
TWENTY-SEVEN

"OK," Syd hissed half an hour later, "They're coming out. Three-two-one — and off we go!"

As Ellis and Lola appeared in the registry office doorway, with their beaming guests jostling and peering over their shoulders, Guy pressed the first remote firing button.

On the nod, Syd started his computerised music score.

Exactly on cue, to the bubblegum blare of Ellis's chosen 'Yummy, Yummy, Yummy', the towering blue and silver fountain archway of fire sparkled into life, creating a twinkling pergola the entire length of the path.

Everyone gasped.

As the first tune ended and the second, 'Goody, Goody Gumdrops', started, the twin multishots on either side of the door, shooting their blue and silver hearts high into the night sky, played waterfalls of stars onto Ellis and Lola, smiling blissfully at one another, as they walked slowly hand in hand down the path beneath the falling fountain.

"Oh!" Lola looked delightedly up at Ellis as finally the colour-co-ordinated lancework heart illuminated to the foot-tapping music of 'Chewy Chewy'. "Oh, this is all too wonderful for words . . . Thank you. Oh, Ellis — I love you so much."

Grinning, he swept her up into his arms. "I love you, too, Mrs Blissit." Then he kissed her.

The guests, still oohing and aahing at the pyro spectacle, clapped delightedly as they crowded outside the registry office.

"Pass me another tissue, love," YaYa sobbed as the fireworks and the music eventually faded. "This is all too much for me."

Clemmie passed a handful of hankies. She hadn't cried, not this time. She was emotionally exhausted. And still stunned by the efficacy of Allbard's Magik Green.

"What I still can't get," YaYa dabbed gently beneath her eyes, "is why she changed her mind. And what part you played in it. And why, come to think of it, you and Guy are always using that fab green firework every time there's a bit of a problem."

"It's just me and my silly bit of homespun folklore," Clemmie said with what she hoped was ringing conviction. "You know, green being the colour of all things magical. I always try a bit of hocus-pocus when there's trouble."

"Yeah, right." YaYa blew her nose. "You mean it's something weirdly scientific that a mere accountant wouldn't understand? Oh, you keep your silly pyro secrets, love — I'm not fussed. I'm just so pleased they got spliced. And now we can all go off and have a little bop at that cute little pub, and hopefully celebrate

Guy's birthday too; not that he deserves it, the way he's been behaving."

Clemmie looked across at Guy, standing with the pyro crew, being congratulated by Ellis and Lola and their friends, and shrugged.

"He's got his reasons. And he might not even want to go back to the Crooked Sixpence — if he's really that bad-tempered, he might go straight back home to Winterbrook."

"Let him," YaYa said with a shrug. "We can still go and have a bit of a celly, can't we?"

Clemmie, who really didn't feel like celebrating anything at all, nodded.

Ellis and Lola, still entwined, were now scrambling excitedly back into the limo, and the guests, laughing and talking, were flooding back to their own various modes of transport.

Waiting until the tail lights had disappeared, and the registry office staff had switched off their lights and locked the doors, the pyro crew, including Clemmie and YaYa, moved silently to clear away the last traces of the display.

"I need a drink," Syd said, slamming the last sand bucket and fire blanket back into the van, and making sure the computers were stacked carefully. "Anyone else?"

There was a general yell of agreement and, in seconds, The Gunpowder Plot's vans had joined the Steeple Fritton-bound convoy.

"What about you?" YaYa asked Guy. "Fancy a drink, birthday boy?"

"Not really."

"Oh, stop being such a pain in the arse!" YaYa snapped. "You're such a spoilt brat! Your bad temper has made Clemmie want to leave us! And I hate you for that!"

"YaYa . . ." Clemmie groaned.

"Sorry, love — but it had to be said. We all tippy-toe round him and his bloody moods — I love him to bits, but I won't let him drive you away!"

Guy pushed his hair away from his eyes and squinted at Clemmie. "Is she right? You're leaving?"

Clemmie nodded. "I was going to hand in my notice straight after New Year, but YaYa asked me to stay a bit longer. So I did. And I wanted to see tonight through and now I have. Well, anyway, I've got my resignation letter in my bag and I might as well get it over, so —"

"Don't you dare!" YaYa spat. "Now you listen to me, Guy Devlin! I'm your best and oldest friend! You talk this over with Clemmie. Now. Properly. Like grown-ups. I'm going to go and sit in the car and have a fag, or maybe two. And when I've filled myself with nicotine, I'll come back and if you haven't managed to sort anything out, then I'll accept that Clemmie's leaving because she wants to and not just because she can't stand the sight of you any longer!"

And swaying away on the scarlet killer heels, YaYa left them alone in the hazy darkness.

"She's very kind," Clemmie said faintly, "but she's wasting her time, isn't she?"

"Apparently."

Clemmie shook her head. "Oh, no. Don't take that sarky tone with me. None of this is my fault. We were getting on just fine before and I was really happy with the job, more than happy — and we were good friends, weren't we? And then —"

"And then?"

"God, you're so annoying! Don't just repeat what I've said. Say something!"

"OK . . ."

Guy shifted his weight onto one hip. It was a very sexy movement which Clemmie tried extremely hard to ignore.

They stared at one another. Clemmie, feeling slightly hot, dropped her gaze first.

"No." She shook her head. "Don't try the smouldering bit on me, either. I know what you did. It was so cruel. You could have just told me to back off, not go through that bloody charade with Helen."

Guy peered at her. "Now you've lost me."

Furiously, Clemmie glared at him. "Crap. You made me think that you liked me — maybe more than liked me — because you knew — *knew* — how I felt about you, didn't you? And you're such an arrogant bastard that instead of just breaking it to me gently, you had to have a laugh about it. You decided to invite me to dinner and then you pulled that viciously cruel stunt. And ever since, you've ignored me, frozen me out, treated me like some menial idiot; so, how the hell do you expect me to stay working with you after that? Go on — you tell me!"

"You stood me up."

368

"What?"

"You heard me," Guy said quietly, his eyes expressionless. "That Friday night. I was waiting for you and you didn't show up. You stood me up."

"Did I hell!"

"Yes, you did." Guy sighed. "We arranged to meet at about seven. I'd found a lovely little Turkish restaurant that did takeouts, planned the menu, lit the candles, and me and Suggs were waiting — and waiting — and waiting . . ."

"All fantasy!" Clemmie snapped. "You didn't do any of that for me. You did it for Helen!"

"I can assure you I didn't."

"Yes you did. You invited Helen to stay for Christmas. Asked Helen to open the door to me when I arrived. Asked Helen to make sure I knew you and she were reconciled and were planning a family Christmas! She even hinted you were in bed — with her."

Guy laughed harshly. "I haven't been in bed with Helen since — well, years and years ago. And Helen didn't come to stay for Christmas! God I'd rather have slit my wrists. I spent Christmas entirely alone with Suggs. Helen only popped in that night, completely unannounced and unexpected, on her way to one of her other exes, to collect the obligatory presents for the brats which in her usual avaricious way she knows I'll buy out of guilt for disliking the poor little sods so much, and as it was way before seven I jumped in the car and drove off. I told her she had twenty minutes to collect the presents and get out of the house before you arrived."

Clemmie sniffed. "Yeah, that sounds really plausible."

"It happens to be true. I stayed out of the way while she was there, and she was gone when I got back." He paused and frowned. "You mean you did turn up while I was out and Helen was there? Earlier than we'd arranged? And she opened the door and said — and you believed her?"

"Well . . . yes." Clemmie nodded. "And she didn't leave a note or anything to tell you I'd called or that she'd spoken to me, did she?"

Guy shook his head. "And I was really worried about you, in case you'd had an accident, so I kept calling your mobile but after a while I just assumed you didn't want to talk to me. That you thought I should have got the message by not turning up."

"You thought I'd stood you up and I thought — oh, God — I thought it was your way of telling me to push off. Helen said that you and she were . . . were . . ."

"Helen is the biggest cow in the world," Guy snarled. "She knew how I felt about you. How close we were. She hated it — hated it! And she — oh, shit!"

Clemmie bit her lip. Oh, shit, indeed.

"I bet she didn't give you the champagne either, did she?"

"No. But then that would have proved that you'd called, wouldn't it? God, she must have loved that — guzzling champagne from you to me."

Clemmie pushed her hair behind her ears. Why on earth hadn't she said something to Guy sooner? Why hadn't he broached the subject? Why had they both been so ridiculously, stubbornly, pointlessly proud?

370

"We've been a bit stupid, haven't we?" Guy said with a rueful grin. "These have been the worst weeks of my life."

"Worse than when you split up with that girl in your youth?"

"Far, far worse — I've never felt like this before. I wanted to die. Honestly. There seemed no point in anything any more. And, to make it even worse, I've been a bastard to you while you've been going through all that yourself. Splitting up with your boyfriend; YaYa told me."

"That's not exactly true." Clemmie smiled, her heart doing a little jig under her ribs. "He didn't actually exist. YaYa sort of got a bit carried away. And when I was so upset about — about well, Christmas and Helen and everything — and couldn't tell her the truth, it seemed easier not to disabuse her of the notion."

They gazed at one another

"So where do we go from here?" Guy asked. "Can we put all that crap behind us and start again? Or do you still want to leave — oh God, you do, don't you?"

Clemmie, her hand in her bag, shook her head. "I'm not about to whip out my resignation letter. Actually, I was going to give you this . . ."

She handed him the rainbow maker.

"Happy birthday — although, as you'll guess from the wrapping, it was really your Christmas present."

"I bought you a Christmas present too. It's still wrapped up in the sideboard. You'll have to have it when we get home." Guy quickly unwrapped the rainbow maker and whooped. "Wow! It's superb!

Thank you! Clemmie — I love it! I've always wanted one of these! Suggs'll love it too — he'll spend forever chasing rainbows."

"A bit like us, then?"

Guy nodded, holding out his hand. "But not any more. Oh God, Clemmie, I've been such a fool. I'm so sorry."

She smiled at him, shivering, as his fingers closed around hers then catching her breath as he pulled her against him.

"Thank God we didn't need to resort to using the Allbard's Magik Green, having used it up on Lola," she said faintly against his leather jacket. "Although I did think I might try it out on you if —"

Guy laughed. "It would have been OK. I brought one, too. For you. Just in case . . . But clearly it won't be needed. Now come here: I've owed you this since Hassocks Hill, haven't I?"

Then he kissed her, and all the fireworks in the world fizzed vibrantly through her body and exploded vividly around them.

"Oh . . ." Eventually surfacing, she looked up at him. "Oh, wow . . ."

"Oh, wow just about cuts it for me, too." Guy stroked her hair away from her face. "I don't know about Ellis and Lola, but this has to be the best night of my life."

"Mmmm . . . Mine too. Do you know," she said dreamily, "if you count Suzy and Luke, we've been involved in three weddings and a funeral."

"We have." Guy kissed her lips again, gently, teasingly, temptingly. "And that sounds slightly wrong to me . . ."

"Well, loves," YaYa chirped happily from the darkness. "There's only one thing left to do, isn't there? Three weddings and a funeral — wrong. Four weddings . . . well, you're the brainy ones so I'll leave you to do the maths."

"I'm way ahead of you," Guy laughed. "Now bugger off and leave us alone."

YaYa giggled as she sashayed away towards the 4×4. "With pleasure, loves. As long as I can be a bridesmaid in black net with white lilies. Now, I'm off to the pub to join in the celebrations. Might see you there, later?"

"Much, much later," Guy said softly. "As this is Valentine's Day and my birthday, it seems like a heaven-sent opportunity for me and Clemmie to have a little private celebration all of our own."

Also available in ISIS Large Print:

Love Out of Season

Ray Connolly

Perched between bleak moors and the cold sea, the North Devon Riviera Hotel is an unlikely destination for February. But, for the guests and staff there, it's about to become the setting for a weekend they will always remember.

Amy Miller has fallen in love with a famous married man and has gone into hiding at the hotel, pursued by the press. While waiting for her lover to call, however, she begins to question their affair. Then, into her life comes Tim, a musician. As the hotel prepares for its Valentine's ball and the tabloids circle ever closer, Amy, Tim and everyone else at the North Devon Riviera are about to discover that love — whether it's young love, old love, shared love or unrequited love — does indeed make the world go round, and sometimes in the most unexpected ways.

ISBN 978-0-7531-8022-8 (hb)
ISBN 978-0-7531-8023-5 (pb)

I Did a Bad Thing

Linda Green

Sarah Roberts used to be good. Then she did something bad. Very bad.

Now, years later, she's living a good life, working as a local newspaper reporter and living with her saintly boyfriend Jonathan. She has no reason to think her guilty past will ever catch up with her.

Until Nick walks back into her life. And suddenly what's good and bad aren't so clear to Sarah any more.

ISBN 978-0-7531-7912-3 (hb)
ISBN 978-0-7531-7913-0 (pb)